EVERYTHING FOR LOVE

KATE SMITH

for my daughters

CHAPTER 1

Emily

EMILY STROLLED DOWN THE BOARDWALK, gazing at the expanse of water. Maybe he was doing the exact same thing, even if it was a different ocean on the opposite side of the country. How was he managing as a full-time parent? Was Savannah settling into her new life?

Shame touched her. She'd avoided contacting Aiden and Savannah. She wasn't oblivious to the damage she'd done but …

"Aunt Emily." Her niece skipped toward her, balancing a precarious scoop of ice cream, a rivulet of sticky caramel trickling down her wrist in the hot California sun. "Look what Mommy got me."

Natalia arrived seconds later. She fished a napkin from her pocket and dabbed at the girl's arm. "Eat it before it melts." Her rueful look at Emily said it all. "I couldn't say no."

Emily smiled gently. Her sister was compensating for Isabella's absent father. Again. Yet how could she judge after witnessing Savannah's devastation when she lost Ross? Sometimes a steady stream of love and indulgence was what it took to dull the pain.

"Emelia?" Nat nudged her with an elbow. "You're thinking about him again, aren't you?"

Isabella bounced across the sand, a seagull hopping away from the energetic girl.

"You are so good with her, Nat. How do you manage?"

"What else can I do?" Her sister glanced at the dark-haired angel as she dropped to her knees, examining something buried in the sand while taking the occasional swipe at her ice cream with her tongue. "It would be easier with a partner."

She avoided the knowing look coming her way. "He'll be fine," she said under her breath.

"Will you?" Nat arched her brow.

"Ha, no. Jenna is adamant about my part in the wedding." The recent text from Jenna conveyed irritation about the secret Emily had kept from her, oddly followed by a phone call an hour later. The warm thank you for being there for Aiden and for keeping said secrets been a pleasant surprise. "That means the grand combination of pissed off man and his bitchy ex-wife."

"She's still the maid of honor?" A horrified look appeared.

"Apparently. Jenna is sweet and gentle and she hates hurting anyone's feelings. She's keeping the peace in hopes Tiffany will come to her senses."

Nat smirked. "You and Jenna are soul sisters."

Emily sighed. Natalia was right. She'd paste on a smile and attend each and every wedding-related event without a single complaint, even if being near her ex-boyfriend was awkward and painful. Over the months of dating Aiden she'd grown close to his friends, especially Jenna, and the woman made it clear that the break-up was no excuse to abandon her bridesmaid duties.

"Let me suggest an easy solution to the pissed off man part of the equation, Emelia."

She squinted at Nat, shaking her head.

"What have you got to lose? You have the vacation time booked, and you know he has room. If he doesn't, Jenna would let you stay with her and Tom."

"I have to leave some space. Let him adjust to being a single parent."

Nat scoffed. "I love you, Emelia, but you're completely insane to let an eligible guy like Aiden go."

"There's more to a relationship than—"

"Uh-huh. Don't pretend this thing between you and Aiden doesn't encompass everything a woman could possibly need." Nat pointed her index finger. "One. He's that perfect combination of adorably sweet and impossibly sexy."

"Right, which means fighting off more flight attendants and supermodels."

"Yet the fictional Dani and legendary Jazlyn are in his rearview mirror." Nat wrinkled her nose. "Two." A second finger came up. "He's got a great career."

"So he works long hours." She cringed at Nat's glare.

"Three." She held up her hand, waggling her extended fingers. "He's an involved and caring dad with the bonus that he makes beautiful babies."

"And he has a bonus crazy-ass ex-wife who hates me."

"Really, Emelia?" Nat glowered. "Four. He's financially stable."

"I don't need a rich guy to take care of me."

"Five." Her sister splayed her fingers, fanning them in Emily's face. "You're in love with him."

Emily clamped her teeth onto her lower lip.

"Ahh." She grinned. "Six." Nat lifted her other hand. "He's in love with you."

"Not anymore. Besides, the minute crazy-ex comes to her senses, she'll want her husband back."

Her sister tapped her pursed lips. "How many years ago was that divorce?" Natalia raised another finger. "Seven. You lov—"

"Stop." Emily clapped her hands over her ears, but her sister tugged them away.

"Unless you want to hear the rest of my many reasons, then get on a plane. Take a chance. He's worth it."

Emily shook her head. Tomorrow she'd board her flight to Chicago and get on with her life. No matter how many reasons her sister thought of or how much her heart ached, the relationship was too complicated. Too messy. Definitely over.

⌒≺

"Bye." Isabella wrapped her arms around Emily and kissed her cheek. "Do you have to go?"

"Sorry, cariño." Emily hugged the girl tight, pressing her face into her soft fragrant hair. A familiar ache built as it always did when she left. "I'll miss you, but I'll visit again soon." She released the girl and turned to her sister. "Love you, Nat."

Her sister embraced her and whispered, "Thank you, Emelia. I found the envelope. One day I'll repay you."

She gave her sister a squeeze. "No need."

"You help Mama and Jules too, and you have medical loans. How can you afford it?"

Emily blinked hard. "I do pretty well as a doctor and you're family."

"You're an angel."

After a last hug, Emily slid into the back of the taxi and waved, sinking into the seat and closing her eyes as the car merged into traffic. Soon she'd be unable to help her sister and niece. The only reason she could now was because Aiden waved off every attempt to contribute to the monthly bills. Not that she could admit that tidbit and provide her sister more ammunition.

As they drew closer to the airport, Emily dug into her bag for taxi fare and pulled out the boarding pass for her flight to Chicago. "Thanks." She

3

smiled and accepted her bag from the driver. She weaved her way through the crowded concourse, spying the check-in.

Emily joined the queue, staring at the pass in her hand. *To jump or not?* When she finally reached the agent she asked, "How do you get from LAX to Martha's Vineyard?"

"Generally through Boston." The agent held out her hand.

"Can I exchange my ticket for a flight to Boston?" She clenched the paper between her fingers.

The woman sighed.

"It's important. There's this guy …" Emily bowed her head and set her paperwork on the counter as the woman curled her lip.

"Honey, there always is." The keys clacked as the woman slammed her fingers against them. "One seat left on the next flight." Her lips twitched as she glanced at the economy booking in front of her. "First class. The last minute fare is … much, much more, Dr. Anderson. The Chicago ticket is non-refundable."

Emily peered at the number on the screen and shook her head. How could she swing it after giving Nat half of her last pay check and knowing she'd soon have to pay a damage deposit and rent for a new apartment?

The agent's smile widened. "The next flight isn't for seven hours. I have economy on that one. Care to wait?"

Emily shook her head again. Aiden wouldn't be that happy to see her anyway. Maybe fate was telling her to forget the entire ridiculous idea.

"So we'll just check you in for your Chicago flight, then?"

The ache built. She had no choice if she wanted to see Aiden. "Let me find my credit card." Emily tugged her wallet free from her bag, pausing. Maybe this was a bad idea. "Never mind, I'll just—"

"Upgrade her ticket and get her on the first Boston flight, please." A large hand came into view. One holding a platinum card. "Book the connecting flight for the Vineyard too."

Emily lifted her chin, peering up at the owner of the deep voice, taking in the broad shoulders and solid muscular chest straining under a dark button-down shirt.

"My treat." He winked. "I believe in paying it forward."

"Thank you, sir." The woman behind the counter directed a smile at the man, batting her big blue eyes before she checked Emily's bag and issued a boarding pass and an itinerary with details on her connecting flight. "Have a nice flight, sir."

Emily slung her bag over her shoulder and snatched the papers from the agent's hand, turning away with a scoff. "How is it the men always get the good service?"

"Don't take it personally. I'm a frequent flyer." The man fell into step beside Emily as they headed toward the security line.

"Yeah, that's it, I bet." She laughed as she took in the guy's tall muscular frame, strong jaw, and sparkling blue eyes. "It has nothing to do with the fact you're tall, blond, and handsome. She practically launched over the counter and tackled you to the floor."

"Aww, darlin', I'm flattered." He grinned and motioned for her to precede him into the queue.

"I don't know how to thank you. If you give me your address, I'll repay you."

"No need." He handed her a gray bin for her belongings and opened his bag, separating his electronics into his own bin and adding his shoes and carry-on bag to a second tray. "You're a doctor?"

"Mmhmm. Emergency medicine." Emily eyed the man before handing her boarding pass to the uniformed security officer and stepping through the metal detector.

Once the man joined her, she extended her hand. "My flight will be called soon … I don't even know your name."

"Our flight. I'm also headed to Boston." He gathered his belongings. "We should go."

Emily glanced his way, unsure of what to say. Had this man bought her ticket because he expected a hook up? She raised her chin and straightened. "I'm involved with someone. I'm sorry if you thought …" She arched a brow at his low chuckle.

He held up his hands. "I'm not hitting on you, I swear." His grin widened as they continued toward the departure gate. "I heard the part about the guy and I'm a sucker for a grand gesture of love."

Her cheeks reddened, heat burning her ears. "Why waste your time on someone who's taken?"

"Since when is making a new friend a waste of time?" He guided her into the priority boarding line. They presented their passes and he followed her onto the plane. "Look at that. We're neighbors." He winked as he settled into the plush seat beside hers.

"How did you manage that?"

"You really are a suspicious woman, Dr. Anderson. Relax. I'm an investment advisor, not a weirdo stalker."

Emily laughed. "Sorry. It's just that guys usually …"

"Want to get laid?" He shook his head. "I'd never interfere between you and your man. Some things are sacred."

The flight attendant appeared. "Would you like a warm towel? Something to drink while we board the rest of the passengers?"

Emily sighed in contentment as she accepted the delightfully warm square of smooth cotton, the gentle heat relaxing her as she brushed her fingers across it. She only experienced the little luxuries of first class when she traveled with Aiden. The difference from economy still amazed her.

The man ordered a scotch and his meal before motioning to Emily. "What would you like, darlin'?"

"Vodka and cranberry." After she'd selected her meal, she stared out the window, idly tracking the movements of the ground crew as they loaded the baggage. What to say to Aiden when she appeared with no warning? She feared a cooler welcome than on her last surprise Vineyard visit.

"How about you and this guy?" The blond man asked once the flight attendant had served their drinks.

"It's stupid, really." She gulped a large mouthful of tart cranberry. "We broke up, so I doubt he'll want to see me." Emily drummed her fingers on the arm rest. "You wasted your money on a first class ticket."

"Yet you're on this plane. That means hope." The man leaned back and crossed an ankle over his knee, taking a leisurely sip of the amber liquid in his glass. "How long since you broke up?"

"Five weeks. Plenty of time for him to hook up."

"Do you always have so little faith in men?"

She drained the cold liquid, swallowing hard. "I've dated a series of cheaters and liars." Even her own father had joined the love 'em and leave 'em club when she was young. Her broken-hearted mother struggled as a single parent, leaving Emily with zero tolerance for infidelity.

"Which one is this guy?"

"Neither." Emily closed her eyes. "He's just … complicated."

The flight attendant worked her way up the aisle. "We're ready for departure …"

The routine words drifted over Emily as she adjusted her seat into the upright position and forced herself to breathe while they bumped across the tarmac. The engines roared and her stomach did the familiar flip as the aircraft sped down the runway and lifted from the ground. She clenched her hands in her lap until they leveled off and the seatbelt light went out.

"Anything I can get you?" The flight attendant asked.

"Another vodka-cranberry, please." Emily drummed her fingers on the arm rest. This flight would pass quicker and easier once she took the edge off.

The man across from her ordered another scotch, studying her silently until they had fresh drinks in hand. "Explain complicated."

A nervous laugh escaped. How to even begin? "I've known him for years. We worked together and he's an amazing doctor." She glanced at the man.

"Yeah, bad idea to get involved with a colleague, right?" She sucked back half of her drink. "Especially a guy like him. He can have anyone, but he chose me."

The man smiled and nodded. "And?"

"One day he asked me to dinner. We'd gone out for drinks after a crap shift many times, mostly with a group, but this invitation had a different vibe." Emily shifted in her chair, taking another sip. "Somehow he managed tickets to a sold out play I'd been dying to see. Brought flowers. Picked me up in a limo. Took me to an expensive restaurant." She sneaked a look at him, noting the wide grin. "Yes, the date ended with mind-blowing sex." A flush crept up her neck. "Did I really did just say that to a total stranger?"

"Ahh, darlin'. I'm not judging."

She ran a finger around the rim of the glass, blinking rapidly. If this man only knew how she judged after that passionate night. How secure it felt being in Aiden's arms, the sweet way he'd treated her, but then allowing insecurity to creep in. How could a man like Aiden value a simple woman like her, raised on the wrong side of town? "He's so perfect."

"What's the problem then?"

She focused on her drink. "He has a teenage daughter and he's moving to Boston."

"Hmm. Is it the teenager or Boston that's the issue?"

"His daughter is lovely and he's an amazing dad. I grew attached to her really quickly."

"So it's Boston?"

"It's so … fast. What if he regrets it? I'll have left my job and followed him and then he's stuck with me. He's sweet and generous and … it's confusing." Emily sighed. "And then there's the ex-wife. What if he can never love me like he loved her?"

"You're worried about Shar—" The man shifted and cleared his throat. "I wouldn't worry, Emelia. She's the ex-wife for a reason."

"Maybe." Confusion rushed in and she shot him a look. "How do you know my name?"

"Uhh, I saw it on your ticket?" He scrubbed a hand through his short, artfully messy hair. "Maybe you need to tell … this guy … to slow it down. Chicago isn't so far from Boston. If you love him, then it's worth the complications. So the question is, do you?"

Emily contemplated him. "How do you know I live in Chicago?"

He shrugged. "You aren't tanned enough to be a resident of L.A. and you were heading to Chicago, so I assumed. Do you live there?"

She narrowed her eyes, but nodded. "Where are you from?"

"Chicago originally, but I went to Stanford and ended up with a job in L.A. Once my contract is up, I plan to move so I can spend more time with my niece and nephew. I miss my friends."

"And your family?"

"Sure, though my parents are divorced and I'm not close to my older sister. I consider my friends as family."

This man reminded her of Aiden. "Funny, he says the same thing. He's not close to his parents, which should be a huge red flag but oddly isn't. He's an only child but his friends are amazing people."

He rewarded her with a warm smile. "Maybe you're overthinking this. Why not take the chance?"

"He seems too good to be true."

"What if he's the real deal?" The man turned serious blue eyes her way. "How does he make you feel," he said, tapping his chest with his index finger, "in here? Can you picture a future?"

She pressed a hand to her chest, wishing she could stop the ache inside. Aiden made her feel so incredibly special all the time, and like Nat, she could easily identify what she loved about him. His generosity. His smile. The wonderful way he had with kids, especially his love and patience with Savannah. How sweet he'd been with her family. The list was endless. "I do, you know."

The man turned her way. "What?"

"I love him and want babies and the ring and … just everything with him. Even when I hate him, I love him. When he's infuriating and stubborn and so damn impossible, I love him even more." She cupped her hands over her face. "I'm terrified of what he'll say if I show up on his doorstep. What if he's with someone else? What if he doesn't feel the same?"

"He's not and I'm sure he does." The man rose. "I'll be back in a minute."

"How do you know?" Emily whispered. This man either had remarkable powers of deduction or he knew something she didn't. Once he'd entered the tiny bathroom at the front of their section, she snagged his briefcase from the floor and searched the front pockets, smothering a sob as she came up with a pack of business cards. "Ryan Hartmann." The familiar name brought tears to her eyes. She tucked the cards away and set his bag in its place, a shiver running through her.

"You cold?"

The voice startled her and she turned her burning tear-filled eyes his way.

"Hey." Ryan crouched beside her seat. "Don't cry, darlin'. It'll all work out with your guy."

"How would you know?" Emily scoffed and dashed the back of her hand over her eyes. "Is it because you and Aiden talk about me? Do you, Ryan?" She sniffled. "You've known all along who I am. Nobody calls me Emelia besides Aiden."

"Sorry," he said, placing a hand over hers, "but it's not what you think."

"You're not spying on me so you can report back to him?" She pulled away. "Sucker for love, my ass. What a dickhead move. You did this for Aiden."

"Yeah, but I also did it for you." Ryan sank into his seat. "You clearly have regrets and you're in love with him."

Emily turned away, brushing at the tears flowing down her cheeks. "Which you know because you tricked me into telling you everything. Now you can all laugh over what an idiot I am for trusting you."

"Nobody would ever laugh at you for loving Aiden. He's one of my best friends. I want him to be happy." Ryan sighed. "When we get there, I'll take Vanna to Tom's so you two can sort things out."

Emily turned away and closed her eyes. Any intention of visiting the Vineyard faded. Every wish and thought had been exposed, including her stupid comment about having Aiden's babies. All revealed to a supposed stranger she thought she'd never see again. What if Aiden never wanted any of those things?

"I'm sorry. I never meant to hurt or embarrass you," Ryan said softly. "Aiden will fucking annihilate me for that."

"Good," she muttered. "You deserve it. Now leave me the hell alone." She didn't know who to be angrier with; Ryan for luring her into divulging the information or herself for trusting some random guy. Hot tears scalded her cheeks as she curled up facing away from him. That would teach her to trust men.

⁓≺

Hours later they landed in Boston. Emily averted her gritty, red-rimmed eyes from Ryan and exited the moment the crew opened the door. She longed to be home, except she had no true home. The penthouse belonged to Aiden. Going there meant facing the memories. Not going there meant the guest room at her mother's tiny apartment and endless explanations.

"Emily." Ryan caught up with her on the concourse. "Where are you going? The gate is that way." He motioned and then glanced at his expensive gold watch. "Our flight leaves in twenty minutes."

"It's not *our* flight, Ryan. My flight goes to Chicago." She glared at him. "What you did was low."

Ryan scrubbed a hand over his face. "Why are you so angry?"

"I told you things thinking I'd never see you again. Aiden doesn't even know half of it, yet you do? I feel so"—she wrapped her arms around herself—"stupid." *Vulnerable.* Trusting a man with her heart was hard enough, and his

9

friend holding power over intimate information scared her. This man could destroy everything.

"I swear I'll never breathe a word of our conversation to anyone. You tell him what you want when you want."

"Assuming I can trust you. Which I clearly can't."

"When I saw you, and heard what you said, I knew." He tugged her out of the flow of passengers. "Aiden is like a brother to me. I needed to help you get to the Vineyard because he does, Emily."

"Does what?"

"Love you, you beautiful, crazy, stubborn woman." Ryan tugged on her hand. "Please get on the plane. I promise you won't regret it."

"I already regret this."

"Aiden will be pissed if I ever tell him. That would involve confessing to screwing up his chances with the woman he loves. He'd never speak to me again."

"Ahh. It's about saving your own ass."

"You get a free trip to the Vineyard out of it." He widened his eyes. "Do I have to beg?" The man dropped to his knees, clinging to her hand. "Emelia Anderson, would you please take pity on a stupid man, forgive his grievous errors, and save his friendship?"

"Get up." Her cheeks burned as odd looks came their way.

"Not until you say yes." His grip on her hand tightened. "I'm not lying about how he feels. He'll want to see you."

She stared into his hopeful face. Even though this was the first time she'd met Ryan in person, the man had been mentioned many times. *Aiden confided his innermost secrets to Ryan almost as often as he did to Tom.* Emily nodded.

"Let's go." Ryan bounded to his feet and hauled her toward the gate and they arrived just as the last of the passengers disappeared down the jetway.

"Cutting it close." The attendant checked their tickets and ushered them through the gate.

Ryan held her hand tightly until they reached the plane, allowing her to precede him onto the small aircraft. They barely got seated before the door clunked closed and the safety demonstration began.

"Thank you, Emily. This is the right choice."

"I sure hope so." She closed her eyes, preparing for the inevitable stomach flip. Now she had to figure out what to do when she arrived.

CHAPTER 2

Aiden

AIDEN SUCKED IN A BREATH, propelling himself through the water with powerful strokes, driving hard for the last few feet to the dock. He hauled himself from the water and lounged on the wooden planks, propped on his hands with his head tipped back, savoring the last rays of sun. With eyes closed, he inhaled, hoping the combination of warm ocean air and physical exhaustion would get the woman off his mind and allow him to sleep tonight. An imagined whiff of lavender brought another wave of pain. Her scent.

"Aiden."

He exhaled. Now he was even hearing that tender voice during his waking hours.

"How are you?"

A frown creased his forehead as gentle fingers caressed his brow, brushing back his damp hair. Only Emily did that. He must be hallucinating.

"Aiden?"

He opened his eyes and tilted his head. After two hard blinks to clear his vision, he decided the woman kneeling beside him was real. He straightened, holding his breath. Waiting.

A smile flickered as she tucked the skirt of her sundress beneath her and dangled her feet in the water, but it faded. She stared wide-eyed, twisting a strand of her dark hair around a fingertip. "Say something." Her lashes fluttered over shining green eyes. "Anything."

The lump lodged in his throat made that impossible. The burn behind his eyes warned him of his impending breakdown. His mind warred. Even as instinct demanded he run, he reached out and tangled his hand into her dark mass of waves, reassuring himself that he wasn't dreaming. He sucked for air, drawing her toward him, burying his head in the crook of her neck. No matter how hard he tried, he couldn't move, couldn't speak, couldn't let her go.

She curled her arm around his back, one hand ruffling his hair. "I missed you."

Those precious words he'd longed to hear. The pounding of his heart drowned out the next ones as his breath hitched in his chest.

She shifted, sliding a leg over him, her fingers entwined in his hair, her soft lavender scent engulfing him. "I love you." Her warm breath wafted against his cheek and she pressed her lips to his temple. "Shhh."

Aiden's embrace tightened. He never wanted this moment to end, the pain and anger already fading away. None of it mattered. The woman he loved was in his arms and he vowed to avoid repeating past mistakes.

He slid his hands up, cupping her face between them, finally daring to look at her.

A shimmer appeared in her eyes, the cloud of dark hair around her making her look like his very own angel. Her lips parted, the nibble to her lower lip and darkening of those beautiful jade eyes sending a shudder of desire through him.

He captured her lips in a hungry kiss, the way she pressed her hips against him and the soft moan low in her throat inviting him to continue.

Emily nipped at his lip and dug her fingers into his back. Her other hand traveled down his bare belly to pluck at the band of his swim trunks.

As he caressed her velvety thigh, a vague thought flitted through his mind. This wasn't the best place for what was about to happen … but … fuck the consequences.

⚮

As his eyes drifted open, contentment crept over him. The warmth of her naked body cradled against his as the sailboat rocked reminded him this was real. Emily had returned.

She shifted, regarding him with sleepy eyes. "I'm starving."

The snicker escaped. "Should we plan a raid on the fridge?"

A radiant smile appeared. "You do speak."

"Mmmhmm." He leaned close, hovering just above her. "It's just that sometimes actions are better than words." The salty tang lingered on her skin and he nuzzled her neck.

"I love that." Her breathless whisper and tender touch sent a shiver down his spine. "Don't stop."

He had no intention of abandoning his goal of keeping her close. This woman drove him out of his mind and time blurred, leaving him in a state of blissful exhaustion with hazy images of silken limbs, heated satiny flesh, and his name falling from her beautiful lips as he loved her. Thoroughly. Completely. Endlessly.

She emitted a mellow, satisfied sigh, dragging a handful of dark waves off her face before she snuggled against his chest and draped a toned leg over his. "Where do you get the energy? I can barely move."

"Me either." Not that he wanted to. Despite his brave words earlier in the summer, he hadn't been fine. He'd been empty, struggling to navigate life without Emily in it. "I'm happy you're here."

Her dark lashes fluttered. "I almost didn't get on the plane."

"But you did." He pressed a kiss to her temple.

His phone dinged from somewhere outside in the darkness. He sighed. It chimed again, followed by three more notifications in quick succession. "Damn. It's on the dock." He wiggled free. "It might be Vanna."

Emily smacked his bare ass as he opened one of the drawers under the bed. "Bring me my dress while you're at it."

He wiggled his brows and tugged on a pair shorts. "I like you the way you are."

"I can't return to the house naked. Imagine if Savannah's there?"

"She's not. Jenn and Alex planned to take her to a movie and keep her overnight." He squinted. "Rather convenient last minute plans actually. Though Ryan's another story. He might show up at any time."

Emily bit her lip. "They didn't know I was coming."

The flash of guilt passed so swiftly he almost missed it. "Hmmm." He contemplated her before stepping onto the deck. His eyes adjusted to the darkness and he padded to the deck box and reclaimed his phone.

Hear you have a house guest. Vanna's staying with us for a few days.

He read Jenna's note again then sent his response.

How did you know?

While the dots danced across his screen, he viewed the texts from Vanna, stating she would stay with Tom and Jenna. He answered his daughter as the dots stopped, then started again. Finally the text appeared.

Ryan was on the same flight. He's staying here too.

Another notification popped up seconds later.

Jenn wasn't supposed to tell you. Don't make it a big deal with Emily, but met her on plane. Tell you later.

Aiden frowned as he replied.

Tell me what??? Big deal how??

Have fun. Don't do anything I wouldn't.

Aiden snickered. That left endless possibilities.

Say nothing about the flight.

"Hey." Emily emerged from the cabin of the sailboat wearing one of his oversized t-shirts. "Everything okay?"

"Yeah, fine." He locked the screen and set his phone on the box face down. "We have the house to ourselves."

"Lovely." She wrapped her arms around him from behind, resting her head against his back. "Though I was looking forward to seeing Vanna."

He covered her hands with his, wishing they could stay like this forever.

"It's beautiful and peaceful here. Not at all like California beaches." Emily sighed.

He turned in her arms and tipped her chin toward him. "What were you doing there?"

"Visiting Nat. Isa's gotten so big."

"How's Nat managing? Is Andy helping?" He scoffed as she shook her head. "Asshole. So you gave Nat half of your pay check?"

"Isa has to eat." She lifted one shoulder. "You think I'm crazy."

"No. I love your big heart." He cupped her face. "What changed your mind about getting on the plane?"

"I can't explain it." She gnawed her lip.

Aiden hoped for something more definitive than the equivalent of I don't know.

"You're disappointed." She squeezed his hand.

"A little," he said, "but I'm still happy you came."

"I missed you. I missed Vanna." She blinked hard. "I love you, Aiden, I do, but this situation is so complicated. I need time."

"The Boston offer is still open."

Her eyes widened. "Let's just enjoy this time together. I promise we'll talk more about it, but not now. Please?"

Aiden fought the urge to push the issue, but he sensed talking would get him nowhere. If he let his heart speak, if he showered her with love, showed her how perfect they were together, how life together could be, maybe then he'd have the answer.

"Hungry?" he asked.

"Starving."

He entwined their fingers and led her toward the house.

"You left your phone on the dock. And my dress."

"It's private property. Have you ever had a moonlight picnic on the beach?"

"We never left Chicago in the summer, so no."

Once they reached the house, she disappeared into the bathroom while he selected two bottles of wine and packed a variety of food into the hamper. When she reappeared, he handed her two blankets.

"You'd almost think you've done this before." She eyed him as they headed toward the sand.

"Sure. We spent summers here for years." He set the basket near the fire pit.

Emily wandered to the edge of the water, the waves lapping at her feet as she crossed her arms and stared into the darkness.

Aiden selected wood from the box he kept nearby, arranging it into a small stack. In moments, flames flickered to life.

"That looked easy." Her voice carried over the shush of the waves as he spread one of the blankets, dropping the second on top still neatly folded. "Done that a few times too?"

The sand felt cool under his feet as he joined her, curling an arm around her waist. "What's wrong, Em?"

"It's been a long day, is all." She pointed. "The water's glowing."

"Bioluminescence. Later, we can swim."

"In that?" A smile appeared as her stomach rumbled. "Food first. What did you bring?"

Once she was settled on the blanket, he poured her a glass of wine and sliced the baguette, laying out the meat slices, fruit, and cheese.

"A gourmet moonlight picnic. It looks delicious." She graced him with a smile and ate several bites. After a sip of wine she asked, "How's Vanna?"

"Better. Now she has the aunts and uncles around, she seems less anxious."

"Good." Emily swirled her wine. "I'm sorry for the drama at the end. I worried she'd never forgive me."

"But she did. She'll be excited to see you."

"Is she coming to the wedding?"

"Hell no. Jenna worried herself sick over how we'd manage the strange dynamics." It hadn't been an easy decision, but he planned to surprise Savannah with a trip to Portland to visit her friends that weekend. "Tom suggested rescinding Tiffany's invitation."

"Why didn't they?"

There were so many things he couldn't divulge about his ex-wife, especially to Emily. "I asked them to leave it alone. Tiffany already hates me. Why make it worse? Or complicate the wedding plans because of my messed-up life?"

"The delicate division of friendships after divorce?" Emily smiled sadly. "My sisters both went through that."

"The divorce isn't the issue. It's her stupidity over Savannah." He scrubbed a hand through his hair. "Sweet Jenn thinks Tiff will come to her senses, but until she dumps Harrison, it's unlikely."

"Until?" Emily's brow arched.

"Until, unless … whatever." He shrugged off the question. This conversation was leading into dangerous territory.

The look she sent his way was searching, as if she was interpreting words unsaid. "You've done these little romantic nights a lot, huh?" Her lips tugged downward, the motion of her hands encompassing their surroundings.

Here we go again. Where had that overactive imagination led her?

"Who's Maya? Is that her middle name or something?"

"Who's middle name? Tiffany?" At her slight nod he said, "No, she's Tiffany Gabrielle. And this"—he pointed at the picnic—"I thought you'd enjoy." He rose, cradling his glass as he stepped into the cool water, swishing his foot through the waves and studying the glowing patterns the movement created in the shallows. He'd thought, or at least hoped, they'd gotten past the assumptions about his life.

Emily came up beside him and curled an arm around his waist. "I'm sorry. The thought of your ex-wife makes me crazy and I don't …" She sucked in a breath. "That's not true. I know exactly why."

Aiden tipped his head toward her and raised a brow.

"It's obvious you loved her. Maybe you still do. Maybe you'll never love another woman the way you loved her."

"Fuck, I hope not." He guzzled the last of his wine before closing his eyes and pinching the bridge of his nose. At the end of his marriage, he'd sworn to never love a woman again.

Emily's arm dropped to her side and she sniffled, turning her head away.

"Another relationship like that would end me." He massaged his temples with one hand. "Please don't get passive-aggressive and jealous over someone I divorced ten years ago. There are many reasons the marriage didn't work, but they don't apply to us."

She lifted her chin, revealing tear-filled eyes. "You two have a lot of history here."

"We don't have to stay if it bothers you. One day, maybe I'll sell this place." He hated the thought, but what she said was true, even if the history was ancient. If it was between the house and Emily, he knew which he'd choose.

"Isn't this your grandmother's house?"

"It was until Grandfather died and then Gramma signed it over to me. It's the closest thing I have to a childhood home." He glanced at her. "I never bring women here. This is my place. Where I escape to when I need space. Where I reconnect with my friends. Yes, Tiffany has been here, but not since we were fifteen."

She cupped a hand over her mouth, her eyes widening. "And I barged in. Twice. I am so sorry."

"Don't be. I invited you. This time anyway." His lips twitched. "The first time ... you were such a hot mess, how could I kick you out?"

Her cheeks flushed a bright pink as she covered her face with her hands, peeking at him through splayed fingers. "Urgh. Every girl's dream. The unforgettable hot mess."

"Unforgettable in an incredibly sexy way." His smile faded. "This amazing, breathtaking, and impossibly complicated woman showed up without warning and stole my heart." He caught her hands in his. "You made it the best Vineyard getaway I'd had in a forever."

The slight hitch of her breath, followed by the shimmer of those beautiful green eyes drew him in. Their gazes locked and he felt it. That snap of attraction, the quickening of his pulse, the rapid beat of his heart, the longing to hold her in his arms. He leaned in, hesitating for a split second before catching her lower lip between his, deepening the kiss, giving in to temptation.

He rested his forehead against hers, forcing himself not to ask. There would be a time and place, but this was not it. "How about that swim?"

CHAPTER 3

Emily

EMILY PADDED ONTO THE LARGE patio attached to the master bedroom, stretching her arms skyward and admiring the magnificent view of the ocean. The spacious deck was bathed in bright sunlight, the wicker furniture and bright flowers in the planters inviting her to linger, stretch on a lounger, and soak up the warm rays.

She drew in a long breath, savoring the mixture of salty air and light perfume of greenery topped by the light aroma of fresh brewed coffee. Her mouth watered. Every morning since her arrival three days ago, Aiden had spoiled her with breakfast in this private oasis.

Moments later he appeared and set the tray on the low table near the wicker sofa. "Sleep well?" He wrapped her in his arms, brushing her lips with his.

She nodded, cuddling closer, loving the outdoorsy earthy scent clinging to his skin while running her fingers through his damp hair. "Been out for a swim already?"

"Mmmhmm. I met Tom and Ryan for a workout."

"It's only eight-thirty." She fought the urge to ask about the discussion between the three men, thankful for Aiden's blissful lack of awareness of her revelations to Ryan. "I'm barely awake and you've finished a half-marathon and made breakfast."

"You needed the extra sleep." He smirked and poured a cup, adding a splash of cream and the tiniest bit of sugar, and offering it to her. "This should help, as will breakfast."

"Why, thank you. It looks amazing." She helped herself to a bowl of granola, fruit, and yogurt. The man was sweet, leaving her to lounge in bed while he did everything. They were sinking into a familiar routine, but not. Here the distraction of work and daily life was absent.

"We're invited to Tom's for a barbecue tonight." He sat and dug his spoon into his own bowl.

"Sounds like fun." She focused on scooping up fresh raspberries while heat rose in her face. A barbecue meant facing Ryan again when she'd worked so hard to avoid him. A touch of guilt ate at her for sharing intimate details with Aiden's friend that she wasn't comfortable saying to him. Not yet. Babies, a ring … She was nowhere ready for either of those things.

"We don't have to, Em." Aiden set his half-empty bowl aside. "If you'd rather it be just us for a few more days …"

She struggled to maintain a neutral expression, avoiding Aiden's keen look.

He scrubbed his hands over his face. "Do we even have a few more days?"

That was a question she couldn't even answer for herself. When she arrived at LAX, she fully intended to return to Chicago, not end up here with Aiden. She clutched her bowl in her lap, gnawing at her lip as she struggled to formulate a response.

"I was hoping you'd stay until the end of August like we planned." Aiden rubbed the back of his neck before he rose and leaned on the railing with his head bowed.

"Don't, please?" Emily blinked hard. "Can't we just go day to day? Things got so messy, so fast, and I boarded that plane missing you, but"—she hauled air into her burning lungs—"what that means, I still don't know."

He kept his head bent, massaging his temples.

"Commitment is hard for me. Look at what happened to my mom." Tears blurred her vision. Those endless, raging battles ending with the swift exit of her father still burned. "My sisters barely remember my father."

"I didn't have either parent, yet we both turned out okay." He swept a hand through his hair, his steely gaze boring into her. "I'll do whatever is necessary to make sure my daughter has at least one parent, and avoids the woman who doesn't give a shit. Even if that includes moving to another state."

"You're right," she whispered. "You've taken on a teenager. That's a huge commitment, and I understand why you left, but it doesn't make it any easier."

"I suppose not." He sat across from her. "That leaves us in the same spot. You there, me in Boston."

"Why is it all or nothing? We broke up without even discussing the other option."

"What? Long distance?"

At her nod, he shook his head. "Relationships are hard enough without a thousand miles in between. It never works."

"Why not? People do it."

"Rarely successfully, and I can't drag Vanna back and forth once she's in school. Add on your shifts, my shifts, and any weekend activities she gets involved in, we'll be lucky to see each other twice a month."

"You can't move back?" Even as she said it, she knew the answer. Aiden had signed an employment contract, paid a substantial deposit on a private school for Savannah, and bought a penthouse apartment. Not to mention the overshadowing Tiffany situation.

"There are positions open in Boston."

"Don't," she whispered. "I can't."

"Or you won't, but it means the same thing." Aiden pried the bowl from her hands and placed it on the tray. "What do you need, Em? What would convince you to take the chance on us?" He caught her hands between his. "Marry me."

"What?" Her eyes widened, her palms growing damp and clammy as terror crept over her.

"I love you. I need you. I want to marry you."

"Aiden, stop." Her voice shook and she yanked her hands away. "You don't mean it. Just … don't."

"Why did you even come here?" He rose to his feet in a smooth motion, avoiding her gaze. "You should leave. Now. Before Savannah comes home."

"Aiden …"

"I'll give you space so you can pack. Take the Mercedes and lock the keys in it when you get to the airport. I'll pick it up later." He finally looked at her, a perfectly flat expression on his face. "It's best you don't see Vanna."

"I don't want it to end like this."

"Yet this is the end." His voice was low and controlled. "You looked petrified. How do we come back from that?"

A sob broke free from her chest.

With a deep sigh, he pulled her into his arms and buried his head against her neck. "I won't survive a long distance relationship, but you'll be miserable in Boston. That would kill me, and it would eventually end us anyway."

"Shh." She silenced him with a finger placed over his lips before replacing it with her own lips, kissing him deeply before resting her forehead against his.

"Take care of yourself, Emelia." He extricated himself from her embrace and retreated into the house.

She wrapped her arms around herself, shivering at the missing warmth of his arms, trying to block out the sound of footsteps on the stairs, followed mere moments later by the thunk of a car door, the purr of a precision engine, and gravel under tires.

A shudder ran through her as her eyes stung, followed by a heaviness in her chest as tears trickled down her face. She loved Aiden, but those words *I want to marry you* struck panic in her heart, and he'd seen it.

After dragging several breaths into her burning lungs, she stumbled into the bedroom and sank onto the edge of the bed, staring at her phone for the longest time before dialing. "Aiden," she whispered after his voice mail kicked in. "I'm sorry, but I'm just not …" The words locked in her throat. She hung up and pressed the phone to her aching chest.

A ragged sob tore free as she curled into a ball in the middle of the king-sized bed, hugging his pillow and stuffing her face into it, wishing he hadn't left. Even if it was easier this way. Her tears flowed freely.

Finally, she crawled from the bed, dabbing at her eyes with a tissue. Saying that goodbye to Savannah in Chicago had been hard enough. Going through it a second time was unthinkable. Time to pack and get to the airport. She threw her belongings into her bag and then splashed cold water onto her face and dressed.

She took a last look around before grabbing Aiden's oversized sweatshirt from the back of the chair and pressing it to her face. It smelled like him, that comfortable masculine earthy salt and sun scent. Without a second thought, she stuffed it into her carry-on bag.

CHAPTER 4

Aiden

IDEN FORCED ONE EYE OPEN and peered at the man hovering over him.

"Hey." Tom prodded him again. "Oh good, you're alive."

"What time is it?" He sat, ignoring the pain exploding in his temple. "Where's Savannah?" A frisson of panic raced through him as the bright light beaming through the glass assaulted his eyes.

"Don't worry. We didn't allow her to see the disgraceful state you were in last night. Get your ass up, shower, and shave so you don't look like you slept in a ditch like a vagrant." Tom wrinkled his nose. "Or smell like one."

Aiden flopped back and shielded his face with one hand. "Shit. I'm sorry, man. You must be sick of rescuing my ass."

"You should be sorry, but don't apologize to me. Someone else needs one more than I ever will." Tom dumped two tablets into Aiden's hand and offered him a large glass of water. "Take these. There's a bag of clean clothes in the bathroom."

After Tom left, Aiden hauled himself from bed, wishing he were dead. A headache hammered away and his stomach rolled, but he'd done it to himself. He cranked the water on full blast, stumbling into the stall.

The hot shower did little to calm the pounding in his head, and he dragged himself into the kitchen. If only he could return to the comfort of bed. Burying himself under the covers would make it easier to pretend the real world didn't exist, but Tom would never permit it, so he'd deal with it. He poured a large cup of coffee and slumped into a chair, massaging the back of his neck with his fingertips.

"Are you okay?" Tom asked in a low voice.

Aiden gave a half-hearted shrug before taking a large gulp of coffee.

"That's what I thought," Tom said. "What happened?"

Aiden stared into the black liquid in his mug. Pain lanced through him every time he thought about Emily. Last night, alcohol had eased his devastation, but now he had nowhere to hide.

"I'll pry it out of you, so … tell me."

Aiden sucked for air. The events of the preceding months weighed him down, threatening to drag him under. Moving forward or even expressing his despair seemed impossible.

Tom sank into the chair beside him, the light pressure of the man's arm looping around Aiden's shoulders reassuring. "I'm sorry."

"What does it matter?" Aiden muttered. He looked away. "We had a wonderful start that went to shit. I thought Emily was different. That she'd be the one who'd stay. Turns out I'm delusional. Women never stay." *At least not with me.*

"No chance you can fix things?"

"What's to fix? She doesn't want any of it. I can't …" The words stuck in his throat and his eyes burned. Aiden focused on his hands, allowing the pain drumming through his temples to drown out the torment in his heart.

"No wallowing, self-pity, or falling apart allowed. Six months ago, you might have binged and drowned your sorrows in alcohol and hot blonde ex-girlfriends, but not this time."

"Nothing happened." Aiden hung his head and dragged in a ragged breath. Vague images flitted through his mind. Why Jazlyn had appeared in the bar last night he didn't know, but he'd never allow himself to travel that bleak road ever again. Especially not with her.

"I hope not, but that's another discussion. Focus on the little girl who needs you to be strong. She's already lost too much. You're the only stable and solid thing holding her together."

"She's not so little. What the hell was I thinking agreeing to be her guardian?" Aiden covered his eyes with one hand. "What the hell was Ross thinking? I'm not equipped to parent a teenager."

"Yet here we are, so you'd better figure it out. Fast." Tom gave him a stern look. "Don't you dare let her down, or I'll kick your ass." The gentle tone of his voice belied the harshness of his words. "You're doing a great job with her, Aiden. And remember, you're not alone."

He forced himself to his feet. Even if he'd never expected anything to happen to Ross and hadn't anticipated the overwhelming and debilitating grief when the man had passed, he'd promised he'd take care of Savannah. The sacred words of one father to another remained forever unbreakable. "Can you drive me into town for my car?"

Tom squeezed his shoulder. "That will give you time to pull it together. Jenn has a few words for you."

"Yay." Aiden sighed. "I can't wait."

An hour later, Aiden let himself in the front door. The sound of water rushing through the pipes alerted him that Savannah was in the upstairs shower.

Alex rose from her seat at the counter, holding out her arms and offering him a sad smile.

"Sorry," he whispered, pressing his face into her soft hair. He took comfort in her familiar and soothing vanilla scent. "Thanks for taking care of her."

"It's not a problem, honey." She drew back and kissed his cheek. "Never scare me like that again."

"You sent Tom after me."

"Only because I love you." Alex cupped his face between her palms. "Ryan almost missed his flight for London, and Joel's in Chicago."

He blinked hard. "I'm worried about Vanna. She's lost another important person in her life."

"Kids are resilient." She tilted her head as the water shut off. "I'll go so you can talk to your daughter." After bestowing another soft kiss to his cheek, she slipped out the door.

Aiden squeezed his eyes closed and placed his flattened palms on the counter, hoping to steady his trembling legs. Ross would have known what to do. Carrying on without him was hard. Why had the man believed Aiden could act as a proper father to this girl he'd only begun to know?

"You're here." Savannah appeared in the doorway, her hair still damp from the shower. "I tried to text and call but you never answered."

"I'm sorry. It won't happen again." Deep shame filled him at the disappointment and sadness reflected in her eyes. He bent his head, searching for the right thing to say but his mind remained a complete blank.

"Where were you?" Savannah sniffled, her curtain of hair hiding her expression. She shuffled toward him. "You're tired."

"Mmhm, I am." Bringing her to the verge of another breakdown made the guilt even worse. Aiden slid his arms around her, wrapping her into an embrace. "I'm so sorry," he whispered.

"I …" She issued a choked sob before bursting into tears. "You missed the barbecue and you d-didn't c-call me. I worried you'd g-gone."

"Oh, sweetie, no." Aiden buried his head against her hair. "I'd never leave you. It's been …" His eyes burned as he fought back his own tears. This not-so-little girl was his weakness. The one person in this world who regularly brought him to the edge. The one who evoked raw emotions and to whom he would never deny his true feelings. The person he owed everything.

"I miss Emily. She left us. Why?"

"She didn't leave us. She left me." Saying it out loud reminded him of his current reality as a terminally single father embarking on a solo journey into parenthood. "You're everything. I will never leave you." He rocked her against his chest. "It's you and me."

They stood there for some time before she whispered, "Promise you won't leave?"

"I promise." He dropped a kiss on her hair. "Dry your tears, sweetheart. We'll head over to Tom and Jenna's for the afternoon." As much as he'd missed Savannah over the past few days, he wasn't in any condition emotionally or physically to be good company.

He locked the door behind them and they headed up the beach.

Jenna dashed across the sand and wrapped her arms around him, not letting go for the longest time. When she finally did, she turned shiny, red-rimmed eyes his way. "Don't do things like that, you big jerk." She smacked his arm with her fist as a tear trickled down her cheek.

"I'm fine, Jenn."

She sniffled and brushed away the salty drop. "Savannah, sweetie, why don't you see if Tom needs a hand in the kitchen?"

Vanna nodded and trudged across the beach, glancing over her shoulder before she disappeared into the house.

"I screwed up, Jenn. I'm really sorry and I'll do better. You and Tom don't need this right now."

"No, honey, don't apologize." She placed a hand over his heart. "You love her. Losing her hurts. Did you talk to Tom?"

"Your future husband dragged my sorry ass out of the bar at some appalling hour." Aiden grimaced. "This morning I got the talk."

"Ahh, all that icky sharing of feelings. Gotta hate that." She smirked, but it faded. "Why were you drowning yourself in alcohol? Tell me your side as I'm sure it'll be discussed between the girls."

"Great. I'm entertainment for the masses."

She squinted and pursed her lips.

"Fine. It came down to me or her career." He shrugged and looked away.

"And?" Jenna grabbed his arm, forcing him to face her. "What aren't you telling me?" She cupped his cheek in her palm. "Don't give up so easily."

"Nothing about that woman is easy." He scoffed. "Our relationship's reduced me to begging and hanging around for a scrap of affection. What's the point of that?"

Jenna tilted her head, her expression softening. "Love?"

"I asked her to marry me and she said *you don't mean it.* And the terrified look on her face … that said it all. If that's love, I can do without."

Her eyes widened. "You asked Emily?"

A humorless laugh escaped. "Complete stupidity, right? Enough is enough, Jenn. I recognize a hopeless case."

"Love isn't hopeless. It's wonderful."

Aiden squeezed her hand. "The love between you and Tom truly is, Jenn. Don't ever doubt you are his everything." He kissed her cheek, grateful this woman was still a staunch supporter even after the mess with Tiffany.

"About the wedding …"

"Don't stress over it. I'll be good. No drama, I promise."

"Uh-huh." Her light laugh and wry smile brought the tiniest of grins to his face. "Thank you for everything you're doing. Hang in there. It'll get better."

"I've been through this before, so I'll manage, even if I've added the teenager. Or maybe it'll be easier." He pasted on a smile. "Savannah's never been to New York. Maybe I'll close up the house early and take her on a road trip. A little father-daughter bonding time and back to school shopping before we head to Boston."

Jenna linked her arm through his as they headed toward the house. "What teenage girl wouldn't like that?"

"Exactly." Tonight he'd talk to Vanna and make some reservations in New York. If he stayed, all he'd do was battle memories of Emily.

No matter how deep the pain, he'd make it through this wedding and move on with his life. It was only two weekends to celebrate the marriage of two of his closest friends. What could go wrong?

⤚≺

Aiden glanced at the clock and forced himself from bed. Summer had faded away, he'd completed his first shift in Boston as an attending physician, and Vanna was ready for her first day of school.

He wandered through to the living room where Savannah munched on a muffin, her eyes riveted on the TV. "Shouldn't you be getting ready for school?" He picked up the remote, intending to turn it off, when the name and images scrolling across the screen caught his eye.

"Senator Harrison Taylor is being arraigned today. Charges include money laundering, bribery, and suspected cases of involvement with a minor. Senator Taylor and his representatives have refused to comment."

"Isn't he engaged to Tiffany?" Savannah tilted her head, fixated on the flickering images as an officer forced Harrison into the back of a black sedan.

The newscaster's voice droned on as his daughter turned toward him, a frown embedded on her features.

"That's him."

"Did you know?"

"No." An odd sense of relief flowed through him at the welcome news. With any luck, the unscrupulous man and his sidekicks would suffer the consequences of their actions.

"Is she still marrying him?"

Aiden shook off the thoughts of retribution and shrugged. "No idea," he said. "You have orientation today. Hurry, or you'll be late."

Vanna shot a look at the clock before kissing Aiden on the cheek. "Bye, Dad. I'll leave your dinner in the fridge."

Aiden hugged and kissed her before she headed out the door. He wondered what this news on Harrison would mean for him and Vanna going forward. Would Tiffany finally break off her engagement? And then what?

Aiden spent the next two hours organizing the final boxes from their move, groaning as his phone rang yet again. As hard as he tried to ignore her, she'd been persistent. He gave in and answered.

"Are you home?" Tiffany asked.

"What do you want?"

"We need to talk."

His stomach lurched at the four words that never failed to bring him misery.

"It'll only take a minute."

"Fine. Come up, but make it quick." Aiden sighed and headed for the foyer. The elevator door swished open moments later. "Tiffany."

She stood ramrod straight, her shoulders squared and chin tipped up. "Can I come in?" she asked, her crisp, imperious voice grating on his nerves.

"You're already in," he said under his breath as she shoved past him, her heels clicking on the tile.

"You saw the news?" She spun and flipped her hair over her shoulder, her eyes narrowing. "Why did you do that?"

"Do what?" He folded his arms over his chest.

"Harrison. You turned him in."

Aiden heaved a sigh. "Wrong, though I see the old-boys network is spinning along as usual. Go find someone else to yell at."

She looked away, shoulders sagging as her bravado evaporated. "Sorry," she whispered. "It's horrible. He's innocent."

"Uhhh, right. Keep telling yourself that."

"You think …?" Her eyes filled with confusion. "No, you're wrong."

"Whatever. I don't give a crap what Harrison has or hasn't done. Is that it? I have a shift and you shouldn't be here. What if Vanna had been home?"

"I waited until she left." She stared at the floor. "I didn't mean to hurt her, or you."

"Too little and far too late to worry about it. I don't want or need your apologies." A shiver ran through him at the thought she'd been keeping tabs on them and that she even knew where he lived. "You should go, and … quit stalking us. That's plain creepy."

"I'm sorry." Her eyes pleaded with him. "Forgive me?"

"Nope. If you think coming here unannounced, accusing me of turning in your idiot fiancé, and offering a half-assed apology is even remotely adequate, then you're more delusional than I imagined."

"I get it. I'll leave you alone, and I won't come here again. But … we have to get through Jenna and Tom's wedding. Can we at least agree to get along for the next few weeks? We're the best man and maid of honor. Not an inspired choice, but here we are."

"Agreed. I promised Jenn we'd get along for her big day." He propped a shoulder against the wall. "What have you planned for the bachelorette?"

"The girls are getting together on Saturday night, the weekend before the wedding. I thought I'd throw a party at my place, though it'll be a tight fit. You?"

"I booked a private room for dinner, a limo to a VIP room at a club for afterward, and hotel rooms for Tom and the groomsmen. Jenn and Tom requested we skip the typical … entertainment."

Her corners of her mouth twitched. "Code for no strippers and strip clubs?"

"Right. I'll probably regret this, but the ladies could join us at the club after your party."

"I'll get a consensus, and send the numbers." She tilted her head. "Your Chicago penthouse is spacious …"

"And?"

"Could I host the bachelorette there? For Jenna?"

"Hmmm. You'd have get Emily's agreement. Alex could ask her. But"—he shook a finger at her—"behave. This is only because it's Jenn."

"Emily's living in your penthouse?" Tiffany's eyebrows shot upward. "I heard you broke up."

"If there's nothing else regarding the wedding, please leave." He narrowed his eyes. "Remember your promise. No calling and never come here again."

"Yes, Aiden, I get it."

"Oh, one more thing. You're not bringing Harrison to the wedding or the club."

"So it's okay for your ex to be part of the wedding, but not okay for me to bring my fiancé?"

"You're my ex-wife, and you're in the wedding party."

"You know what I mean."

"Emily isn't a political figure charged with major criminal offenses." He scoffed. "Harrison's appearance will cause a media circus. We don't need stalking paparazzi." He held back the smirk. "Do it for Tom and Jenna."

She glowered. "I doubt he'll want to come anyway."

"That's settled. Now leave before Vanna comes home." He ushered her toward the elevator, thankful when the doors closed behind her. He stood there for several seconds, wondering why she'd bothered to make the trip to Boston when a phone call would have accomplished the same goals. Not that it mattered. He'd wasted far too much of his life on her already. After the wedding, he'd move on and forget the impossible women and damage they'd inflicted.

⌒≼

Aiden tacked Savannah's class schedule on the board beside Tom and Jenna's wedding invitation. As he double-checked that he'd marked the dates in his calendar, he noted the missed call from the familiar number.

Vanna watched him through narrowed eyes. "What's wrong? Who called?"

"Nothing is wrong." How did she know? Keeping his emotions in check was a full-time job. He steeled himself against the comments he expected were coming. "And nobody."

"Will you ever call nobody back?"

"Who?"

"Emily calls, but you ignore her." An eye roll accompanied her words.

"How would you know?"

Vanna shrugged, dropping her gaze. "You hate her, but we still talk. She asks about you."

Aiden sighed and rubbed his face. "I don't hate Emily, but there's nothing left to say. Talk away. It's fine. Just don't expect we'll get back together. It won't happen." Before he could prevent it, the question escaped. "How is she?"

"If you're so interested, why don't you call her?"

He squinted at her. Teenagers were experts at adding those little sarcastic inflections, but he wouldn't let her get away with it.

"She's fine," she said. "She asked me to forgive her for leaving without saying goodbye."

He should have expected it. Emily wasn't a mean or cruel person. He'd always thought she was wonderful. At least she'd made the effort for his daughter. Maybe Vanna wouldn't lose the precious and much-needed connection she developed with his ex-girlfriend.

"She invited me to visit her in Chicago." A sad look appeared. "I told her I didn't think you'd let me."

"You could go one weekend after you're settled in school." He busied himself sorting the mail.

"I can see her?"

"Why not?"

"Oh. Good." Vanna tilted her head. "She'll still be at the wedding?"

"Yes. Tom and Jenna wanted to invite you, but there won't be any guests your age. I'm the best man, which means I'll be busy the entire weekend. It wouldn't be much fun."

A small scoff left Savannah. "Don't you mean that Tiffany doesn't want me there?"

"Vanna—"

"It's fine." She waved a hand. "I'm over it. Anyway, spending time with my friends in Portland will be more fun."

"I'm sorry. I wish things were different."

"Just don't pretend," she whispered. "It makes it worse, not better."

"You're right." He leveled his gaze at her. "I told Tom and Jenna not to make the situation more awkward or hurtful than it already is, even though they'd have loved you to be there. I'm sorry for not saying it, but I hate how hard this is for you."

She lifted a shoulder. "You're protecting me, right? So, let's drop it." Savannah peered at him. "Call Emily." She looked away, picking at a nail.

"Savannah." He moved closer, placing his hands on her shoulders. "I'll always care for Emily, but we won't be together. I'll talk to her at the wedding, and we'll figure out when you can see her. That's all I can promise."

Savannah nodded, leaning in to hug him. "I miss her."

"I know you do, sweetie." He kissed the top of her head, grateful for her resilience and understanding.

Chapter 5

Emily pasted a smile on her face as she entered through the sliding glass doors into the ER. Another day of work should thrill and excite her, but it failed. It took superhuman effort to make the daily trek.

"Hey, boss. How's it going?" The new chief resident waved from behind the front desk.

"Great. Let me drop off my things and you can update me."

Boss. A word she'd longed to hear but now rang hollow in her ears. A meaningless word, considering what she'd done to Aiden. Even thinking of him made her stomach bundle into knots, but she refused to dwell on the lingering emptiness left by his absence. Emptiness tinged with irritation. In the two weeks since she left the Vineyard, he hadn't returned a single phone call or shown the slightest interest in the *why* of it. Why she'd run. Why the idea of marriage had etched that look of terror on her face.

"Dr. Anderson." Tara trailed her into the lounge. "You look off. I hope you're not coming down with something. Isn't the big wedding coming up soon?" The nurse heaved a sigh. "Isn't Aiden invited?"

A feigned illness might be a brilliant way to avoid the whole situation. The thought raced through her mind. Now she was back to pissed off man and bitchy ex-wife, she longed to escape. *Nope.* She'd put her own feelings aside. Abandoning Jenna was unthinkable after she'd promised to be the perfect bridesmaid.

"Earth to Dr. Anderson?" Tara crossed her arms as a smirk appeared. "What did I say to turn you green? Things not so rosy with our fine Dr. Hamilton these days?"

"I'm great." She waved off the concern.

As sweet as the nurse pretended to be, Emily knew she harbored a grudge. Over time it had become clear that Tara wanted far more from Aiden than she admitted. The woman had been downright nasty after he'd quit, placing the blame on Emily for his move to Boston.

Dragon Lady hadn't helped either. Emily wasn't sure who was happier at the apparent demise of her relationship with Aiden—Dana or Tara. Both for different reasons, but all the same, it hadn't been pleasant working in the ER after Aiden walked out that door.

***

Emily rushed through the door of the bridal salon. Her lateness couldn't be prevented. Two trauma patients had arrived in the ER only minutes before the end of her shift. With no other attending doctors available, she'd stuck around to supervise the senior resident until the surgeon had escorted the injured parties to the surgical floor.

"Grayson/Maxwell?" Emily asked the receptionist.

"They're in the fitting area. Go on in." The receptionist pointed with a smile.

Emily waved and headed through the opulent dress displays to the back. She paused as the long honey-blonde hair came into view. Her immediate thought was of Savannah and how much she physically resembled this bitter and distant woman.

"Sorry, I'm late."

An *I'll pretend I like you* smile appeared on Tiffany's face. "Nice of you to show up," she muttered as she inspected one of the designer shoes from the display.

Emily pasted on a bright smile. "How wonderful to see you again, Tiffany."

"I'm so glad you're here." Alexis wrapped her in a warm hug, throwing a dark look toward Tiffany. "Jenna is about to do her big reveal."

"Alex." Emily embraced her friend, grateful for the support and genuine welcome.

Jenna stepped from the change room, lifting the skirt of flowing ivory gown to step onto the raised podium.

"You look amazing." Emily circled her friend, admiring the delicate lace detailing and sweetheart neckline. The dress had cost a fortune, but Jenna seemed unconcerned with the expense.

Emily shook off the image of herself in an incredible gown. Nothing but a seductive fantasy, and she'd be better off without harboring any of those ridiculous illusions. Marriage often ended with cheating bastard husbands and nasty divorces, as proven by both her mother and two younger sisters.

"The perfect dress." Alex sighed, pressing her palms together and bringing them to her lips.

"Beautiful, Jenna," Tiffany said.

"The bridesmaids' dresses are ready too. I can't wait to see them on." Jenna motioned toward the dressing rooms.

"Since Aiden's best man, I'll need heels before they do the fitting." Tiffany held up the expensive designer skyscrapers with immaculately manicured fingertips. "Can I get these in a seven?"

The wedding consultant nodded and disappeared toward the storage room to retrieve the shoes.

"Speaking of Aiden," Tiffany said, a sly smile creeping across her face, "I saw him the other day."

Emily's stomach rolled. The man never phoned her back but allowed that woman to visit? Even if he'd been adamant he had no desire to see Tiffany and had avoided her all summer, the two had a long and convoluted history that included love, marriage, and a baby, even if not in that order.

"You saw Aiden?" Alex looked confused. "He didn't tell me he was in Chicago."

"I visited Boston." Tiffany sent a triumphant look at Emily as she accepted a shoebox from the saleslady. "He bought an amazing penthouse in Back Bay. Totally gorgeous. And the view. Spectacular. Not sure which place I prefer." The woman tapped her pursed lips with her index finger. "Which one do you think is best, Emily? You're still living in his penthouse, aren't you?" Her perfect brow arched.

"I haven't visited his new place." Emily kept her expression neutral, but she couldn't prevent the tremble in her voice.

"Oh, that's right. You and Aiden split up." The woman purred the words in a saccharine voice. "We didn't get around to much … discussion." A smirk appeared before she stepped into a changing room.

Emily blinked hard, her lips tugging downward as she pulled the curtain closed on her own changing room, but not before she registered the pitying looks directed her way by Alex and Jenna. Her cheeks flamed as she sank onto the bench. She wished she'd never agreed to be part of the wedding.

Emily forced a cheerful smile before she slipped on her heels for her fitting, but keeping the happy expression pasted there for the entire ordeal and through an excruciating dinner at a nearby restaurant was nearly an insurmountable task.

"What are the plans for Jenna's bachelorette?" Alex asked the moment the bride excused herself to use the restroom.

"Oh." Tiffany combined her sideways glance with a smug grin. "Aiden offered his penthouse for the party. You don't mind, do you, Emily? So many of *our* friends are attending and my place is tiny."

Irritation rose. How dare he permit his ex-wife to invade their private space? "I don't know—"

"For Jenna? It's too late to book another venue, so it would totally ruin the party."

How could she refuse? "If Aiden said it was okay …" She shrugged, wishing she had time to find a new place to live before the spectacular party.

"Perfect. I'll arrange everything." Tiffany glanced at her watch. "I should run. I have an early meeting at my gallery." She rose and gathered her things, stopping to say goodbye to Jenna on her way out.

"Are you okay?" Alexis stared at her, deep concern mirrored on her face.

"Why wouldn't I be?" She pasted on a smile.

"Don't let Tiffany get to you. I'm sure nothing's going on with Aiden." Alexis patted her arm.

"Why should I care? Aiden's a free man. He can see whoever he wants."

"You lack both killer instinct and a poker face." Alex shook her head. "It makes you perfect for Aiden, but it leaves you at Tiffany's mercy."

"That's why she went at you with those insinuations about Boston and a romantic interlude with Aiden." Jenna slid into her seat. "I don't get it. You could be with him, yet you're here, listening to Tiffany's BS stories."

"We know he asked you to move." Alex sounded disappointed. "Why didn't you go with Aiden?"

"Why? Give up my career to chase after a man? What happens in two months when we break up?"

"Right, well"—Alex pursed her lips—"keep telling yourself that, but you'll kick yourself one day. Guys like Aiden are a rare and precious commodity."

Jenna shared a conspiratorial look with Alex before turning to Emily. "Wasn't there something else he asked?"

"Is nothing sacred?" Given the expressions on their faces, Emily had little doubt he'd spilled about his marriage proposal. "It doesn't matter because he didn't mean it." She gripped her glass.

"Aiden wouldn't make any proposal he didn't mean." Jenna shook her head. "What did you say? I'm stupidly in love with you, but I'll hang around Chicago and hope you come back for me? In the meantime, I'll let your ex-wife taunt me and drive me insane with the idea you're having hot, illicit sex with her?"

Emily twirled her glass on the coaster. "I didn't know what to say. It freaked me out. Admit it. Marriage, babies, all of that … it ends badly every single time."

"Well. Thanks for that." Jenna said with a humorless laugh.

"Sorry, I didn't mean—" Emily blushed.

"I love Tom. I'm willing to take that chance, because living without him isn't an option," Jenna said. "But this discussion is about you and Aiden."

Emily gulped a mouthful of her drink. Jenna and Alex were both shaking their heads. This lecture was far from over.

"The only word that should have come out of your mouth was a big fat YES." Jenna thumped her fist on the tabletop. "Or please, Aiden, make me the happiest woman on the planet by allowing me to marry your fine ass. Why would you turn down a lifetime of married bliss?" Her eyes shone. "With someone ... you love. You ... Oh, Emily." Jenna pinched the bridge of her nose.

"You wonder why he refuses to call you? What could he say to you after he ... and you ... and ...?" Alex threw her hands up.

Jenna squeezed Emily's hand. "He'll be in town for the bachelor party next weekend. If it were me, I'd be doing some hard thinking before then."

Tears stung Emily's eyes. "It's not an option."

"Do you love him?" Jenna asked. "If you do, you need to fix this. Call him."

"Why? He's ignored every attempt I've made. Anyway, he'll get back together with Tiffany."

"Wipe that thought from your mind," Alex said. "Aiden will never go back to her. The end of their marriage was a disaster, and now I know the whole story, I'd kick his ass if he even let it cross his mind."

"Alex is right. None of us would allow him to get entangled in that mess again, but it doesn't mean he won't move on with someone else. I'm ..." She shrugged. "I'm sad and disappointed."

Emily frowned at her friend. "Why?"

"Because you two are an amazing couple. What happened? It had to be more than the ridiculous notion he lacked sincerity." Jenna sighed.

"He said it on a whim."

"You're dead wrong." Jenna set her lips in a flat line.

"No. You're wrong. Our relationship is far from perfect. He expects me to drop everything and follow."

Alex tilted her head. "So his move had nothing to do with the fact he lost his job? Or his need to do what's best for Savannah?" she asked. "He's a full-time father to a teenage girl. His situation requires tough decisions and sacrifices."

Emily twisted her napkin between her fingers.

"Hmm." Jenna stared into her drink. "Try harder to talk to him." She lifted her gaze to meet Emily's. "Never give up on true love."

"Who says we have anything resembling true love? What is that anyhow? Non-existent fantasy is what." Emily scoffed. "The man can't even return a damn phone call. And you heard Tiffany."

Jenna heaved a sigh. "You'd have to be blind not to see how the man feels. You're letting him go because of your stupid pride. Stop making ridiculous excuses and start planning that hot and sexy outfit for Saturday night. Take back your man."

"He's not mine."

"Only one way to find out." Alex arched a perfect brow. "Shopping. Tomorrow night."

"But ..." Emily let the objection die on her lips. In the face of these two determined women, how could she say no? Besides, nothing said she had to follow through.

CHAPTER 6

Aiden

THE CROWDED ROOM RANG WITH conversation and laughter and the drinks flowed. Tom appeared happier than ever now the official countdown to starting his life as a married man had begun.

"Yo, Aiden. When are the ladies showing up?" Ryan threw an arm around his shoulders. "Any gorgeous single ones I should keep my eye on? The wedding party has a sad lack of available women. Very disappointing."

"Trust you to be lining up your prospects. Tiffany texted and they're on their way. I'm sure out of the thirty joining the celebration, there'll be one or two single hotties for you."

"That's what I wanted to hear. Good man for inviting them."

Aiden patted his long-time friend on the back. "Anything to help you find the girl of your dreams." He glanced at his phone as it buzzed. "Speaking of which … Are you accepting a position on the welcoming committee? The doorman asked me to confirm who's with us to keep out the party crashers."

"Hell, yes." Ryan followed and they wound their way through the crowd to the entrance. "Ohh. Shark in the water." He nodded toward the door. "A damn sexy shark, but still …"

Tiffany bestowed a dazzling smile on the doorman as she shrugged out of her coat, revealing a slinky black dress paired with stiletto heels. She swept her hair over her shoulder, her hips swaying seductively as she moved through the crowd.

"Damn. Don't know how you deal with her." After a pat to Aiden's back, Ryan danced his way over to greet the group of new guests and point them toward the private room.

Aiden approached the bouncer. "Thanks."

"No problem." The man grinned. "Doesn't hurt business one bit."

Aiden hid his own smile. A large group of well-dressed women flooding through a club's door tended to liven up the joint, and any men in line witnessing the arrival would wait hours to get inside.

Tiffany appeared at his side, pressing her lithe form against him as she whispered into his ear. "Thanks for the penthouse. We had fun." Her hand lingered on the back of his neck as she played with his hair.

"What are you doing?" He pushed her away.

"Sorry." A coquettish smile played across her lips and she batted her eyes. "Old habits and all that."

"That habit should die, don't you think?" He spotted Emily as she entered the club and removed her coat.

Her head tilted as she narrowed her eyes, her icy stare passing over him to rest on the woman by his side before she turned away.

Aiden's mouth went dry at the sight of the bare skin exposed by the low back of the sexy red satin dress that clung to her in all the right places. He longed to tangle his hands into the dark, wild curls cascading down her back and take possession of her luscious red lips …

"Aiden?" Tiffany tugged on his arm.

"We have the private room at the back. I should say hi to Jenn." He brushed her off and wove through the crowd. Once he reached the group of ladies, he looped arms around Jenna and Alex, giving Emily a nod. "Can I interest you in drinks?"

"Thought you'd never ask." Jenna kissed his cheek. "Thank you for lending us your place."

"You're welcome, honey." He led them to the bar set up for their private function and motioned toward Jenna, Alex, and Emily. "These three are on my tab."

"This is amazing. The turnout's great." Alex surveyed the room after they'd ordered drinks.

"It is." He sighed at the venomous glare from Emily as she accepted her cocktail from the bartender. "Is she plotting to stab me or what?"

"Someone's a little jelly. She saw you with Tiffany. I'd avoid the blonde bombshell ex-wife if I were you," Alex said against his ear. "She's still in love with you."

"Is that too much to drink or delirium speaking?"

"You weren't at the apartment. Those two were ready to kill each other." Alex lifted a brow. "So take your pick." She stretched on tiptoes and planted a kiss on his cheek. "I vote for Emily." With a smile, she danced into the crowd.

Aiden searched the room and spotted Emily socializing with one of Tom's colleagues. He signaled the bartender for a shot, downing it and motioning for another. Not being allowed to hold her close was unbearable. Her flirting drove him insane, but it wasn't his place to interfere.

After fortifying himself with more shots, he threw himself into the role of host, mingling and greeting the guests as he moved through the room, keeping as far away from Emily as possible. Focus. That's what he'd do, and soon it would be over.

Hours later, the party had devolved into a free-for-all, everyone moving in and out of the private room, dancing, drinking, and circulating with the rest of the crowd in the club. Aiden had spent an excruciating, endless time with Tiffany's nails sunk into his arm, finally shaking her off when someone asked her to dance.

"Is it over yet?" he asked as he joined Ryan at the bar and tossed back the shot offered by the bartender. "Keep them coming."

Ryan tapped Aiden's shoulder and pointed at something behind him.

Aiden turned, his gaze drawn to a dark-haired beauty as she joined the other three women moving sensuously to the music on top of the gleaming bar only a few feet away. His mouth went dry at the sinuous movement of her arms as she swept up her hair as she swayed her hips and tipped back her head, lost in the beat.

"Whoa." Ryan's voice brought him to the present. "Time to get them to the hotel before the striptease begins." His friend sported a huge grin.

Aiden scanned the throng the performance had attracted. More than a few of the male guests issued shrill wolf whistles, stamping their feet and clapping.

"Sir, they shouldn't be up there." The bartender motioned to the women. "Should I call for backup?"

"We'll handle it." Aiden pushed through the throng, holding his hands up to Jenna. "Come down, sweetheart."

"Thanks, honey." She giggled as he swung her to the floor, planting a light kiss on his lips before wobbling toward Tom.

Joel appeared and reclaimed Alex, while Ryan pursued a belligerent Tiffany who swatted at his hands and sashayed to the far end of the bar.

Aiden stared at Emily, their eyes locking on each other as she brought her hands down and around his neck, allowing him to scoop her off the bar. He held her against his chest for a moment, enjoying the warmth of her body and her intoxicating scent tickling his nose.

"Let me go." She released her hold, wiggling to break free. The second her feet touched the floor, she shoved his hands away and disappeared into the crowd.

Tiffany dodged Ryan and moved toward Aiden. He grabbed her off the bar and draped her over his shoulder. As he set her to the ground, she wound an arm around his neck and locked her lips onto his.

"Don't." He unhooked her arm and stepped away. "Let's get out of here. Everyone's half-wasted."

Ryan frowned and cast a glance at something over Aiden's shoulder. "You got that right. I'd watch your back. Someone's not happy with your little sideshow."

By the time Aiden turned, Emily and Alex were supporting Jenna and weaving toward the exit with Tiffany only a few steps behind. As they reached the door, Tiffany glanced over her shoulder.

Aiden recognized that look, the unmistakable invitation reflected in her eyes. "You warned me, man. Shark." With a shake of his head, he headed toward the door.

⌒≼

The hotel Aiden had chosen was within stumbling distance of the club. It didn't take long before they were piling into the elevator.

"Take Alex and get her to bed, Joel. Ryan and I will take care of the bride and groom." Aiden inserted the card key, and they hauled Tom into the room, followed by Jenna, Tiffany, and Emily.

"Thanks. Night all." Joel's voice carried in from the hallway.

Jenna pirouetted in circles, swaying as if to some imagined beat in her head as Ryan and Aiden tipped Tom onto the bed.

Aiden worked on his coat. "Sit up, Tom. You need to help us out. Jenna, time for bed."

"Uh-huh." Jenna shimmied out of her dress and wobbled over, flopping onto the mattress.

Emily pulled off Jenna's shoes and tucked her under the covers before collapsing onto the couch.

"That's our girl." Ryan laughed. "Not an ounce of shy."

"Nope. Remember those beach parties?" Aiden raised a brow at his friend as they stripped Tom down to his boxers and tuck him under the covers.

"Who could forget?" Ryan located two water bottles and a bottle of pain tablets, placing them on the side tables. "Tom okay?"

Aiden checked on their friend. "He'll hate life in the morning, but he'll be fine. I forced him to drink water along with those shots. Stomach pumping in the ER ruins the fun." He peeked at the sleeping Jenna and adjusted the pillow beneath her head before smothering a yawn. "She has the right idea."

"I'm turning in." Ryan performed a subtle eye roll toward where Tiffany waited with her arms crossed and foot tapping, then to the inert form of Emily slumped on the couch. "Hey, Tiffany, I'll walk you to your room. Aiden can finish tucking them in."

"Yes, you two go." Aiden kept his face straight, sending a silent thanks to Ryan.

"I'll st—" Tiffany yanked her arm away. "Hey!" She wiggled, attempting to free herself as Ryan steered her through the door and closed it behind them.

Aiden picked up clothing and tidied the room before turning off the lights, leaving one on in the bathroom. "Em, you awake?"

"Barely." She yawned and surveyed him through bleary eyes.

"I'll walk you to your room."

"Call me a cab?" She stumbled to her feet. "Nobody told me to book a room."

"Didn't Tiff … Right. Why would she?" he muttered as Emily scowled. "You should stay."

"Here?" She waved a hand as they exited into the hallway. "In this over-priced palace? If I even tried to check-in at two in the morning, they'd assume I'm your hooker."

"Don't act crazy. A hooker wouldn't book a …"

Her glare silenced him. "Your little wifey obviously decided this would be entertaining. I'm surprised I even received an invitation to the party, but someone told her she could use your apartment." She leaned against the wall and slid into a heap, dropping her head onto her knees. "Wifey hates me."

"She's not my wife." Aiden scooped her into his arms, his heart rate quickening as Emily's head sank against his chest. He carried her the few feet down the hall and opened the door to his suite, lowering her to her feet. "I told her to ask about the apartment."

"Well, she did, but she cleverly combined it with a heavy load of guilt. My place is soooooooo tiny." Emily's voice rose to a high falsetto. "It'll totally ruin the party." The woman's expression darkened as she flipped her hair over her shoulder in a perfect imitation of his ex-wife. "If I said no, she'd brand me as the unreasonable bitch freeloading on the rich guy."

Yikes. She'd unsheathed her claws. *A wise man would say nothing.*

"Why didn't you tell me yourself?" She glowered. "She scarcely let you out of her sight. It's sickening." She pushed away the moment he set her on her feet. "I'm surprised she's not banging on your door."

"She's engaged."

"Yeah, she showed great concern over her fiancé as she hung all over you." Emily's eyes blazed with fury. "That"—she jabbed a finger into his chest—"was quite the kiss."

"Whoa." He caught her hand. "I didn't kiss her. That was all her."

"And the Boston booty call?"

"The what?" His eyebrows rose.

"You don't deny she visited your apartment?"

"What's to deny?" He narrowed his eyes. "I've got nothing to hide, and it's none of your damn business anyway."

"It's none of my business that you're hooking up with other women?" She stepped toward him, her eyes flashing as she struck at him with an open palm.

He forced her hand to her side. "Is that what you think of me, Emelia?"

She glared, but her lips parted, her breasts heaving as he held her wrist. Her eyes shimmered as their gazes locked.

Aiden froze, unable to take his eyes off her. They stared at each other for a moment before he grasped her face and captured those sweet lips.

Emily moaned into his mouth, an arm winding around his neck as she pressed her body against him, pulling him closer.

He couldn't resist as their kiss deepened and desire rushed through him along with a heady mix of emotions. He loved this impossible and infuriating woman. If he could only have this single moment, he'd take it.

Chapter 7

Emily

Warning bells rang in Emily's head as she wound her arms around Aiden, sliding a hand to caress that tight ass. She nipped at his bottom lip as he unzipped her dress and it slithered into a silky pool. The edge of the mattress pressed against her legs and she sank into the sheets, hauling him down with her.

Her anger and frustration poured out as she ripped at his shirt, sighing as she encountered the smooth bare skin of his chest. "Aiden," she murmured, tipping her head to the side, allowing him access to the sensitive spots on her neck. Her fingers grazed along his side, and she slid her hands under the waistband to cup his butt, pushing her hips against him. She'd longed to discard every stitch of clothing between them.

She entwined her fingers into his hair, kissing and tasting his hot flesh, arching against him, savoring the weight of his hard body on hers. "Please don't stop," she whispered.

Those same warning bells jangled when Emily opened her eyes hours later, registering the warm naked body pressed against hers. In the dim light of morning and with her relatively sober mind, the regret rose and a small sob escaped her lips as the images of the night before flashed before her eyes.

She listened to his deep breathing and stared at his broad back. A small part of her longed to brush her fingertips over it, to caress his smooth skin and heal the red marks she'd left in those moments of uninhibited passion.

Emily lifted her weight from the bed, careful not to disturb him. After a quick and silent trip to the bathroom to don her recovered clothing, she located her clutch and slipped into the hallway, the door clicking shut behind her. She sagged against the wall, closing her eyes and sucking in a long breath. "What have I done?" she whispered as panic raged through her. Every time the man appeared, she became incapable of resisting the compelling and powerful attraction.

"Where are you slinking off to so early?" asked the owner of a deep, masculine, and yes, *familiar* voice.

She straightened as heat rose in her cheeks. "I could ask the same of you."

"I have a plane to catch." Ryan motioned to his suitcase. "It's inconvenient, but tomorrow I'm due in London for an early morning meeting. Are you heading home?"

She nodded and combed her fingers through her hair, wishing she'd taken more than a moment to splash water on her face and run a brush through her tangled curls.

"My driver's meeting me downstairs shortly, but I planned to grab a quick bite first. Why don't you join me for breakfast?" A smile quirked his full lips. "I hate eating alone."

"I'm surprised you're hungry after last night." Emily followed Ryan into the elevator, swallowing hard to control the lingering queasiness. She longed to be home, but her stomach twisted, warning her to rehydrate before risking the car ride. "Maybe water … and a coffee."

A small crease appeared in his brow but he remained silent until the hostess seated them in the hotel café and filled their glasses. He ordered coffee and opened his menu. "You sure you don't want anything?" At the shake of her head, he gave his breakfast request to the server. "Thanks," he said with a dazzling smile.

"So business in London?"

He nodded. "I don't mind accruing the frequent flyer miles, but it doesn't make life easy. It's hard on relationships when you're always out of town."

"I can relate after spending eight years in school and then another three or four trapped in a hospital during residency. It doesn't leave much time for a personal life." She sipped her ice water, grateful as it soothed her dry throat.

"Our group drifted, but we've become a family. That's the point, isn't it? That you stick around and support the important people in your life?"

Emily contained the rueful laugh. "Is that my forced epiphany? My man will wait until I regain my senses?"

"Is he yours?" The corners of his mouth tugged downward as he studied her. "Should he bother to hang around while you figure out your shit?"

She opened her mouth to respond, but what could she say? The man's words struck a chord.

"I formed the distinct impression you didn't say goodbye." Ryan raised a brow. "I accepted the challenge of blocking Tiffany, yet you're throwing my efforts away?"

The flush rose in her cheeks as she tipped her chin, allowing her hair fall in a curtain across her face, remembering the humiliating moment when her eyes met Ryan's last night. His knowing smile and nod toward Aiden, acknowledging that she'd spent the entire evening tracking the man's every move. "It's not the first time you played wingman so he could have his fun."

"That's a touch harsh, considering where you spent the night." A grin crept across his face. "Besides, I was your wingman, not his."

"Mine?" She peeked at him. "Why?"

He pointed as his own chest. "Sucker for true love, remember? I did my best to eliminate the threat posed by his pesky ex-wife."

Of course he'd noticed how Tiffany clung to Aiden, all fake bright smiles and irritating loud laughter. The woman had dogged her ex-husband's footsteps all night, scarcely leaving his side.

"Yeah, Sharkie dug in her teeth, didn't she?"

"Sharkie?" A snicker escaped Emily. "You named her…?" Her smile faded. What did this man call her now she'd damaged his friend?

"Fitting, don't you think?" His gaze met hers. "She tore him apart. Left him for dead. Now he's healed from those wounds and found someone else to love, she wants him back and she won't let anything get in her way. Especially a woman like you."

"But we're not—"

"That's why you were sneaking out of his hotel room? Keeping tabs on him all night? Because you're not?" He raised a hand to stall her objection. "I like you, Emily, but take it easy on the guy. Last night he played his role as best man and host of the party, but"—he frowned—"it doesn't define him. I figured you'd understand the difference between his public persona and the inner person."

"Right, and next you'll say it's okay that every single woman put their hands all over him, and I imagined him kissing Tiffany."

Ryan thumped his cup onto the table. "He's known those people for years and last night he flew solo. Who broke up with who?" His eyes narrowed. "Stop running and let him catch you, or let him go. Quit leading him on and"—he wagged a finger—"forget punishing him for Tiffany's behavior. No matter how strong he appears on the surface, he can't take it. He's one of the good ones. Why can't you see it?"

Emily blinked back the tears, hunching forward, wishing she could disappear.

"Don't cry." Ryan sighed and squeezed her hand. "You're seeing what you want to see, or you're buying into what Tiffany wants you to believe. That woman detests seeing you anywhere near Aiden. Trust me, if she finds out you spent the night in his bed, watch out for the volatile reaction."

Volatile. Aiden's exact description of his marriage. "Maybe I'll keep it to myself."

Ryan sat back as the server placed his plate in front of him and refilled their beverages. Once she'd left, he took a large bite, his silent observation making Emily squirm. After several more bites he said, "Don't count on keeping last night a secret, darlin'. Everyone's spotted the raw chemistry between you and our boy."

She concentrated on adding a splash of cream to her cup, pondering his words. The man's sharp observation skills and his apparent lack of filter caused her lips to twitch. "You're direct."

"Who has time for silly games?" He dabbed at his mouth with his napkin and pushed away his empty plate. "I'm sure my car is here."

"I'll catch a cab."

"Don't be ridiculous. I'll drop you." He tucked his credit card into the folder. "I insist."

After he'd settled his bill, Emily followed Ryan toward the exit, glancing across the marble foyer directly into icy blue eyes.

Tiffany turned her nose up before flipping her wavy blonde ponytail over her shoulder and stalking toward the elevators.

Emily sighed as Ryan ushered her into the sleek black sedan. Soon she'd be home, but the reprieve would be short. Next weekend, she'd face the other woman's animosity at the wedding. Now she wished that she'd walked away while she could. No one would escape this awkward situation unscathed.

Ryan settled into the seat beside her, giving the penthouse address to the driver. "Talk to him, Emily," he said as the car merged into traffic. "It's not fair that you …" The man glanced at his phone as it chimed four times in quick succession. His eyes widened as he swiped his fingers over the screen. "Fuck."

"What? Is everything okay?"

"Fine." He scrubbed a hand over his face. "Just something with work." His brow furrowed and he drummed his fingers on the armrest as he glanced at his watch.

"Are you sure?"

"Yup." A smile appeared, but not the usual cocky relaxed one she associated with this man.

She clutched her hands in her lap and stared out the window until they pulled up in front of her building. "Thanks for the ride."

"No problem, darlin'." He peered at his watch again.

"Bye." She slid from the car and headed for the front door. By the time the doorman had it open, the sedan was halfway down the block. Something had changed in the last ten minutes, but she wasn't quite sure what. And she wasn't sure she wanted to know.

CHAPTER 8

Aiden

A TINKLE OF LAUGHTER RANG THROUGH the air as Aiden slipped through the doors and walked between dark wooden pews toward the front. The ornate stained glass windows created a spectrum of colors in the late afternoon.

"Look who made it." Tom clapped him on the back. "We should start the rehearsal as we have dinner reservations."

"Sorry, some idiot refused to check their over-sized bag and delayed my flight." Aiden gave his friend a brief hug and waved to Joel and Ryan who were chatting with Alex. "Get a load of this place."

"Five hundred guests. My mom went crazy with the list. We tried to cut it back, but you know how it goes."

"Poor bastard. You should have eloped."

"My parents would have freaked if I hadn't let them plan the event of the season." Tom's expression became serious. "You're a good man, tolerating a wedding with two exes."

"Shall we begin?" The officiant cleared his throat.

Aiden followed Tom to the altar, listening to the directions before the bridesmaids entered.

Every few seconds, Tom glanced at him as Emily strolled up the aisle with Ryan.

"Shut it," Aiden muttered under his breath. He'd aimed to keep things level after Emily's disappearing act the previous weekend. Waking up to an empty hotel room had acted as a stark reminder to expect nothing. She'd never change her mind.

Aiden struggled to focus, but he stole glances at Emily. She looked gorgeous. Her thick dark hair cascaded in silky waves and her green eyes were bright and vibrant. Her joyful smile made his heart skip as she laughed at something Alex said. He'd missed that laugh. The ache resurfaced. *Why lie, even to himself?* He missed everything about her.

The rehearsal didn't take long, and once they finished, everyone chatted while gathering their belongings.

"See you at dinner? Seven?" Tom asked.

"After I check into the hotel and change. I'll meet you there."

"Hey." Ryan caught up with him near the front door. "Can I catch a lift? I need to change."

"Sure. The car is waiting."

"I told Emily we'd give her a ride." Ryan lifted a brow.

"Idiot," Aiden muttered, but he couldn't refuse. He waited as Emily retrieved her purse and followed them to the car.

"Thank you," Emily murmured as the driver opened her door.

Ryan followed, settling across from Aiden with a smirk.

"How's Vanna?" Emily asked as the limo slid from the curb.

"She's settling in. The new school is working out." If he could keep the neutral conversation going, the ride to the hotel might be swift and painless. It would be even easier if Ryan engaged, but his friend stared out the window, drumming his fingers against the armrest.

"I phoned her," Emily said.

"She told me, it's ... fine ... good. Just because ..." He cleared his throat.

"Any more panic attacks?"

Aiden shrugged. "She's okay."

Emily fiddled with her purse strap and angled her body toward the window with a soft sigh.

The rest of the trip to the hotel passed in silence.

⌒≺

"Thanks for the lift." Emily waved and headed toward the elevators.

At the check-in desk, Aiden claimed his room key as Ryan waited.

"Well, that was awkward." Ryan said once they were in the elevator.

Aiden narrowed his eyes. "What did you expect after what happened last weekend?"

"You should tell Emily about Savannah. She needs to know Vanna's in counseling. Maybe she can help."

"We're not together. It's dangerous for Savannah to become dependent. After this weekend, Emily will be gone for good." Aiden brushed off Ryan's hand, intent on getting to his room. He couldn't get this weekend over fast enough.

The rehearsal dinner ended up being a marathon of speeches with Tiffany glued to his side. She'd tried his patience numerous times, but finally, it was over.

"We're hitting the club." Ryan's voice snapped him from his thoughts. "You in?"

"If Tom's going."

"Right, best man duties. It'll be the wedding party as the older folks want something more sedate."

The group piled into limos, and within a few minutes, they entered the club.

The thumping music and dim lighting added to the atmosphere, the party starting as the ladies headed for the dance floor. Aiden ordered a round of shots for the table which became a second round and then a third. The added drinks on top of the wine and drinks at dinnertime allowed everyone to loosen up. The effects of the alcohol sang through Aiden's veins.

"Oh, gotta get out there." Tom motioned to Jenna who was on the floor, surrounded by her bridal party. The group of ladies had attracted more than a few interested guys.

"Have fun." Aiden watched for a moment but turned away as one man moved closer to Emily. Seeing a random guy hitting on her drove him nuts and his fist curled. Aiden quelled the inclination to deck the man as it wasn't his place. He waved down the shot girl instead and ended up tipping back several more.

"Careful, you're hitting those rather hard." Ryan eyed him with concern. "If this is too much, then go. I'll take over duties for tonight."

Aiden shook his head, tipping back yet another shot.

"Want to dance?" The stunning woman appeared out of nowhere.

"Yes." He tipped back his last shot before allowing her to lead him onto the dance floor. The woman wore a short, sexy red dress, and was blessed with long, thick, dark hair. Definitely his type, his friends would say. *Well, why not?* An irresistible and undeniably attractive distraction had presented itself ...

Aiden turned his full attention to the dark-haired woman. He rested his hands on her hips, pulling her closer as they moved to the beat. The alcohol rushing through his system relaxed him, and the music took over as he turned his back to the group. He couldn't watch the guy flirting and putting his paws all over Emily.

The dark-haired woman inched closer and offered a seductive smile. She trailed her hand over his chest, then up, working at the knot and loosening his tie. White teeth clamped on her full bottom lip as she arched a brow, her nimble fingers fumbling with the top button of his dress shirt.

Aiden's chest tightened. The music faded out as his vision blurred. He sucked in a breath, fighting to regain focus, but everything remained hazy except for the brazen invitation in the woman's eyes. A sudden urge to escape both her and the crush of gyrating bodies overtook him. The dance floor seemed overcrowded, and he fought for breath as his heart pounded.

With a shake of his head, he shoved the woman's seeking hands away and fled, retreating to their empty table. He bowed his head, struggling to catch his breath, pinching the bridge of his nose.

He stiffened as the arms encircled him from behind, the softness of a warm body pressing against him and the woman's fingers tracked across his chest before gripping his biceps and forcing him to turn. His own hands rose, intending to force the invader aside, but he froze.

The woman's half-closed eyes glittered as she tipped her head, her wild, dark curls cascading over her shoulders. She tugged on his collar, her nimble fingers releasing the second button before the tips brushed across his cheek, one tracing his lips.

His moment of panic faded to a distant memory as she molded to him, the crush of bodies in the club forcing her closer. He grazed his hands over her curvaceous hips, sliding one around to caress the smooth exposed skin at the small of her back. The soft floral scent of her perfume enveloped him, creating a deep yearning for her kiss.

Her gentle touch to the nape of his neck sent a shiver racing down his spine. She twined her fingers through his hair, sending her own invitation as her lush lips parted and she pulled his head downward.

He met her halfway, the softness of her mouth and sweetness of the liquor on her tongue intoxicating, hunger galloping through his body. Time halted.

Powerless to resist, he devoured her lips and plundered her mouth, her passionate response compelling him to tangle his hand into those satiny locks and draw her closer.

"Let's get out of here," she whispered in a faint breathy voice.

A request he couldn't refuse. He maneuvered them through the crowd, winding their way to the door as he tapped a message to their driver.

The limo waited at the curb as they emerged. The moment they were inside with the door closed, he hauled her into his lap, fumbling for the switch to shut the privacy glass.

Emily entwined both hands into his hair as she straddled him, her dress riding up to reveal smooth tanned thighs, encouraging him to stroke the exposed skin. A soft moan left her as he plied butterfly kisses to her neck, hitting each pulse point with gentle suction before reclaiming her luscious lips, losing himself in her.

A soft rap on the glass startled him, and it took a moment to realize where they were. He eased her off his lap. "We're at the hotel," he murmured against her hair. He straightened her dress before the door opened.

She clung to his hand as he offered a polite nod at the driver. They sailed past the doorman, Emily's stiletto heels echoing against the marble tile as they crossed to the bank of elevators.

He poked the button, lacing his fingers through hers. After an eternity it opened, and they entered the empty car, the doors sliding shut as he pressed her against the side, their bodies molding together. He buried his head against her neck and trailed his mouth across the tempting, satiny flesh.

The moment they were inside his suite, she stepped into his arms, their lips meeting as they exchanged ravenous kisses.

Clothes hit the carpet. Two steps, shirt. One step, dress slithering down creamy skin into a silky pool. Two more steps, the jangle of his belt buckle. Another step, his pants falling into a heap, followed by her lacy bra. A final step, lowering her onto soft, luxurious sheets.

His fingers played through her hair, across her silky skin, her limbs wrapping around him. He lost all sense of time and space, caring about nothing other than this passionate, amazing woman in his arms.

CHAPTER 9

Emily

ER HEAD POUNDED AS THE morning light hit her eyes. Emily slammed them shut, covering her face with a hand before forcing them open again, orienting herself while her vision adjusted.

A warm hand ran over her hip, and she wiggled onto her side. "Aiden," she said, coming to the reality they'd spent the night together. Again. "What time is it?"

"Almost eight." His voice had a rough, low, not-quite-awake quality, and his body radiated heat. He blinked his red-rimmed eyes and pulled her closer.

His steady heartbeat thudded against her fingertips as she pressed them against his smooth, firm chest. "Eight? I should dress." She struggled half-heartedly to untangle herself from the mess of sheets, managing a half-sitting position.

The comfort of his loving arms snaked around her, pinning her against him as he drew her down into the cozy bed. She closed her eyes and sighed, wishing she could stay there all day. This seemed so right, like old times … but it wasn't. He lived in Boston. They weren't dating.

Her eyes popped open. "I have to get—"

"Good morning." He cut off her protest with a long slow kiss. "Just a few minutes longer …"

The way his voice trailed off made her shiver and she fought the urge to submit to his teasing kisses. Memories of long lazy mornings in the Vineyard ran through her mind. As satisfying as it would be to remain in bed with Aiden ...

Emily rested her palm against his cheek. "I need to go."

He sighed and loosened his grip.

She ruffled his hair and crawled off the mattress to collect the path of strewn clothing.

"Aiden? You in there?" A knock and Joel's voice carried into the room. "Get your ass out of bed. Aiden?"

Aiden reached for his pants. "Someone's sure to complain about the crazy man in the hallway."

Emily scooped up his shirt and slid it on before snatching her clothes from the end of the bed. She padded into the bathroom and shut the door, grimacing at the messy halo of hair surrounding flushed cheeks and the gritty red-rimmed eyes. A shower and strong coffee would help, but an even better bet was Aiden's small toiletry bag. *Ahhh.* The small bottle of pain relievers and vial of eye drops were welcome sights. The man thought of everything.

The drops stung, but they soothed the gritty redness, and the two extra-strength tablets she washed down with a handful of icy water would kick in soon. She dabbed at her watering eyes and leaned against the counter, straining to hear the faint voices in the next room.

Did Joel know she was here? What would Aiden's friends say about their swift exit last night?

The soft tap on the door brought her back to reality.

"Joel's gone."

Still clutching her dress and bra in one hand, she opened the door and eyed him, taking in the tousled hair and sexy scruff on his face. She admired his bare chest, the tight six-pack, and the zipped but unbuttoned jeans slung low on his hips.

Shame we don't have time ... What would he say if she acted on her lascivious thoughts? *Did he know what I was thinking?* Her cheeks burned as his eyebrows rose, the corners of his mouth twitching.

"Busted?" She bit her lip, controlling the urge to step closer.

His look lingered on her mouth before roving downwards. "Yup, expect comments." Aiden leaned in, pausing for a split second before caressing her jawline with enticing butterfly kisses.

Emily closed her eyes and tilted her head, playing with the soft tendrils of hair at the nape of his neck. The tingle in her belly grew, a shiver shaking her as small bumps prickled the bare flesh of her arms. She swayed, her knees threatening to buckle, the warmth of his hands seeping through the soft cotton of the shirt.

The ding of her phone made her open her eyes. "What are we going to do with you?" she whispered against his lips. "Last night shouldn't have happened."

Aiden dropped his hands to his sides and stepped back. "Go shower." His voice sounded flat, and he turned away. "We have a busy day and you should be downstairs having breakfast with the ladies. Headache?"

Emily bowed her head, examining the pattern on the carpet. "Nothing a couple of pain tablets and some strong coffee won't cure. I left the bottle on the counter." She grabbed her clutch and hurried toward the door.

"Emily."

She spun toward him.

"You might want to"—he motioned at her—"button that up?"

Heat rose in her cheeks at the gaping fabric between mismatched buttons, revealing an expanse of bare skin. No wonder he'd stared. "Thanks," she muttered as he disappeared into the bathroom.

After donning her dress, she dashed out the door, returning to her room to change before hurrying to the hotel's café.

"About time you showed up." Jenna greeted her with a mischievous grin.

Tiffany's only greeting was an icy glare as she sipped her coffee.

Emily smiled, willing herself to ignore the treacherous blonde. "Sorry, overslept. I need coffee" She gave a little wave, and the server approached to fill her cup.

"I ordered, otherwise you wouldn't have time to eat." Alexis smirked. "I'm guessing you need to rebuild your strength after last night?"

"Joel snitched?"

"Like he had to after the hot lip action followed by the hasty exit." Jenna's exaggerated wink brought a hot flush to Emily's face.

Tiffany sniffed and rolled her eyes as she looked away.

Alexis smiled behind her coffee cup, her eyes sparkling as she peered over the rim.

Emily narrowed her eyes. If the woman so much as mentioned marriage and Aiden in the same sentence, she'd have her killed.

"I trust you two had a good talk and worked through your issues." Jenna spread strawberry jam on a triangle of toast. "Last weekend, now again last night …"

"They weren't doing a whole lot of talking." Alex giggled.

"Stop." Tiffany slammed her cup onto the table. "No one wants all the down and dirty details. You're making me nauseous." She folded her arms across her chest. "Tramp," she said under her breath.

"Excuse me?" Emily straightened, clenching her hands around the white ceramic cup.

"You're all over him like a worthless little gold-digging tramp. You live in his penthouse despite your break-up, and every time he comes to town you answer his booty call. You're his plaything."

"This from the engaged woman who crawls all over him at every opportunity. Go home to Harrison and quit throwing yourself at my guy. Besides, what we do is none of your damn business." Emily lifted a brow. "Refresh my memory. Why was it that Aiden dumped you?"

Tiffany's face reddened. "You should talk."

"Enough." Alexis glanced around the restaurant. "This isn't the time or the place for this discussion."

Tiffany shoved her chair away from the table, her malevolent glare making Emily cringe. "See you at the salon." She tossed her napkin on top of her half-finished meal and stalked from the restaurant.

Emily's cheeks burned. "That was inappropriate … I'm so, so sorry." She bowed her head, blinking hard against the tears. What if people believed she was a gold-digger taking advantage of Aiden's generosity?

"I'm glad you defended yourself. She has no right to judge." Jenna patted her arm. "Everyone's seen her moves on Aiden. It's not cool."

"Still, I'm sorry. This should be a celebration, not a catfight. All over a damn man." Emily dabbed at her eyes.

"He's a damn fine man, so fight for him. Things haven't been the same since the whole deal with Vanna." Jenna shrugged. "Understand, he's putting on an act to avoid ruining my wedding, and I love him for it. I'd hoped we could all be adults about this, but Tiffany's pushing the limits."

Emily sat back, allowing the server to set the omelet in front of her.

"Eat." Alex motioned to the plate.

Emily forced down several bites, but her appetite had faded. Last night with Aiden had been amazing, but she'd destroyed the warmth and closeness with careless words.

Her stomach clenched and embarrassment flooded her. Everyone seemed to know everything about her relationship with Aiden. Perhaps they were tolerating her to allow the wedding to proceed without overt drama.

She'd do her best not to let her mortification show, if only to make sure Jenna had the special day she deserved.

Chapter 10

Aiden

As Tom and his groomsmen settled into the limo, Aiden shot a text to Tiffany. He bit his tongue and bided his time, even with the anger coursing through him. Today's goal was to avoid losing his temper and get through this wedding.

"To your last single moments," Ryan said, pouring them each a tumbler of Macallan. He tapped his glass against Tom's as the limo proceeded toward the church. "We wish you all the best."

Aiden focused on the day ahead. He had a million things to remember but his ultimate wish was to make this special for Tom and Jenna. He'd sort his messy life later.

"You have the ring, right?" Tom fidgeted in his seat. "And the license?"

"It's under control." *Except my vow to stay strong and prevent Emily from annihilating my heart.* He pushed the thought aside as the limo stopped in front of the church. "Let's get you married." Aiden led them through the side door and into the room assigned to them for their last-minute preparations.

Tom's eyes widened. "I forgot her gift."

"No, you didn't." Aiden held up the bag. "I'll deliver it while you relax. Joel, maybe get water for Tom before he bursts into flames."

He shook his head in amusement as he made the short trip to the other side of the church. His heart flipped at the sight of Emily in her blue chiffon dress. The sweetheart neckline and fitted lines emphasized her trim figure and tiny waist. "You look beautiful."

"Thank you. I'm glad Ryan will prop me up or I'd never make it up the aisle on these heels." She accepted her bouquet—an array of deep greenery and bright colorful flowers—while Aiden inspected her stilettos.

He never understood how women managed the towering heels, but they sure looked good. "What women do for beauty."

"What bridesmaids do to make the bride happy." She brushed imaginary fluff from his tuxedo. "You look …" A soft smile touched her lips.

He swayed toward her, drawn in by the inviting look in her eyes, visions of the night before dancing through his head. "Em …"

Tiffany's hand clutched his arm, her grasp like an eagle's talons digging into his flesh. "Don't let me fall on my face."

Damn. The woman had the worst timing. *Or did she?* He cleared his throat. Today wasn't about him. "Jenna. I have something for you." He presented the velvet jeweler's box.

"Oh." Tears sprang to her eyes, an audible inhale issuing from her as she revealed a sparkling diamond necklace. "It's gorgeous."

"May I?" Aiden lifted it from the box and motioned to her slender neck. "Tom hopes you'll wear it today." He circled behind her to drape and fasten the exquisite piece.

She stared in the full-length mirror, a hand rising to her chest. "Wonderful man. Tell him …" Her eyes shimmered.

"You look gorgeous, Jenn." He hugged and kissed her, careful not to squish her dress. "He can't wait to see you walk down that aisle."

"Thank you, honey. I can't believe this is it."

When he returned to the groom's room a few minutes later, he found Tom pacing back and forth. "Mission accomplished. It's time for Joel and Ryan to join the ladies. How are you holding up, Tom?"

"I'm nervous as hell. She is here, right?"

Aiden placed his hands on his friend's shoulders. "Just wait until you see her. She's gorgeous." Soft strains of music carried through the air. "You're up, bud."

They escorted Tom's mother and his grandmother to their seats before taking their places at the altar, both turning their attention to the end of the aisle. The music changed and the flower girl and ring bearer toddled up the aisle, followed by the long slow march of the bridesmaids.

Tom shifted from one foot to the other and bowed his head before peeking toward the doors.

"Almost at the finish line," Aiden murmured. "Breathe. Just breathe."

Tom rolled his eyes Aiden's way, but the comment seemed to work. His friend drew a long breath, his shoulders relaxing.

At long last, the bridal march filled the air, and the guests rose. Jenna entered on her father's arm, a stunning vision in ivory silk. Her rosy cheeks and bright eyes glowed as she floated toward Tom. The lovely woman heading toward them had Tom riveted.

Even with the complete joy for his friends, a piece of Aiden remained mired in agony. The woman he loved wasn't so eager to make this level of commitment. If only one day Emily looked at him the way Jenna was looking at Tom … If only she … *Not about me.*

He focused on the bride and groom, but his attention kept wandering to Emily with her glowing skin and shiny upswept hair revealing her slender, delicate neck and lovely green eyes. His very own angel.

Not mine. A mental shake cleared the thoughts he feared to voice. If Emily even suspected the depth of his love, she'd run. Nothing had changed.

Tom's shaky smile and trembling fingers as he reached for the diamond eternity wedding band compounded the feeling. The sheen in his eyes and the quick intake of breath betrayed his crumbling emotions.

Jenna blinked misty eyes as her new husband slipped the ring on her finger.

Aiden shifted, clasping his hands in front of him, not daring to move. Emily had rejected his proposal in the worst possible way. Seeing her expression now would be unbearable.

The change in music signaled the end of the ceremony and he presented Tiffany his arm for the processional to the doors, an odd thought overtaking him. He and this woman, who now seemed a complete stranger, never had the big white wedding. If they had, would it have changed the fate of their marriage?

The exit from the chaos of the swarm of wedding guests and snapping cameras into the peaceful air-conditioned interior of the white stretch limo was a relief. It was over. He'd survived. Barely.

Aiden produced the expensive bottle of champagne and crystal flutes, wishing the joyous couple well. The happiness of his friends meant everything, and he hoped it would last forever.

It was now after one in the morning. At least the reception had flown by, courtesy of his best man duties. He'd even managed to avoid Emily.

As the ballroom emptied of all but a few couples, he leaned against the bar, savoring the sweet tones of his favorite single malt scotch. At the sight of the familiar honey-blonde hair and crystal blue eyes, he drained the amber liquid and signaled the bartender. "A double. Neat."

Tiffany set her empty glass on the gleaming counter. "Aiden."

"Need something?"

"We got through the day with no major mishaps. That calls for a celebratory drink."

"Already have one." He waggled his glass and stared across the floor to where Emily talked and laughed with Ryan and Tom's cousin, Ken, who'd been at her side all night. He narrowed his eyes as he noted the proprietary hand resting on her back.

"My treat. We could … catch up." She ran her hand up his back, curling it around the nape of his neck. "Emily's busy so …"

He grasped her wrist, dragging her into the deserted coat check to the right of the bar.

"Mmmm. Privacy." She looped an arm around his neck, pressing against him.

"Whatever damn game you're playing needs to stop. Now." He caught her left hand and held it up, his lip curling at the glitter of diamonds. "You're wearing another man's ring, for fuck's sake."

"It doesn't mean—"

"Your ring didn't mean a damn thing during our marriage, either. Go home to your fiancé and leave me alone. The wedding's over and done, and so are we."

"Emily's fucking Ryan."

"Don't be ridiculous."

"It's true. I saw them together in the Boston airport in August, Ryan on his knees. Perfectly indecent. The morning after the bachelorette, she left the hotel with him."

Aiden scoffed and stalked from the room, heading straight for the bar and slugging back two shots in quick order. His phone dinged and he peered at the screen, pain searing through his chest. One of his best friends in the world … on his knees in front of Emily, clutching her hand with the airline departure board behind them.

Seconds later another message appeared.

I really did see them in Boston.

Three more pictures followed this missive. Ryan and Emily, hands linked together on an airport concourse. Ryan and Emily eating breakfast. Ryan and Emily climbing into the back of a black sedan.

He pinched the bridge of his nose, sucking for air.

"You good?" Ryan appeared beside him, signaling the bartender for another round.

"Fuck off." He closed his eyes, fighting the burn.

The man paused with his drink halfway to his lips. "What did I do?"

Aiden slid his phone toward his friend. "What the fuck, Ryan?"

Ryan squinted at the screen. "Shit. Sharkie sent you that?"

"How did you know it was from her?" Aiden scoffed as the realization hit. It was all true. "She sent them to you first. A little blackmail?"

"Yeah. The morning after Tom's bachelor party, but I didn't think she'd stoop so low as to send them to you. It's not what it looks like. I'd never, Aiden."

Aiden glanced at the dance floor where Emily swayed in Ken's arms. "Just like she'd never hook up with another guy right in front of me? Whatever. She and I are done."

"Not whatever." Ryan sighed. "I ended up behind her in line at the airport. She was wavering, afraid to get on the plane to Boston, so I bought her the ticket. Tricked her, really, so she'd visit you."

"What?" Aiden shook his head, trying to clear the muddled thoughts. "Why would you …?"

"I avoided introducing myself, but she caught on. When she realized, she was livid but I begged and practically dragged her onto the connecting flight. The other pictures are after she spent the night in your suite. I bought her a coffee and gave her a ride home."

"Why hide it?" Aiden scrubbed a hand over his face. Something was missing from this picture.

Ryan blew out a breath. "She'll kill me for this, but she told me some things." He held up a hand. "Don't ask what, but she assumed I was some random guy she'd never see again."

"Things." Aiden sucked back another shot. "Personal things about our relationship?"

Ryan shrugged.

"Things she couldn't say to me?"

His friend sighed. "Sorry. I made a huge mess, but I did it because she truly loves you. There's some sort of commitment fear there."

"No shit." Aiden motioned to the dance floor. "And that?"

"That's for your benefit. You disappeared into the coatroom with Sharkie," Ryan said. "Emily's been keeping tabs on you, my friend. All those women flocking around you drove her mad."

"Yeah, right. It's all fun and games between those two. I'm nothing but their boy toy." At his wave, the bartender poured him another shot.

"Slow down, man. Why don't you sleep it off?" Ryan lifted the glass from Aiden's fingers and downed it, pointing toward the door. "Go. We'll talk when you're sober, but nothing happened between me and Emily, I promise."

The room blurred as fatigue washed over him. The many nights of scarce sleep and too much drinking had overtaken him. "I believe you." He hugged Ryan and headed for the exit.

Once in the elevator, he sagged against the wall with his eyes closed as the doors slid shut, but then reopened. After a bleary stare at the interloper, he tipped back his head.

"Avoiding me?"

He clenched his jaw.

"I'm surprised Wifey isn't tagging along. Or are you sneaking away to hook up with her?"

"Are you fucking kidding me?" he muttered. "She's. Not. My. Wife. She's engaged."

"Huh. I notice Harrison is missing."

"I uninvited him to avoid the media circus."

"How could she hang all over you with her fiancé in the room?"

"Oh, stop. I have as much going on with her as you do with Ryan." He bit back a comment about her coziness with Ken.

"Ryan?" Her eyes widened. "Why would you say that?"

"You just never know with all those phone cameras, do you, Emelia?" Aiden tapped his screen and turned it toward her. "Look familiar?"

Her eyes widened. "Where did you get that?"

"Doesn't matter. What does matter is you hid it."

"You don't trust me?" Emily crossed her arms. "Is that what was going on with Ryan at the bar just now?"

"It sounds more like you don't trust me." The elevator stopped at his floor and he stepped into the hall, fumbling in his inner jacket pocket for his key.

"Don't think I missed the fact you disappeared into the coat check with her." She followed him into the hallway.

"Did you time us?" He scoffed, facing her as the doors slid closed. "The quickest quickie in history. An entire thirty seconds of earth-shattering mind-bending sex with the ex. Not that it's your business."

"It's not a joke."

"Says the woman who flirted with half the men in the room." Aiden shook his head. "Go back to the party, Emelia. We're done."

"Nothing happened with Ryan."

"Yeah, it did." The truth was unavoidable. "You told him things you refuse to tell me. Things about us and our relationship."

She closed her eyes and sniffled. "So now you know."

"Nothing's changed since you left the Vineyard. Whatever you want, it sure the hell isn't with me. Take care of yourself."

It took full effort to leave her standing there, to move forward without a single look back. Time to quit torturing himself over a woman who had no intention of committing. Emily wasn't his and never would be. Not in the way he wished.

CHAPTER 11

Emily

EXHAUSTION OVERWHELMED EMILY AND SHE pulled the pillow over her head, fighting the nausea plaguing her. The past two mornings it had been brutal, making it impossible to eat until well past noon. This morning she called in sick, the thought of the crowded train, the endless paperwork stacked high on her desk, and the job that had already lost its initial charm only months after she'd started impossible to bear.

Was it her turn to fight the flu that ran rampant through the city? She wasn't so sure, but she lacked the courage to find out. The slim white package sat unopened on the bathroom counter, taunting her.

Three weeks. Three lonely, sad weeks since the wedding, the small changes creeping over her, one by one. Each night by seven her eyelids drooped and she fell asleep on the couch until hours later when she crept to bed. Breakfast lacked appeal. The bathroom visits more frequent. She rolled, swallowing hard, flattening a palm against her belly. Nothing seemed different there, but then she cupped one of the breasts spilling over the top of her pink camisole. Fuller. Aching. An incontrovertible sign.

She propped herself against the pillows, munching on saltines and sipping ginger ale until she dared move to the edge of the bed, hauling in long breaths.

Her soul ached. If only Aiden were here. Would he be happy? Excited? Or just plain livid? She wished she dared phone, but he was adamant. They were done.

She dialed her sister's number.

"How are you?" Natalia asked.

All that came out was a long ragged sob.

"What's the matter? Are you okay?"

"I messed up. He'll never forgive me, and …"

"Who? Aiden?" Natalia's soothing voice flowed down the line. "Did you fight with him again? What did he do to my big sister?"

"I haven't spoken to him since the wedding. What would I even say?"

"Still? I hate that you're sad, but it won't get better unless you talk to the man."

Emily sucked in a breath, pressing a hand to her belly.

"Em?"

"I think I'm pregnant."

"No way." Her sister's voice dropped. "It's his?"

Emily sniffled. "It has to be … if I am."

"So no test yet? Do you have one?"

"I'm scared to take it. It changes everything." Emily massaged her temples. "Aiden will lose his shit if he even talks to me. How do I tell him?"

"How about … Hey, doc hottie? Remember that physical you—"

"Stop." Emily grimaced.

Nat gave a soft laugh. "Then say … Dude, you knocked me up."

Emily exhaled a sigh. "You're not helping."

"You don't even know for sure. Take the test. Now."

"Nat …"

"You're torturing yourself. Go. I'll hold."

Emily set her phone aside and padded into the bathroom. She tore the plastic wrapping from the stick and recapped it once she was done. "I'm back," she said as she returned to the bed with the wand in her hand.

"And?"

"It takes up to five …" She closed her eyes, fighting the wave of nausea washing over her at the sight of little pink plus sign materializing in the window. "What am I going to do?"

"Is that a yes?" Natalia asked. "Tell him, of course."

"You weren't there. He was so angry about the thing with Ryan."

"And he'll be even angrier if you hide this. At least give him the chance to be there for his baby. You know how often I wished my dirtbag would visit his daughter?"

She could never fault Aiden as a father. How he doted on Savannah was proof enough of his qualities in that department. "Aiden will want to be involved in everything. Every decision."

"Exactly. So get it together and tell Daddy about his impending bundle of joy. Right away."

"I have to get him to listen." Which meant she needed the courage to call.

Emily gave a half-hearted wave at the two ladies seated in the booth. It had been a tough week of fighting fatigue and nausea while trying to make that crucial call to Aiden. She couldn't seem to get past the first ring of his phone, hanging up every time.

"There she is." Alex said from her spot beside the tanned and beaming Jenna.

"How was the trip?" she asked after giving both women warm hugs.

"Amazing." Jenna flashed her perfect white smile. "We ate too much wonderful Italian cuisine, and the gelato was heavenly." The woman radiated happiness.

"You look like you need a drink." Alex frowned at Emily. "You've lost weight and look exhausted."

"Thanks so much." What would they say if she told them her rough appearance was due to lack of sleep and constant morning sickness, courtesy of a night of hot drunken sex with one of their closest friends? "I'll have water."

"You're pale." Alex patted her hand. "What's wrong?"

"She needs a doctor." Jenna sipped from her own glass. "The diagnosis will be a severe deficiency of someone that starts with *A* and ends with *n*."

"Very amusing. I'm recovering from the flu."

"Speaking of Aiden, he's staying in our guest room." Jenna smirked.

"He's here?" Emily perked up. It presented an opportunity as much as she dreaded the confrontation. Along with the nausea setting in, a twinge of guilt crept over her. Aiden owned the penthouse, yet he'd arranged to stay elsewhere.

"Nothing to do with him, huh?" Alexis giggled. "Yet you sound mighty interested."

Jenna's long, silent gaze was punctuated by a deep sigh. The woman produced her phone with a flourish and she hit speed dial. "What are you boys up to?" She trained her eyes on Emily. "Join us for dinner." She slid from the booth and wandered a short distance away, murmuring into her mobile. "They're at the house finishing a game of pool," she said when she returned. "They'll be here in a few minutes."

Emily started an inner pep talk. There'd be no escape. Did she even want to escape? Panic rolled over her. The honest answer was yes, yes she did. Her feet itched as she glanced at the door.

"Don't even think about ditching us." Jenna wagged a finger.

Emily met her friend's gaze.

"Imagine my surprise when I learned you're still living in his penthouse. Admit you're terrified of breaking that final bond." Jenna stared at her. "Tell me I'm wrong. Convince me you're not in love with him. Prove you don't regret walking away."

"What does it matter? He'll never take me back. He refuses to talk to me, so how could he love me?"

"Huh." Jenna's brows rose. "No denial in those words. Stop this stupid behavior and pack your bags for Boston."

Alex's lips set into a flat line. "If you aren't clear about how Aiden feels, you haven't been listening. And," she squinted, "a few half-assed incomplete calls aren't close to enough. If you want him back, earn it."

A tear trickled down her heat-filled cheeks. "Does he even want me back?"

Alex shrugged. "Ask him."

Jenna narrowed her eyes. "You'd better take this final chance to say whatever it is you need to say, or you'll regret it for the rest of your life." Her friend offered a faint smile. "You have something important to tell him."

Emily's eyes widened. Did Jenna know? *She couldn't, could she?* She whispered, "He's too angry."

"Procrastination won't make seeing him any easier. Either beg him to take you back or say your piece and kiss him goodbye. It's not fair to him or Savannah," Alex said.

Emily stared at the menu. Deep down, she feared she'd already used up her final chance. Adding in a baby would only make it messier, but she had little choice.

She looked over her shoulder as Jenna waved toward the door, noting how Aiden froze, his eyes narrowing.

If Tom hadn't put a restraining hand on his arm and leaned in to say something, she suspected he would have bolted, but he trailed Tom and Joel to the booth.

"Emily," Aiden said with a small nod, taking the last open seat beside her after he'd greeted Jenna and Alex.

She blinked hard, hating the cool reception and the way he avoided touching her, a space separating them as he perused the menu.

"A Macallan. Neat," he said when the server offered drinks.

"How are you?" she asked after everyone had ordered their meals.

He lifted one shoulder. "You?"

"Fine." Emily closed her eyes, fighting the urge to wiggle closer, suddenly craving the warmth of his arm around her shoulders. The subtle scent of earthy aftershave tickled her nostrils. *Heavenly.*

Aiden studied her. "Are you okay?"

"I'm great." Her stomach twisted and rolled and her palms grew clammy as the heat rose in her face. Having him so close hurt, and she squirmed under the intensity of his gaze. *What if he guesses my secret?*

The slight narrowing of his eyes and almost imperceptible tilt of his head suggested he hadn't bought it.

Her pulse quickened. He must hear her heart trying to pound its way out of her chest, along with the inner voice shrieking at her for being a damn coward. She sipped her icy water, forcing a smile as conversation swirled around her.

Aiden contributed nothing, his mouth set in a flat line as he twirled his glass of Macallan, taking the occasional sip. When the server came by, he ordered a double, earning a look from Tom.

Jenna arched a brow in Emily's direction.

Now or never. "Can we—"

"Ma'am?" The server stood at the edge of the table with steaming plates of food.

She leaned back as he served their dinner, sending a silent thanks to the universe for the reprieve. Emily forced small bites into her mouth as everyone chatted and joked, noting the covert looks passing between the other four at the table.

At long last, the waiter cleared the empty plates.

"Tom still owes me a rematch on that last game." Joel pushed his glass away.

He and Tom slid out of the booth, followed by Jenna and Alex.

Jenna threw a guilty smile over her shoulder as she walked away.

The group of four busied themselves chalking up cues and pretending they weren't watching Aiden and Emily.

"Damn. They set us up," Emily muttered. She couldn't even look at Aiden.

"Don't worry. I'll leave you to your evening." Aiden slid from the booth and grabbed his coat. "Take care."

Emily stared at his back as he stopped at the bar and offered his credit card to their server.

Jenna appeared at her side. "Get up," she whispered. "Don't you dare let him walk out that door."

She shook her head, cringing as Jenna directed a stern look at her. "Okay, I'm going." Emily forced herself to her feet, covering the few steps to the bar. She grasped his arm. "We need to talk."

"That doesn't sound good." He accepted his card from the server and tucked it in his wallet. "What did I do?"

"Why do you assume you did something?"

"Whenever a woman says *we need to talk,* it's never good." His brow rose.

"Oh, right." Now she had to decide how to proceed. "Can we sit?" She led him to their empty booth, ignoring the looks coming from the other side of the pub. "I'm sorry how we left it after the wedding."

"I—"

"Please, let me finish. I need to get this out." She angled toward him. "You did what you needed to do for Savannah. Me being upset because you left was unfair."

She stared at him, raising a hand, craving his touch, longing to feel closer. As she brushed his cheek with her fingertips, she bit her lip, unable to tear her gaze from his. She swayed toward him as he placed his hands on either side of her face, searching her eyes. Without warning, he bent his head, taking possession of her mouth, a tingle running all the way to her toes. She sank against him, melting into his arms, powerless to resist.

He pulled away. "Sorry." His hand wandered through his hair, then down as he rubbed the back of his neck. "That shouldn't have happened."

"Aiden …" She reached for him, reeling from the intensity of their connection.

He drew back. "Don't. Please … I can't go through this again."

"Don't leave," Emily whispered. "Not before you tell me if the offer is open?"

"The offer?" His head came up, eyebrows rising as something flickered in his eyes.

Her heart pounded, the words catching in her throat as she dug deep for the will to continue. No matter what she had to sacrifice, he was worth it. "I miss you and I love you. I love you so much it hurts." She closed her eyes. "I want to move to Boston."

Silence fell over them, and she feared looking at him. Thoughts jumbled in her mind, and she fought the desire to cry.

"You're serious?" His words drew her to the present. He stared at her with the oddest expression on his face. "You want to move?"

"If you'll have me. Please forgive my selfishness in putting my career before our relationship." She cupped his cheek in her hand, stroking it with her thumb. Did he still want her, or love her, or had she destroyed everything?

"Why now? Before, you refused to discuss it." He shook his head. "I don't know."

Tears flooded her eyes. "Please? Give me another chance."

He gave her a long look. "What's different? So I get my hopes up, and you change your mind and disappear on me?"

Emily brushed a tear from her cheek. "I'm sorry for everything. I should never have let you go."

He opened his mouth, but she pressed her fingertips to his lips.

"I worried we'd end up like my parents." How she wished she could interpret that look.

"Oh, Emily, how …" He pulled away. "I'm getting my life together, and Savannah's stopped missing you. No. We're not doing this." Aiden slid from the booth and left without a backward glance.

Emily bowed her head, fighting the urge to break down, sucking in a long breath before snatching up her coat and purse.

Alex appeared by her side. "What happened?"

"He said no, and … I didn't get to tell him, and … I h-have to g-get out of here."

"Tell him what?"

"Let me go." She pushed past Alex, sucking in the icy cold air as she rushed out the door. A flood of tears accompanied her departure from the pub, and she brushed at them with the back of her hand. The terrible thought she'd lost everything overtook her. She'd thrown it all away.

"Emily." Alex fell into step, the woman's steadying arm curling around her. "Are you okay?"

"I want to go …" A sickening realization crept over her. It wasn't her home, but his. She swallowed hard, praying her dinner would stay down. "He hates me. I've ruined everything."

"Oh, sweetie. Aiden will never hate you. He loves you, but we blindsided him. That was wrong."

"It's over." Emily felt hollow. Empty. "He doesn't want me in Boston. You're wrong. He doesn't love me."

"Oh no, he does." Alex clutched Emily's arm, halting her progress. "You must understand the residual fear and damage caused by unhealthy relationships." Alex sighed. "Be patient and gentle, and don't give up. He is so worth it."

"I can't allow myself false hope." She shrugged off Alex's hand and walked, the sidewalk blurring as her friend's words struck her heart. "He's adamant it's over. How can I blame him?"

"Give him time."

"I have so much to tell him, and … it has to be soon, but he didn't give me the chance."

"What could be so urgent that you can't wait—" Alex froze in her tracks. "You're pregnant."

Emily turned. "He has to hear it from me."

"I won't say a word, but …" Alex approached. "Emily, you can't keep this from him, you have to—"

"Don't lecture me. I'll tell him … but …" She bowed her head, brushing at her cheeks in an attempt to stem the tears. "I don't want him to take me back because I'm pregnant. I want him to take me back because he wants to be with me. Can't you understand that?"

"Oh, Emily. You're making this far too complicated. He loves you, you love him but you're both so scared of making the leap. Damn it, tell him."

"He may not even want any of this." Emily sniffled.

Alex dug into her pocket, producing a pack of tissues. "Dry your eyes. Just tell him, or he will never forgive you."

CHAPTER 12

Aiden

FROM THE MOMENT HE WALKED into the pub and saw her, he'd known seeing her was a terrible idea. And now, he walked along the chilly Chicago streets, hands shoved deep in his pockets, convinced he was wrong.

Terrible was a gross understatement. It had been a complete and total disaster. One of those moments when you saw the road rushing up to meet you, but your stubborn limbs refused to reach out and break your fall.

I want to move to Boston should be wonderful words, but he couldn't accept them as real. This time he'd stay strong. Last time he'd relented and paid the price. It would be insanity to believe she'd stay. Women never stayed.

When his phone vibrated, he silenced it without a single glance. He knew who it would be. Jenna had been texting him non-stop since he'd left, but he had nothing to say. Even if his friend figured she was doing the right thing, she'd betrayed him.

A shiver ran through him as he got his bearings. He'd been walking for at least an hour and his fingers were numb. The sound of music blaring as a door opened and closed drew his attention to the familiar pub. That would do.

Warm air blasted over him as he rubbed his hands together. He claimed one of the last empty seats at the bar, ordering a double. By the time the dark-haired woman slid onto the stool beside him he was on his fourth round.

"Tracked you down." Alex waved off the bartender.

"Leave me alone." He threw her a dark look. "So not funny, Lex. What the hell was that?"

"I'm sorry." She squeezed his hand. "It was ill-advised, but Emily needs to say something important."

"Ha, I call bullshit. She's hung up every damn time, so what could possibly be that urgent?" He tipped his glass, draining it in two gulps. "I'm getting it together. Why would I take her back now?"

"Taking her back would be bad because?" Alex turned his way. "You love her, and I'm damn sure she loves you. You two are destroying each other, but your damn pride's in the way."

"Fuck pride." He rubbed his gritty, tired eyes. "She reels me in, then leaves. She's done it over and over. If she changes her mind again, I won't climb out of that deep dark pit." He refused to look at her. "It's for Vanna too. Emily leaving took a piece of her."

"But you still love her." Alex slipped an arm around him, leaning her forehead on his arm. "You'll regret leaving without one more discussion."

"I'm not strong enough," he whispered. "If I see her, she'll take what's left."

"Honey. She's not …" She sucked in an audible breath. "She's not Tiffany."

"Don't even go there." He yanked out his wallet and threw money onto the bar. "I'm sick of women and their shit."

"Where are you going?" She caught his arm.

"Boston." He hauled his coat from the back of the chair. "There's no reason to stick around."

"But there is."

"Yeah, right." Aiden scoffed. "You know what's stupid? When she said we needed to talk, I had this weird idea it would be one of those conversations where she'd say *guess what?*"

Alex cupped a hand over her mouth, the truth evident in those shimmering blue eyes.

The pieces clicked in his muddled brain. He tipped his head back, cursing the universe. "Fuck me." His entire life was about to blow up and Alex knew it. He glowered at his friend. "She fucking told you before she told me."

"Ask Emily."

"Right." He looked away.

"She tried to tell you, but you didn't want to hear her."

"I'm damn sure the words *I'm pregnant* weren't included anywhere in that conversation, unless I've developed amnesia." He turned his collar up, preparing to face the wind. "Go home and stay out of my business."

***

Aiden's first instinct was an immediate visit, but instead he walked, allowing the stupor of alcohol to lift while he considered his options. Approaching Emily drunk and angry would only make this worse.

Two hours after leaving Alex outside of the pub, he entered the warm lobby and waved at the doorman before stepping into the elevator and pressing the fob against the panel. Moments later, the doors swished open.

A dim glow came from the kitchen of the silent apartment. After shrugging off his coat and sliding out of his shoes, he tiptoed through to the master bedroom and crawled onto the bed, draping an arm over her.

With his forehead against her back, he closed his eyes, savoring her soft scent and the warmth of her body. He allowed himself to relax, and he drifted, existing only in that single moment.

Her sharp inhale snapped him to reality. "It's me, Em."

"You scared the crap out of me." She rolled, her eyes wide and glittering in the glow from the clock. "You haven't learned how to phone? Instead, you walk in like—"

"I own the place?" At her look, he moved to the edge of the bed, rubbing his hands across his face. "Sorry. This was a bad idea. I'll go."

"No." She kneeled behind him, wrapping her arms around his shoulders, her breath warm against his neck. "You're freezing." Emily's fingertips trailed across his back in a gentle caress. "And drunk."

"Mmm." His eyelids drooped as he rested his head against her shoulder. "I tried to walk it off."

Emily pulled him onto the bed, wrapping a blanket over them before resting a hand against his cheek. "Relax."

He raised a hand to cover hers and let his lids sink shut. This was what he'd feared. Being powerless in her presence. The love he'd buried under the layers of pain might prove too strong to resist.

"I'm glad you're here," she whispered. "I have so much to say."

He forced his eyes open. "Tell me."

She sniffled and brushed at her cheeks.

The sight of those red, shiny eyes wrenched his heart. "Why are you crying?"

"You said no."

Aiden pulled her closer, his resolve weakening further. He wanted to accept the words but didn't trust they'd hit a turning point. Hope meant giving her the opportunity to drag him under, but maybe he had no choice. A child carried a whole new level of complicated. "It's not only about me. I don't think—"

"Shh." She placed her fingertips over his lips. "Please listen. It's a lot to ask for another chance, but you know why I didn't come. I'm terrified of commitment."

"We're hurting each other an' I need it to stop."

"Tell me we're not over." She brushed her eyes. "I've never kept my past relationship troubles a secret, but I didn't want a bad ending for us."

"It's already ended badly." Aiden closed his eyes, struggling to gather his thoughts. "Not even trying is what's crazy. Fear rules you." *Stop talking.* "Not trying broke us. How can I allow you to do it again? I won't survive another round of this messed-up game."

"It's not a game," Emily whispered, "but I'm terrified. I'm begging for another chance. I love you, Aiden."

"Then what? We have a few great weeks before your commitment phobia emerges, and you leave?"

"It won't be like that."

"You promise? You won't freak out and disappear?"

"We'll always have a connection."

"Huh, that's not the answer … I was expecting more …" He longed for her to say it out loud. To tell the truth.

"Do you love me? Say it. Tell me you want me to come to Boston."

He sighed. "Don't do it because of the baby."

Emily blinked hard. "She told you."

"No, you did in your roundabout way. *We need to talk?*" He cupped his palm over her belly. "How far along?"

She bit her lip. "Seven weeks."

Aiden let out a long slow breath. "You've known for a while."

"Are you angry?"

"A little, but more about how I found out, not about the baby. Why didn't you call me?"

"I tried, but after the wedding … what would I say?"

The fat tears streaming down her face made him come undone. This woman always managed to scale each and every wall he tried to build. He had no defenses. He loved her far too much to turn away from her pain. "Em—"

"A child is an enormous, crazy, wonderful commitment and I have no right to ask, but the thought of our child growing up without their father because I'm scared to take the chance on someone I love …" Her head wagged from side to side.

"My child won't grow up without me."

"No, but long distance parenting isn't what I want from you."

"What do you want?"

"You. And our baby," she said. "Please say we can be a family. In Boston."

Her words sank into his brain as he cupped her face in his palms. A family was something he'd wanted forever, but he'd given up. He pulled her onto his chest, burying his face into her hair and cradling her against him. The fear of reaching out and taking it overwhelmed him. Things blurred around the edges and he wished he could think clearly. Tomorrow he might wake up and find it was all a dream.

⚬

Aiden silenced his mobile, grateful it hadn't disturbed Emily. He headed into the kitchen and hit the call button.

"Where are you?" Alex asked. "Tom and Jenna haven't seen you and it's almost noon."

"Why? Is Jenna planning to drop another ex into my life without warning?" He tried for sarcasm, but how things had turned out made it impossible to be upset.

"Don't tell me." Alex chuckled. "Did you two kiss and make up? Or maybe more than kiss?"

"Something like that."

"Glad to hear it. How's she doing?"

"She's sleeping, but we talked."

"That's it?" She sighed. "I'm sorry about last night. Forcing you into that awkward situation was incredibly stupid. We love you, Aiden, and watching this Emily situation play out has been painful."

"No kidding. That crap didn't help. Thankfully I regained my senses and calmed down before I talked to her."

"How far along is she?"

"What? Something she didn't tell you?"

"Ouch," she said. "No need to be a grouch."

"She's due in June."

"That's exciting. Congrats, Daddy. What's next?"

"Getting her moved to Boston before she changes her mind?" Aiden sank onto a stool.

"She won't."

"But she might."

"Have some faith and be patient. You're meant to be together."

"Wow, that's cheesy."

"But true," she said. "Call Jenna, she's worried sick about you. You'll come to dinner tonight?"

"Probably. I'll ask Em when she wakes up." Aiden swept a hand through his hair, contemplating his next move. Definitely a call to Jenn. Despite his initial anger, the woman always wanted the best for him, and he could never hold that against her.

Chapter 13

Emily

Emily snuggled deeper under the warm covers, Aiden's soft breaths puffing against her neck, his arm slung over her as he slept. It had been a late night at Tom and Jenna's house, and at midnight, she'd pleaded exhaustion as she fought to keep her eyes open after an amazing night with their friends. Tom and Jenna had revealed they too were expecting a child.

Aiden had tucked her into bed, and she'd fallen into a contented sleep within minutes.

"Morning, beautiful." He brushed the hair from her neck, kissing and nuzzling her sensitive nape.

Emily closed her eyes again, enjoying his caresses. "Wonderful man. I …" She brushed his lips with hers. "Love," she whispered, kissing him again. "You … mi vida."

"Back at you, sweetheart." He entwined his hands in her hair.

Emily savored the sweet taste and earthy masculine smell of him. How she'd missed having this man in her arms and in her bed. Without him, the universe lacked sufficient air. She luxuriated in his gentle touch as they made love before drifting to sleep.

Hours later, she opened her eyes, a smile touching her lips as she snuggled into the warm bed. The weight of his arm draped across her hip soothed her and the sound of his breathing reassured her he was there to stay.

She glanced at Aiden, who had his head buried in a pillow as he sprawled in the bed. Her smile grew wider as she considered him. He deserved this well-earned rest, and she intended to let him sleep, but moments later he opened his beautiful brown eyes.

"Mmm, let's wake up like this forever." Emily stretched.

"Done." He smiled and grazed his fingers over her skin. "I can't wait until you move to Boston."

"What do you think Vanna will say? She'll get a sister or brother out of the deal."

"My prediction is thrilled." His flattened palm rested on her belly. "How about I make you some tea and we'll call her? I'd like us to tell her together. We can't keep it secret for over two weeks, nor should we."

Emily nodded. Even if she couldn't see Vanna in person, the girl's reaction was not to be missed.

With a sigh, she dragged herself from the bed, fighting the usual round of nausea before showering and joining Aiden in the kitchen. She accepted a cup of tea and nibbled on the light breakfast of fruit and granola before they cuddled on the couch.

"Hi, Dad." Savannah's cheerful voice came over the speaker.

"Hi, Vanna, how are you?"

"Good. We're going to a movie."

"Hi, Vanna." Emily smiled at Aiden and entwined their fingers.

"Emily. What are you doing there?"

"I live here?"

"Dad's with you at the apartment?"

"He is. We have a question for you. How do you feel about me moving to Boston?"

Dead silence fell over the room. Emily stared at the phone wondering if they'd been cut off.

"You're moving?" Savannah shrieked, both Emily and Aiden wincing as the phone crackled. "No way."

Thumps that sounded like jumping echoed through the phone, followed by a muffled squeal.

"I can't believe it. I'm sooo excited."

"She likes the idea," Emily said.

Aiden shrugged, even though he had a huge grin on his face. "Maybe just a little. There's something else."

"More good news?"

"How do you feel about being a big sister?" Emily linked her fingers through Aiden's.

This brought another round of squeals from Savannah. "What? When?"

They filled Savannah in on the details and finally disconnected the call. To Emily, it had turned out perfectly, though she knew the toughest days were yet to come. Everything in her life was about to change. Absolutely everything.

Monday. Emily entered the ER, the envelope with her resignation letter tucked in her bag. A smile crept across her face. She wouldn't miss Dragon Lady. Not one teeny tiny bit.

Dana would be disgruntled, but she'd have to deal with it. Emily belonged with Aiden, and it had already taken her far too long to realize it.

"Good morning," she said as she arrived at the front desk.

"It's Monday." Tara frowned. "Did you win the lottery? Or maybe you've got a new boyfriend?" The woman arched a brow, studying Emily. "This is the best mood you've been in for months."

"The benefits of a relaxing weekend." Emily wasn't about to feed the beast. The news would travel like lightning after she quit.

"Dr. Anderson." Dana's voice made her jump.

"Good morning, Dana," she said.

"You look much better today. Did you manage to rest on your days off? We have a lot of new projects coming up."

"Do you have a minute? I need to speak to you in private." Emily motioned toward the empty lounge.

Dana nodded and followed her in. She plucked the offered envelope from Emily's fingers, perusing the letter with a disdainful look on her face. "I don't understand. You're resigning? Barely six months and you're gone? Is the responsibility too much? That's it, right? You can't handle this job. I should have known you were too soft. No. Stick it out for a full year, Dr. Anderson. That's what I expect."

"I can handle the job."

"Then why quit? My finger's on the pulse of the medical community, and there aren't any positions available. I have no attending positions. If you resign, you must leave the hospital and work in some clinic."

"I'm moving to Boston."

Dana frowned, then a smirk appeared. "Would that have anything to do with a certain Dr. Hamilton? I heard a rumor he asked you to go, and you refused. Now you're chasing after him?"

Emily shrugged. "I'll give you two weeks to get the search underway. I'm moving by the end of November."

"Hold off on those relocation plans. I refuse to let you go."

"You can't stop me. There's nothing in the employment contract to force me to stay."

"I disagree. You'll hear from our lawyers."

Just like that, Emily's mood slid downhill.

Twenty minutes later, Tara was at her heels again, trailing after her as she entered Exam 2.

"I heard a rumor."

"Where do they hide those darn sample kits?" Emily dug in a cupboard.

"Are you moving to Boston?"

Emily crouched in front of a lower cabinet, pushing aside a pack of gauze.

"There's only one reason you'd leave." Tara reached into an upper cupboard. "Here." She held out the kit. "Didn't you fire Aiden's ass? And break up with him?"

Emily accepted the samples. "Thanks." She headed toward the room where her patient waited.

"Are you engaged?" Tara trotted behind her.

"No. I'm just moving." She fought the instinct to rest her hand on her belly. Nobody in the ER had clued in and for now, she'd keep it secret.

The day wore on, and the disgruntled and imperious looks Dana shot her way marred her happiness. Those, along with the way the woman snapped orders. With any luck, the Dragon Lady would calm down by the end of the week, but Emily wouldn't count on it. All she wanted was to get through these last weeks in peace.

By break time, Emily's eyes burned with unshed tears. The hormones rushing through her system didn't help. She'd been so level and happy the entire time Aiden had been in town, but Dana's foul mood had driven her into a funk.

She slumped onto the couch in the lounge and dialed Aiden's number, craving the sound of his voice.

"Hi, sweetheart. How are you?"

She sniffled. "Aiden, I …" A single tear trickled down her cheek. "I …" A flood of tears followed, along with the sob that dragged from her chest.

"What happened?"

The only reply she could give was more sobs and an inelegant snuffle as she blew her nose.

"Why are you crying? Damn. I'll be on the next flight."

"No, no, it's Dana. She's been horrible." Her lips twitched. She fought the smile, laughing at herself for sounding like a little girl complaining about the schoolyard bully.

"You're okay? And the baby?" he whispered.

"I didn't mean to scare you. I'm turning into a crazy hormonal mess. Usually, I can handle her, but …" She pressed a hand to her belly, taking several breaths to calm herself. It seemed unreal that their child would arrive in only a few short months.

"It's been an emotional few days. Should I fly out? I can switch shifts."

"Don't do that. You have Vanna, and I'm being stupid. I needed to hear your voice." She dabbed her eyes with a tissue.

"I'm glad you called. You handed in your resignation?" His deep calm voice soothed her.

"Why do you think I'm upset? She's raving mad and being an impossible bitch."

"Ignore her. She can't do anything about it. You're giving fair notice. If she keeps hassling you, let me know."

"Do you think she'll make legal trouble?"

"Not if she knows what's good for her. She and I had a run-in over me walking out, so I suspect she learned her lesson."

"You always make me feel better." She sighed. "My break is almost over. How's Vanna?"

"Excited. She can't stop talking about you moving or being a big sister," he said. "Don't worry, okay?"

"I love you too." After she hung up, she closed her eyes, practicing her deep breathing. Gradually, the knot in her stomach eased.

Aiden was right. Dana didn't have a valid cause, but if she made problems, then what? More deep breathing and she gathered the courage to head onto the floor. She only had to hang on for a couple more weeks. Then everything would be fine. Being with Aiden was all that mattered.

~

Emily stretched and stepped from the exam room after finishing with her final patient of the day. The only thing she could think about was getting home and sinking into a hot bath filled with relaxing lavender bath salts.

Tara appeared. "A fancy power suit is asking for you. He looks familiar, and damn, he's hot. Married though, or he wears a ring to keep the chicks off."

"No doubt the hospital lawyer threatening to sue my ass," Emily mumbled as she shuffled toward the front. This day kept getting better and better.

Tara trailed her. "Do the hospital's lawyers wear Armani and look like Mr. GQ?"

Emily's eyes widened as she took in the tall dark-haired man leaning oh-so-casually on the desk.

"There's my girl." Tom smiled and opened his arms to her. "How are you?"

"What are you doing here?" Despite the comfort of his warm embrace, unease settled in her stomach. "Everything okay? Jenna?"

"Everyone's fine, but I hear you're having trouble." Tom kept his arm around her shoulders, giving a light squeeze.

"Aiden called you?"

"I'm here to escort you to dinner with the ladies."

Emily shook her head. "I can't believe him. You're checking up on me."

"Mea culpa." Tom held up his hands. "You're family. He'd do the same for any of us. He's worried and needs reassurance. Don't be mad, please? He means well."

"He threatened to get on a plane." She lowered her voice and drew Tom to the side. They were attracting attention, and the last thing she wanted was to feed the rumor mill.

"Sounds like Aiden. He'll always take care of his family. In fact, we all have your back. I'll let him know we have it under control."

"Thanks, Tom. I didn't expect you to drop everything to rescue me."

"We can't let Dragon Lady impede true love." He winked. "She gives you any trouble, call me."

"Shh, someone will hear you." Emily looked around in a panic. "I can't believe he told you her nickname."

"Aiden tells me a lot of things, but I'm a vault." He grinned. "Get your stuff."

"I'll be quick." Emily entered the lounge and opened her locker.

"Is that Tom Grayson?" Dana appeared behind her.

"You know it is."

Dana narrowed her eyes. "Are you taking legal action against the hospital?"

"Tom's picking me up for dinner. But now you mention it … can we end this in a civilized way? I'll do what I can to help with the transition, but I'm not staying. I need to be with Aiden. I should never have taken this job."

"The job you were willing to do anything to get? You could have let me ask him to leave."

Emily gave a humorless laugh. That wasn't how she remembered it. "You didn't give me much choice, but I still made the wrong one. I gave up the man I love for a stupid job."

"You'll sacrifice your career for a man? Ridiculous. He may be rich and good-looking, but he's noted for his string of ladies. Most women are lucky to get three months of mileage." Dana's head bobbed as she relayed this information. "The two of you barely lasted six months before he left."

"We've been together almost a year." Emily wrapped her scarf around her neck, desperate to leave.

"I followed a guy once. It lasted an entire two months. Then I started over at a new hospital. The next time it happened, I chose my career. I've never regretted it. Not one single time."

"No wonder you're so unhappy. You chose career over family. I love Aiden more than any job." Emily pushed her locker shut.

Dana stepped into Emily's path as she headed for the door. "A family?" The woman squinted. "You didn't have the flu. It's not you he wants, but his Hamilton heir."

"You're wrong. He asked me to move before he even left, though I don't deny I'm pregnant."

"Good luck, Dr. Anderson. Run after him. He'll toss you aside after the baby is born, and you'll beg for your job back."

Emily froze, but only for a moment. "We love each other."

A smirk appeared. "Keep telling yourself that." The woman stalked from the lounge.

Emily blinked hard to stem the tears. Why was this woman so cruel?

She straightened and pasted on a smile. No way would Dragon Lady to see her cry. She stepped from the lounge, Tom's warm smile lifting her heart. Her future held great things with an amazing man and wonderful friends. She wouldn't face it alone.

Still, Dana's comments preyed on her mind and Emily remained silent for the short drive.

Tom said nothing, but he sent constant worried glances in her direction, even if he sensed she wasn't ready to talk.

"Emily." Jenna met them at the door. "Glad Tom caught you. We'll meet Alex at the restaurant."

"Have fun, ladies." Tom kissed Jenna and waved as they exited.

It only took a few minutes to walk to the restaurant, but Emily was grateful to be out of the windy and chilly November weather.

"You seem distracted," Jenna said as they sat in a booth toward the back.

"Is it obvious?" Her shoulders slumped. "Rough day, you know? I woke up alone and puked my guts out. Then I went to work and dealt with the Dragon Lady," she said, curling her lip, "who threatened legal action if I move to Boston."

"I'm sorry, but it'll get better." Jenna patted her belly. "Let's order potato skins while we wait for Alex."

"I could eat. Continual hunger is my nemesis." Emily fiddled with her glass as Jenna placed their order.

"Tell me more," Jenna said.

"Well, Aiden panicked and sent Tom to check on me." Emily brushed at an escaped tear. "Here I go again."

Jenna handed her a tissue. "You miss him, is all."

"Like crazy." Emily sipped her ice water, grateful for how it eased her aching throat. "Dragon Lady reminded me that he's never kept a relationship together more than a few months." Her voice broke as she sniffled. "He'll toss me aside like a piece of trash the minute his child is born."

Jenna slid her arm around Emily, pressing another tissue into her hand. "I could slap that woman."

"She'd slap you back." Emily let out a tearful snicker.

"Nope. She knows who I married." Jenna rolled her eyes. "If she says anything further about legal action, call Tom. He'll take care of it."

"That's sweet, but I can't afford Tom."

Jenna arched a brow. "Tom is Aiden's oldest friend, so if you need legal help, ever, call him. No arguing."

"Thank you." She pushed the ice in her water around with her straw. "She has a point though. He said no until he found out about the baby."

"Oh, Emily," Jenna said with an exasperated sigh. "He's been asking you to move for months. Aiden had plans, but you made it clear you didn't and he backed off. He almost gave up."

"Ignored me is more like it. He refused to call me back."

"You're trying my patience. He asked you to marry him long before the baby news. Damn it, don't you get it?" Jenna lifted her chin. "He's terrified. Have you ever thought you were with the one and had them turn on you?"

"Most people have." Her mind wandered to her ill-fated relationship with Jason.

"When things fell apart with Tiffany, he was devastated and hasn't committed since." Jenna met Emily's gaze. "Tom believes he's chosen women who'd expect nothing from him. Until you."

"Hmmm." Emily drew her brows together.

"Tom was at ground zero when it all went down. It was a monumental mess."

She considered Aiden's comments early in their relationship. "He said I was crazy to get involved with the messed-up guy."

"He jokes, but it's taken Aiden ten years to recover and settle down." Jenna offered a tiny smile. "How long have you known him?"

"Years, though it's only in the last few months he's divulged anything remotely personal."

"What does that say?"

"He changed the entire dynamic of our relationship overnight. I went with it. It felt comfortable."

"You two are a perfect match." Jenna gazed at her. "Don't you dare break his heart. If you run now, there'll be no putting him back together."

~≺

It had been a long day, and she struggled to keep her eyes open, smothering several wide yawns before she excused herself from the restaurant shortly before ten.

She'd let Alex and Jenna carry the majority of the conversation, smiling and nodding while mulling over her talk with Jenna. She couldn't decide if the information made it better, or if it built on her insecurities. Aiden had loved Tiffany and it had taken him forever to let her go. Their experiences and their daughter had forged a strong and enduring connection.

Emily brushed her teeth and crawled into bed, curling up on Aiden's pillow. The distinctive scent soothed her and she rested a hand on her belly. She had her own special connection with the man. The tiny miracle growing inside her would forever link them.

She dialed Aiden, eager to hear his voice.

"How are you?" he asked.

"I'm okay. Tom checked on me."

"That meltdown worried me."

"I know, mi vida. I love you for it. You had my back, and you always will, won't you?"

"You're family. Soon you'll be my wife and the mother of my child. I'll always be there, forever," Aiden said, his voice low and soothing.

Emily closed her eyes, pretending he was there with her. She missed him so much it became a dull ache. "I hate being apart. I want to be there." The tears tracked down her cheeks.

"I miss you too. Only three days until Friday, so hang in there."

She smiled faintly. "When you asked me to marry you this summer, you were serious."

The silence stretched out before he said, "Why wouldn't you believe I was serious?"

"It came out so easily that it felt unreal." Emily tightened her grip on her phone, her heart pounding.

"It was anything but easy." He exhaled a long drawn-out sigh. "Are you having second thoughts?"

"Never think that. I love you. But let's discuss it when you're here."

"No. Now," he said. "What's bothering you?"

How could she put that slight unease flitting around her peripherals into words? "It's an adjustment, Aiden. Please don't worry."

"But?"

She settled deeper into the pillows. "Don't freak, but ... Dana made comments. She figured out I'm pregnant."

"What did Dragon Lady say?" Annoyance infused his voice.

"Umm." If she told him, he might be on an earlier plane.

"Just tell me. It's obviously an issue." The man's tone told her he'd never let it rest until she unburdened herself.

"That chasing after you would be a huge mistake. But," she said, "those are her words, not mine. In her opinion"—Emily cringed—"you're with me for the baby."

"Damn it, Emily." The heavy sigh did nothing to ease her worry. "Ignore everything that woman says. I'm sure creating issues in our relationship is her revenge. Her boss ass-kicked her for her legal antics when I quit."

"You never told me."

"Things weren't rosy between us, were they? We barely talked about it," he said. "And you never asked."

"I'm sorry," she whispered, sad that she'd been too wrapped up in her own misery to show interest in what Aiden had gone through during those months.

"It's done, so let's move on. No looking back. Dana's one of those annoying little yappy dogs, full of bravado and tons of noise. Don't let the old Dragon get to you. She has no clue about our relationship. Promise."

"I promise," she whispered. "It's been such a stressful, awful day. I miss you."

"I can't wait for you to be here. You, Emily, I want to marry you, because I love you. There's no ulterior motive."

"I can't wait until Friday."

"I'll be on a plane in the morning," he said, chuckling.

"No, you have work and so do I." A smile twitched her lips as she rested her flattened palm on her belly. "We love you, mi vida."

"You sound exhausted. Get some sleep and things will seem better tomorrow."

After sending him air-kisses, she rolled onto her side and snuggled into the cozy bed with a smile. Huge changes were coming, but Jenna's advice was solid. Go with it, let it happen, don't freak out, and most of all, don't run from it. She needed to trust him and their relationship. Emily closed her eyes and drifted into sleep.

Emily stared at the towering gray building before continuing through the ambulance bay and entering the sliding doors. Soon this place would be history. She'd even started crossing the days off of her calendar.

The antiseptic odor bit at her nostrils as soon as she walked in, making her mouth water, but a few deep breaths and several sips of tea relieved the nausea. Once at her locker, she popped a handful of trail mix into her mouth, hoping the small starchy snack would keep the morning sickness at bay.

She prepared for her shift, musing about the weekend. Having Aiden and Savannah around had been wonderful. They'd both pampered her by making all the meals, allowing her to sleep in, and helping pack and sort through the apartment. On Thursday night, the movers would collect her personal items, transporting her entire life to Boston.

"Good weekend?" Tara asked as she opened her locker.

"Morning, Tara, and yes, it was." Emily smiled. Perhaps Tara had accepted her relationship with Aiden.

"Where's Aiden?"

"Boston." Emily slid on her lab coat and slung her stethoscope around her neck. After two hours on the floor this morning, she'd escape to her office and complete the pile of paperwork. She'd promised Dana she'd tidy up whatever she could for whoever took over her position.

"He seems to have a new attachment. Who's the teenager?" Tara asked. "Savannah's an unusual name."

"Perhaps you should ask Aiden."

"I heard a crazy rumor." Tara propped a shoulder against the wall and folded her arms over her chest, an arch expression appearing. "Is it true?"

Emily glanced at the woman, lifting her shoulder in a slight shrug. The rumor mill must be spinning like mad, but she wasn't about to offer more information than necessary.

"Someone said that teenager is his kid."

Emily sighed, weighing whether or not she should respond, but denying the truth seemed counterproductive. The talk would die quicker if she admitted the relationship. "Savannah's his daughter." She met Tara's gaze.

"They're right?" Tara's eyes widened. "How old is she?"

"Fifteen."

"Where's her mother? Why's she with Aiden?"

"If you want to know more, then ask Aiden."

"How long have you known?"

"Long enough."

"So you're moving, getting married, and you have a ready-made family." Tara smirked. "Guess he wanted a mommy for his kid."

"Enough." Emily glared at Tara. "What is it with the catty women around this damn place? Could you be happy for me?" After enduring Dana and her crap, she's run out of patience with the crass comments about her relationship. Was it so hard to believe the guy loved her?

Tara looked taken aback at her outburst. "Sensitive, aren't we? Is it that time of the month?"

Emily slammed her locker shut and left the nurse standing there. The Zen feelings from the weekend evaporated and now she wanted to cry and throw up.

She dashed into the bathroom, tears trickling down her face as she heaved into the toilet. Finally, the sickness abated, and she leaned back against the door, closing her eyes and taking a deep breath before stepping out of the stall.

Emily jumped as she spotted Tara leaning against the counter. "Can't get rid of you." She washed her hands and rinsed her mouth.

"Guess that's the reason you're moving." A gleam appeared in Tara's eyes as she crossed her arms. "One sure way to catch the rich guy is to get knocked up. He has quite the track record. A fifteen-year-old daughter and another kid on the way."

"Go back to work." Emily inspected her makeup and pinched her cheeks to add color. She took several deep breaths before lifting her chin and giving the woman a frosty look. "Enough of the gossip and quit staring at me. A couple more days, and I'll be out of here."

"Off to be a kept woman and live the good life."

Emily raised a brow. She recognized Tara's words for what they were and ignored them. Instead, she turned and strode into the ER, determined to take on the world.

⤙

Two days later, Emily ambled through Logan International Airport, her small bag slung over her shoulder. Despite the weather delay and the wait while they de-iced the plane and plowed the runway, she'd arrived.

"Emily." Savannah's voice carried over the murmured conversations and calls of other families who were awaiting the passengers from her flight. The teen bounced over, wrapping her into a big hug. "I'm so happy you're here."

The girl dragged her the few remaining feet to where Aiden waited and Emily let the bag slide from her shoulder. It hit the tiled floor with a small thump as she threw her arms around him. She inhaled, enjoying the spicy scent of his aftershave and his warm embrace as he lifted her from her feet.

"I missed you," he murmured.

She lifted her gaze to his, stretching on tiptoes to kiss him. "This week was interminable."

Aiden gave her another firm squeeze before he scooped up her bag. He entwined their fingers as Savannah latched onto her other hand and they headed toward the parking lot.

"You'll love it here. Have you seen the apartment?" Savannah skipped along beside her.

Emily shook her head. "Just the pictures you sent. I've only been here once on vacation, so you must show me around."

"I have three days off work so we can get you settled." Aiden squeezed her hand.

His grin and Savannah's excitement overrode her misgivings, even though this move was crazy. She didn't even know if she liked Boston, or if she'd find a job, or if she'd like the apartment—or anything, really. However, she was here now, and she owed it to everyone to give it a fair shot even if it terrified her to depend on a man.

Emily shivered as the frosty air hit. "It's as cold here as it is in Chicago."

Aiden laughed. "The winters aren't any warmer, but I think you'll like Boston." He stowed her bag before he opened her door.

Emily settled into the seat, turning on the heater. "I'll get used to it, I'm sure."

It seemed like no time and they were turning onto a side street, then into the underground parking garage. Emily glanced at her watch. The trip had taken all of fifteen minutes. "Wow, you live close to the airport."

"We live close to the airport," Savannah said. "You live here too."

"We." It was a strange reality, going from Aiden's place in Chicago to his dwelling here. This was now home.

Aiden retrieved her bag and ushered her toward the bank of elevators, and in moments they were rising upwards. The doors opened into a foyer much like the one in Chicago.

She gazed around as they stepped inside, raising her eyebrows. The apartment was luxurious and almost nicer than his other penthouse.

Savannah took her hand. "I'll give you the tour."

Emily turned to look at Aiden, and he gave her a nod, so she let the girl lead her through and point out the various rooms. By the time they reached the master bedroom, Aiden had stowed her bag. They'd stacked her boxes from Chicago along one wall, and a peek into the walk-in showed her clothing hung on one side.

"It's beautiful."

"I'm happy you like it. We're close to work, Vanna's school is a few streets over, and it's only a few short blocks to the Commons."

"Maybe you can show me around tomorrow." She smothered a yawn.

"You're tired." Aiden rubbed her back. "Do you want tea? Or a warm bath?"

"Both. I was up early, and it was a busy day."

Vanna nodded. "I have the cinnamon tea. Would you like some of that?"

"Please."

Savannah disappeared down the hallway.

Aiden took her in his arms again. "You okay?" He placed his palms against her cheeks, studying her face.

"I'm exhausted. I need sleep."

Aiden kissed her nose. "I'll fill the tub." He went into the bathroom and moments later she heard running water.

Emily grabbed her toiletry bag and some sleepwear, following him in. He'd added lavender bath salts, and she allowed the scent to calm and soothe her mind.

He rubbed her back and dropped a kiss on her forehead, then left, clearly recognizing her need for quiet time to acclimate.

She stripped and sank into the tub, leaning back against the bath pillow with a sigh. The warm water eased the tension in her muscles as she closed her eyes and relaxed.

A few minutes later she heard the tap on the door and Aiden let himself in. "Tea."

"Thanks. The two of you are pampering me."

"Vanna's been super excited all day. She organized your clothes, made sure we bought all your favorite foods, including extra-healthy stuff for the baby." He set the steaming cup on the ledge within her reach.

"It's cute. I'm glad she's okay with me house crashing."

"House crashing? Never. This is your home."

"I know, but huge changes are coming, right?" She ran a hand over her belly. "How's she going to deal with a screaming baby at two in the morning?"

"It'll be fine. The big sister role is a dream come true for her. She's already offered to babysit whenever we need. We have a few months to get used to it before then." He reached down and took her hand. "We've missed you."

Emily smiled, unable to answer, but she gave a small nod.

"I'll let you bathe in peace. Come out when you're ready."

"Thanks. It's been a long day."

"This is a big move for you."

Emily sipped the tea and lingered in the bath until the water cooled. She yawned, longing for soft sheets and her pillow. Aiden had left a fluffy towel within her reach, and she dried off before sliding the soft fabric of her sleep pants and top over her body. She lifted her shirt and ran her hands over the tiny swelling of her belly, rubbing in gentle circles before she padded into the bedroom.

Aiden had turned on her bedside lamp and had his eyes closed but she knew he wasn't asleep.

"Vanna said goodnight. She wanted to wait, but I told her to relax as we have lots of time," he said in a soft voice as she slid under the covers.

"Thanks, no point in her staying up for me. I'm ready to pass out." Emily turned off the light. She wiggled closer to Aiden, resting her head on his chest. "Mmm."

Aiden wrapped an arm around her, dropping a kiss on her hair. "I've missed this, Em. Having you here is amazing."

"It'll be an adjustment, but it'll be great." It felt wonderful being held in his arms. "I love you." A simple mantra ran through her mind. Everything would be okay. It would all work out.

CHAPTER 14

Aiden

Two weeks after Emily's move to Boston, Aiden headed to New York to meet Ryan.

Ryan waved as Aiden strode into the hotel lobby. "You made it." The man drew him in for a hug. "Big changes on the home front, huh? Congrats, man. I'm excited to be an uncle again."

"I'm freaking out." Aiden chuckled, but he was only half-joking. The next days of his relationship with Emily might move them forward … or send her running.

Ryan gave his own small laugh as a smug grin appeared. "No need. This is the right move. Trust me."

"I guess you'd know better than me."

The grin disappeared. "I'm truly sorry, though I'm not sure if I actually regret my actions." Ryan gripped Aiden's shoulder. "We're good, right? You've forgiven me for meddling in your business with Emily?"

"Well, I don't know. Maybe you could make it up to me." Aiden raised a brow. "Why are you so convinced this is the right move?"

His friend emitted a deep laugh as a broad smile spread across his face. "Wondered when that was coming, but I'm surprised you haven't gotten it out of Emily," Ryan said as they exited onto the busy New York sidewalk.

"I've just left that one alone, waiting for her to talk, but she hasn't." Aiden rubbed at the back of his neck. "It pissed me off that she could tell someone she assumed to be a stranger, yet she still hasn't trusted me. Is it that earth shattering?"

"It was then, but now?" Ryan shrugged. "She admitted how much she cared. That she saw a future. It seemed she wanted the next step, otherwise I would have let her go."

"Are you sure?" If he went by her reaction that day on the patio, Ryan was dead wrong. "She didn't seem that into marriage." He paused outside the doors of the store, gazing in the window. If he did this, and she said no … "You didn't act that surprised about the baby. Why not?"

"Damn. Do you ever miss anything?" Ryan shook his head. "Look. She said she wanted marriage and babies and … that life with you. Do I think she did the baby thing on purpose? No, because she wanted you to slow it down, give her some time and space. Which you didn't. You pushed and she bolted. This baby is more like … fate. If you believe in that sort of thing."

Aiden massaged his temples. Valuable information, given far too late. "Should I do this? Or is it pushing her again?"

"Time to go all in, Aiden. She's worth it."

He tipped his head back, closing his eyes for a moment before he glanced at Ryan. "If this goes south, you're to blame."

"Shut up." Ryan shoved him toward the door. "Quit acting like a pussy and buy the damn ring already. Besides, you've done all the work on designing, choosing stones, so …" His friend shrugged.

"But will she say yes?" To Aiden, that was the real question. Emily, in her roundabout way had begged him to slow down, but he hadn't picked up her cues. His biggest mistake was refusing to accept the compromise of a long distance relationship, and they'd both paid the price. A misstep now would be devastating.

⁓

Apprehension hit the moment Aiden walked into the doctor's office. His palms felt damp and his heart skipped when he scanned the waiting area and she was nowhere to be seen.

The receptionist looked up from her computer. "Can I help you, sir?"

"Emily Anderson. We have an appointment today."

"She's in the first room on the left. They took her in a few minutes early. Go on in."

He tapped on the exam room door.

"Come in?" Emily sat on the edge of the exam table in a gown, flipping through a magazine. "There you are."

"Am I late?" He leaned in for a kiss.

"You know you're not." She patted his cheek. "I can always count on you, Aiden. I appreciate that."

"Back at you, beautiful."

She patted her belly. "I need to buy clothes. I resorted to leggings today because I couldn't do up my jeans." She laughed. "Just like high school. You know when you have to hop around and wiggle into them and then lie flat on the bed so you can zip them?"

"Can't have that. We'll grab a snack after our appointment and go shopping. Vanna's in class, anyway."

They both looked up as the doctor entered the room. "Sorry to keep you waiting. I'm Dr. Ritchie. I understand you're new to Boston. I received a referral and your chart from Chicago. Let's do an exam. Does ..." She consulted her notes. "Oh, Dr. Hamilton. What's your specialty?"

"Emergency Medicine."

"Aiden, right? I thought you looked familiar. You work in the ER." Dr. Ritchie smiled. "Did you want to wait outside or are you comfortable with being here for the exam?"

"I want him here." Emily peered at him. "Aiden?"

"I'll stay." Aiden moved to the head of the table and held her hand while the doctor did the exam and measured her belly.

"Everything looks perfect. I'd like to do an ultrasound, check the fetal development, and listen to the heartbeat. You haven't had one yet."

Emily gripped Aiden's hand.

The doctor squeezed gel onto Emily's belly and moved the wand. The rapid heartbeat filled the room.

Emily looked up with glistening eyes. "Wow. Our baby."

Aiden's heart pounded and his eyes burned as he listened to the whooshing sound filling the room. "Can we see?"

The doctor turned the screen. "Eleven weeks seems right based on the fetal development. Heartbeat is strong and steady as you can hear. I'll print a picture of this for the baby book."

The doctor spent several minutes asking Emily questions, but Aiden's thoughts drifted as he held her hand. It took him back in time. He'd been here before, but this time it would be different. No one would take this precious baby away. He vowed to be there for every moment, every step, and every sleepless night. He never let Emily or their child down.

***

Aiden opened the front door of the apartment, and Emily struggled out of her coat and boots, dashing into the bathroom. She spent tons of time there these days, which was normal, but he didn't know how she combated the morning sickness and hormones on top of it all.

He hung up her coat and tidied up the shoes before carrying her bags into the kitchen, making a stop to turn on the kettle.

Emily appeared behind him. "You read my mind." After a quick rub to his back, she carried her bags into the living room and pulled out one of the loose flowing tops she'd purchased. "Do you like this?" She held it against herself.

"It looks amazing." Aiden almost rolled his eyes. He'd heard this all afternoon and had reassured her at least three times about this same top. She'd tried on so many outfits his mind was spinning, but at least she seemed happier.

"Ha ha, good answer." She ran her palms over her belly. "We heard our baby's heart beating. It's much more real now we've seen the ultrasound. I wonder if it's a boy or a girl?"

"Truly a miracle." Aiden stepped bent down to give her belly a kiss. "You're excited?"

"Of course." She rubbed her hands over his hair as he straightened. "I'm adjusting, don't worry."

"Am I that obvious?"

"This is huge for all of us, but I love you, and I want to be with you when our baby is born."

"It means everything that you're here." He leaned his forehead against hers. "Are you happy?"

"Am I that obvious?" Her lips twitched. "I'm incredibly happy, Aiden. This feels like I'm finally where I'm supposed to be."

"So you could tolerate me for another fifty or sixty years?"

"I don't know?" A tiny smile appeared. "You'd have to make it worth while."

"Hmmm. What would that involve, I wonder?" He wrapped an arm around her waist, pulling her against him. "Are you ready for that commitment, Emelia?"

"Are you …?" She hauled in a breath as she wrapped a hand around the back of his neck, gazing into his eyes. "I am," she whispered. "I love you. I love this baby. I love Savannah. So, yes." She stretched to kiss him, her lips tender against his.

He exhaled softly and rested his forehead against hers. "You're ready to get engaged?"

"I can't wait to marry you, Aiden." She smiled tearfully. "Mi vida."

"Then we should make it official." He caught her hand, leading her toward the bedroom.

"Savannah will be home soon." Emily giggled, wrinkling her nose.

Aiden smirked, but ushered her to one of chairs by the fireplace before heading into the walk in closet. He retrieved the box he'd tucked away while debating on the when and how.

"What are you doing?" She straightened and slid to the edge of the chair as he approached her. "Why do you look so serious?"

He blew out a breath. It should be easier now, but somehow it wasn't. His heart raced as he kneeled before her and produced the velvet box.

Emily's eyes teared up as she pressed her fingers to her lips.

"Emelia Anderson, will you marry me?"

She swept her fingertips under her eyes, and nodded. "Yes, mi vida." Her eyes widened as he opened the box, a radiant smile appearing as he slid the ring onto her finger. She turned her hand, the stones sparkling as they caught the light. "That's incredible." Her smile widened as she cupped his face between her palms, bestowing a long sweet kiss.

Aiden sank into her embrace, his life feeling complete for the first time in a very long time. Everything he ever wanted was here. The trick would be keeping it.

CHAPTER 15

Emily

EMILY HUNG UP AND GRINNED. "I got it. It's only part-time attending, but I'm excited. I start next week." The phone rang almost immediately. She frowned as she sent the call to voice mail.

"I knew you'd get it." Aiden hugged her. "Who was the other call?"

"My dad." She sighed. "Natalia told him I'm getting married. I've hardly heard from the guy over the last few years and now he's interested."

"I'm sorry." Aiden rubbed her back.

She lifted a shoulder, not knowing what to say. Aiden knew her views on her father. No point in allowing those memories to turn her into a tearful lunatic. *Again.* "He'll want to walk me down the aisle, but I don't want him there."

"It's okay if you don't invite him." Aiden kissed her nose before heading into the kitchen. "Want some tea?"

"Please." Emily sighed as her phone rang again. Her family had started in on her the moment she'd announced her big news. "Hi, Mamá." She massaged her temples with her fingertips.

"Cariño. I have some ideas for the wedding to keep the costs down…"

Aiden's mobile vibrated and lit up and she idly spun it as her mom nattered on about how expensive weddings were. *Tiffany* appeared before the screen faded to black. What could that woman possibly have to say to Aiden?

"Emelia?"

"I'm here, Mamá." She tried to concentrate on her mother's diatribe. Trust, or the lack of it, was a major hot button in their relationship after the *Dani-the-flight-attendant* issue.

Seconds later, his phone buzzed and lit up once more and a voice mail notification appeared. That woman had left a message? Her fingers itched and extended toward his cell phone, but she snatched her hand away and tucked it into her lap.

"Emmy?" Her mom's voice reminded her she was mid-conversation.

"I'm here."

"Send me the details. Natalia and Juliana will get measured so we can pick the bridesmaids' dresses. When I visit over Christmas, I'll bring my dress and we can pin it. Oh. That little hall would be perfect for a wedding reception. We'll make all the food—"

"Aiden and I haven't even decided on the guest list yet. I appreciate you want to help, but slow down. I'm buying a dress, and I don't want to rent the hall or make the food ourselves. And Natalia and Juliana aren't my bridesmaids."

The line crackled. "What?"

"I've asked Jenna, Alex, and Savannah."

A heavy inhalation was followed by an equally deep and forbidding silence. "Why not your sisters?" Nina asked.

"They both live on the other side of the country, and neither have the time or energy to plan a wedding. They're both fine with it."

"Hmmph." Her mother huffed. "I wish you'd reconsider my dress. The gowns are far too expensive. Why buy a new one when …?"

Another lengthy ramble ensued. One that had Emily ready to yank out her hair. She yearned to hit the little red disconnect button as the pain crept into her temples. "Mamá?"

"We can do this …"

"Mamá?"

"Your sisters …"

"Mamá."

Dead silence fell.

"I'll talk to you tomorrow. Do nothing on the wedding."

"But Emmy …"

"Promise me. Aiden and I need to discuss our plans."

"I promise. But tomorrow we need to figure it all out if we're to pull this wedding together on such short notice."

"Love you, Mamá." She hung up with a massive sigh.

"You good?" Aiden arched a brow as he set a steaming cup on the table.

"My mother insists we should throw together a wedding right away before I show." Emily placed her palms over the firm roundness of her belly. "Too late, but I didn't tell her. Anyway, I don't mind sporting the bump, but she wants me to wear her dress."

"She kept her wedding gown for … thirty years?" Aiden's lips twitched.

"Don't laugh." She shook a finger at him. "Thirty-four years. She's insisting, maybe because my sisters avoided it." Emily grimaced. She envisioned herself walking down the aisle, and how Aiden would look at her. Her perfect day didn't include an old-fashioned, buttoned-to-the-neck gown. "It's sweet, but it doesn't show an inch of flesh. And these"—she hooked a thumb toward her ample cleavage—"won't fit. Let alone this." She patted her belly again. "She's fretting about the cost, and wants to book her church and the little community hall plus do all the cooking."

"Just say no."

"It's not that easy. She did this for both of my sisters."

"Quit stressing about it and buy your dream gown." Aiden's intense gaze made her wonder what kind of expression she had on her own face. "We won't rush the wedding to keep up appearances. You'll look incredible, beautiful and amazing."

Emily smiled. This man was incredible, beautiful, and amazing... He always supported her. Her love for him welled up.

"Before I forget, this came for you." He handed her an envelope.

"What's this?" She slit it open and pulled out the enclosed card. "This looks like a credit card with my name on it."

"Maybe because it is a credit card with your name on it. Sign the back and you're in business."

"What's my limit?"

"There isn't one, so have fun." He winked. "You can charge Vanna's dress, shoes, and stuff on there so it doesn't cut into her allowance." Aiden sipped his coffee. "Jenna sent the name of their wedding planner. We should pick a venue right after we finish the guest list. It needs to get booked soon if we are doing this in February."

Emily's head spun. Wedding planner? Guest list, dresses, and invitations... Her chest constricted and she dropped her head in her hands as the dizziness hit. The tears rose unbidden, her throat closed up, and she gasped for air. She was getting married and having a baby after uprooting her entire life.

"What's wrong?" Aiden kneeled in front of her, concern written on his face. "Talk to me."

Emily took several deep breaths, desperate to control the shake that had taken over her entire body. "I'm fine."

"You're pale and diaphoretic." He placed his palms on her cheeks and studied her. "Em?" He pressed his fingertips to her wrist, timing her pulse.

"It's only a little nausea." Emily pulled her arm away. "Quit worrying."

Aiden strode into the kitchen to pour her a glass of ice water. He set it on the table in front of her, still looking concerned. "Nausea brought on by the mention of a wedding planner and guest list." He rubbed his face and wandered to the large windows, staring through the glass at the snowy vista.

Emily sipped her water, letting it soothe and loosen the lump in her throat. After several deep breaths, she rose from her seat, noting the stiffness of his shoulders. She could almost hear what he was thinking.

"Aiden." The few steps across the room seemed interminable, like covering a wide chasm between them. After a moment of hesitation, she wrapped her arms around his waist from behind and leaned against his back. "It's overwhelming, but I love you. I want to marry you. It's my family. They're too much on top of everything, and now ... a wedding planner?"

A deep sigh escaped as he turned and embraced her, his cheek resting on her hair. "A planner will keep track of the details and do all the legwork and take the pressure off. I understand, Emily. You're pregnant, starting a new job, and planning a huge event." He placed a hand on her belly. "It's better for everyone."

"A planner is expensive and my mom is already panicking over the budget. It's doubtful my father would offer, and I don't want him to pay for it anyway."

"Nina only needs to buy a dress and show up. Don't worry about price tags. I've got it covered." He grinned. "You can order everyone around."

Emily frowned. "How? You don't know how much it is."

"Jenna shared their cost per person, so I have a ballpark."

"Their wedding was like every woman's fantasy. We can't afford that kind of wedding."

"Why not?"

"I'm only back to work, and my student loan payments alone will eat up my income. You've just started as attending, so your income can't be that high yet. Tom earns way more than us combined."

"Uh, Em?" An odd expression appeared. "Not to burst your bubble of denial, but ... in addition to my full-time job, I own half of the shares in Hamilton Grayson and have substantial investments in equities and real estate. I owe nothing. We can afford it."

Emily's head snapped up. She'd never calculated his net worth. A picture of his grandmother's house flashed through her mind, followed by a vivid image of his Chicago apartment. Plus he owned the Vineyard house ... and this place. She assumed the raging pregnancy hormones had given her temporary amnesia and turned her into a complete idiot. "I'm clueless."

"You've never considered my family's wealth?"

She shrugged. "I've never asked about your finances because we've both had our own incomes. It's fair I contribute to the wedding, but I have student loans and I need a new car. Impossible on a part-time income." The last word hiccuped out with a sob. The ability to pay her own way created a sense of pride, and she hated the prospect of relying on anyone.

"It's okay." He nestled her against him as she wept, her tears leaving wet spots on his immaculate shirt. "You'll be working part-time, and you can always return full-time after you have the baby. But until then, if you need anything, it's covered."

"It's what I do. I have bills to pay." She snuffled. "I can't freeload."

"It's not freeloading. What I do for you is because I want to, not because you expect it."

"I never considered staying home with the baby."

"Now you have choices. If you want to work, then work. If you don't, then don't. You could stay home with the baby for a few months if you'd like... or not. Up to you."

"So many details." She peered at him.

"We have a busy year coming up, but don't freak out, please? Let's deal with it one thing at a time. One day at a time." He held her face between his palms, brushing his thumbs over her cheeks. "Do you want to push the wedding date to next fall? This should be a happy day, not a stressful marathon."

She dropped her hand to rest on her belly as she gazed into his eyes. Despite what Jenna maintained about his fear of commitment, each and every day he'd proven himself.

"No, it's February. I can't wait to marry you." She smiled. "Let's hire the wedding planner. You're right. I'm dealing with too much on my own."

"And I can't wait to marry you." His lips caressed hers as his hand slid down to cover the one she'd placed on her small bump.

She sank into the kiss, wrapping a hand around his neck to keep him close. When they pulled apart, the tension had dissolved, not only from her body but from his too. After another long embrace, she stepped back, wiping at her eyes. "I'm a mess. I'm a massive, hormonal, weepy, half-crazed nightmare."

"It's not that bad." Aiden smirked.

"Liar." Emily blotted at her tears with a tissue. "My face is red and puffy, and I've left half of my makeup on your shirt. I'll freshen up, you change, and then we'll tackle the guest list. My mom will be back at me tomorrow."

"I'll call the wedding planner, and we can set a date to meet her when we're in Chicago." Aiden gave her a kiss. "Don't worry about Nina. I'll calm her down."

"Lay on the Hamilton charm?" A grin twitched at her lips. Aiden had a way with people, and she had no doubt he'd settle Nina down. She should have suggested it earlier.

"Of course. We're planning our big day, and nothing will get in the way. It'll be perfect. Absolutely perfect."

Allowing Aiden to take care of her, even a little, would be one of the biggest adjustments. That wouldn't be easy for a woman who'd learned the art of self preservation at such a young age.

CHAPTER 16

Aiden

A S HE STEPPED INTO THE coffee shop, Aiden spotted the familiar blonde woman sitting at a table. "Hi." He slid onto the opposite chair.

Tiffany smiled faintly. "Aiden." She clutched a large coffee cup and pushed a second one across the table. "Extra hot, with a touch of cream and sugar."

Aiden hesitated before accepting it. "Thanks."

"Don't worry, I know how you like your coffee." Her eyes narrowed. "I didn't poison it. I didn't even spit in it."

"Good to know." Aiden hated that she'd guessed what he'd been thinking.

"Why are you in Chicago?" Her voice was even and conversational although she scrutinized him.

"I wanted to see Gramma ... and everyone." He kept his tone light to match hers.

"You kept the friends. I'm the evil ex." She sipped her coffee, her icy gaze fixed on him.

He rubbed a hand over his face. "I didn't want to make things difficult, Tiffany. No one was to take sides. This is between you and me." He sighed. "It doesn't mean I'll ever understand how you walked away."

As she picked at the lid on her cup, she half-shrugged. "I can't explain. Things are over with Harrison. I'm waiting until after his trial, but I've stopped planning the wedding. Then the engagement will be over." She twisted the diamond ring on her finger. "You were right about him. Why did nobody tell me?"

"You refused to see him for who he is, blinded by all the political bullshit that brought you down this path. I don't even recognize you anymore."

"You're the one who kept all the friends, and you lecture me?" The sheen of tears sparkled in her eyes, and she looked down and fidgeted with her cup. "I've been replaced by your flavor of the week. My best friends chose Dr. Perfect."

Aiden sat back and crossed his arms. "Emily happens to be my fiancée."

Tiffany's head snapped up. "You're getting married? Are you returning to Chicago?"

"Emily moved to Boston," he said. "Savannah's made new friends at school. I'd hate to uproot her when she's happy. Have you noticed the world is still spinning?"

Her eyebrows rose. "My entire world has changed, and there are days I can't help but wonder. If I hadn't gotten pregnant, or we'd protected her from our families, what would our lives be like now? Would we still be together?"

"It's doubtful. I never wanted a career in politics or all the fundraisers and parties you live for. I love being a doctor, and I'm sure being an Emergency Physician isn't prestigious enough to make you or your daddy happy. Our divorce thrilled him."

Tiffany hung her head, not even denying that David Baxter had never liked him.

"My life is perfect. I have a family. I'm happy ..." He observed her quietly. "We're having a baby."

"That's why you're marrying her?"

"No. I love her."

"I heard Jenna's due in June, but she didn't call me. Alex rarely speaks to me, and you scarcely tolerate me as you made clear at the wedding. Ryan refuses to look at me."

"What do you expect?" He narrowed his eyes. After talking with Ryan, they'd decided to let it go, but since she'd brought it up ... "You tried to drive a wedge between Ryan and me with Emily as the bait. Why did you do that? Why can't you let me be happy and get on with my life?"

"I didn't mean it."

"Sure you didn't. Don't worry. Your worst nightmare will go elsewhere. Shouldn't be too difficult as I live in a different state."

"And the only reason you called was for this." She slid a small box onto the table, keeping her hand on top. After staring at him for a moment, she pushed the package away and placed her hand in her lap.

Aiden hesitated for only a second before pulling it toward him. "Thank you." He resisted the urge to open the lid. "I'm amazed you still had it."

"I hadn't thought about it for years." She lifted one shoulder. "I'd packed it in a storage box and hoped to forget. It's fitting you take it now as you ... have her." She shifted in her chair and tucked a long strand of hair behind her ear. "How did she find you? You never told me."

He cleared his throat. "You never cared enough to ask." Her gaze didn't waver as he took a sip of coffee, which had been sweetened with a touch of sugar and a splash of cream. *Perfect.* "The train derailment last winter."

Her eyes widened.

"The hospital sent me to the scene, and I treated both her friend Leanne and Savannah at the accident site. She heard my name in the ER."

"She was your patient?"

"Weird, right? Fate intervened."

"It's all because I couldn't bear for her to not have anything of us," she said. "You'll be a great dad. Well, you already are a dad. But I remember how you were there for me. I'll never forget, so ... I guess Emily's a lucky woman. Maya Gabrielle, remember?"

"You ...?" Aiden didn't know what to say. A compliment from Tiffany was unexpected, and to have her voice that name even more so.

"I've been hard on you. You took a lot of chances, and it was wrong to claim I was alone. I'm sorry."

Aiden nodded, studying her, unsure where this was coming from or why. "You should have these," he said as he pulled out his wallet. "Ross gave me this"—he tapped a finger on one photo—"not long after the DNA testing. She was two days old." He extracted a second picture and set it beside the first. "This one's from this past summer."

A choked sob escaped her as she viewed the image of the baby girl. "She was perfect. You have other pictures from when she was little?"

He nodded and sipped more coffee to ease his aching throat. "I should go. Keep those. I have other copies." He slid his coat on and picked up the box. "I appreciate you bringing this stuff. I'm glad you kept it. Take care, okay?" Time he walked away, but it wasn't so easy. After today, he doubted he'd see her again. "Tiffany?"

Her red-rimmed eyes rose to meet his, her brow knitting into a frown.

He rested a hand on the table. "She's beautiful and amazing," he said in a low voice. "Don't let who you've become destroy your chance to know our daughter." He sucked in a breath. "Regret is a hell of a thing to live with. I endured it for fifteen years, but you're choosing it. Why the hell would you ever throw away your final opportunity to be part of her life?"

Her eyes welled with tears, her fingers trembling. "I can't, Aiden," she whispered. "It's too hard."

"Have you forgotten what she meant?" The tears no longer affected him. "You're pathetic." He spun and stalked out, refusing to look back. He couldn't.

The words had been impulsive, and he wasn't sure why he'd said them, but she'd needed to hear it. Now he'd let her live her life however she wanted.

Half an hour later, he parked in the underground garage at his apartment and exited on the ground level, leaving the box in his car. The walk to Tom and Jenna's house took less than five minutes.

"What took you so long?" Tom clapped him on the back and extended a beer.

"Sorry, my appointment ran long. Hey, Joel." He accepted the ice-cold bottle, taking a long pull. The visit had rattled him more than he cared to admit. "Where are the ladies?"

Joel tapped Aiden's beer bottle with his. "They're upstairs buried in wedding talk and bridal magazines. Alex brought a pile of stuff to show Emily, and they're planning the trip to New York."

"Ah, right. Vanna's up there with them?"

Joel nodded. "I've heard she has pictures of the perfect dress. Vanna is so damn cute. I can't get over the fact your daughter is almost sixteen. That's crazy. And she looks so much like—"

Vanna chose that moment to skip into the kitchen. "Dad. You're here. Emily tried to call you about our trip. Can I miss a day of school?" She chattered on about the trip but he didn't interrupt, grateful for the reprieve from the typical nerve-wracking Tiffany conversation.

Emily appeared and slid an arm around his waist. "Hi."

He leaned in to give her a long kiss, one hand coming to rest on the slight roundedness of her firm belly. "How are the plans coming?"

This launched a discussion that carried them through dinner. Everybody had comments and suggestions on everything from the dress down to the food. Not that he minded because Emily's eyes sparkled in delight when they discussed the upcoming trip to New York.

Jenna kept shooting quizzical glances his way until she cornered him in the kitchen when he offered to help her clear the supper dishes. "What's going on with you?" She crossed her arms and narrowed her eyes.

Aiden leaned against the counter. "I could ask the same of you. You've been giving me weird looks throughout dinner."

She heaved a sigh. "Tiffany phoned while we were upstairs earlier, which was super awkward." She placed her hands on her hips as her mouth formed a grim line. "Your appointment was coffee with Tiffany? What in the hell were you thinking?"

"Why are you making it into a federal case?" Aiden grasped Jenna's shoulders. "We met in a public place for all of fifteen minutes. She had something I needed."

"That's it?"

"What did she say to you?"

"She's pissed off. She discovered I'm pregnant."

"Not from me." He shook his head. "She already knew. I informed her I'm engaged, and that Emily is expecting."

Jenna squinted. "What did she have that was so important?"

"I'm not getting into it, Jenn."

"Tread lightly, Aiden," she whispered. "Did you hear about the altercation on my wedding day? Alex teased Emily about spending the night with you, and Tiffany lost it and called her a gold-digging tramp."

Aiden froze. "Tiffany said ... What?"

"Emily didn't tell you?"

"We were busy discussing other things, not your breakfast conversation. I can't believe she said that to Emily."

"She's jealous. Alex and I have known for a while. If things went south with Harrison, she'd be plotting to get you back. I'm sure part of what went wrong that weekend had to do with the gold-digger comment." Jenna patted his cheek. "Promise me you'll stay away from your ex-wife. Emily already knows you've been in touch with her, but you haven't shared the reasons."

"How ...?" Aiden closed his eyes. "Damn it. She's been snooping my phone?"

"Absolutely not. Your phone was on the table, and she saw the call display. Stop with the secrecy, Aiden. Don't be sneaking around. If Emily finds out that's where you were today?" Jenna slashed a finger across her throat. "Tell her, or she'll think you're hiding something. She's hormonal and struggling with the changes already."

"I'll explain it to her tonight."

"Don't screw this up. You owe Emily complete transparency and honesty." She shook her head. "I'm still pissed that you kept Savannah from us for fifteen years. You're so bloody stubborn and secretive. Quit with the damn half-truths." Jenna grasped his chin, forcing him to look at her. "Promise me."

His friends had a right to be angry. He should have trusted them no matter the consequences. "I hear you. I promise, and I'm sorry. It's stupidity on my part."

She nodded, surprising him by wrapping her arms around him and hugging tightly. "I love you. You've been my friend forever. I wish eternal happiness for you, and Emily's your girl. No matter what, never let her go."

"I don't intend to, Jenn." Not ever.

CHAPTER 17

Emily

OVERALL, IT HAD BEEN A good day. They had set the dates for the New York trip. Jenna had contacted the Bridal Salon and booked an appointment, relaying the specifications for both her gown and the bridesmaid dresses to the associate.

Emily smothered a wide yawn, exhausted after the hours of planning, followed by the boisterous family dinner.

"I'm off to bed." Vanna hugged her. "Today was fun. Night."

"Have a good sleep and say hi to Chase for me," Emily said, knowing Savannah would be on the phone for at least an hour talking to her boyfriend.

She stretched her arms upwards, rolling her neck to work out the tension. It was late and the urge to yawn swept over her again. Definitely time for cozy pajamas and her nightly tea.

Aiden appeared and set a box on the granite counter. He moved close behind her, wrapping one arm around her waist and pushing aside her hair with the other. His soft kiss at the nape of her neck caused a shiver to run down her spine.

Emily leaned against him, turning her head to look at him. "Want tea?"

"Sure." He captured her lips, his mouth lingering against hers as his warm hand caressed her belly. "I'll make it. Why don't you put your feet up? I'm sure you're exhausted."

Emily shuffled into the living room, flipping the switch for the gas fireplace. She sank onto the sofa and elevated her aching feet, cuddling under a throw. Her eyelids drooped as she listened to the comforting sounds of Aiden working in the kitchen.

It wasn't long before he joined her and offered her a cup of tea. After dimming the lights, he settled beside her.

"That was fun." She curled up and leaned against his chest. "I miss living close to everyone."

"Me too, but they'll visit Boston for New Year's, and then you'll be off to New York." He sipped his tea before sighing and closing his eyes.

"What's up between you and Jenna? She gave you the eye all night, and then ..." Emily shrugged, not knowing how to ask, but dying to hear the details. She'd caught the constant exchange of looks, which in itself was strange. Once they'd returned from the kitchen, they'd both looked so damn guilty.

"Nothing much." He trickled his fingers down her arm. "Jenn likes to keep me in line, is all."

"About what?"

"Tiffany phoned her while you were all upstairs in the bedroom."

"That's why she acted cagey?" Emily took his hand, linking their fingers. "You were talking about Tiffany?" She angled her body so she could see his face. His expressions often gave him away even if he was adept at hiding his emotions.

"I need to tell you something, but let me finish before you say anything. Please?"

Emily's stomach flipped, and she closed her eyes. "Boy, that's almost as wonderful as starting a conversation with *we need to talk*."

"It's nothing bad. It's only a small confession," he said with a sigh. "I met Tiffany for coffee. As soon as I left, she phoned Jenna."

Emily bolted upright, jostling her tea. "You saw Tiffany?"

He nodded. "This"—he placed his fingertips on top of the box—"is what I was after." Aiden placed a palm against her cheek. "Don't worry. I have no intention of seeing her again."

"But you told me because Jenna called you out?"

"Em." He shook his head. "I never intended to hide it, but these things seem to turn into a big deal. And you should talk. Jenna told me about the lovely breakfast conversation at her wedding. You didn't tell me Tiffany spoke to you like that. Don't ever let her—"

"These things tend to turn into more than they are." Emily held up a hand. "I held my own, so calm down. Anyway, I'm more interested in knowing what's in this ever-so-important box."

"I haven't opened it yet, and it's been sixteen years so ..." He flipped open the lid revealing an assortment of photos and other small keepsakes.

Emily spotted the scan that rested on the top of the pile. "That's an ultrasound."

"It's Vanna."

"This is for Savannah?"

"She's expressed curiosity and is excited to see her new sibling. It got me thinking." He dropped a kiss on her hair. "I contacted Tiffany to ask if she had any pictures. She phoned me a couple weeks ago."

"Jenna told you I saw the call display." Emily narrowed her eyes, reading the truth on his face.

"If you want to be mad, be angry at me. I should have told you right away that I'd phoned Tiffany and why. I didn't want to upset you, but I was stupid not to realize keeping it secret would upset you more than if I told you outright. I'm sorry." He took her face between his hands. "I'm not good at sharing. Secrecy has been drilled into me. It's a part of me I need to change, and I'll try to do better and be more open."

"Did Jenna tell you about not being so damn secretive?"

"More like demanded it. She's right. You're the perfect woman for me. I love you, and it'd kill me to lose you."

"I'm not mad, but you can't sneak around to see exes." A soft smile appeared. "These are important keepsakes. Vanna will love them. Have you told her much about Tiffany and how it was when she was pregnant?"

"Bringing up Tiffany isn't easy, but over time Vanna will have questions. I've never told you everything that happened when I met Vanna for the first time, or about the initial visits to Portland. Maybe I've blocked some of it out. And then with her losing Ross, and the difficulties between you and me, I've hesitated to bring Tiffany up and cause more confusion."

"Tell me."

"Over time I will, but not tonight, okay?"

"I understand." Emily sipped her tea, allowing him time to sort through his own emotions. "Does she know you and Tiffany were married?"

"I don't even know how to tell her." Aiden sighed. "Marrying Tiffany was stupid and impulsive. I tried to save a relationship when there was nothing left to save. It's history. An unhappy life lesson." He rested his forehead against hers. "Now I recognize true love. Those months apart made me miserable. I missed you every day, every hour, every single damn minute. You're the piece of me I didn't even know was missing."

Emily inhaled as the words sank in. He told her he loved her all the time, but he rarely opened up like this. A surge of love surfaced along with a measure of relief. She hadn't realized how tense she'd grown until now. She held out her hand. "Come to bed."

～≺

Emily tapped on the door, steeling herself for a long and painful afternoon.

Nina opened the apartment door. "Cariño. Let me look at you." Her mom enveloped her in a warm hug before holding her by the arms, eyeing her closely. "You're too thin. Good thing I made Paella." She patted Emily's belly.

"It smells delicious." Emily's mouth watered in anticipation as the aroma flooded her nostrils, but her heart sank as she noted the state of the apartment. Decorative items covered the coffee table, littered the couch, and overflowed boxes on the floor. A bonanza of wedding-related paraphernalia that would need to be returned or given away. "What's this?" She forced a smile, thinking of the hours she'd already spent discussing the details with Aiden, their wedding planner, and her bridal party.

"It's not every day your eldest daughter marries. Everyone has been keeping their eyes out for decorations and color ideas and—"

"The flowers, decorations, and invitations have already been ordered. And we booked the caterers and venue last week."

"I can't help?" Nina dabbed her eyes with a tissue. "My Emelia is marrying at long-last, and I can't lift a finger to make it easier?"

"Oh, Mamá." Emily hugged her. As exasperating as Nina could be, she'd been an amazing mother. She backed up a half-step, holding her mom's shoulders in a gentle grip. "Aiden and I can afford the wedding planner."

Her mom turned away, surreptitiously brushing at her eyes. "Whatever you wish, Emelia."

"You still have an important part as the mother of the bride." Emily bit back a sigh. "Besides, you'll be able to enjoy the wedding without worrying about the details. I don't want my family serving and attending to the guests. Aiden's friends and family won't be expected to do any of that."

"Our lunch is ready." Nina patted her arm.

Emily followed her into the kitchen, washing her hands before reaching for the tray.

"No, no. You sit." Her mom guided her toward the table, casting a glance at Emily's belly.

"I'm pregnant, not an invalid."

"Sit. Once baby arrives, you'll be even busier. Besides, if I don't help with the wedding, you don't help with lunch."

Emily rolled her eyes but lowered herself onto a chair as her mom placed the dishes on the table.

Emily took a bite of Paella. "Mmm, it's delicious. This is my favorite meal. I bet Aiden would love it."

"I know it's your favorite, Emelia." Her mom nibbled from the end of her fork and gazed at her. "Papá called, and we need to discuss it."

Emily gnawed on her lip. "What did he say?"

"That his eldest daughter refuses to speak to him? Aren't you inviting him to the wedding?"

Emily set down her fork. "Why is he suddenly interested in my life?"

"He cares, but you've been unreceptive." Nina squeezed her hand. "Why won't you talk to Papá?"

"How can you not know?" Emily frowned, resisting the urge to yank her hand away. "He left us and broke your heart by sleeping with anything and everything that moved. I heard it all when he abandoned our family. Why should I invite that cheating bastard?"

"Emelia." Her mother wagged a finger. "Aiden should meet your papá. You've met Aiden's parents and his abuela. Su hija lives with you."

Emily closed her eyes. The news his parents weren't invited to the wedding wouldn't make her mom happy, but no need to share that information. Not yet.

"Cariño." Her mom gripped her hand tighter. "What happened was between me and your papá. I appreciate your concern, but he did nothing to you. You avoid seeing him. He'll want to know his grandchild and he wants to meet Aiden. Don't hold a grudge. Share your special day with him. Let him walk you down the aisle."

Emily sighed. This would be anything but easy. She should have run away and married Aiden, avoiding all these familial obligations and hassles.

CHAPTER 18

Aiden

AIDEN STABBED AT THE ELEVATOR button, brushing the light flakes of snow from his hair. Moments later, the doors swished open, and he stepped into the warm apartment. A fragrant and spicy aroma filled the air, along with Nina's warm laugh.

The kitchen was a hub of activity, Emily dodging around Nina who seemed to be into everything. He watched the two dance around each other effortlessly. Whether from years of practice in the kitchen, or Emily's skills in a crowded trauma room, he wasn't certain.

"How was work?" Her eyes lit up, her bright smile making his heart skip a beat.

"The usual for Christmas Eve." He bent down to bestow a kiss on his lovely fiancée, giving her belly a mandatory rub. "Smells wonderful."

"Seafood chowder, roasted lamb with baby potatoes, and Mantecados for dessert. Our traditional Spanish feast. Mamá always makes it for La Nochebuena." Her cheeks glowed a delicate shade of pink, but her eyes reflected her flagging energy.

"Sounds amazing." He grasped her shoulders, halting her progress. "What can I do to help?"

"Nothing. We've got it."

Aiden looped an arm around her waist and whispered, "Stop and take a breath. You look exhausted. Sit. I'll get Vanna, and we'll help Nina finish the meal. Please?"

Emily patted his cheek. "Stop being such a worrier."

"You're driving yourself too hard." He guided her toward a stool. "It's only the four of us."

"You worry—"

"The right amount," he said with a small soft smile. "It's great you're energetic, but don't overdo it." He rested his hand on her belly. "Emily?"

"Listen to mi hijo mio. You relax and take care of my grandbaby." Nina waved a hand.

"Fine." She grinned at Aiden. "I'll order you around. I like being in charge."

"Do your worst. Where's Vanna?"

"In her room. She's a touch grouchy but refuses to talk about it, so we gave her some space." Emily's tone softened. "The first holiday is the worst."

"I'll coax her from her room." He poured her a glass of juice and set it in front of her. "Drink and don't move."

Emily gave him a mock salute but stayed in her seat.

He narrowed his eyes and wagged a finger at her in a silent warning.

"Come in," Vanna said when he tapped on her door.

Aiden peeked in, noting the open notebook in front of her. "Why are you hiding out?"

She closed her book before sitting and pulling her knees to her chest. "It's different being here for Christmas."

Aiden perched on the edge of the bed and wound an arm around her. "Holidays are the hardest, aren't they?"

Vanna nodded and brushed her cheek.

"Why don't you join us? Nina could use help finishing dinner, and then we'll attend Midnight Mass."

"We're not Catholic."

"Nina is, and it's important to her."

"Do I have to?"

He pressed a kiss to her hair. Though he understood her hesitation, getting her out of the house and giving her something to focus on besides the pain of her losses seemed essential. "Will you do it for me? This is our first Christmas. It doesn't matter what we're doing, as long as we're together. Tomorrow we can do some of your traditional things."

Vanna nodded. "I'll go for you and for Emily, because Nina's her mom."

"Thank you. Could you help with dinner? Em is overdoing it." He held out his hand.

⌒≼

Aiden woke early on Christmas morning, his arm over Emily with one hand resting on her belly. He'd fallen asleep cuddled against her, but it seemed like he'd drifted even closer during the night.

She looked peaceful, her breathing deep and even. Yesterday, she'd run herself ragged, scarcely keeping awake on the ride home after Mass. There were even points during the service where he swore she drifted to sleep, leaned against his shoulder.

He disengaged himself, careful not to wake her. After a hot shower and donning fresh clothes, he headed for the kitchen.

Vanna hunched over a cup of tea, still in rumpled pajamas. From the wild mess of her hair, he assumed she'd just rolled out of bed.

"Morning, sweetie." He dropped a kiss on her hair and rubbed her back. "Merry Christmas."

Vanna dabbed her red puffy eyes with a tissue. "Morning," she whispered.

"What's the matter?" He curled an arm around her.

Vanna leaned into him, sobbing. "Just … missing them." She swiped at her eyes and rested against his shoulder, taking several deep breaths. "Mom and I had a tradition of making cinnamon buns. Would it upset Emily if I made some? She's worked so hard on planning the meals."

"Emily adores cinnamon buns." He smiled. "Would it be okay if I helped?"

"That would be fun. I'll help with the rest of breakfast so Emily can relax. I'll dress and we can start."

"I'll make coffee."

He kept himself busy organizing the ingredients for breakfast until Vanna reappeared, looking far more cheerful. They set to work and had the buns baking and the breakfast prep done before Emily wandered in, looking bright-eyed and well-rested.

Emily closed her eyes and drew in long breath. "Do I detect cinnamon rolls?"

Vanna peeked through the glass of the oven. "They're almost done."

"Wonderful. What can I do?"

"Relax and drink your tea." Aiden poured hot water into the cup he'd prepared for her and set it on the counter. He leaned across to give her a kiss. "Merry Christmas, Em."

Emily looped a hand around his neck, holding him there for a moment. "I love you."

⌒≼

Making breakfast, followed by the gift opening, seemed to brighten Savannah's spirits, but by early afternoon she'd descended into a deep funk. She curled up on the end couch with a sad, lost look in her eyes as Nina grilled Emily about the wedding plans.

Vanna sighed and rose to her feet before wandering toward the kitchen. When she didn't return within a few minutes, Aiden followed.

She stood by the fridge, running a fingertip over the scan tacked to it. "How big is the baby?"

Aiden leaned against the counter. "Tiny. About the size of a pea pod." He used his fingers to demonstrate. "But the baby is fully formed, kicking, and moving. We've even heard the heartbeat."

"An entire teeny tiny person." She tilted her head. "Can I come the next time they do a scan?"

"I'm sure we could work it out. I'll talk to Emily."

"You go to all her appointments."

"I like to know what's happening, and Emily appreciates me being there." Aiden sensed this might be the optimum time to introduce the subject that had been preying on his mind. "Come with me. Bring your tea."

Vanna arched a brow but took his hand and they proceeded down the hall to the master bedroom.

Aiden pointed to the sitting area and flicked on the gas fireplace before digging out the small package he'd built over the past week. He handed her the gift and settled onto the couch with his coffee. "Go ahead."

She shot him a curious look before setting it on her lap. A slight frown creased her brow as she removed the ribbon and peeled back the paper. "What …?" Her eyes widened as she revealed the small album. After another glance his way, she opened the cover "Who's this?" She tapped a fingertip on the ultrasound pictures.

"The top scan is you at around nine weeks and the second one was twenty weeks."

"It's me?" she whispered, her eyes shimmering. "I can't believe you've never shown me these before. You were there?"

"I remember both. Hard to forget the first time you hear your child's heartbeat. During the second one, we found out you were a girl," he said. "I didn't have them until last week."

Vanna froze as her gaze darted to his face. "Who …? Oh." She stared at the photo. "Tiffany kept these?" A single tear trickled down her face.

"She did. When Emily and I went for our first appointment and we heard the baby's heartbeat, it brought back memories." He handed Savannah a tissue.

She wiped her eyes. "You went to the appointments?"

"Uh-huh."

She pointed to the name in the corner of one document. "Who's E. Black?"

"An alias. Using our real names was too scary. Hamilton and Baxter weren't incognito names. David Baxter was running for Mayor. Both my grandfather and my father were high profile lawyers." Aiden shrugged. "We went to a clinic on the opposite side of town."

Savannah smiled tearfully. "You lied?"

Aiden gauged how much he should say. "Our families ... well, you have some insight into them now. Anyway, we were in boarding school, followed by the usual summer vacation at the Vineyard. By some miracle, we kept you a secret until the end of August."

Tears streamed down her face. "You always tell me to ask for help. Why didn't you?"

"Neither of us had a trusted adult," he said. "Eventually, our luck ran out and her mother noticed. Tiffany disappeared and it took several days before she contacted me with the news they'd shipped her to her aunt's house in Portland. By that time, I'd returned to boarding school. After that, I'd sneak away from school on the weekends and fly to Portland."

"Nobody in your family figured it out?"

"Nope. I signed out and told the school I'd be visiting my parents or at my grandparents' house. I had convenient access to the travel account."

Vanna tilted her head. "And?"

"Tiffany would schedule appointments for Friday afternoon and tell her aunt she didn't want her there. Our subterfuge worked until November, then all hell broke loose."

"What happened?" Her eyes grew bright and interested and her tears dried.

"My grandfather received the travel agent's statement and noticed the flights and hotel bills. They dragged me home from school, but I took advantage of the opportunity and flew to Portland." He flipped a page of the album. "We boarded a bus to Canada and ended up in Vancouver. We hoped to disappear, but they caught up with us." He pointed to a photo taken by a kind stranger during their time in Vancouver. "This is us at the Seawall."

"You ran away?" A tiny grin appeared. "Who knew my dad was a badass." She examined the picture. "I never knew you had photos when she was pregnant."

"Your mother was almost eight months in that picture."

Vanna inspected the next page. "Maya Gabrielle Hamilton? You named me?"

"We planned on keeping you," he said. "We made a list of names. We made plans. It wasn't ideal, but we wanted you. Always."

"But I was an accident. A mistake."

Aiden reached for her hand. "You weren't planned, but I've never considered you a mistake. We did our best, but it wasn't enough. After they caught up with us, they separated us. I missed your birth. And then you were gone. We had no way of finding you."

A furrow appeared between her brows. "The closed adoption."

He nodded. "You ended up with great parents. I'm sure they did better than two fifteen-year-old kids could have managed, especially with our dysfunctional families."

"Why doesn't Tiffany want me now? She kept all of this."

Aiden slid an arm around her shoulders, drawing her close. "I can't explain, because I don't understand myself. She's changed. Life and the people in it affect you. Some in good ways, some not so good."

"You think she's made bad choices about the people in her life?"

"I do. The decision to cut her from our lives is difficult." He exhaled a sigh. "I can't force her. That would make me no better than our families."

"My dad told me when I first met you that you were respecting her wishes, but I thought you weren't protecting me. But you were, right?"

He nodded.

"Now we have Emily."

"Together we're a family. You have aunts and uncles, and Gramma Grace, and Gramma Nina too."

"Abuela Nina. She told me to call her Abuela, even if she's not my grandmother. And they aren't really my aunts and uncles."

"Sure they are. I'm closer to them than my actual family. They're true friends and always there when I need them. Don't forget that, Vanna. They'll be there if you need them. Family is more than a biological relationship."

She leaned into him. "Thank you for showing me this and sharing the story. I love you."

He wrapped her into a tight hug. "I love you, my sweet girl. Always."

"Dad?" Vanna whispered. "Would you be upset if I changed my name?"

"To what?"

"It's more adding on a name. I want to use Hamilton. Savannah Jayde Phillips Hamilton. It's the perfect combination of who I am."

Aiden closed his eyes and gave the girl a squeeze. "We'll get Tom working on it after the holidays." Some of their memories were gone forever, but this small thing was a tiny building block on their way to creating new ones. This holiday he was thankful for the chance to know this amazing young woman who was growing up all too fast.

CHAPTER 19

Emily

As she hung her clothes in the closet, Emily sneaked a glance at Aiden.

An occasional thump and bursts of giggles broke the silence, reminding her that Savannah and Leanne were sharing the luxurious suite.

"They're thrilled to be together again." Emily slid her arms around him.

"No doubt. They've been best friends for years."

"I'm glad Leanne could come for dress shopping and Vanna's birthday. You have a sixteen-year-old. That's craziness."

"I try not to think about it too hard. We're having a baby and my daughter is only a year away from graduation."

"Mmm, my old man." Emily took his face between her hands, kissing him and pressing her belly against him.

He laughed. "Considering you're older than me, you'd better not complain. I should call you my old lady."

"Only by two months. I hit the big three-two this year."

"You're still sweet and beautiful." He glanced at his phone. "The car's here."

"You won't be saying I'm beautiful when my ass is huge and I'm bigger than a baby beluga."

"You'll always be beautiful. I love you."

"I love you too." She cupped his cheek with her palm.

They both looked over at the sound in the doorway.

"Quit with the sappy stuff." Savannah shifted from foot to foot. "Is the limo here? Are we going soon?"

"Put your coat on." Aiden waved a hand at her, his gaze following as she left the room. As soon as she disappeared, he captured Emily's lips in a deep kiss.

Twenty minutes later they arrived at the busy restaurant. The hum of conversation filled the air as the doorman ushered them inside.

"Good evening, Dr. Hamilton."

Emily raised a brow even as Savannah frowned. He hadn't opened his mouth, and he was greeted by name.

"Good evening, Pierre." Aiden winked at Emily and checked their coats.

Moments later, the host escorted them to their table near an elegant four-sided stone fireplace.

"That was quick." Savannah gazed around the opulent room. "This is amazing."

Emily didn't say a word, but she recognized the place. They'd come here for dinner with Aiden's parents. No doubt the mere whisper of the name 'Hamilton' had the staff scrambling to provide impeccable service. As if to prove her correct, the waiter arrived, offering beverages and menus.

Conversation flowed, centering on the wedding and the baby, with a few tidbits added by Leanne. The girls didn't seem to want to talk about their friends in Portland even though Aiden asked several well-placed questions.

"Where's the ladies' room?" Savannah asked after their server had cleared the table from their main course.

"That way." Aiden pointed, and both girls headed off. "Never understood why women go to the restroom in a pack."

"It's a girl thing." Emily linked their fingers, squeezing his hand. "Surprised we came here."

"Vanna picked it. Don't worry. My parents are on their annual Christmas trip. They never return before mid-January."

"They recognized you."

"I dine here every few months. They knew my grandparents too." He shrugged. "It's high-scale, but it's her sixteenth birthday. We don't do it all the time."

"True. Sorry, I have to abandon you for a couple of minutes." Emily folded her napkin and rose, heading toward the restrooms.

Familiar voices carried from the sitting area of the well-appointed bathroom. Savannah and Leanne were seated on the small benches in front of the mirror, chatting with a well-dressed woman as they fiddled with their hair and makeup. Emily's breath caught as the woman's gaze lifted to hers.

Caroline Hamilton's eyes widened as she scanned Emily from head to toe, her gaze riveted on the belly outlined by the evening gown. "Emily."

"What are you doing in New York?"

"I live here. I was having a nice chat with these young ladies. Aiden's here?" Emily nodded.

"He didn't call about your engagement," Caroline said in a flat voice. "I'd love to see the ring. And nobody mentioned a baby."

Savannah's gaze darted back and forth between Emily and Caroline. "You know my dad?"

Caroline's head snapped toward the two girls, recognition dawning in her eyes. "Savannah." She observed the teen for a moment. "I should have seen the resemblance to your mother," she whispered, "but I never expected to see you in New York."

Vanna threw a confused look at Emily.

"Aiden's never told you about me?" Caroline's face dropped.

"Why would he?" Emily crossed her arms. "Vanna, are you done? You should head to the table. Dessert will be there by now."

"Wait." Savannah's eyes glistened as she stared at Caroline. "You're Caroline Hamilton. I saw pictures. You're my grandmother, and…" She brushed away her tears before pivoting and dashing from the bathroom.

Leanne watched the whole show with her mouth open. Her head bobbed back and forth between Emily and Caroline, like viewing a tennis game.

"Leanne? Can you check on Vanna?"

Leanne nodded. Still looking dumbfounded, she pushed out the door, throwing one final glance over her shoulder.

Emily glared at Caroline before locking herself in a stall, finally exiting to find that Caroline hadn't moved from the bench.

The woman sat with her head bowed, hands folded in her lap. "You're not inviting me to the wedding?"

"Why would he invite you?" Emily narrowed her eyes. "You chose James and your life in New York over your son. Why is the effort always from him?"

"I'm his mother." Caroline's eyes filled with tears. "You're having a baby and he didn't say a word. When are you due?"

"June." Emily wasn't sure whether Caroline's weeping was real or simply theatrics. She didn't trust the woman.

"Boy or girl?"

Emily shrugged and turned her back, concentrating on washing her hands and fixing her hair.

"I'd like to meet my grandchild. Will you send me a birth announcement?"

Emily lifted her chin. "What about the grandchild you already have? Why would we include you in the life of this child when you have a beautiful granddaughter you've never cared about?" She stalked from the bathroom without a backward glance.

⁓≼

Savannah stared out the window of the limo during the ride back to the hotel, one trembling hand wrapped around her pendant.

Leanne sat stiffly, peeking out of the corner of her eye at her friend and shooting nervous glances at Aiden.

"Maybe we should go skating in Central Park?" Aiden said softly. "Or … we could go for one of those carriage rides and stop at that amazing little café for hot chocolate."

"Great idea." Emily grasped his hand, squeezing gently. "What do you think, Vanna?"

Vanna shrugged, hunching over and gnawing on her thumbnail.

Aiden shared a look, the sadness reflected on his face. He'd tried so hard to make the birthday dinner special, and it clearly pained him to see Vanna so despondent.

The moment they arrived back at the hotel suite, Savannah disappeared into the bedroom, slamming the door behind her.

Emily rested a hand on Aiden's arm. "Can I try?"

Aiden studied her for a moment and nodded. "Call if you need me."

"I will." She gathered her thoughts before tapping on the door. "Vanna?" Muffled sobbing was the only sound, so Emily opened the door.

Vanna sprawled across the bed with her face buried in her pillow.

Emily sat on the edge of the mattress. "I'm sorry. We had no idea Caroline would be there. Usually, she's on vacation in some tropical destination."

The girl only sobbed harder.

"Feeling unwanted hurts, doesn't it? I've never told you about my father."

Vanna turned her head, her eyes red and puffy. "Your father?"

Emily handed her a tissue. "My father left when I was nine. Me and my two younger sisters. He left us for another woman."

The teen sat, dabbing at her tear-streaked face before accepting a fresh tissue. "He cheated?"

"Multiple times. He chased younger women and he was never home. It ended with a raging fight. They screamed and threw things and he left. Over time he forgot about us and disappeared from our lives."

Savannah tilted her head. "Kind of like Tiffany and my grandparents, except they've never been part of my life. Aiden says not to take it personally because they don't see him, and he's their son."

"They've never given him the support he deserves. When he says it's not you, believe it." Emily inspected the girl's tear ravaged face. "I saw how it went

121

down last year in New York. They may never be part of your life. It's something you have to accept."

"Caroline doesn't want to know me." She smoothed a hand over the pillow in her lap.

"I'm not sure that's true, but she's let her husband rule her, ruin her relationship with her son, and ensure she'll never have the chance to enjoy her grandchildren. Aiden won't let them or Tiffany within ten miles of you. I'm sure the same will go of this one." She patted her belly.

"He's overprotective, but I like it when he is. Does that sound weird?"

"Not at all. There's a great deal of security in having a father like Aiden." She rested a hand on her belly. "It's who he is, maybe because he felt no one cared about him when he was growing up."

"He doesn't talk about it often, but he didn't … doesn't … trust them."

"He's become self-sufficient and dealt with major issues alone. You're luckier because you have people around you can talk to."

"It still sucks knowing my grandparents don't want me."

"Don't let it get you down. It took a long time to get over being abandoned by my father. It hurts some days, but the best way to deal with it by never giving up. It's about their issues and not yours. Don't let Tiffany's problems or Caroline's misgivings prevent you from living."

"So, pretend they don't exist?"

"The main thing is to focus on the good things in your life, and the people who support and love you every day. My father's absence at my wedding could ruin my day, but I won't let it. I refuse to let anything get in the way. My advice is for you to do the same."

Savannah tilted her head. "The only one who needs to be happy is me?"

"Bad things happen. You'll deal with adversity and nothing will ever be perfect."

Vanna smiled. "You're right. I've managed fine without any of them."

"Exactly. Now, we should let your dad take us out and have some fun for your birthday. What do you say?"

She nodded. "That would make Dad happy. Let's go."

The next afternoon, Emily and her entourage arrived at the brightly lit salon. Jenna murmured to the receptionist while everyone else perused the racks of gowns.

"This is amazing." Vanna's eyes widened at the sheer number of dresses. "Look at these."

"Welcome, ladies. I'm Meghan and I'll be assisting today." Meghan consulted her notes. "I see you'll be twenty-three weeks on the big day, and

I've pulled out several of dresses. Shall we?" She escorted them into the large fitting area.

The selection was far beyond Emily's expectations. Tulle, lace, satin, and beading adorned every imaginable fabric and style, along with racks of veils. Her heart pounded and her palms grew damp as she twisted the spectacular ring gracing her finger. In only a few weeks she'd be Aiden's wife.

Savannah and Leanne searched through the selections, chattering in excitement while Nina wandered through the aisles, stopping now and then to inspect a gown.

"Oh, this one." Jenna pointed to a dress with a full skirt made from yards of tulle.

Alexis waved from the other side of the room. "And this. You'll look gorgeous."

Meghan's assistant noted the numbers while Meghan ushered Emily toward a fitting room.

Jenna shot a saucy grin her way. The woman was enjoying this a little too much.

"Can I help?" Meghan peeked around the curtain as Emily wiggled into the first frothy sea of tulle. "Beautiful."

Emily took a deep breath and stepped out, the train swishing behind her. The room fell silent for a moment.

"So beautiful." Alexis nodded.

"This one has to go into the consideration group," said Jenna.

"Cariño." Nina dabbed at her shimmering eyes.

"Amazing." Vanna said.

Emily stepped onto the podium, checking the dress from every angle. "I like it, but I have several more to try."

She spent the next hour in and out of dress after dress after dress. Rejected ones were whisked away as more were added. Emily's head spun with the sheer number of gowns.

After three hours, she collapsed onto the bench in the change room, blinking back tears. "I've tried on half the store, but I haven't found the one."

Meghan patted her shoulder. "Don't worry, it's here. Can I ask you something?"

Emily nodded as she sucked in a deep breath.

"You clearly have a vision, as many brides do. Is there a tiny bit of room in your budget?"

"My fiancé wants me to find the perfect dress. He intends for this to be my only wedding, ever."

"That's sweet. Seems like you have a keeper." Meghan smiled and lifted Emily's hand. "This is a magnificent display of diamonds. Someone has exquisite taste."

"Aiden. It's a custom piece." She pressed her right hand to her chest. "I bet you're tired of brides gushing over their future husbands like they're the second coming, especially when half of them will be divorced within ten years. But Aiden has overcome so much adversity and become this amazing, loving man. When I close my eyes, I picture his face and the look in his eyes ... this dress needs to put that smile on his face."

Meghan squeezed her hand. "I predict that you'll beat the odds as long as you remember one thing. When Aiden sees you walking down the aisle, that look won't be about the dress, but about the beautiful woman wearing it."

Emily closed her eyes and nodded. "What do you suggest?"

"My assistant has been dying to see you in one particular gown from the moment you arrived. It's above your price range, but not by much. Will you try it?"

"Why not? I've tried every other one in the store."

Meghan waved a hand outside of the room, and a dress appeared in it as if by magic. "Michel has a marvelous eye for fit."

The lacy strapless creation brought a smile to her face. The beading, scalloped hem and swath of tulle took her breath away. "It's gorgeous."

"Wait until it's on. The color will set off your skin tone and dark hair much better than white. The lace is hand-beaded, the train is exquisite, though not overwhelming, and it will drape perfectly." Meghan motioned for Emily to turn and she refastened the small rounded pillow with a strap before helping Emily into the dress and clipping the back. "One last detail." Meghan stepped in front of her, producing an elegant veil and placing it on her head.

Emily skimmed her hands over the lacy fabric before she stepped into the main room.

Vanna's eyes popped open as her jaw dropped. The girl clapped her hands over her mouth.

Dead silence fell as all eyes turned toward her. Emily allowed Meghan to help her onto the podium, and she stared in the mirror, tears springing to her eyes.

"That's the one." Savannah said.

"Gorgeous." Jenna beamed.

"It's the dress." Alex stepped toward her, reaching out to brush the back of her hand against the full skirt.

"It's not too much?" Emily's heart raced as she stared at her reflection in the mirror. She pivoted, checking from each angle, falling more in love with the gown every second. "The back isn't too low?"

"This dress is perfection." Alex toured around Emily. "Aiden won't take his eyes off you."

Emily turned to inspect the low cut back. The detailing on the bodice was exquisite, showing off her well-endowed chest. The chapel length train and full skirt with the metallic beaded lace were perfect. It was elegant, classy, and exactly what she'd dreamed of wearing.

"This is it. Magnificent." Jenna nodded.

"Emelia." Her mother reached up to squeeze her hand. "You must wear this one."

The tears welled in her eyes as she stepped down to hug her mother. "You think so?"

"Yes, cariño. You're so beautiful."

Meghan beamed, scanning Emily's glowing face and wide smile.

Michel appeared with champagne flutes. "Non-alcoholic for the bride." He winked at Emily as he handed her the glass. "You look amazing."

"Thanks to you." She gave him a quick hug. "How did you know?"

He shrugged and smiled before retreating, leaving her surrounded by her friends and family.

CHAPTER 20

Aiden

AIDEN STEPPED INTO THE SUITE, unwinding his scarf as he set the packages on the side table. After ushering the ladies into the limo for their shopping trip, he'd stopped at the jewelry store for Emily's wedding gifts and run several errands.

He glanced at his watch. Emily would be busy for several hours with picking her gown, so he'd have time to work on his study proposal. Within a few moments he'd settled on the sofa with his laptop and paper, but a knock on the door interrupted his train of thought.

"Probably forgot her key." He opened the door,. "Did you forget some—" He crossed his arms and planted his feet. "Why are you here?"

"I can't visit my son?"

"It would be a first. How did you know where we're staying?"

"This is where you stayed last time. Can I come in?"

"I assume it won't take long?"

She shook her head. "I only need ten minutes. Please, Aiden?"

He stepped back, allowing her into the room.

Her eyes scanned the pile on the table. "Oh, what's all this?"

"I'm developing a medical study."

"They went shopping?"

"What did you want to talk about? I thought we'd said everything last Christmas."

Caroline perched on the edge of the couch. "Aren't you going to offer me some tea?"

Aiden hid the eye roll as he turned on the kettle in the kitchenette and poured her a glass of water, planting it on the coffee table. "What's going on? I wouldn't have gone to the restaurant if I'd known you'd be there. You and James are usually lounging in the sun about now."

"We're getting a divorce."

Aiden breathe caught in his chest. "What?"

"I've lost so much. My only son, my granddaughter, and I don't want to miss my next grandchild growing up."

Aiden stared at her. "You and James have separated?"

Caroline blinked and bowed her head. "Maybe this is too little and too late, but I don't want to miss any more. I sit alone in the apartment or go for lunch with a group of insipid women who chatter on about their next salon appointment or latest trip. It feels empty. I let him take you away. I let him talk me into leaving you in Chicago with Grace, and …" She shrugged.

"Now you realize? Where were you when I was fifteen? I'm thirty-one. I don't need a mother, Caroline. If you think it's that easy, you're wrong." He smacked his hand onto the counter.

Caroline cringed. "No," she whispered. "I don't think it'll be easy. I've made huge mistakes but please let me try. Let me meet my grandchildren and find meaning in my life. I missed seeing my only son grow up."

"That was your choice. What is it with women?" He crossed his arms, narrowing his eyes.

Her brows rose. "What are you talking about?"

"You and Tiffany. I don't understand how you can be so cold and close your heart to your own child. Both of you decided your high society lifestyle was more important. Your family meant nothing. So many people can't even have children, as hard as they try, yet you take it for granted and act like I should be grateful."

"Aiden, I—"

"Could you shut up and listen for once in your life? Lots of women manage their family and a career, but your engagements at the Country Club were always more important. You think I'll let you do the same thing to Savannah as you did to me?"

"I'm sorry. I should never have turned you or Savannah away." Caroline sniffled, brushing tears from her eyes. "I wish I'd told James to go to hell. Last night, I realized what I was missing. She's so beautiful, and turning into a wonderful young woman, and I've missed it."

"So did I, but not because I chose not to be there. They forced me to give her up, Mother. You gave me up willingly, so excuse me if I don't feel sorry for you."

She stared at him, her eyes wide. "I didn't know about her until last year. I'm so sorry. Allow me to make it up to you."

"After all this time?" Aiden folded his arms over his chest. "I let you in and then what? You decide to go back to James and leave again?" He shook his head.

"Never. I'm moving to Chicago. Please. If you could find it in your heart to forgive me."

Aiden sat beside her on the sofa, running a hand through his hair. "You're serious."

"I want to know my granddaughter and be there for my new grandchild. Whatever you think or believe, I regret not being there for you. I missed everything, and now you're getting married. Please don't cut me out forever. I love you."

⚊⚊

Aiden lay on the bed staring at the ceiling. The last thing he'd expected was his mother to show up and beg him to include her in his life. She hadn't much cared about him for the past twenty years. Why now? His head pounded and his eyes burned. Everything had been flowing, but now …

Emily appeared in the doorway. "Mi vida."

"How'd the search go?"

"I found it." Her smile brightened. "After the millionth one I tried on. It's ordered and on its way to Chicago. Bridesmaid dresses too, and Mom found one. I hope you don't mind, but I bought her dress, otherwise she'd have gone to Bargain Barn or something." Emily's cheeks flushed an adorable pink.

"Don't apologize for her being frugal. She raised three girls on her own. I have great respect for her. She did it however she could and never gave up."

Emily brushed her hand over his hair and slid onto the bed beside him. She caressed his cheek, turning his head toward her. "She was a great mom, no denying it. I want her to fit in and be comfortable. Your guests will be well-dressed. It's my day and …"

"Whatever makes you happy. The important thing is you meet me at the altar and say I do." He captured her hand and kissed it.

"What happened? You look upset." Emily studied him.

"Caroline."

"She phoned?"

"She left James. They're divorcing."

"What?" She sat upright, staring down at him. "She dropped the news on you now? Are you okay?"

"I don't know how I feel." He rested the back of his hand across his eyes. "She begged and pleaded to be invited to the wedding, and she wants to know her grandchildren. She hasn't been part of my life since I was thirteen and flitted in and out of my world like a ghost. Now she's layering on the guilt. If I invite her, I'll worry about her turning into a drama queen and ruining everything. If I don't, I'll feel like shit for not inviting my mother to my wedding. Your family will think I'm an asshole."

Emily emitted a long, deep sigh. "I'm sorry. Your mother is insane and my father is a virtual stalker. I totally understand."

"Right?" He almost laughed, despite how unfunny the situation seemed. "Paul make his usual call today?"

"Yup and left his daily message. He isn't getting the hint." She flopped on the bed, rubbing her belly. "It's as if he wants in on my happy family. Same deal. He could turn this into a huge drama or pick a fight with my mom. He hasn't earned the right to be there or to walk me down the aisle. And the idea of giving the woman away is antiquated. I'm nobody's possession."

Aiden propped himself on one elbow, resting a hand over hers. "No, but it's more tradition now than anything. Nobody will read anything into it if you have someone walk you down the aisle."

"Oh." Emily's eyes widened.

"Are you okay?"

"Feel this," she whispered, guiding his hand onto her belly.

A smile stole across his face. "Incredible. It's the first time I've felt our baby move."

"I've felt tiny flutters before, but this is the first strong kick. Maybe the baby is trying to tell us something?"

"Mmm, maybe." Aiden moved in to kiss Emily before sliding down to drop another onto her rounded tummy. "Hey, baby, what do you think? Should Caroline and Paul be invited?"

Emily giggled. "Oh, feel this. Is that a yes or no?" She placed his hand higher. "Baby's active today. I'm glad you're here."

"Me too. Our little miracle baby."

"All babies are miraculous."

"This little person made you reevaluate your life and say yes to getting married. This baby changed our lives and brought you back to me."

"It's a wonderful thing." Emily put her hand over his. "This baby made me realize where I wanted and needed to be. I love you."

"And I love you." He slid upwards and kissed her temple, pulling her so her head rested on his chest.

She snuggled closer, draping a leg across his. They lay in comfortable silence for several minutes. "What should we do about Caroline and Paul?"

"Don't know. Caroline seems to mean it, but what if she runs back to him? Vanna isn't having nightmares or panic attacks, and the wedding is coming together. If I open the door to her …" He sighed.

"I wish I knew. I hardly know the woman."

"Neither do I. The sad truth is, I have absolutely no idea if it's real or an act. Do I take the chance and risk it blowing up on our wedding day? I can't remember the last time I spent more than an hour with her at a stretch, and I hadn't seen her in over a year."

"It's up to you. What if it is real, and she truly wants to be there for her grandkids? Maybe you should give her the chance. It'll be okay, you know. Invite her. Make it clear James isn't welcome. I can deal with it. I won't let it ruin our day."

"You know we have to move around the seating arrangements and—"

Emily put a finger to his lips. "Stop. Call and ask her to dinner. We'll talk to her and set out some rules. Then we can talk to Vanna and invite Caroline to the wedding if we believe she's sincere."

"Ah, you're so smart. Now we have to decide what to do about Paul. I understand why you don't want him to walk you down the aisle."

"Even if I invite him he shouldn't be the one, considering he's been absent for so many years."

"Why don't you ask Nina? She's been there, Em. Always. She wants more of a part, and I can't blame her. I know she's driving you nuts, but on the other hand, you're her daughter and she desperately wants to be there for you."

Emily gave him a long look. "Now who's being a genius?"

"I'm really glad you found your dress. I can't wait to see it." He pressed a kiss to her lips and cuddled her against him. Times like these made everything worthwhile.

CHAPTER 21

Emily

EMILY PAUSED OUTSIDE OF THE hotel doors to inhale the crisp cold air. She loved the time with her friends and family, but she was desperate for quiet time after everyone fussing over her. After adjusting her scarf and pulling on her gloves, she started along the sidewalk.

The streets were peaceful as she enjoyed her early morning stroll, stopping to glance into store windows.

"Dr. Anderson."

Emily jumped, startled by the burly man who'd appeared from nowhere. She peered at him in concern.

"Come with me." He grasped her arm, propelling her toward a dark sedan at the curb.

The scream lodged in her throat as she struggled against the man's firm grip.

"Settle down." He released her arm and opened the car door.

"Don't panic, Emily. It's only me."

Emily frowned, hesitant, but at least she wasn't being kidnapped. "What do you want?"

"I won't keep you long. Come inside, it's chilly out there." James beckoned.

She glanced at the large man who stood between her and the sidewalk. What what would happen if she refused?

"Please?"

Against her better judgment, she slid into the car, the door closing behind her.

"I wanted to talk to you, but I know my son would never allow me to visit at the hotel. I heard you were in New York, and I've seen the wedding announcements."

"That's what this is about?" She shook her head. "My marriage would be over before it began if I invited you."

He waved a hand. "Aiden would have me bodily removed before I got halfway to my seat. This is business."

"Oh?" She arched a brow. What could James Hamilton want from her? "What sort of business?"

"My son is a wealthy man, Emelia." His stern expression made her shudder. "That makes him a target for women who wish to be pampered and indulged."

"I suppose, but—"

"You're not one of them, are you, Emelia? I know you come from … humble beginnings. You worked your way through school, but you've acquired significant debt even after your scholarships. It's tempting to marry a man like my son."

"I love Aiden. I don't care about the money."

"Of course not, but even the best of relationships can fail. It's best to be clear going into the marriage on where you stand. As much as my son thinks I don't care, I do."

Emily froze, unsure what James wanted or where he was headed with this conversation.

"It's hard to prove love and devotion, isn't it? You two were pretty much over, but then a baby appears on the scene, and he asks you to marry him. It's the right thing for him to marry you, Emelia, and give that child you're carrying his name. Provided the child is his, of course."

This was unsettling. The man seemed to know an awful lot about her relationship with Aiden and about her finances. Not that it was a huge secret within their circle of friends but still …

She placed a protective hand on her belly. "He doesn't doubt it, so why should you? I'm marrying him for love. I want a family with him."

"I'm sure that's true, but it's been tried before and the girl roped him in. It ended with a nasty divorce though we contained the damage on that unfortunate incident. Things look rosy until they aren't."

"What do you want? There must be something you're circling around here."

"His grandfather and I tried to protect Aiden, even when he was a teenage boy. He doesn't see it like that, but the agreement we made with the girl's family was for his benefit. Everyone got something out of the deal."

"What did Aiden get?"

"His freedom. The chance to live his life free of the burdens of raising a child at such a young age. Seems harsh, but it's true. It was all for the best even if he's thrown that in my face. How is the child, Emelia?"

"She's good." An involuntary shiver ran through her at his cold and emotionless inquiry in Savannah's well-being.

"Excellent. I thought she looked well, but … pictures never tell the whole tale."

Emily kept her expression neutral at his words. "Why are you concerned?"

James held out an envelope. "A present for you, Emelia."

She stared at it, keeping her hands folded in her lap.

"Oh, come on. Don't you want to see what's inside?" James raised a brow. "No?"

"I want nothing from you."

A displeased look fleeted across his face before the bitter smile reappeared. He opened the envelope and held up the document, waving it in front of her face. "It's a substantial sum, Emelia. It's payable to you, and you alone." James flicked imaginary lint from his sleeve. "You could have a good life with this money. You wouldn't need Aiden at all."

She broke out in a cold sweat as fear trickled down her spine. "Why would I want your money? I love him."

"That's what they all say. Did you sign a prenuptial agreement?"

Emily clasped her hands to prevent the shaking.

"Ah, you didn't. Tom isn't protecting my son." James sighed. "What do you think? Last chance. You can walk away, give your child a good life, and Aiden never needs to know why you left."

Emily snatched the check from his hand, shredding it before flicking the pieces at him. "Are we done?"

"Feisty one. Aiden always had a weakness for hellcats, and I suspect he always will." James smirked. "Have it your way, but don't come crying to me when it all goes bad." He gave her a wolfish smile that didn't quite reach his eyes.

Emily shivered. The man's eyes seemed like cold, hard, obsidian, and so very different from Aiden's. The more she looked at James, the less he resembled his son. When she looked into her fiancé's eyes, there'd always been a soulful warmth. Even when he'd been livid at her actions, he'd never hidden his softer side. This meeting convinced her James didn't possess a softer side. All she felt was a cold unyielding fear.

She swallowed hard to relieve the lump in her throat. "Let me out of the car."

"Relax, Emelia. All in due time." He narrowed his eyes and wagged a finger at her. "Under no circumstances will you speak of this meeting to anyone. And I mean no one, Emelia. There are consequences if Aiden finds out about this ..."

Another tremor shook her body as Emily fumbled for the door handle, but it opened from the outside, and she scrambled from the car. The sedan pulled away from the curb as she blinked away the tears, unsure what to do next. As she wrapped her arms around herself she forced air into her lungs, wishing she were anywhere but there.

Emily snuggled closer to Aiden, peering at him. He looked so peaceful in his deep sleep though his arm tightened around her as if he was protecting her. It comforted her being with him even if she had a certain level of fear residing in her heart after the run-in with James. Aiden's warning words from that night in Portland came back to her with clarity.

It made her wonder what his father was capable of but she was certain she didn't want to find out. The man hadn't shown even a flicker of human kindness. Her blood ran cold every time she remembered being trapped in that car.

She wiggled from under Aiden's arm, careful not to wake him. It had been a late night, involving an intense discussion about both Caroline and Paul, although Emily had avoided any mention of James. Her mind waged the war; to tell or not to tell?

She scooped her nightgown from where it lay in a silky puddle and slid it over her head. It took effort to ignore the insistent buzzing of her phone as she tiptoed into the bathroom. In no rush to answer the persistent calls, she lingered, washing her face and brushing her hair. She shifted to inspected her profile, pressing a cupped hand over her belly, contemplating her figure. "Time to eat, right, baby?" A contented grin broke out at the fluttering sensation as the baby turned and kicked. "I bet your daddy could use breakfast."

Emily emerged and padded toward the bed. Her phone buzzed yet again, and she sighed. At this time of the day, it could only be one person. And Emily had made a promise to Aiden after spending hours pouring out her feelings.

"He's called at least three times."

Her hand flew to her chest, and she gasped. "Oh, I didn't know you were awake. And yes, I know, but the baby was on my bladder." Emily offered him a hopeful smile.

"Now that's taken care of, call Paul and arrange a visit with him for when we get back to Boston." Aiden's plumped up his pillow and tucked an arm behind his head.

Emily smiled at his adorably tousled hair, picturing her fingers running through the silkiness, messing it even further. He looked so damn sexy propped up in the bed, covered with a wisp of sheet that did nothing to hide those beautiful washboard abs, tapered hips, toned biceps, and his smooth, tanned skin.

"Em?"

She exhaled, dropping her head.

"Come here." Aiden extended a hand toward her, pulling her onto the bed. "What's the matter?"

Emily curled up in his arms, trickling a hand down his belly. "You interrupted my memories of last night, along with a few indecent thoughts." She brushed her fingertips over the light scruff on his face, caressing his lips with hers.

"Sorry," he murmured. "It was amazing, as always." As he buried his face in the crook of her neck, he nuzzled against her, his warm breath tickling her skin. "You're tempting me, but stop the feeble effort to sidetrack our conversation." He tucked a lock of dark hair behind her ear. "What else is bothering you?"

She couldn't hide her fears. Not the ones about her father, anyway. She'd broken down this man's defenses and invaded the virtual fortress he'd built around himself over the years. Now she had to let him enter her world. "After all this time, I don't know what to say. Hey, come to Boston for lunch? It seems inadequate. I keep trying to figure it out and I come up blank. What if he wants to stay with us? It would be awkward."

"Don't stress over it. Call him and let him initiate the conversation. Hear him out. Then invite him if you like, but book him into a hotel room which I'll pay for, or we can fly to Chicago on the weekend and avoid the issue of where he stays." His fingers swept up and down her arm, his touch light and gentle. "I'll be with you. If it goes bad along the way, we walk away."

Emily enjoyed the comfort of his arms and his soothing voice. "Thank you. You can drag me away before I claw his eyes out. He was horrible to my mom and dumped her for the younger model, leaving her to raise us by herself."

"Nina has forgiven him, so perhaps you should too. You're only getting married once, Em. This is it and I don't want you to have regrets. Our messed-up families have created plenty of remorse and sorrow and disappointment. Give him one chance. If it doesn't feel right, then say no and you never have to see him again."

She raised her chin and stared into his eyes. "You're determined we'll last forever."

Aiden rested his palm on her cheek, stroking with his thumb. "I can't imagine loving anyone but you. You're the one I can't live without. I feel it to the bottom of my soul. I want to spend the rest of my life with you."

Her heart thumped and her palms grew damp as he dipped his head to capture her lips. It was overwhelming to have anyone, let alone this incredible, wonderful, sexy man, say they couldn't live without her. She wrapped her arms around him, not wanting to let go. Ever.

Emily checked her call display as her phone rang. Her father. Again. She hadn't gathered enough courage to call him back.

Aiden looked up from his paperwork and raised his brows. He recognized the ringtone she'd assigned to Paul Anderson and there'd be no more avoiding it. He'd kept his promise, now she needed to keep hers.

"Hello?"

Dead silence hung on the line for a moment before he said, "Emmy?"

"Yes." Emily wound a strand of hair around her finger, avoiding Aiden's gaze. She knew he was soaking in every word.

"You answered. Thought I'd have to track you down. Your mom said you moved to Boston with your fiancé. I saw an engagement announcement in the paper."

"What did you want?" She wandered into the bedroom, sinking onto the bed and folding a leg beneath her.

"To talk to you. I haven't been the world's greatest dad, but I'd hoped you'd allow me to come to your wedding. I'll walk you down the aisle."

Emily traced the design on the duvet with a fingertip while she considered his words. "I'm not sure there's much to say." She kept her voice low. "You left us."

"It wasn't you I left, it was your mother." His tone was soft and level.

"You never visited. You forgot about me, Natalia, and Juliana. I grew up without you."

"I never forgot you, Angel Eyes. Never. It seemed best for everyone if I left. I wish I'd tried harder to be there for you and your sisters. I wish you could forgive my mistakes."

The tears burned and one escaped and trickled down her cheek. She hadn't heard her nickname in years. It touched her heart, causing her breath to catch in her chest. She propped her head up with one hand, the other clutching the phone. "And now I'm getting married, you want to drop into my life? And then what?"

"I don't want to mess things up, but I should meet this young man of yours. Make sure he's treating you right. You only deserve the best."

"Don't trouble yourself." Sarcasm tinged her voice, even as she choked up. "You of all people have no right to judge my fiancé. Not after how you treated my mother."

The whoosh of breath expelled from his lungs carried down the line. "I deserve your anger, but you're still my little girl. It would kill me to miss your big day. Please, Emmy."

"Aiden's nothing like you," she whispered.

The line crackled. "I'm sorry, Angel Eyes, for everything. I've missed so much. Can you find it in your heart to forgive me and to let me make it up to you? Please let me see my Angel get married. Maybe one day I'll even have grandbabies."

"Aiden makes me happy." Emily brushed away another tear. He had to know the nickname would get to her. "Do you want to come to Boston and meet him?"

"When? This weekend?" His voice rose a touch. "You'll let me see you and meet your fiancé?"

"Yes." Emily didn't have the heart to refuse. "Mom didn't tell you about the baby, did she?"

"You're pregnant?"

"I'm due in June."

"Wow, a grandbaby. You're not marrying him to provide for the child or to console Nina? Please tell me you're not being forced into this, Emmy."

"I love him. We're both excited about the baby." She hoped he wasn't disappointed in her. Why it still mattered what her father thought, she didn't know. Over the years, she'd worked hard to put it behind her, but one phone call and her resolve melted. "Do you still want to visit?"

"I want more than a visit, Angel. I want to walk my girl down the aisle and be a grandpa."

"We'll book you a room. It's only a visit for now. The other stuff we'll discuss when you're here. One step at a time."

"I can live with that."

They worked out the details, and she hung up as secure, warm arms wrapped around her. She looked into Aiden's eyes.

"You okay?" He brushed her tears away with his thumbs.

She leaned into his chest, resting her forehead against him. "He and my mom are ganging up on me. She says I should forgive him and it was her fault as much as his when he left."

He rocked her against him. "Ahh, sweetheart. It's not easy, is it? So much time and distance between you and your dad. I saw how you looked even talking to him on the phone. You miss him, don't you?"

She nodded. "When I was little, he had this nickname, and he called me by it. To get into my heart, I'm sure. It worked, damn it."

"What is it?"

"Angel Eyes. It reminded me of when he taught me to ride a bike, and how he used to take me for ice cream. He wasn't always a terrible father, but I hated his fights with Mom and who he turned into those last few years."

"Hmmm." He lifted her chin with a fingertip. "Fitting. You do have the eyes of an Angel."

"Don't tease."

"I'd never tease you about your dad or your nickname. Maybe we'll have a baby girl with her mommy's eyes. I'd have my own little Angel Eyes which would be amazing." He snuggled her against him again. "You invited him for a visit?"

She nodded. "I told him we'd talk, but I'm sure I'll cave and at least invite him to the wedding. My mom said she'd keep the peace. As long as he promises the same and abides by the rules, he'll be there. I want him to meet you so he knows."

"Knows what?"

"That I love you. That he shouldn't worry about me, and I'm not making the same mistakes as Nat or Jules. Their husbands were like him. You're nothing like him."

"I bet we have one thing in common." Aiden rubbed her back. "In fact, I'm absolutely certain."

"What could you possibly have in common with my father? He's a drunk, self-employed plumber who abandoned his family."

"We both love you. Maybe it's time to forgive him and let him into your life. Make a new start. We're beginning a new journey together, and I don't want regrets and enmity surrounding us. We have so much to look forward to, and I don't want to spoil it." He rested his hands on either side of her belly. "Our child needs a family. Grandparents included."

Emily smiled. He was right. Maybe it was time to put it all behind her. Grant a few second chances.

CHAPTER 22

Aiden

Emily clung to Aiden's hand and shifted in her chair. "How long must we wait?"

"Relax. We're early." Aiden pried her hand open and gave his fingers a shake. "You're cutting off my circulation. Calm down, it's only a doctor's appointment."

"She's doing a scan today. Should we find out? Do you want to know?" Her eyes lifted to his, her brows raised. "Everyone keeps asking if we're having a boy or a girl?"

"Yes." Aiden grinned at her.

"Yes, find out?"

"Yes, it'll be one or the other."

Emily smacked his shoulder and rolled her eyes. "That's not what I meant, smart ass."

"Just because people ask doesn't mean you're obligated to tell them. But yes, I'd like to know." He shrugged. "Then we can think about names and decorate the baby's room. I'll arrange the painting for when we're on our honeymoon."

She batted her eyes at him. "Where are we going?"

"Ha. That might work on your dad, Angel Eyes, but it's not working on me. It's a surprise. We renewed your passport so you're good to go."

"What should I pack?" She leaned in closer, running her hand up his back, resting it on the nape of his neck and playing with his hair. "A teeny tiny hint? Pretty please?"

"Uh-uh. It's handled." Aiden smiled, capturing her fingers.

"Did I miss it?" Vanna appeared in front of their chairs. "Tell me I didn't miss it."

"Nope, perfect timing." Aiden motioned toward the other side of the room as a nurse appeared in the doorway.

"Emily Anderson?" The nurse beckoned.

Happy for the distraction, Aiden pulled Emily up from her chair. She'd been bugging him non-stop to find out where they were going on the honeymoon, but he wasn't breaking. She'd learn the destination when they were on the plane, and not a moment before.

"Wait here. The doctor will perform an exam first." Emily indicated a chair.

"I'll come get you, don't worry." Aiden patted Vanna's arm before following Emily. He waited in the exam room while the nurse weighed her and she changed into a gown.

Dr. Ritchie breezed in. "How are you feeling, Emily?"

"Wonderful." She reached for Aiden's hand.

"We'll do the measurements and a scan today." The doctor chatted as she went about the exam. "Let's see this baby. Are we finding out the sex?"

Aiden raised his brows at Emily.

She shook her head. "I want to be surprised. Don't tell us."

Dr. Ritchie glanced at Aiden as she squished gel onto Emily's exposed belly.

He shrugged, hiding his disappointment. Even though he understood her point of view, he would've preferred to know. The birth of the baby was still months away, and he wasn't sure he could wait.

He'd considered proposing a trade of the honeymoon location for the sex of the baby but decided that seeing her expression when he revealed his plans would be worth it. Besides, a healthy baby was more important than discovering the sex.

The doctor ran the wand over Emily's belly, concentrating on the screen. "Hmmm."

"Everything okay?" Aiden frowned.

"It's perfect." She smiled at Aiden. "I'm ensuring all the appropriate parts are in place. I'll turn the screen in a moment. Ten fingers, ten toes, development is right on track. Amniotic fluid level looks great, perfect, strong heartbeat." She hit a couple keys. "I've ordered the prints from several angles, and you'll receive a recording."

"That would be great." Emily looked relieved. "The baby is good?"

"Baby is terrific. Your weight gain has been reasonable though you could stand to gain a few more pounds."

"We're getting married." Emily sneaked a glance at Aiden. "I've been doing a lot of walking and I'm on my feet all day at work. I eat well."

"Exercise is positive, and I understand the pressures, Emily, but it's better to gain extra weight, rather than too little. Continue exercising, but make sure you're eating a good portion of protein and lots of vegetables every meal. Schedule relaxation time, especially with the extra stress of getting married."

"I'll ensure she takes breaks," Aiden said. "I'll grab Vanna. She'll want to see this next part."

"I'll do the final measurements while you get her." The doctor concentrated on the screen.

Aiden stepped out and motioned to Savannah. "We're getting to the good part." He led her into the room and moved to hold Emily's hand.

Savannah smiled, bouncing on her toes as the doctor turned the monitor.

"Here's baby." She ran the wand over.

Emily teared up. "Our baby's sucking their thumb."

"That's amazing." Savannah watched as the doctor pointed out the various parts—excluding the one Aiden wanted most to know about.

The doctor lingered over the image for a moment, chatting with Savannah and Emily, both of them entranced and staring at the screen.

He squinted and examined the form, a grinning as he spotted what he was looking for. It might upset Emily if he shared the secret, so he'd keep it to himself.

⌒≼

Aiden scanned the restaurant, spotting the group as Tom waved from a nearby table.

"Aiden." Tom stood and embraced him, patting him on the back. "You made it. Good thing. It's hard to party without the groom."

Joel and Ryan rose and clapped him on the shoulder, Ryan waving at the waitress to bring a round of drinks.

"How are things?" Ryan asked.

Aiden shook his head. "Emily is driving herself half-crazy with all the preparations, even with the wedding planner. I made reservations for Valentine's and then the pre-wedding events swing into full gear."

"Jenn and Alex scheduled their time so they could help and keep her grounded. I've heard all about it in infinitesimal detail." Tom grinned. "She's a happy woman, my friend, so go with it."

"Oh, I will. Trust me."

Joel nodded. "Hell ya. After the drama, and how bumpy the road has been, cold feet aren't allowed."

"Ha ha, Joel. Not a chance." Aiden lifted a gift bag. "Valentine's covered, and I picked up her wedding gift so she can wear it as her new item."

"Jenna showed me the pictures," Tom said. "Evidently, the wedding gift is a perfect match for the dress."

"That's why I sent them to Jenn. Two styles grabbed me so Jenna had final say. She and Alex packed Emily's suitcase for the honeymoon."

"Wow, nerves of steel keeping your destination from the pregnant woman." Joel laughed. "I could never have held up against Alex when she was pregnant with Daniel. You find out yet? Boy or girl?"

"It's one or the other." Aiden raised his brow. "Em didn't want to know, so it'll be a June surprise." He looked at Tom. "How about you and Jenna?"

"I'm under a strict secrecy code. If I tell, it'll be certain pain. It's another mystery bundle for this summer."

"Secretive bunch." Ryan rolled his eyes. "Why can't you find out? You're all whipped puppies."

"Says the single guy." Aiden smirked. "Wait until you're in this position, and then we'll see who's whipped. We know better. It's part of being in a happy committed relationship."

"Especially when they're pregnant and hormonal," Tom muttered under his breath.

"Amen to that, brother." Aiden waved at the waitress, making a circular motion with one hand and pointing to his glass.

"How's Vanna?" Ryan asked once he'd been served another drink.

"She's good. Gramma Grace is entertaining her for a few days."

"You let Vanna invite her boyfriend and her friends from Portland?" Joel tipped back his beer.

"There won't be many her age, and Leanne has spent time with us in the Vineyard and in New York. They're close. I figured allowing Vanna to bring friends might make it more fun. After the wedding ceremony, Emily and I will be busy."

"Still, four teenagers in a swanky hotel overnight. You're a brave man. Do you have guards posted at the girls' door?" Ryan raised a brow.

"Gramma Grace is taking them back to our place after the reception. She'll manage."

Joel snickered. "She didn't keep us in line. Wasn't it Easter weekend we spent at your grandmother's? The one where we all sneaked out and met the girls? A little something happened over that weekend, didn't it, Aiden?"

"Don't make me think about it. Hey, I could keep them at the hotel and let you chaperone them." He smirked. "Kids always find a way no matter what restrictions you put on them. We sure the hell did."

Ryan frowned and played with his coaster. "You're not worried about your daughter?"

"Always." Aiden sipped his drink. "Em and I have done all we can to help her make better choices than I did as a teenager. Now I'll trust her to make good decisions."

"You're awfully cool about it," Joel said.

"It's the strangest thing, but I remember what it was like to be her age. It's all coming back to me. Wait until Daniel's a teenager, and you'll get it."

"I have lots of time. He's only a baby." Joel stood. "Enough chit-chat, ladies, let's play some pool before the real party starts."

Chapter 23

Emily

THE SMELL OF FRESH COFFEE wafted through the room. Emily opened her eyes as soft lips touched hers and she ran her hands up into Aiden's hair. Mornings like this were heavenly, especially when they had the apartment to themselves.

"Happy Valentine's." He smoothed her hair back. "Ready for breakfast?"

A smile stole across her face as she pulled him into the sheets. She worked her fingers under his shirt, savoring his warm skin. "You're overdressed. It's not often we find ourselves here ... alone."

"Don't have to ask me twice," he murmured against her neck, dropping soft kisses on her collarbone.

"Happy Valentine's, Aiden." She wrapped her arms around his shoulders.

When she woke again two hours later, the smell of bacon wafted to her nostrils. Her mouth watered as she stretched and wiggled from the bed, wandering into the bathroom. She went through her morning ritual, ending it standing in front of the mirror, checking from all angles.

"Oh, no." She grimaced as she inspected her ass. Was it bigger than yesterday? Damn Aiden for making her eat bigger meals, even if they were healthy.

The exotic homemade ice cream had to stop, or she'd need to alter her gown to squeeze into it, along with whatever she'd wear on the fantastic and mysterious honeymoon he'd planned. The guy remained tight-lipped about the destination, and so far, neither Jenna nor Alex had ratted.

She sighed and adjusted her skimpy nightgown to hide her growing butt. At least the wonderful basketball-sized bump hadn't raged out of control.

"Em?" Aiden peeked into the bathroom. "So much for breakfast in bed."

"Your child performed the usual morning gymnastics on my bladder. Is it ready?" Her tummy rumbled in anticipation. "I'm starving."

He pulled her into his arms for a deep kiss before leading her to the bed. After some fussing and propping her up with pillows, he set a tray table across her legs.

"This is amazing." She scanned her eyes over the serving of Eggs Benedict, hash brown potatoes, and bacon strips, accompanied by a colorful fruit salad topped with a touch of yogurt and granola. A red rose in a bud vase adorned the corner of the tray. She sniffed the soft fragrance. "I think I'll keep you."

He laughed as he poured her the one small cup of coffee she allowed herself daily. "Eat before it gets cold."

She savored each bite, sighing in contentment as she scooped up the last of the hollandaise sauce. "So good." The flutter in her belly made her smile and press a hand to the little bulge of a foot. "The baby agrees."

"You're welcome. I'll get this out of the way." He carried the dishes from the room, returning a few minutes later to flop across the bed. He ran a hand over her belly until he found the tiny body part pressed against her stomach. As he traced his finger over, he followed the baby's movement. "I'll never tire of feeling the baby move. Incredible."

"We're over halfway there." She rested her hand over his. "Time is flying by, but the birth still isn't arriving soon enough."

"I can't wait to meet our new little person."

She kept her hand covering his as her mind drifted. This baby had happened with no planning or discussion, and they'd gone with it and rode the wave. "It's incredible that there will be sixteen years between your kids."

"Scary, isn't it? I never got to do this part. I missed her birth, her first steps, and her first words." He rested his forehead on her rounded belly. "No way I'm missing any of it this time."

"You'd better not." Emily twined her fingers into his hair, moving down to the back of his neck. "You know what's great, though? You'll be there to see Vanna graduate high school, go to university, and get her first job. Maybe one day she'll get married and you can walk her down the aisle. You'll be there to welcome your first grandchild."

Aiden laughed. "Can you imagine? We might have grandchildren before our kids graduate high school, or even before our kids even get to high school. That's insane."

"We'll be the young and cool grandparents. You could be a grandfather before you're forty." She giggled. "So you want more after this one?"

"I'm sure I will. When you told me you were pregnant, it seemed right. We never even discussed any options."

"I'd always hoped for a child, but I'd focused on my career. Then our relationship was too new, and ..." She shrugged.

"Too volatile? Too messy?" He shared a wry grin. "Those months weren't the best."

"Neither of us could wrap our minds around committing, let alone bringing a baby into the picture."

"Not true, Em. I was ready even if you weren't." He held up a hand as she opened her mouth to protest. "You couldn't force it and I understand. I worried you'd never get there, or that I wasn't the guy you wanted to commit to."

"Then I came to my senses and realized how horrible I'd been, and how crazy, and how scared. I wondered how you could be so sure, and what you saw in me. You forgave me so easily. Even after you lost your job, and I ruined our holiday."

Aiden gazed at her steadily, a frown furrowing his brow. "You keep saying *easily*. Do you think, even for a second, that any of it was ...?" He rolled onto his back, one hand shielding his eyes.

Emily's heart dropped as silence fell. The only sound in the room was his breathing. The magical moment they'd been sharing evaporated. She crawled from her cocoon of pillows, brushing her hand across his hair. "I'm sorry. I didn't mean—" The words caught in her throat as she tried to gather her thoughts. "I only meant you forgave me."

"And you think that was easy? Are you fucking kidding me? It was the hardest thing in the world. The first time when you came to Portland, I expected it would be okay. Then you told me in no uncertain terms how pissed you were that I'd considered finding a job elsewhere. I assumed it was over when you didn't bother to come to Boston. Then you showed up in the Vineyard and did it again, and then again the weekend before the wedding by sneaking out without saying goodbye. The common theme is, if I said anything about our future, all you could say was *don't* and run. Fuck." He rolled off the bed, keeping his back to her as he stalked from the bedroom.

Emily flinched at the crash of dishes, holding her breath as silence fell. She tiptoed down the hall to the kitchen. As she suspected, he was there, leaning on the counter with his head bowed. A pile of shattered ceramic and glass littered the sink.

"Aiden," she whispered as she closed the distance between them and ran her flattened palms up his back, rubbing before wrapping her arms around him. "That came out all wrong. I didn't mean it was easy to handle or get over."

He didn't respond but didn't push her away or leave either, so he was at least listening.

"I love you. I've made huge mistakes, and you've had this amazing capacity to forgive. You've given me more chances than I deserve, put up with my poor choices and my insecurities. If only I could replay those moments and change how I responded. I wish I'd told Dragon Lady to shove her job."

"Do you?"

"I missed so many chances to make it right but I didn't mean for it to be that way. Even showing up unannounced at the Vineyard, I didn't consider what I was doing or how it would affect you. I needed to be with you, but it got too damn real and I fell apart. The only way I got through it was by pretending I hadn't hurt you as much as I'd hurt myself."

"Are you about done?"

"Oh." Tears rose to her eyes. "Sorry, I needed to explain—"

"No." Aiden turned, placing his palms on her cheeks. "Are you done running? We're getting married in four days and …" He dragged in a rough breath. "I wouldn't survive losing you. Not again."

Tears flooded her eyes, and the sob escaped.

"Every time you've left, you've taken a piece of my heart. Even after you moved to Boston, you weren't fully committed. Do you know what it's like to constantly worry you'd disappear?"

"You thought …?" Fresh tears streamed down her face, pain stabbing her heart at the torment she'd put him through. She'd tried so hard to hide her insecurities, her worry, and her doubts, but she'd done a poor job. He'd been reading her all along, but he'd kept it all inside, hidden and securely wrapped. He was his own bundle of fear and insecurities, burying the scars and pain she'd inflicted.

Such a complete fool. She thought she'd scaled the walls, torn down the barriers, and invaded the fortress, yet here she was, still sitting outside the castle gates. Where had he found the courage to allow her into his life?

"So are you?" He brushed his thumbs over her cheeks.

She nodded. "I love you, and I can't wait to marry you. Thank you for loving me and for accepting me even with all my faults and insecurities. I'm sorry for every moment I've ever made you feel that way. Truly sorry. Can you forgive me?"

"I already have, or we wouldn't be here. I love you, Emelia Alejandra Anderson. So much."

Emily gazed around the room, a warm haze hanging over her. She noted Nina and Caroline chatting near the bar, and her dad in discussion with Tom. The rehearsal had gone well, and by this time tomorrow, she and Aiden would be husband and wife.

"Time to get you home. You need to rest for your big day." Jenna tapped her watch.

"Let me say good night to Aiden." Emily scanned the room, searching out her husband-to-be and heading his way. "Hi." She stretched on her tiptoes, rubbing the back of his neck and planting a kiss on his lips. "Jenna's decreed it's time for my beauty sleep."

He slid his arms around her waist. "You're already beautiful, but you need your sleep." Aiden ran a hand over her stomach, searching for movement.

Emily smiled at the ritual. "Baby's sleeping. Sorry you missed it today."

"Tomorrow night we'll be together," Aiden said. "Looks like everyone is behaving."

"They promised and nobody has dared get into their differences or—" She did a quick slashing motion across her throat. Paul, Nina, and Caroline had been warned to get along before their invitations were issued, and so far, they had.

"We hold the trump card." He caressed her belly.

"They're excited about being grandparents and don't want their privileges revoked. Just be thankful we live in another city or my mom would drop by without calling." She winked. "Unannounced visits could cramp our lifestyle."

"Em?" His voice trembled ever-so-slightly. "You're ready to do this?"

She placed her palms against his cheeks, looking deep into his eyes. "I'm ready. Remember? I've hung them up."

"I love you, Emily." He wrapped her in a warm embrace. "I can't wait until tomorrow when I get to see you walk down the aisle." He rested his cheek against her hair and whispered, "It'll be strange for you to be away from me tonight."

"I hate sleeping alone."

"Two nights in a row."

"Then we'll be on our honeymoon, and I get you all to myself. You're still not telling me?"

"Nope." He winked. "Your keeper is about to drag you away."

"I'll see you tomorrow afternoon. I love you, and our wedding will be perfect." Emily brushed her fingertips down his face, giving him a last kiss before she allowed herself to be led away.

⌒≼

Jenna tapped on the bedroom door as Emily finished wrapping the box in brown paper.

"A courier dropped this off at the concierge desk while we were out." She waved the large brown envelope.

Emily plucked it from her fingers, apprehension running through her. "Thanks." She slit the top and peeked inside.

"Are you okay?" Jenna's brow wrinkled. "You look pale."

"I'm fine." Emily set it aside. "I'll be out after I change."

Jenna threw a concerned look over her shoulder, but she left, pulling the door shut behind her.

Emily sat on the edge of the bed, rubbing her damp palms and taking a deep breath before shaking the contents onto the bed. Her breath caught in her throat and tears rushed to her eyes at the photos clipped to the front of the glossy magazine. She picked up the first one with a shaking hand, not wanting to believe any of it. A sick feeling welled up as she recognized the woman.

She closed her eyes, her whole body trembling before she had the courage to look through the rest. A sob ripped from her throat as she swept the pictures to the floor.

So much for Aiden being nothing like her dad. She had proof in living color. Here he was, pictured with luscious blonde model, Jazlyn Leitner. With trembling fingers, she opened the magazine to the marked page and pressed her fingertips to her lips.

Together again? The headline screamed, a picture of Emily looking at the lip-lock between Aiden and Jazlyn. Further headlines revealed her as the jilted lover.

"Asshole." She yanked the ring from her finger and tossed it onto the bed before stalking toward the closet to grab her suitcase. Time to pack and get the hell out of here. Her worst fear had come true. Aiden betrayed her, she was homeless, with only a part-time income, and she was having the cheating bastard's baby. *A baby I already love.*

"Emily?" Jenna tapped on the door before peeking in. "What's going on?"

Her friend's eyes widened at the photos scattered across the floor, Emily's tear-stained face, and the open suitcase.

"I have nowhere to go." Emily sobbed as she slumped onto the bed.

Jenna picked a picture from the floor. "What is this? Who …? Jazlyn?" She lifted the magazine from the duvet and scanned the page. "Who sent this?"

"I can't marry him." Emily brushed at her eyes, avoiding the hurtful pictures. She'd endured more than enough women hanging all over him in the past few months.

"At least give Aiden a chance to explain. You'd throw it all away without even talking to him?"

"There's nothing to say. He's wearing the shirt I gave him."

Alex appeared in the doorway. "What's up? Vanna and I were making—" She snatched the magazine from Jenna. "What's this?"

Jenna shoved the pictures into the envelope and seized the magazine from Alex's hands. "I'll be right back. You stay with Emily."

"I want to be alone." Emily curled up, grabbing the throw from the end of the bed and hauling it over her head. "Please, leave me be." All she wanted to do was hide from the unimaginable pain.

CHAPTER 24

Aiden

Tom patted Aiden's shoulder and handed him a drink. "Relax. She won't disappear. Jenna has her tucked in at your apartment and Emily will be there tomorrow."

"We've had little time together the past few days." It had been a flurry of last-minute errands, lunches with the parents, the bachelor party, and the bachelorette for Emily, followed by tonight's rehearsal dinner. "I miss having our alone time."

"Mmm, right? It was like that at our wedding." Joel laughed. "Just think, three weeks away, just the two of you." He wiggled his brows. "She'll love it. Alex thought it was the best place ever, and it was so relaxing."

Aiden sipped his drink, his nerves jangling and his stomach twisting. Tomorrow he'd stand in front of everyone, say I do, and promise to love and cherish her forever.

Most days, loving her would be easy, but some days, perhaps not so straightforward. Emily's fiery Spanish heritage played its part, and the woman was unpredictable and exasperating, not to mention stubborn and frustrating. After Valentine's Day, he hoped she understood that he loved her with all of his heart.

Joel lined up his cue, taking the shot as Tom's phone lit up.

"It's Jenna. She'll want to say good night." His friend bounded upstairs.

"Your turn." Ryan prodded Aiden, a grin spreading over his face. "Last game, then you need your beauty sleep."

Aiden rolled his eyes. "Like any amount of sleep will help."

Joel lifted a shoulder. "Maybe not, but tomorrow will be a long one and we've all been partying a little too hard these past few days. Lucky for us, we don't need all the primping and salon time the ladies do, so we get to sleep in."

"Aiden." Tom beckoned as he came down the stairs. "Just Aiden." His best friend held up a hand to stop Joel and Ryan from joining them and led him upstairs into the office, shutting the door.

"What's up?" His heart pounded as he noted his friend's serious expression. "Did something happen? Is Emily okay?"

Tom leveled a long look at him, tapping the legal-sized envelope on his desk with a fingertip. "Before you open this, promise we'll talk this out before you do anything. Promise, Aiden."

"I promise?" Aiden raised his brows. "What's in there? What's going on?"

Tom sighed and held it out.

The last time he'd been in this position it had been Savannah sitting across the table with her mystery envelope. He peeled open the tab, pulling out the photos and a glossy gossip magazine. "What the …?" Everything blurred, a headache building as he flipped picture after picture. "Where did these come from? Shit." Panic rose as he opened the magazine and scanned the headlines.

"A courier delivered these to Emily."

"Emily saw these?" A sick feeling built in his stomach. "This isn't what it looks like. Who sent these …?" He scrubbed his jaw and then closed his eyes. "I need to see Em."

"It would be better if you didn't. Give the ladies a chance to calm her down. Jenn will call."

Aiden took several deep breaths as the fear rose within him. "So she thinks …?" The words stuck in his throat as he dropped his head into his hands.

"Hey." Tom moved around the desk, sitting beside him and grasping his shoulder. "Talk to me."

Aiden kept his head down, struggling to clear his thoughts.

"Tell me when this was."

"It was after Emily left the Vineyard. I was drunk, but I didn't sleep with Jaz. It was only a kiss."

"This was a rebound?"

"No, because nothing happened." Aiden tried to breathe. "Emily's angry?"

"She's upset. Give her a few minutes."

Aiden ignored the advice and hit his speed dial. "Emily, please call me." After disconnecting, he texted her before he tried to call again. "I should talk to her in person," he said when it went through to voice mail.

"Not a good idea, Aiden."

"Why?" he whispered. "I can't lose her, Tom. We need to deal with this. What does it say if I hide? How did she even get those photos? Who gave them to this tabloid?"

"No idea. You don't think Tiffany would …?"

Aiden narrowed his eyes. "There's no love lost between her and Emily. Do you think she would?" His heart ached. This could break them. "I need to see Emily." He was out of the office before Tom said another word.

Tom arrived at the front door and slid on his coat.

"What are you doing?" Aiden asked.

"The groom goes nowhere without his wingman."

"Well, don't count on being best man. There won't be a wedding at this rate."

Five minutes later, Aiden pressed the fob against the panel and leaned against the wall as the elevator rose.

"You okay?"

"No, but what's new?" Aiden rubbed a hand over his face, contemplating how Emily would react when he arrived. "She'll probably tell me to go to hell and we'll be over for good."

The doors slid open, and he strode through the apartment, following the sound of muffled voices coming from the master bedroom.

"Aiden." Jenna's eyes widened as he appeared in the doorway. "You shouldn't be here. It's bad luck."

"Can you give us a minute?"

Emily sat on the bed with her shoulders slumped, a box of tissue beside her. "I don't want to talk to you."

Aiden motioned Jenna and Alex toward the door, waiting until they'd pulled it shut behind them.

He shoved his hands into his pockets and gazed at her steadily, but she refused to look up. "We have to talk about it."

She snatched a tissue from the box, wiping at her face. "Leave me alone. There's nothing you could say to fix this."

"That's it? This is how it ends? You don't even want to hear what I have to say?" At her continued silence, he bowed his head and stared at the floor. "Well, I guess you're right. If this is how we're handling our issues, we shouldn't get married. You've already convicted me and decided the wedding is off."

He closed his eyes and sighed, hoping she'd say something. Even a little yelling or screaming would be better than this horrible, oppressive silence. When she said nothing, he turned and stepped into the hallway.

Her failure to respond broke his heart. Now he needed a drink. Tomorrow he'd deal with canceling the wedding, but at this moment, there was only numbness and the knowledge he should have known better.

"And that's what cheating bastards do. They leave." Emily stalked after him, grasping his arm. "Why would you do that? With her." Her eyes blazed as she struck out at him, pummeling her fists against his chest. "You're such an asshole."

Aiden caught her wrists and pulled her against his chest as she burst into tears, sagging in his arms.

"I h-hate you." Her chest hitched as her knees buckled and she sank to the floor, wrapping her arms around herself. "Why?" she whispered.

He kneeled, half-afraid to touch her, but aching to soothe her fears. "You left me. I never expected you to return, but I guess the circumstances don't matter."

She brushed at her cheeks and sniffled. "Damn it, I hate this part." Her chin dipped. "Seeing another woman all over you is upsetting enough without pictures and an embarrassing tabloid article. It's been constant over the past few months, and I'm having a hard time dealing."

"Well, so am I." He slid an arm around her, thankful when she only sobbed and rested her forehead on his shoulder, one palm pressed against his chest. "If I could change how things went down after you left, I would," he whispered. "But I'm human. It hurt."

Emily buried her face in the crook of his neck, one arm looped around his neck.

"If we can't get past our mistakes, it's better we end it now." He grasped her face between his hands, tipping her chin up. "Please don't wait until tomorrow to call it off. Don't make me wait for you." He sucked in a breath and forced out the question he didn't want to ask, but not knowing was even worse than the expected answer. "Are we over?"

"Was she the only one? Were there others?"

The question burned, but if he wanted this relationship to survive … "It was one kiss and nothing else."

"Nothing happened with her?"

Aiden blinked. Honesty might end this forever, but he had no choice. "Jazlyn and I dated three years ago, but I haven't been with her since then."

"Not after us?"

"There's nobody after we became us. It's not," he said, sighing in frustration, "how I deal with things." *Anymore.* The temptation to dull the pain with Jazlyn had been fleeting. The memories of past mistakes had risen in his mind. No question regret would follow if he slept with another woman while his heart still belonged to Emily. This moment proved him right.

"You kissed her." A sob broke free from her throat, but she cuddled closer, one hand caressing the nape of his neck.

"I'm sorry. I wish I could take it back," he said against her hair. "I love you. Only you."

"Forgive me for being crazy," she whispered, burying her face against his sweater. "I promise to be better about resolving our issues."

"You'll be there tomorrow?"

She nodded.

He buried his face into her hair and tightened his embrace. Neither of them seemed in any hurry to break the contact, but he finally stood and helped her to her feet. He turned her hand, noting the bare ring finger.

Her teeth clamped onto her bottom lip as she peered at him from red-rimmed eyes.

Panic threatened to engulf him, that awful feeling lingering in his belly. "Where is it?"

Emily bowed her head, but turned, tugging him into the bedroom and shutting the door behind them. She headed straight for the bed, crawling onto it and running her hands over the duvet. "It's here," she whispered. "I promise it's safe." A choked sob escaped her as she patted the covers. "It has to be here."

Aiden blew out a long breath. How could he make a big deal out of it, considering the fate of his first wedding ring? "Relax. We'll find it." He tugged her from the bed, gathering the duvet and shaking it gently over the mattress. *Nothing.*

She sniffled, dashing the back of her hand across her nose, catching one of the salty drops trickling down it.

He kneeled and peered under the edge of the bed, the diamonds catching the light. He slipped the ring onto the end of his finger before sitting beside her.

"I've made such a mess of this." She covered her face with her hands. "We're supposed to be getting married tomorrow."

Aiden sighed and looked at his watch. "Today. It's after midnight." He twirled the platinum band. "Is that what you want?"

"I love you." She placed her hand over his. "Is it what you want? Or have I ruined everything?"

After a tiny shake of his head, he took her hand, hesitating for only a second before he slipped the ring onto her finger. As he curled an arm around her waist he asked, "Do you know who sent the pictures?"

"I'd guess … James?" A shiver ran through her.

"Why do you …?" He contemplated her. "You're scared. Of James?"

She brushed the back of her hand over her eyes. "When we were in New York, he dragged me into a car and offered me money to go away."

"And you didn't tell me this … why?" He narrowed his eyes as his anger built. "Did he threaten you?"

Emily clenched her hands in her lap and nodded.

"I'm so sorry," he whispered. "Tell me everything."

Aiden rolled over and squinted at the clock. It was still early, but he was wide-awake and it was unlikely he'd get any further rest. He crawled from bed and paced to the window. The first rays of sun were touching the lake, creating a frosty glow. Aiden itched to be moving, desperate for a distraction from the details crowding his mind. The day of truth was upon him.

Tom tapped on the door. "You're up."

"I'm debating on a run by the lake. I need air."

"Let me know if you want company." Tom held up a package. "A courier dropped this off."

"What's in store this time?" Aiden stared at the box. "The sending address is our apartment. Here goes." He ripped the paper in one motion and flipped open the lid. Relief surged through him.

"What?" Tom raised his brows as he peeked into the box. "Will those fit?" A smirk appeared. "That purple is rather girly, but suit yourself."

"Not my usual color, but I like them." Aiden gazed at the running shoes nestled in tissue paper, fighting the grin. "You had to be there."

Tom tilted his head and patted Aiden's back. "I kind of was."

Aiden met his friend's look as the reality of his situation hit him. "Am I making a huge mistake?"

His friend lifted a shoulder. "In love there are no guarantees, but you learned that a long time ago."

"So I am?" Aiden closed his eyes, replaying the previous night in his head. That moment when it became far too real … far too much like the end of his first marriage.

"Hey," Tom said in a low voice. "Don't second guess it. Last night could have been a disaster, but you worked it out."

"Could have been?" Aiden scoffed. "Why do women always need to ask that fucking question? It felt like a return to hell."

"I don't know, but does it matter? This isn't the same situation. Not even close."

Aiden sank onto the edge of the bed. The man had not only propped him up last night after Emily's meltdown, but during the end of his marriage to Tiffany and the path of destruction that followed. He trusted his friend was right. "So what do I do?"

"You already know the answer." Tom headed toward the door. "Are you ready for that run?" He thumped the doorframe with one hand and glanced over his shoulder. "Aiden?"

"Let me change." Aiden dug into his bag for his work out gear before pulling one of Emily's running shoes from the box. The woman had tested his commitment time and again, pushing him to the breaking point. The inescapable fact was he loved her and some things were worth fighting for and always would be. He hoped she felt the same.

Chapter 25

Emily

EMILY STRETCHED AND STARED AT the ceiling, resting her hands on her belly. It felt strange sleeping alone in this bed. She wouldn't see Aiden until this afternoon when she walked down the aisle to meet him. *If he showed up.*

She closed her eyes, forcing several deep breaths as flutters tickled her stomach. *Was it the baby or nerves rising to the surface?* She wasn't sure. After last night, she worried Aiden might have had enough. It had only taken a little gossip and a couple of photos to whip her insecurities into a frenzy. She hated the situation, but she'd been the one who left. *Even if something had happened with Jazlyn, could I blame him?* It was unfair to punish him.

The muffled sound of feet shuffling in the hallway alerted her. Vanna must be up, and more voices rang through the air. Jenna and Alex. Time to get up, but her limbs wouldn't obey her command to move. *I'm marrying Aiden ... Keep breathing.*

She straightened her engagement ring and held it up to the light, picturing his sadness as he slid the magnificent piece of jewelry onto her finger early this morning. That moment when she worried he would bolt.

Jenna rushed into the room with a huge smile on her face. "Time to get up. By the time you're ready, so will breakfast. Then it's spa time. You have a pre-natal massage booked, a mud wrap, then makeup, hair, and nails. Plenty of pampering in store for the bride."

They'd done the same when Jenna married Tom. She reminded herself to thank Aiden with a big kiss for insisting on the wedding planner. At her sister's wedding, they'd been up at the crack of dawn, rushing around to ensure the cousins had done their duties. They had squeezed in the bride's hair and makeup right before the ceremony. In comparison, her day would be simple and relaxed. Or so she hoped. *Only if the groom shows up.*

"I'm up, I'm up. Give me five minutes to dress." She waved Jenna away, and her friend retreated. After taking a few moments to rinse in the tile shower, Emily pulled on her oversized, comfortable *Bride* sweatpants and a sweater.

She'd soon be Aiden's wife. *Breathe. Keep breathing. I love him and it's only cold feet. Breakfast. Spa. Dress. Get in the limo. Walk down the aisle. Say I do. I can do these things.*

The garment bag covering the froth of lace, tulle, and satin hung in the closet. She unzipped it, a smile teasing her lips as she contemplated how Aiden might react when he saw her in this dress.

Alex peered in the doorway. "You'll look breathtaking."

"If I can get myself down the aisle," Emily whispered. *Breakfast. Spa. Dress. Get in the limo. Walk down the aisle. Say I do, because I can't live without him.*

Alarm flitted across Alex's face so rapidly Emily almost missed it. "Bridal jitters are normal." The woman approached her and traced the lace on the bodice with a fingertip. "You'll never regret marrying Aiden."

Emily closed her eyes, taking a deep cleansing breath. "You're right, but there's a tiny part of me that's terrified. I don't want to end up like my parents. Or his."

"Oh, Emily." Alexis slid an arm around her. "You and Aiden are nothing like Nina and Paul. Or James and Caroline, either. Did you know his parents' marriage was about as close to being arranged as you get in our social circle?"

"What are you talking about?"

"Their parents pushed them into marriage. The right girl marrying the eligible bachelor. The right educations, the proper connections, and the socially acceptable families. But did they love each other? I suspect not."

"I can't imagine being forced to marry someone for appearances." She shuddered, remembering the day in the limo with James and the wintry darkness lingering in the man's eyes. Even the mention of the man had her nausea rising. "James Hamilton is a ruthless man."

"Your man is nothing like his father. You're marrying Aiden because you love him and he loves you. Stop fighting it. Quit worrying about what could go wrong. Cherish the wonderful things awaiting you. Enjoy what's right. Let yourself be happy."

Tears rose at her friend's wise words. "The man has infinite patience. I woke up this morning and realized today's the day. A few months ago, I swore this day would never come. I wasn't even sure I believed in weddings and marriage, yet I'm about to walk down the aisle."

"In fifty years, when you celebrate your anniversary with Aiden, you'll recall this unforgettable day. I've never seen him so tied in knots over anyone. You have his entire heart. Don't crush it."

If she made a misstep today, she'd better keep on walking. As patient and loving as Aiden had been, she was certain his capacity to forgive her had run out. If she showed even a tiny glimpse of hesitation, he'd bolt.

"I love him more than anything." Emily straightened. Marrying him was everything she wanted, and she would marry him for the right reasons, no matter what some people seemed to believe.

Jenna peeked into the room. "Let's eat. We need to stay on schedule."

⌒≼

"This is so much fun." Savannah sat beside Emily, the manicurists fussing over their nails.

"It is. Jenna's a sweetie for arranging this." Emily regarded the girl as the ever-present wedding photographer snapped pictures. Her smile widened. She doubted Aiden loved receiving the same treatment from his own photographer as he dressed.

Emily found it easy to smile with everyone chattering and keeping her mind occupied. She didn't even mind Nina fussing over everything from her nail color to her hair.

"We should book these days regularly. It's been just what I needed." Emily had endured primping and pampering, waxing and buffing until she shined. Jenna had insisted Emily submit to a major waxing session as soon as she'd arrived in Chicago to prepare for the wedding and honeymoon. Now the final touches were being put on her nails, and they'd be on their way home to dress.

"All dry," The manicurist said. "You look stunning."

"Thank you." Emily touched the exquisite antique diamond tiara she'd received from Gramma Grace and tucked in her hair.

"Time to dress. The wedding planner called and they've finished decorating. The flowers and cake arrived on schedule." Jenna shooed them toward the front door. She'd been the perfect matron of honor, keeping them to a strict timetable.

"I'd be a basket case without the planner." Emily smiled, picturing the multitudes of cream and red roses and soft fabrics turning the chamber into something out of a fairytale without her lifting a finger.

"She's a gem." Jenna ushered them into the limo. "After the ceremony, her crew will move the flowers and decorations into that magnificent reception hall. The rooms you picked are so elegant."

"I'll be waterlogged." Emily laughed as Jenna handed her yet another bottle of water.

She'd plied them with cleansing caffeine-free teas and lemon infused water during their entire visit at the salon even after a nourishing breakfast that included piles of fresh fruit.

"We'll cut you off from drinking after our snack at the hotel." Jenna grinned. "Can't have you dancing at the altar, but I promised Aiden I'd make sure you ate and drank enough. We don't want you dehydrated and fainting before you say I do."

"He's such a worrier. Keeps making snacks and pretending he's hungry, but I'm on to him." Emily cracked open the bottle and sipped the water. She appreciated his attentiveness. Many men didn't take the time to worry or pamper their significant others.

"He's right, Emily. You're anxious about gaining too much weight and the dress not fitting, but it's not healthy. You'll look gorgeous, and you're not alone, sister." She patted her belly. "Mine is even bigger than yours, and so is my butt. If it's any consolation, Tom does the same to me."

"I'll eat well on our honeymoon." Emily grinned. "I hear the food will be amazing."

"Oh, no." Jenna wagged a finger. "Aiden went to a lot of trouble to make this special, so you'll pry nothing out of me." She ran her fingers across her lips, zipping them and tossing the key.

"I had to try. Did you do a good job packing?"

"I'm incredible." Jenna giggled. "Why do you think Aiden asked me to take care of it?"

"True." Emily had to give her props. The woman was an organizational dynamo. "So, everyone in this limo aside from me knows where we're going?"

"Pretty much."

The limo glided to a halt in front of the apartment. They no sooner got to the suite when the call came from the lobby.

"Caroline." Emily greeted her as she stepped from the elevator.

"I hope you don't mind me stopping by, but I have something for you. I'm playing delivery woman, too." She lifted two gift bags. "I promised I'd get this to you before the ceremony. Then I'm off to the Cultural Center to meet Aiden."

"Thank you, Caroline." She accepted the gift bags and settled onto the couch. The first one was a card from her soon to be mother-in-law. Emily furrowed her brow as she opened the accompanying ring box. "Ohh." Her heart skipped a beat at the glittering combination of sapphires and diamonds.

"It's a family heirloom, and it would honor me if you wore it today."

Emily lifted the ring from the box. "It's gorgeous. I'll be proud to wear it." On impulse, she hugged Caroline, who returned the embrace after a tiny hesitation. "It's beautiful, thank you." She tucked it in the box. "I'll keep it safe until I have my dress on." She dabbed her eyes, touched that Caroline would think to bring such a personal and special gift.

"It's nice to see my son happy. You're good for him." Caroline's eyes looked shiny as she beamed at Emily. "Now this one." She held out the second larger bag.

Emily arched a brow. The second bag contained a card, along with three velvet boxes. The short but sweet note brought a flood of emotions. "I might cry." She fanned her face with one hand as Alexis handed her yet another tissue. The first and smallest box contained earrings which winked and flashed, and tears burned behind her eyes. "They're amazing."

"Open the other ones." Jenna shifted in her seat and pushed the box of tissues closer to her friend. "You might need these."

Emily opened the second box, finding a matching diamond necklace. The last held a bracelet. She dabbed the corners of her eyes, taking in the wedding gifts and the ring. "I'm set with the old, the new, the borrowed, and the blue."

Caroline patted her knee. "You look splendid, Emily. Thank you for letting me share your day. Now, I need to check on my son."

They hugged and Caroline took her leave.

Jenna snickered. "How did you tame Caroline? She has to check on her son? Say what? And that." She pointed to the ring box. "Unbelievable. I never thought I'd see the day."

"Why are you so surprised?"

"Caroline shares nothing, and she's lending you a priceless family heirloom. Trust me, she likes you. You'll look like a million dollars walking down the aisle." Alexis giggled. "And be wearing about that much, too," her friend murmured.

Emily shot a curious look at her friend before staring at the diamond ring glinting on her finger and the array of velvet boxes. She hesitated to ask the value of her custom designed ring.

"Emily, you change into the items on the bed and then we'll help with your gown." Jenna smirked.

"What?" Savannah frowned. "Why are you looking at me like that?"

"Oh, never mind." Alexis giggled. "Put on your dress, sweetie." She waved Vanna toward her room.

"Don't let her see," Jenna said to Emily under her breath.

Emily spotted the fancy box on the bed. It became clear when she lifted out the delicate, but infinitely sexy, robin-egg blue lingerie. "You two." She lingered in front of the mirror, studying her voluptuous figure. The lacy strapless bra emphasized her full breasts, which to her joy compensated for the fact the rest of her had filled out. She turned from the mirror and stepped into her dress.

"Ready?" Jenna appeared in the doorway, still smirking. "Did it fit?"

"Perfectly. Now I'm covered for the blue items. I understand why you didn't want Vanna to see. Not that she's fooled. She's sixteen, not five."

"She doesn't need to picture the wedding night as Aiden gets a load of you in sexy lingerie." Jenna grinned.

"I'm sure she'd rather not think about it. Do me up." Emily turned as Alexis and Vanna joined them in the bedroom.

"Veil." Vanna held out the delicate and elegant matching swath of tulle. She darted from the room, returning with the velvet boxes, helping Emily fasten each of the jewelry pieces as the other two fussed with the row of buttons.

Emily scanned the room. "Oh no. I left my shoes."

"You don't need them." Vanna presented a box. "These are the ones you should wear."

She opened the lid. "You bought them."

Vanna giggled. "They're from Dad. I could never afford those. I told him how much you loved them plus they're blue."

With the elegant veil now perched in her hair and the final adjustments made, Emily slid the sapphire ring onto her right hand and turned to face the ladies.

Silence dropped over the room, broken only by the sound of the camera.

"That bad?" Emily peered over her shoulder toward the mirror as the shutter clicked.

Savannah let out a sob. "You're so beautiful."

Jenna and Alexis both nodded and turned Emily to face the full-length mirror. Her heart pounded as she stared at her reflection. Heat rushed over her and she felt faint, fanning her face.

"Are you okay?" Jenna asked.

"I'm getting married," Emily whispered.

"You look like a princess." Vanna stepped beside her. "Dad will flip."

"Have a few sips." Alexis handed her a glass of ice water. "Remember to breathe."

Emily sucked in a deep breath and nodded. "I will." She glanced at her engagement ring. Aiden would add a simple diamond eternity band to her hand in less than two hours. "Mamá and Paul should be here soon."

They spent a few minutes taking pictures until both Nina and Paul arrived.

"Oh." Paul stepped into the room, staring wide-eyed at Emily. "Angel, you look gorgeous." His eyes grew red and misty.

Jenna's phone trilled. "Hi, Tom." She turned, whispering into the mobile.

"Is everything okay?" Emily asked once Jenna hung up. Her palms felt clammy and her breath caught in her chest. "He's not coming, is he?" She blinked back the tears.

"Nonsense." Jenna patted her arm. "They're in the limo and will arrive at the venue in a few minutes. We'll leave here in less than ten minutes, so they'll be inside before we arrive."

"Breathe. In." Alex demonstrated by inhaling, then blowing out a long slow breath. "Out. Your turn."

"Okay, I get it." Emily laughed. "I'm being silly."

"Incredibly silly." Savannah crossed her arms, looking tearful. "Aiden would never do that to you. If you even think—" The teen turned and fumbled for the box of tissues. "He loves you," she mumbled.

"Vanna." Emily turned to the girl. "I love him, but I'm nervous. This is a huge commitment, and I sometimes wonder if I deserve him."

"Of course, you do. You complete each other. He was miserable when you were apart. When you moved to Boston, everything changed for the better. I may be a kid in your eyes, but I know true love when I see it. This big wedding is all for you. All he cares is that you show up and say I do. You could wear a paper bag and he'd marry you, he loves you so much."

"I know, Vanna," Emily said. "I can't wait to marry him." She hugged the girl, careful not to scrunch their dresses. "Dry those tears. This is a happy day, right?"

"Sorry." Savannah nodded, dabbing her eyes. "I'm scared you'll disappear, like at the Vineyard."

"I won't. I'll never leave again. This is me experiencing pre-wedding jitters."

Alexis slid an arm around the girl's shoulders. "Most brides have these moments on their wedding day. I sure did. It's a huge deal to marry someone, but the only place Emily is going is to her wedding. To marry your dad."

"Okay." A smile peeked out, and the girl's face lit up. "Maybe I have my own jitters."

"I understand." Emily's breath caught in her throat. From the moment she'd met this beautiful, sweet, and loving girl, nothing in the relationship had involved only her and Aiden. His daughter depended on him.

Today, she became a wife and Savannah's stepmother. In a few short months, she'd be a mother again. A married woman with two kids. Aiden turned out to be a different man than she'd bargained for, but in the best of ways.

She looked around the room, dabbing her eyes again. "I love you. All of you. You're all so special and I'm ecstatic you're here."

After accepting hugs from each of them, with an extra long hug from Vanna, she picked up her extravaganza of red and cream roses and let Paul drape a warm wrap over her shoulders.

"You look beautiful, Emelia." Nina brushed her eyes.

They posed for a few final photos and then they were in the limo. It was time.

Emily waited with her attendants and her parents in one of the side rooms. She fanned herself again. Despite the chilly February weather, an overheated flush crept from her toes.

They'd invited three hundred people, and based on the hum of voices and echo of laughter, each and every one of them converged on the hall this afternoon. Her knees shook. *What if I collapse or trip half-way up the aisle?*

"Emelia, relax." Nina handed her a small glass of water. "Aiden's here, looking handsome in his tux. Wait until he sees his princess."

"Mamá." Emily shook her head, holding out her hand to prevent her mother from squishing her into a hug. "Don't start." She pressed the bridge of her nose between two fingers. "I'm going to cry."

Nina smiled. "The red, cream, and gold combination in the hall looks enchanting. You picked the perfect colors."

Emily relented and gave her mom a quick squeeze. She appreciated the attempt at distraction.

Jenna checked the clock. "Paul, it's almost time."

Joel and Ryan appeared at that moment.

"Aiden will escort Gramma Grace to her seat in a minute. They're waiting for Paul." Ryan offered his arm to Savannah. "Ready, Vanna?"

"Totally." The girl took his arm. "Let's get my dad married."

"If we let Emily get away, we'll never hear the end of it." Ryan winked.

"I need a moment with my Angel." Paul cleared his throat, his smile shaky.

Emily accepted Paul's outstretched hands, taking comfort in their warmth. "This is it."

"You've found someone who makes you happy, Angel Eyes."

"I almost didn't get here. I'm scared and I don't know why." Her entire body trembled as she struggled for breath.

"When I married your mother, I was quaking, but the moment she started up the aisle, it all melted away. You love him and he's waiting for you. He sees you, Angel Eyes. You're beautiful, it's true, but he loves what you are inside, Emelia. He sees your soul, your innermost spirit and beauty, that golden heart of yours."

"Thank you, Papá." Emily hugged him. "Thank you for being here."

"I wouldn't miss it for anything, Angel. Focus on Aiden. You'll be fine."

"Okay," she whispered as her chest loosened and she drew in a breath. That she could do that.

"Aiden's waiting. I love you, Angel."

"I love you." She blinked back the tears as he disappeared out the door.

"Okay, last minute stuff." Jenna adjusted Emily's dress, straightening the train and ensuring everyone had their bouquets. "You look amazing," she whispered in Emily's ear. "Now marry that man."

The soft music filtered into the room. Aiden would seat Gramma Grace, and Tom would escort Caroline to her seat during this preamble.

They stepped to the doors, Emily and Nina staying back and out of sight as the wedding planner ushered Savannah and Ryan into their places. With a nod and a quick word into the woman's headset, the doors swung open and Savannah and Ryan were on their way up the aisle.

Jenna did a final adjustment to Emily's dress, her nod and smile reassuring as Joel and Alexis started their stroll. The soft strains of the string quartet floated through the air.

Breathe, breathe. Focus on Aiden. Emily closed her eyes, struggling to quell the trembling of her body.

"Wait until Aiden sees you." Jenna's voice forced her to open her eyes. "I'll be watching him, and you should too."

Emily nodded, clutching Nina's arm as Jenna began her solo stroll toward the group at the front.

Nina loosened Emily's grip and held her fingers. "Relax. He loves you, and you love him."

Emily straightened as the music changed.

Nina kept her hand over Emily's, cueing her to walk. Emily lifted her chin as they stepped into view. She almost froze at the sheer number of eyes trained on her.

"Aiden," her mom murmured, barely moving her lips. "Focus, cariño."

Emily stared straight up the aisle. Her gaze met Aiden's as his eyes widened. Even over the distance, she felt the jolt, the tingle that ran from head to toe. Her breath hitched as he smiled, his eyes lighting up. She forced herself forward, one step at a time.

Her mind vaguely registered the magical flickering of candles and the soft music as they glided forward, but she remained locked on the man she loved, the fear lifting, everything melting away. They were the only people in the entire world.

The smile came from nowhere, her lips twitching as the joy blossomed in her heart. Jenna was so right. The look on his face was everything she'd ever wanted to see. And it was all for her.

CHAPTER 26

Aiden

AIDEN STOOD AT THE ALTAR with Tom beside him, trying to stop the trembling. He shuffled his feet. "You're sure she's still here?" he said under his breath. "She didn't slip out the back door?"

"Relax," Tom said out of the corner of his mouth. "Don't forget to breathe."

Aiden exhaled the breath he'd held. The woman had reduced him to a quivering mass of insecurity and standing here in front of three hundred guests was excruciating. What if she had a last-minute change of heart?

"Breathe, man, you're a wreck." Tom's lips twitched. "Remember. You have her shoes."

Aiden rolled his eyes toward his friend. Tom would never let him forget. Ever. He'd thank Emily for that later, but it loosened him up, at least for a moment as the processional proceeded.

Jenna arrived at the altar, accompanying her bright smile with a subtle wink.

"Quit flirting with my wife," Tom whispered, barely moving his lips. "Get your own."

Aiden almost laughed, appreciating Tom for lightening the mood. "Working on it."

The music changed as Jenna took her place, and his breath caught as Emily stepped into view, pausing before she lifted her chin. His very own fairy princess, her vivid green eyes sparkling as they met his. The current running between them kept him riveted as she floated down the rose petal-strewn aisle.

The smile swept across his face as emotions flooded him. He felt a touch of relief at seeing her, but mostly he felt overwhelming love, his heart pounding and drowning out everything. There was only Emily, and every moment of love and pain seemed worth it to get to this moment in time.

Their gazes locked, and he recognized the look on her face. It was the one he'd longed to see. The complete surrender to her own feelings, love brimming her eyes, a secretive smile on her lips meant only for him, her steps never faltering as she approached. After a brief pause at the bottom of the steps as Nina kissed her cheek and murmured in her ear, Emily reached for Aiden's hand.

He grasped her fingers as his eyes met Nina's for a moment, taking in her small, satisfied nod that said one thing. *Treasure my little girl.*

Aiden's heart skipped a beat as Emily smiled at him. "You look gorgeous." He blinked hard, willing himself not to let the emotions overwhelm him. "I love you."

Her eyes glistened. "I love you."

They joined hands as the minister cleared his throat and spoke. The words washed over Aiden and he tried to concentrate and respond as needed. Her hands felt warm and alive between his, but he couldn't accept he was standing here with the love of his life, committing to her forever.

When the time came, he slipped on the ring, giving her fingers a light squeeze before she did the same for him. The unfamiliar weight of the shiny platinum felt strange but reassuring. He gazed at their entwined hands, catching the glint and sparkle of the diamonds on hers.

"You may kiss your bride."

Aiden cupped her cheeks, leaning down to capture her soft, full lips. He put every ounce of his love for this amazing woman into the kiss, marveling at the softness of her mouth, how wonderful she smelled, and he lost his sense of space and time. Her hand wrapped around his neck, holding him to her.

Tom cleared his throat, pulling him back into the present, and he straightened. "You always have to be the center of attention." His friend chuckled.

Aiden smiled and turned, pausing for the multitude of pictures. After forever and a flurry of flashes, they strolled down the aisle, followed by the rest of the wedding party. He laid a hand over hers, glancing at her as they arrived at the entrance.

Her eyes sparkled as she returned the look. "Pictures, right?"

"Uh-huh."

"Too bad." She winked.

The wedding planner and her assistant greeted them with Aiden's coat and her wrap. "The limo is waiting." She ushered them down the steps toward the waiting car with the wedding party right behind them.

"Congrats." Tom produced a bottle of expensive champagne and popped the cork before the limo even left the curb.

"To the bride and groom." Joel lifted his glass.

The glasses clinked as everyone joined in the toast.

Emily linked arms with Aiden, taking a tiny sip of the champagne.

"That was perfect." Jenna grinned. "So beautiful. Nina and Grace were weeping. Even Paul and Caroline looked like they might shed a tear or two."

Aiden shook his head. "I find that hard to believe. I mean, Nina and Gramma, sure, but Caroline? Never mind. Thank you for making this a special day for us and for all of your help in planning and supporting us through it. We appreciate it."

Ryan raised his glass. "Back at you. You've been there for us, many times. We're happy to be here, and we wish you both a lifetime of happiness and a healthy family."

Tom nodded. "You're the closest I'll ever have to a brother, Aiden. Emily, welcome to the family."

"Thank you." Emily sniffled, blotting her eyes with a tissue. "You need to stop, or I'll be weepy in the pictures."

Jenna pulled out two wrapped bars and snagged two water bottles, handing one to Emily before opening one herself. "Have this. It'll keep you energized."

"You didn't bring those for everyone?" Ryan focused on the treat as Emily ripped opened the package.

Jenna patted her belly. "You can wait, but Emily and I need to snack. It's my job to take care of the bride." She grinned at his downcast face, opening the bag and tossing a bar to him. "Anyone else?"

Emily bit into hers while Aiden lifted her feet onto his lap.

"What are you doing?"

"Changing your shoes." He slid the heels from her feet. "You can't do outdoor pictures in these during the winter." It had taken some doing, but he'd managed several touches to make her day extra-special

"These are amazing." Emily threw back her head and laughed as he slid on the light blue suede dress boots. "My feet and I both thank you."

⌒≺

Emily massaged Aiden's cheek with her fingertips. "My face is frozen from all the smiling. Good thing we have a break." She peeled off her suede boots and rested her feet on his lap.

They'd taken what felt like a million pictures and assembled a receiving line. Now they relaxed in a private room, enjoying a peaceful interlude while their guests mingled and found their seats.

"I have permanent spots in front of my eyes." He massaged her feet, grateful they had a quiet moment before the reception.

"That feels divine." She sighed and closed her eyes. "Thank you for all the amazing gifts, and for making this day so incredible."

"It's been an amazing ride, and it's not over yet. Plenty more to come."

A soft tap sounded at the door and Tom looked in. "Show time."

"Ready?" Aiden helped Emily to her feet.

The rest of the wedding party appeared and Jenna fussed with Emily's dress, adjusting it before they preceded Emily and Aiden from the room.

Aiden restrained Emily for a moment, his pulse rate increasing as she lifted her beautiful green eyes to his. "I love you." He brushed her lips with his. "Now, time to face the masses."

"They're playing our song." A soft smile appeared as the wedding planner motioned them to enter the reception.

They'd no sooner arrived at their seats than the tinkling of the glasses began. Aiden raised his brows before kissing Emily, giving her a small dip and receiving several wolf whistles.

⌐≼

"We'll starve to death." Aiden laughed as Emily tried for a bite of her dinner as yet another round of tinkling glasses abated.

"I'm missing out. These caterers were a fantastic choice." She raised a brow. "Hey, don't laugh. I'm eating for two."

He patted her hand. "Take your time. It's our day, so they can talk and entertain themselves while we eat. After all, it's their fault we're not finished."

"True." She took another bite. "I should enjoy it. I doubt I'll be pampered every day of my life."

"Maybe not, but I sure will try." Aiden lifted his fluted glass and tapped hers.

A smile twitched at the corner of her mouth. "I always suspected you were one of those closet romantics."

"Never." He kept his face straight but she quirked her brow. "Fine," he whispered. "It's our secret."

Aiden surveyed the room. Conversation flowed, and the decorating had been exceptional, giving the exact relaxed and elegant ambiance they'd hoped for. Emily called it romantic and wistful.

After a few heartfelt speeches from the wedding party, it was time for their first dance. Aiden escorted Emily onto the floor as the first notes of their song drifted through the air.

After the first couple of turns, he wrapped his arms around her, and she melted into him, her head resting on his shoulder. The reality sank in. He was dancing with his wife. He marveled at how sweet she smelled and her warm breath against his neck. This was one dance he wished could go on forever.

When Paul cut in for the father-daughter dance, Aiden invited his grandmother to the floor. Gramma Grace was the one who'd been there when he'd needed her. She'd raised him, shared the holidays, all while his mother had been sunning herself on some far-off tropical island.

"Can I have a dance with my son?" Caroline asked after the initial dances were complete. "This has been a beautiful day. Thank you for letting me join you. It's not been easy, but … I love you." She kissed his cheek.

Aiden didn't know what to say. She'd been a non-entity, an under-involved presence in his life. He couldn't bring himself to respond, only kissing her cheek before Tom claimed Caroline for a dance.

"Can I cut in?" Aiden tapped Chase on the shoulder.

"Yeah." Chase stepped back, allowing Savannah to take Aiden's hand.

"I'm happy you and Emily are married." Savannah stretched to kiss his cheek. "She looks gorgeous."

"She does." He glanced across the room to where Emily was dancing with Joel. "How do you feel about having a stepmother?"

"Fortunately, she's not the wicked type. I love having her with us."

"Good." As the song ended, he pressed a kiss to her cheek. "You look beautiful," he said. "Thank you, Savannah."

"For what?"

"For being you. I love you. Now go and have fun, but not too much fun."

Savannah giggled. "I'll be good, I promise. We'll listen to Gramma Grace and I'll be extra-good while you're away. Emily will love the honeymoon."

"Go. Enjoy the time with your friends."

She headed to her table, a smile on her face. He'd miss her, but she'd be in good hands while they were away.

Jenna appeared, reaching for his hand. "I need a dance with my brother." She pulled him onto the floor.

Jenna sure felt like his sister. He wished he'd been more open with her, but perhaps things happened for a reason. He couldn't imagine his life any other way. Any different choice and he wouldn't be in the here and now with Emily.

"It turned out so well." Jenna glanced around. Most of the guests were up dancing or socializing. "I bet you're glad it's done."

"It's been stressful, even with a planner and all the wonderful support. Jenna, thank you for getting her here. Until I saw her walking up that aisle …"

"Oh, honey, this has been rough, but she got herself here. It's worked out how it should. I wish I could take back all the grief we gave you and that we'd supported you better. Your family, Gramma Grace excepted, has been little use."

"Ahh, Jenn. It's bygones. Let's move on. I should've been more open with you. I appreciate how much help you've been in putting this together. I will forever be grateful for your interference. Without your little matchmaking game, we might not be here."

"Oh, no, you two would have found your way. It's meant to be. If I hadn't brought you back together, the baby would have. Emily's loved you through every moment. Never doubt it. She conquered her fear and overcame her reservations about marriage. Now hold her close, and never let her go."

"How'd you get so wise?"

Jenna shrugged. "Must be all the brilliant friends I have. Maybe my fabulous husband's wisdom is affecting me." She patted his cheek. "You and Tom are a lot alike. You're both good men."

"And you're the best sister I could ever ask for. Thank you for everything today. It was perfect."

"Anything for you. Go dance with your wife and your guests. I've monopolized too much of your time, and everyone is lining up for their time with the groom."

Aiden opened the door, tugging Emily in behind him. The moment they were inside, he wrapped her in his arms. "This has been the best day."

"It was magical." Emily's warm breath wafted against his neck.

After another long, deep kiss, he turned to survey the room. A heart-shaped display of rose petals adorned the king-sized bed, and a crystal vase with two dozen long-stemmed red roses sat on the small table, along with an expensive bottle of champagne, two champagne flutes, fresh strawberries, and a variety of other treats. Their overnight bags were on the suitcase stand and the room was littered with gold, red, and cream candles.

"This is astounding."

"The perfect finish to an incredible day." Aiden glanced around. Every little detail was impeccable.

Emily slid off her shoes and sank onto the bed. "Did you do this?"

"With a little help from our awesome wedding party."

"Hmmm, so modest. You thought of everything. I only hoped it could go this smoothly."

"I did my best. You're only getting one wedding, so I hope it was everything you ever dreamed."

"It was." She patted the bed. "Join me."

He loosened his tie as he sat.

Emily wrapped her arms around his neck and stared into his eyes. "Thank you, it was amazing, flawless, and extraordinary. I love you so much."

Aiden pulled her to her feet, admiring how the fabric of her dress clung to her in all the right places. "You look gorgeous, my amazing wife." He held her at arm's length, allowing his eyes to rove over her.

"Perhaps you'd help me out of this dress, my wonderful husband." Emily smiled at him.

"My pleasure." He slid the strap of her silky dress off her shoulder, nuzzling against her neck. "You smell so good."

"Lavender." Emily tipped her head to allow him better access.

"Delicious." The dress slid into a pool around her feet as he dropped kisses across her shoulders. His heart raced at the sight of her lacy lingerie. "You took the blue thing to a new level. I approve," he murmured against her smooth, creamy skin.

"A little gift from Jenna and Alex." She stepped back and performed a slow turn.

"You look as beautiful out of the dress as you did in it."

"I don't know how I ever got lucky enough to have you in my life."

"I feel the same way." He placed his palms on her cheeks. "We're forever, Emelia."

Chapter 27

Emily

Emily's eyes fluttered open, her body wrapped in his arms. Contentment and joy flooded her entire being. Her husband spooned against her back, one arm curved around her belly and a hand splayed across her skin. It was cozy and comforting.

She lifted his hand, staring at the platinum band adorning his ring finger. Her mouth curved upward as she brought his hand up and pressed it to her lips. She entwined her fingers with his, holding them against her chest, snuggling down and enjoying his warm breath tickling her neck.

Her eyes drifted closed as she savored her first morning as Aiden's wife after the perfect wedding day.

"Good morning, my lovely wife." Aiden's soft, sleepy voice whispered in her ear. "Sleep well?" He squeezed her gently.

"I had an amazing sleep, but maybe good afternoon would be more accurate."

"It's only after ten. Mmm, I could do this every day for the rest of my life. It's perfect to wake up with my wife in my arms." He nibbled on the nape of her neck.

"Now you'll never get rid of me." Emily turned her head enough to accept his kiss. "I never want to leave this bed. I'm so comfortable, cuddling with my husband."

"Mmmhmm, except we have a flight to catch. I'll order room service. What do you want for breakfast?" He ran his hand over her belly.

Emily lounged beside him with closed eyes. She listened to the low warm tone of his voice as he ordered an array of delectable treats. Her tummy rumbled and the baby turned, creating a feeling of flitting butterflies. "Baby's performing somersaults in excitement."

Aiden replaced the receiver and rolled toward her, searching for the small movements. A grin appeared as he located a tiny limb. "Found you." He slid down, placing a kiss over the tiny bump the baby created on her belly. "Morning, little one." After dropping a few more kisses, he rested his cheek against her bare skin.

"More entertaining than Where's Waldo is Where's Baby." Emily ran her fingers through his hair. "This kid will recognize Daddy."

"That's the plan." He tracked the movement with his hand, pressing gently as the baby kicked.

"When do we need to check in at the airport?" She propped herself up on the pillows as he continued to caress her belly.

"The car will pick us up around eleven thirty. Excited?"

"I can't wait to find out where we're going."

"Soon. Let's shower before breakfast. It's cold and your hair takes forever to dry." He rolled out of bed, wandering naked toward the bathroom. "Join me?" He waggled his brows before disappearing through the doorway.

She smiled and wiggled out of bed, padding after him.

⌒≼

Emily gazed at the skyline and the river below, one hand resting on her belly. It seemed like a fairy tale she'd stayed at the most expensive hotel in town for even one night. He'd insisted. *Go big, Emily, enjoy it. I want nothing but special memories of this day. We're only doing this once.* Even if this wasn't Aiden's first marriage, she was determined it would be his last.

Aiden nuzzled against her neck, pressing gentle kisses to her sensitive skin. "Our car's waiting. Alex and Joel will be by to pick up our bags. Suitcases for our trip are at the airport." He tucked his wallet and both passports into his pocket. "Let's go." He entwined their fingers as he led her to the elevator, and through the front doors of the hotel.

Emily pressed a hand to her mouth at the sight of the antique Bentley Limo awaiting them. "Aiden." The chauffeur opened the back door, and she slid inside, Aiden following behind her. "This is amazing. Thank you, mi vida." She rewarded him with a long kiss.

"We couldn't have one yesterday given the size of the wedding party, so … since you've always wanted to ride in one."

The driver pulled into traffic and they cruised toward the airport, turning north on I-294.

"Our driver's lost. The airport's that way." Emily pointed over her shoulder.

"He knows where he's going." Aiden linked their hands.

Emily's eyes widened when she spotted the sign for Executive Airport, and they drove through the security gates, making their way onto the tarmac. When they pulled up alongside a sleek white jet, tears sprang to her eyes. "Wow. A private plane?"

"One stop in Boston and we're off to faraway destinations."

"Boston?" Emily took his hand as he led her up the steps. "Oh." She stepped in to find Tom, Jenna, Savannah, and Chase on board. "We're dropping you in Boston?"

"The plane belongs to Hamilton Grayson. It's our most recent acquisition." Tom wiggled his brows. "As managing partner, I insisted on being here for the first flight, plus we needed a ride."

"I realized you would fly home, but …" Emily was almost speechless. "You guys bought a jet?"

"Isn't this amazing?" Savannah hopped in excitement. Her eyes were wide but Chase sat in stunned silence. "You should see this." She dragged Emily through the plane to the back. "There's even a bedroom and there's a kitchen stocked with food and drinks."

Emily glanced at Jenna. "Did you know about this?"

"The boys were secretive about the purchase. Wait till you get a load of the other surprise that comes along with the plane."

"What?"

"Tom and Aiden both got pilot's licenses." Vanna almost squealed.

Emily stared at Aiden. "You can fly this thing?"

"We've both been working on our licenses for a while, and now Tom and I both have enough hours to fly on our own. Tom and I are flying to Boston, and we'll pick up the pilot and co-pilot there." He laughed at her expression. "Want to sit in the jump seat while we take off?"

"I do." Vanna jumped to her feet. "Oh, pick me."

Emily waved her toward the front. "I'm sure I'll have another chance. Talk about keeping secrets." She buckled her seatbelt, leaning back in the comfortable seat.

Vanna disappeared into the cockpit with Aiden and Tom while Chase sat a few seats away, playing on the built-in entertainment center.

Jenna smiled. "How does it feel to be Mrs. Hamilton?"

"Incredible. My cold feet and nerves all seem so silly. Waking up this morning, after last night—" She glanced over, aware Chase was soaking up every word. She changed the course of the conversation. "At work, I'm Dr. Anderson, but for the next week, I'll enjoy being Mrs. Hamilton. I can't wait to see where we're spending our honeymoon."

"I thought you'd be away for three weeks?" Chase asked, barely glancing up from whatever he was shooting on-screen.

Emily frowned. "No, only a week." She shot a look at Jenna, who only shrugged. "Why do you think it's three weeks, Chase?"

The teen shrugged. "Must have misheard." He squinted at the screen before volleying another round.

Emily peeked at Jenna.

"It's nothing." Jenna sighed as the plane taxied down the runway. "Here we go. Your husband is flying this plane. He won the coin toss, much to Tom's disappointment." She sipped from her water bottle, resting a hand on her rounded belly. "Husband. How does that sound?"

"Scary. Both that I have a husband and that he's flying a damn jet. No one would ever accuse Aiden of not keeping his mouth shut. This is a major purchase, you'd think he would have said 'hey, honey, by the way, do you mind if I spend …'" Emily frowned. "How much does a Gulfstream even cost?"

"No idea. Didn't ask as the law firm funded the acquisition. Tom doesn't ask permission to make purchases for the firm, and neither will Aiden. Anyway, these secrets are good. He's done his best to make this trip special, so enjoy it. Go along for the ride. Your life has changed.

"Do I have a choice?" Emily sipped her ice water.

"No, but you knew who you were marrying."

As the tarmac slipped by and the jet rose into the air, the phrase 'you knew who you were marrying' ran in a loop in her mind. The firm had to be doing well for the two men to be investing in expensive toys such as private airplanes, and it was a brand new one based on the immaculate interior and new car smell.

They leveled off and a few minutes later Savannah returned to the main cabin. "That was amazing." She dropped onto the sofa beside Chase. "My dad said you could sit in the jump seat for the landing if you wanted."

"Why, so he can toss me out and call it an aviation accident?" Chase muttered.

Emily smothered a laugh. Although they'd included him in the wedding and paid for the flights and accommodations, Chase had a residual fear of Aiden. Like it was a game where Aiden tried to coerce Chase into relaxing and dropping his guard.

"You're paranoid." Vanna elbowed him in the ribs. "Get over it."

Chase cast a doubtful glance at Vanna, his gaze cutting toward Emily.

She pretended not to be listening, concentrating on the glass in her hand.

Jenna raised her brows. "What's the deal?" she whispered. "The kid is terrified of Aiden. That's weird."

Emily waved off the question, shaking her head. No way would she embarrass the girl by disclosing details. She hadn't been home at the time, but one afternoon Aiden had walked in on something happening between Savannah and Chase, and now the boy expected retribution for the unfortunate episode.

Savannah and Chase seemed involved in the video game on the built-in screen, heckling each other and play wrestling.

"Jenna? This is super personal, but did you sign anything before you married Tom?"

"Like what?" Her friend turned her full attention to the question.

"Well, Tom owns half the law firm." Emily shrugged, "Did he ever suggest a prenuptial agreement? Is that too intrusive?"

"Tom didn't ask me to sign one, but I offered. He said absolutely not." Jenna tilted her head. "Did Aiden ask you for one?" she whispered.

"He didn't even bring it up, though James did. Maybe the pictures were about not having a pre-nup. I only have a vague idea of what Aiden owns and how much he makes. Not that he's hidden it, but it's never been important."

Her friend's eyes widened. "You don't have any clue?"

"I'm an idiot." Emily bowed her head, her hair covering her burning cheeks. "We talked about it briefly when we were discussing the wedding expenses."

"I can see him keeping it to himself when you worked with him at the hospital. Nobody there knows much about his family." Jenna patted her arm.

"I never thought about it, and until now I've earned enough to support myself. It's naïve for me to be clueless about his finances."

"Don't be scared to talk to Aiden." Jenna regarded her friend. "Remember being part of the Hamilton family is like swimming in a tank full of sharks. Sooner or later, you'll have a bite taken out of you. Don't let anyone ask you to sign or commit to anything without talking to Aiden and always ask Tom if you need legal advice. Aiden doesn't keep many secrets from Tom." Jenna turned in her seat to face Emily. "Promise me."

"I promise."

"I'd hate to see you make a huge mistake and keep what I said in mind. Sharks. Vicious, man-eating ones."

"I married a shark?" Emily laughed. "Now you tell me."

"Not Aiden. His family. Big difference. I often wonder if they switched him at birth because he's nothing like his dad or his grandfather. You can trust him, but don't put too much faith in anyone else, even your new mother-in-law. She popped out of the woodwork right as Aiden married and she's fighting with James over assets. Maybe it's genuine, perhaps it's not. You notice Aiden hasn't rolled out the red carpet for her. He allowed her to be there, but he has reservations."

Emily nodded as the seat belt indicator lit up. Minutes later they were touching down onto the tarmac in Boston.

Aiden handed over his house keys to Tom and Jenna and everyone exchanged hugs and goodbyes.

"You be good, Vanna. I'm trusting you while we're gone." Aiden hugged the girl.

"You and Emily will have so much fun. Don't worry about a thing." Savannah turned to Emily, embracing her. "Go with it, he spent a ton of time arranging this," she whispered into Emily's ear.

"I will, honey. You take care and see you soon. Not sure when as it seems your dad has a few surprises in store for me."

"You'll die when you figure out where you're going."

The pilot and co-pilot boarded the plane and Aiden settled Emily into the jump seat and then took the co-pilot seat for takeoff. Her eyes widened as they glided off the runway. She'd never been in the cockpit of a plane, let alone for takeoff.

Once they were at cruising altitude Aiden led her into the passenger cabin.

"What's this?" She pointed at the basket wrapped with a large satin bow on top.

"Now you get to find out where we're going." He sat opposite her. "Go ahead, unwrap it."

She pulled the ribbon and lifted the basket out of the cellophane. As she looked through the various items, she noticed a theme and her excitement grew. By the time she reached the bottom, she was bouncing in her seat. "Oh, Aiden." A tear dribbled down her cheek. "Paris?" She threw her arms around him. "This is incredible."

He hugged her. "I've marked a ton of places you've mentioned seeing, and a few you haven't. We're staying in an apartment not too far from the most incredible attractions. We'll have a busy week."

"This is so amazing."

"Why don't we prepare snacks in that amazing little kitchenette and we can figure out where to start? Then we'll sleep for a few hours. It'll be morning in Paris when we arrive, and it would be best to be well-rested so we can take advantage of our first day."

"You wonderful man. You think of everything."

Emily was in heaven. They spent the next two hours planning their first day, then cuddled on the bed. She drifted to sleep with a smile, dreaming of Paris.

～≼

From the moment the plane landed, the visit was magical. A private sedan whisked them from the airport to the elegant apartment. After a quick tour of the luxurious accommodations, they'd explored.

She walked thousands of stairs, not wanting to pass up the chance to climb the Notre Dame Bell Tower. She couldn't miss the museums, amazing food, shopping, the romantic strolls by the Seine, or the incredible nights snuggled up to her husband in their cozy apartment.

It had flown by, and today they were visiting the Louvre for the second time.

"I thought it was bigger." Emily tilted her head as she stared at the Mona Lisa, ensconced on the wall behind heavy glass.

"Everyone thinks that. The photos suggest it's a huge painting." Aiden studied the piece of art and then stared upward.

Emily followed suit, admiring the incredible mural on the ceiling. She couldn't fathom someone spending countless hours squinting at the ceiling and producing such beautiful and intricate work.

They walked hand-in-hand down the ornate hallway, stopping every few feet to inspect a new piece of artwork. From the moment she'd entered through the glass pyramid, she'd been entranced and stunned at how enormous the Louvre was in reality, and packed with paintings and sculptures.

The previous day they'd spent in Versailles. It took the best part of a day to see it, but Emily loved the entire experience, right down to their stroll through the ornate though snowy grounds. She could barely take it all in. "We must come to Paris again. A week is not enough."

"You're right. There's so much to see. I'd like to take you to Italy too." He smiled. "Time for ice cream."

"I'm getting so fat." She patted her belly. "My ass grew again, despite all the walking and stairs." She followed him out the door and they wandered along the Seine toward Ile St Louis.

"I love every inch of that beautiful ass."

"Until it grows to the size of Kansas." Emily shook her head. The hardest part of being pregnant for her was the weight gain. She'd worked so hard to stay slim over the years, and now her body was running rampant.

Aiden turned her toward him, looking serious. "It doesn't matter. I love you. Every single bit of you. Stop worrying. You're having a baby."

Emily bowed her head. It was like he could see her thoughts. "I'll never look the same. I understand why, but when my mom was pregnant the last time, my dad lost interest."

"Oh, Emily." He wound his arms around her. "I'm not him, and I won't lose interest. You're so beautiful with your baby belly, and I love the extra curves. I fell in love with you, not how you look. It's important you stay healthy and eat right. Quit obsessing over every single pound." He lifted her chin with his fingertip. "Em?"

Emily nodded. "It's hard. I love this baby, and I want to be a mom. I've never told you, but I struggled with eating when I was a teenager. Most of the time I'm okay, but some days it gets the better of me. I'm sorry," she whispered.

Aiden pulled her closer. "Don't be sorry. I'm glad you told me. Be yourself, it's all I ask."

"You're so good to me. I'm such an insecure, hormonal mess. You'll tire of it."

"Never. You don't have to be perfect so don't even try. We all have our issues and insecurities. I certainly have mine." He gazed into her eyes. "Remember our vows? I meant every word. I love you as you are. Right now. What we have is real and incredible and amazing and ..." He shrugged. "What else is there to say besides the obvious. Don't obsess. Your doctor will tell you if she's concerned about too much weight gain, but up to now, it's been too little."

The tears burned behind her eyes. This man offered true, complete, unconditional love. She wasn't sure how she'd gotten so lucky. "I'm trying not to let it overwhelm me."

"You're doing great." He linked his fingers with hers. "Come on, there's still lots to see before we say goodbye to Paris."

⌒≺

Emily looked up as Aiden joined her on the patio. It was chilly, but the view was amazing. He handed her a cup of hot tea, wrapping his arms around her as the Eiffel Tower lit up, the lights blinking and flashing. The past week had been something out of a dream. This was their last night, and she didn't want to go home.

"I wish we could stay forever." She sighed, leaning back against his chest.

"We'll come back one day, don't worry." He rested his cheek against her hair. "We have an early flight in the morning, so it's time to sleep."

"Do we have to? I'm imprinting this in my memory."

"We do, or I won't be able to pry you out of bed. Let's go." He led her into the apartment, securing the door behind them.

Chapter 28

Aiden

THE HONEYMOON WAS OVER AND Emily couldn't hide her disappointment. "I'm not ready to go home." She slumped lower in the seat, unable to keep the grouchy tone from her voice. "At least I can sleep stretched out and comfortable. I won't be squished into a coach cattle car. Even first class would be hard as it's difficult to get comfortable and sit for any length of time." She smothered a yawn with the back of her hand.

"Now you like the plane?" Aiden grinned. "Not such a bad expenditure, was it?"

"You convinced me on the way over here." She gave him a wicked grin. "The flight was … pretty good. Not sure I ever want to fly commercial again."

"Pretty good?" Aiden lifted a brow. "A terrific endorsement."

"You get what I mean." Emily patted his leg. "It was amazing. Is that better?"

"Oh, so flattering, thanks." He returned her eye roll. "Anyway, the plane belongs to the firm, not me."

"It's still incredible. I don't understand why the firm needs a jet, but I'm not complaining." She fidgeted, shifting in her seat. "Once we take off, it's time for a nap. You could join me."

"Perhaps. I could use a nap." He wiggled his eyebrows and winked.

"I might be up for … something." She closed her eyes. "My stomach always does this little flip when a plane takes off."

He took her hand, watching her face as the tarmac sped by outside the window. The flushed cheeks and glowing skin made her more beautiful than ever. Pregnancy suited her, he decided. Everything about her exuded health and vitality, despite the noticeable fatigue after their time in Paris.

Weightlessness overtook him as the plane soared upward. Once they reached altitude, the pilot turned off the seatbelt indicators, and they both stood and stretched.

Aiden held out his hand. "Come on, grouchy, let's rest. I hope you didn't overdo it in Paris."

"I might need a vacation to recover from our honeymoon."

"I'll see what I can do." Once they reached the back, they settled onto the bed. He smiled as she snuggled close, draping a leg over his and propping her belly against him. "I'm your personal body pillow."

"You kinda are. So comfy." Her eyelids drooped, her breathing becoming soft and even as she drifted to sleep.

When he awoke five hours later, Emily was still asleep, though now she clutched a pillow. It would be another four or five hours before they reached their destination. He wondered how she'd react to being kidnapped.

He rolled, watching her sleep before sliding off the bed. Once in the main cabin, he placed the gift box on the seat and visited the kitchen for coffee and snacks. He settled in a seat by the window and opened a journal.

An hour later, Emily appeared looking adorable with her tousled hair. "Hey." She lowered herself into the seat beside him, combing her fingers through her dark locks. "I woke up alone." After planting a kiss on his cheek, she ruffled his hair.

"You needed the rest."

"Sorry for being a grouch. What's this?" She pointed at the box. "More presents?"

Aiden shrugged. "Open it and find out. Can I get you something?" He grinned as she picked at his plate.

"The baby's hungry." She patted her belly and stole half of his sandwich. "You wouldn't deprive your child, would you?"

"There's a full fridge in the kitchen, food thief." He raised a brow but gave up and handed over the entire plate. "Enjoy. I'll make another."

"Good idea." She took another bite of the sandwich before drinking half of his water.

"I see how this will go. Can I get you anything else while I'm there?"

"Tea?"

By the time he returned, she'd set the empty plate aside and was fiddling with the ribbon on the box.

"Open it."

She glanced at him and then yanked on the ribbon. On top was a brochure. "Malé City. Maldives?" Her eyes widened as she spotted the resort brochure. "Are you teasing me with our next trip?"

"We haven't finished our honeymoon. We'll spend two weeks in The Maldives. You'll love it."

"A tropical paradise." She pressed a palm to her mouth.

"Surprise." Aiden winked. "Does it meet with your approval?"

"Are you kidding? You're the best husband in the entire world." She rewarded him with a long, deep kiss. "Another two weeks? How did you manage it? What about Vanna?"

"Ryan offered to stay with her."

"Chronically single, jet-setting, high-financier Ryan Hartmann is taking time out of his busy schedule to babysit? Are you insane?"

"Vanna's a teenager, not a baby." Aiden waved a hand. "Besides, she loves Uncle Ryan."

"Yeah, because he lets her get away with everything. How can you trust that irresponsible party-boy to take care of your daughter?"

"*That* irresponsible party-boy would protect my baby girl to his very last breath. He's more than what you see on the surface." Aiden took her hand. "Give him a chance and you'll see. Now relax, it's several more hours on the plane. We'll explore Malé City for a couple days and then visit one of the islands and stay at a gorgeous resort where you can swim and sleep and eat to your heart's content."

"My heart is already content. I have you."

~≺

Emily gazed out the window, clutching his hand as the vista opened below them. "It's beautiful." She leaned closer to the window as they started their descent. The sunlight glinted off the crystal blue water and palm trees swayed in the breeze.

The seaplane touched down, and they alighted on the dock where they were greeted by the staff, their bags whisked to their private villa. Her delighted smile was all the reward he needed.

"What do you think?" He asked as they lounged on their private deck watching the sea life swim by through glass inserts in the floor.

"I'm speechless. Paris was incredible, but this is beyond." She wiggled closer, staring at the unobstructed view of the ocean. "I haven't been on many tropical holidays, and certainly not to a fancy resort. Who knew you could have your own pool when you're only five steps from the lagoon?"

He leaned in to kiss her. "I wasn't sure how you'd feel about being kidnapped."

"You can spirit me away to this place anytime. I love it."

The next few days were perfect, filled with snorkeling, couples massages, and decadent, delicious meals. Emily seemed enchanted by the underwater restaurant and was thrilled with the over-water villa. Her skin took on a sun-kissed glow, and she looked rested and content. She'd even donned the two-piece bathing suit Jenna packed for her, growing more comfortable with her expanding belly.

"Where are we going now?" Emily took his hand, letting him seat her in the boat.

"You'll see."

A few minutes later, they disembarked onto a private sand spit. Emily's eyes lit up at the sight of the table set up in the sand. A small fire pit was ready to be lit and there were various places to lounge as a couple.

"You're kidding." She threw her arms around him. "This is gorgeous. How many people get to dine alone on a private island? We can watch the sun go down over the ocean and gorge on seafood."

Aiden held her close. She was the key to everything he'd ever wanted, and her complete joy made the struggle worthwhile.

"Can I ask you something?" Emily traced his hand with a fingertip as they lounged on one of the many couches scattered around the sand. "Promise you won't get upset?"

He placed his palms on her cheeks, lifting her chin so she was looking him in the eye. "You can ask anything."

"Why didn't you want me to sign a legal agreement before we got married?"

"Like a prenuptial agreement?"

She nodded. "I would have signed one. I still would if you wanted."

"Damn James, right? He put this into your head?"

Emily flushed. "That day in the limo he made a comment about Tom not doing his job. I've always been too afraid to ask about finances because you're so private about it, but you have much to lose."

"There are many things I hold dear, but none of them are money."

"What if I wanted one?" Emily put her hand over his. "James thinks I'm in it for the money. And he's not the only one."

"I know who put that thought in your mind, but you can't listen to her, or to James. It's interesting how they've managed to guilt you into thinking we need legal agreements."

"We should have one."

"No." He shook his head while silently cursing Tiffany for her gold-digger comment. "As my wife, you're entitled to share everything."

"I've worked since I was a teenager to buy my clothes, put myself through medical school, and I've supported myself for over ten years. I'm not entitled to a damn thing." She rested a hand on her belly. "You'll always take care of our child and that's what matters. The rest is irrelevant. I don't even need to know what you have or own."

"Why not? When we get home, we'll discuss finances and add you to the title of my real estate."

"You don't have to do that."

"Yes, Emily, I do. This is our child, and you are my wife. I never want you to be without. James hit you with his demands when you'd be too frazzled to make a proper decision."

"Am I so easy to read?"

Aiden shrugged. "For him you are. You forget what he does. He deals with criminals. And not the ones charged with possession of two ounces of pot or petty theft. These are hardcore drug and human traffickers, pimps, murderers, members of the cartels and white-collar embezzlers. Over half of them have already done serious time in a Federal Penitentiary. He's learned some dirty tricks and made some unsavory connections in the criminal underworld. You hide little, and you're trusting. It makes you an easy target for my father's personal brand of intimidation."

"I should have told you about New York right away, but I didn't want to start something. Our relationship has been bumpy enough."

"Isn't that the truth." His lips twitched. "Interesting. This conversation is enlightening."

"What is? That I'm a clueless idiot who should have thought about this before I married you and not afterward? I have no idea how much you're worth, and I don't care, but the idea that people consider me a gold-digger makes me want to sign an agreement so you know I'm not."

"Ahh, Emily. You're so damn cute." He brushed her hair back from her face. "I'd never ask you to sign one of those stupid agreements. Those are for people marrying for the wrong reasons. Tom and I talked about it before he married Jenna and again about a month ago. You know our conclusion?"

Emily shook her head.

"That neither of us ever wanted to marry a woman if we needed the protection of legal agreements. If I thought you were a gold-digger, you wouldn't be part of my life." Aiden shook his head. "I trust you and I love you. If I can't share all that I have with the woman I love without jumping through legal hoops, then it's not much of a marriage."

"Now it's my turn to say interesting."

"Why?"

"You're so different from James, it's like you don't even belong to the same family. You're not angry with me?"

"No. And I'm thankful I'm nothing like James. I often wonder if I should thank him for being such a lousy and neglectful father. Anyway, if our marriage is to work, you can't be afraid to talk to me. You're so outspoken about some issues, yet so hesitant about others, it's confusing."

"The idea of having so much money is a foreign concept, and I don't know how to deal with it."

"You'll get used to it. When we get home, we'll get into the finances. For now, let's enjoy the rest of our vacation."

CHAPTER 29

Emily

As the elevator rose toward their floor, Emily rested her head against Aiden's chest, closing her eyes. The honeymoon had been what she'd envisioned and hoped for—a perfect and romantic escape with her new husband. It had been an amazing three weeks, but she was exhausted.

The door slid open, and they stepped into silence. It was mid-morning and Alex was on Savannah duty. Emily figured the two had taken Daniel to the park.

"I'm happy to be home." She gazed at Aiden. "The trip was incredible."

"It'll be heaven to sleep in our own bed, and I missed Vanna."

Emily nodded. They'd been in touch during their trip, but mostly by quick texts with several video chats thrown in. The teen had been under constant adult supervision, so they hadn't worried, but Emily was used to her stepdaughter's presence and being away for so long had been more difficult than expected. "Should we order in?"

He shrugged. "Perhaps the fridge is stocked. How about you check out the food situation, and I'll drop this stuff in our bedroom."

As Aiden headed down the hall with the luggage, Emily wandered into the kitchen. In the fridge, she spotted the pan of lasagna on the top shelf, the foil-wrapped garlic bread, and the lettuce, washed, and torn, all ready to add the Caesar dressing. A note perched on top:

Welcome home. We'll be back around five. Dinner is ready for the oven. Bake at 350 for an hour.

"So?" Aiden came up behind her, wrapping his arms around her waist which seemed to have expanded over the past three weeks.

"They made dinner. Put it in the oven to bake, and voilà." She covered his hand, which now rested on her ample belly. "We have the best friends in the entire world."

"I love that woman. I have something to show you." Aiden led her down the hallway into the room they'd picked for the baby. "Look."

Emily's eyes lit up as she spotted the boxes stacked in the middle of the room and the fresh paint on the walls. "I love the color. You were right, it'll work for a boy or a girl." She patted her belly. "Should we find out?"

"Up to you." He ran a hand over the wall. "He did a fantastic job."

"I thought you'd be jumping up and down in excitement." She narrowed her eyes as he looked away. "Aiden?"

"What?" He turned toward her, smiling.

"You already know." Emily grabbed his arm as he fought the grin. "You dirty rat. Did you see the last time we were in for a scan?"

"See what?"

"Wipe that smug grin off your face. You've known for weeks and you didn't say a damn word." Emily crossed her arms and glared. "No fair."

"Who said life was fair?" He wiggled his brows, the grin widening.

"Tell me."

"Uh-uh. You said you didn't want to know." He hesitated, running a fingertip down her cheek. "Besides, I only caught a glimpse so I could be wrong."

"I knew it," she muttered, and then attacked the ticklish spot under his ribs.

"Oh no, you don't. You know who'll win this." He scooped her up like she weighed no more than a feather and carried her from the room, smirking as she struggled to break free.

"Put me down." She wiggled half-heartedly, enjoying the security of his muscular arms wrapped around her.

"Not until you behave." With one hand, he immobilized her wrists and dropped her onto their bed. He pinned her with both hands above her head and leaned in, hovering like he was about to kiss her.

Emily parted her lips, anticipating the moment their mouths would meet. His warm breath wafted against her face and a shiver raced down her spine.

He let out a low laugh and turned his head to the side. "Give?" he whispered against her ear.

"I give," she murmured, blinking at him as she ceased to struggle and relaxed her body. She batted her lashes. "Such a tease." As his grip loosened, she slid her hands up his arms, lingering over his biceps and caressing his smooth skin. Ever-so-slowly, she grazed her fingertips across his shoulders, entwining one hand into his hair, biting her lower lip and widening her eyes and then wetting her lips.

His pupils dilated and his eyes darkened, smoldering as his gaze rested on her mouth. He scanned her body, following by skimming a hand over her side. "Now who's a tease?" He brushed a strand of hair back from her face with a tenderness that made her ache.

Emily quivered under his touch as the heat rose between them. She pulled him toward her, sighing against his mouth. They shared a sweet and slow kiss that had her longing for more.

"So, so beautiful." He captured her lips again, this time the kiss was deeper and more passionate, creating a ripple of need within her.

Emily sucked in a breath as he nuzzled her neck, his warm, masculine scent surrounding her. She pressed her face against his soft, silky hair as her hands travel down his back, tracing his well-defined muscles with her fingertips before she skimmed one hand upward and curled it around his neck.

These were the moments when all the walls came down, and she knew she loved him more than she'd ever thought it was possible to love anyone.

Emily blinked, feeling disoriented and foggy, finally registering she was home in her own bed, the light dimming as the afternoon faded away. Her cheek rested against warm smooth skin, and Aiden's arm curled around her shoulders. She'd draped one of her legs over both of his, her belly propped against him.

The light brush of his fingertips on her arm alerted her he was awake. She tilted her chin. "How long have you been trapped?"

"Not long. I drifted off. It's so comfortable having you cuddled up to me, I never want to move. And it gives me an excuse to stay in bed with my wife." He ran his fingers through her locks and kissed her. "Your hair has grown." He twirled a strand around his finger, lifting his hand and letting the curl drop against her shoulder.

"All these hormones. Everything's growing."

"You look amazing. I love these sexy curves." The fingertips of his free hand grazed over her hip and lingered on her belly. "Twenty-six weeks and counting. We should get the baby's room ready."

"Mmmhmm." Emily ran her fingers up and down his arm. "So, spill."

"What?" He tucked an arm behind his head, peering down at her.

"Is it a boy or a girl?" Emily poked his side.

"Will you get all crazy if I tell you?"

Emily pondered his words. If he told her, would she regret it? Being surprised would be amazing, but they could choose names and she could buy gender appropriate clothing, plus they could finish decorating the baby's room. "I want to know."

He leaned in close. "Are you sure?"

"Don't tease." She swatted him. "We're in this together."

"True." His happy smile didn't give her any clues, and he slid down to kiss her belly. "Should we let Mommy in on the secret? One kick for yes and two for no."

Emily laughed. "Poor kid. You're forcing our baby to take sides?"

"How about one kick for girl, and two kicks for boy?"

"Quit drawing this out and tell me." She played with his hair as he kissed her belly again.

He crawled up and whispered against her ear, "I can't wait to meet our son."

She fought her own grin. "Are you happy?"

"I'll be thrilled with either. It's more important our baby is healthy and we get you through this pregnancy. But what guy doesn't want a son?"

"How sure are you?"

"Ninety-five percent? We'll ask Dr. Ritchie to confirm my diagnosis at our appointment tomorrow. Don't throw out either name list yet."

"Do you have a favorite name?"

"Yes, but why don't we get our second opinion before we decide."

"Deal. Let's assemble the crib and work on the room."

"Alright, get dressed and we can start."

⌒≼

The room was taking shape. As a team, they'd built the crib and the change table and moved the dresser and armchair into place.

"Someone has energy." Alex appeared in the doorway, bouncing Daniel on her hip. "You'd think after all the sun, surf, and extracurricular activities, you wouldn't have the energy to assemble furniture."

"Nah, we slept most of the way home, plus we had a nap in our silent apartment." Aiden stood and stretched.

"Oh, the jet. How was it?" Alex smirked.

"Both the flight and the honeymoon were amazing."

Savannah bounded into the room. "I missed you guys." She hugged Aiden, then Emily. "Your belly grew." The girl rubbed it.

"Well, I fed h—" Emily caught herself. "Them enough."

Savannah arched a brow, but the asked, "Was it amazing?"

"Gorgeous. I'm thrilled we visited Paris, and The Maldives is beyond incredible."

"I'd love to go again. You look great." Alex set Daniel onto his feet and held out her arms for hugs. "I smell dinner."

"It'll be ready soon." Aiden kissed her cheek. "Thanks for taking care of Vanna." He scooped Daniel into his arms. "How's my little man?" The raspberries he blew on the boy's tummy were rewarded with a volley of giggles.

Emily smiled as he tossed the boy in the air.

"Aiden will be an amazing dad." Alexis slid an arm around her friend. "Right from day one, he's been incredible with Daniel. Last summer he braved the nasty diaper without even being asked."

"I've seen much worse than a little baby poop. It's not a big deal." Aiden tossed Daniel into the air again.

"You'd think a diaper was a toxic waste dump based on Joel's reaction. And don't even consider telling me what you've seen." Alex shuddered. "Yuck. I've no idea how you two stomach it."

"Anyone hungry?" Aiden balanced the boy on his hip and disappeared down the hall with Savannah trailing behind.

CHAPTER 30

Aiden

A IDEN USHERED EMILY INTO THE Chicago offices of Hamilton Grayson and waved at Sadie, Tom's assistant, as they approached his office. He peered inside, spotting the empty chair behind his friend's desk.

"He's in a meeting but said to wait here for him." Aiden wandered into the office.

"I can't get over this place." Emily gazed through the bank of glass.

He wrapped an arm around her, letting his free hand rest on her belly. Some days it felt like a dream. Here he was with his wife, expecting their first child, and life was fantastic. He couldn't wait until they broke the big news. "Just wait. Things are about to get even better."

"Waiting is a lot to ask. You're so secretive." She stood on tiptoe, pressing her warm sweet lips to his.

"Hey. None of that in my office." Tom leaned against the doorframe, a wide smile on his face. "Sadie rounding up refreshments?"

"I imagine so. Everything ready?" Aiden guided Emily to the chairs and seated her.

"This isn't something Aiden needs to do." Emily peered at Tom across the large desk.

"You're wrong. It's important we implement this now you're married."

"None of this is bad." Aiden gripped her hand. "Do you want separate counsel?"

She shook her head. "If I can't trust my husband, I have big problems. Let's get it done."

Tom wasted no time in presenting the paperwork. "Here are the title transfers for Martha's Vineyard, the Chicago penthouse, and the Boston apartment. It excludes the Lake Forest house as Grace has joint ownership."

Emily frowned. "You have holdings with Gramma Grace?"

"I'm on her accounts in case she becomes incapacitated. She needs someone trustworthy to ensure she's taken care of. Otherwise, James would get himself appointed. That would be disastrous."

"Makes sense." An icy shiver ran down Emily's spine. That day in New York still gave her nightmares, but she shook it off and accepted the pen, signing each paper as Tom pointed.

Tom placed another document in front of Emily. "Take a few minutes to read through your will. I'm surprised you've never done one before."

"I've never had anything worth leaving. Nobody wanted my pile of medical school loans." Emily laughed. "Now I have kids, houses, and a husband. Never thought I'd see the day."

Tom smirked. "Kind of sneaks up on you, right? We were about to give up on your man, then you came along." Tom signed and stamped the documents.

Aiden pulled out a check and placed it onto the desk. "Thanks for paying Vanna's tuition while we were away. The wedding scrambled my mind."

Emily laughed. "Getting your own dose of baby brain, are you?"

"Perhaps, though now the wedding and honeymoon are over, my focus is returning."

"While Emily reads, this is for you." Tom slid a paper across the desk. "It's sweet."

Aiden raised a brow as he scanned the document. "This is their first offer?"

"Mmmm, and I'm tempted. It would thrill Jenna if I worked less and I wouldn't mind more time at home."

"Did you talk to your parents?"

"They're cool with it, as is Grandmother."

Emily watched the two of them lobby back and forth. "What is going on with you two? I feel like this is a huge deal, and you'll unload it on us tonight."

"You'd be correct on both accounts. It's life altering, especially for Tom and Jenna."

"Not planning to share?" Emily rubbed his arm.

"Where's Jenn?" Aiden asked. "I think we should discuss this before dinner. Maybe we could meet her at the restaurant early."

"Good idea. I'll give Joel a heads up and he can tip off Alex. This is picking up steam on us, buddy." Tom tapped a text into his phone. A minute later it buzzed and he glanced at the screen. "All set. Jenn will join us in half an hour." He pointed to the page in Aiden's hands. "Bring that."

Aiden ushered Emily into the restaurant, winding through to the private dining room they'd booked for the evening.

"Jenna." He gave his friend a long hug. "You look great."

"I feel amazing." Jenna returned the embrace, then turned to Emily. "I'd catch up, but Tom can't sit still."

"Once you get a look, you won't either," Tom said. "But none of it leaves this room. It's not a done deal until we discuss and negotiate further. Show them."

Jenna plucked the paper from Aiden's hand. Her eyes widened.

Emily let out a choked gasp. "Wait. What? Is that? Are those?" She pointed a trembling finger at the paper. "That's the first offer?"

"We have a huge client list, great lawyers, and a major reputation." Tom patted Jenna's knee. "We've been evaluating the feasibility of opening a second shop in Boston, and Joel wants to buy in. We'd form a new firm called Hamilton, Grayson, and Nichols. We're about eighty percent of the way in planning, and we wanted to run it by you. Joel's asking Alex if she'd be willing to move to Boston."

"No way." Jenna popped out of her seat. "Alex and Joel are moving to Boston and leaving me here by myself?"

Tom frowned. "Thanks, honey, I love you too."

She dropped her head into her hands. "I only meant that Alex and Emily will be in Boston and I won't."

"Or maybe you will." Tom raised a brow. "If we accept this buyout, we'll move. I was weighing the pros and cons, anyway. That's why we bought the jet, for commuting between Chicago and Boston, and for transporting partners."

"Why didn't I hear about this earlier?" Jenna crossed her arms, glowering at Tom.

"I didn't want to get everyone excited until we knew if it would work. No point in dredging things up if there was no possibility it would happen. Now we have an offer on the table, and we have everything in line." Tom squeezed her hand. "Would you be interested in moving? The buyout of Hamilton Grayson would give us more than enough money, and we can set up the new firm so I share more duties with Joel. I could spend more time at home."

Jenna's eyes brimmed with tears. "Aiden? What do you think?"

"I'm willing to sell, but it's for you and Tom to decide. I get a fatter bank account, but day to day it affects you and Tom more than me and Em."

"It's a huge decision. Can I think on it?"

Tom put his arms around her. "There will be plenty more discussions. You're my wife and my partner in life. I won't sell or make changes unless you'll be happy."

Alexis tapped on the door. "Hi." She blinked her shimmering blue eyes. "My husband dropped a massive bomb on me."

"Join the club." Jenna rose to give her a hug. "Sounds like we'll be having some interesting dinner conversation tonight."

Aiden slid under the covers as Emily slathered her belly with cream. "What's in that stuff? It smells delicious."

"Cocoa and Shea butter, along with other natural oils that reduce stretch marks. It does smell rather good." She finished her ritual before ambling to the bed, her gaze cutting to him and back to her task of plumping her pillows.

"Out with it."

"What?" She stared at him.

"Don't think I haven't noticed you ogling me like a damn zoo exhibit. What's on your mind? You don't think I should sell?"

"It's not my place to decide. I understand why you're deferring to Tom and Jenna. He's the one who puts in the hours to keep the firm running." She sank down onto the edge of the bed, her shoulders and back stiff.

"So what then?" He plumped his own pillow and flopped back. "Did I do something? Every time I touch you, you get all tense."

"I knew you were wealthy, but I'm in a serious state of shock. Why do you even have a job?" She threw her hands into the air. "When you left Chicago, I thought it was because you needed to work, but that is so clearly not the case. All we went through, and you could have stayed."

"I left because I lost my damn job and needed a meaningful one to utilize my skills." He folded his arms across his chest. "Being a spoiled wastrel lying around on a beach isn't my style. I busted my ass to be a doctor. No one gave it to me. I damn well earned it."

A wrinkle appeared in her brow, but she stared at him in confusion.

Aiden rolled over and flicked off the lamp on the bedside table. "Whatever." He buried his head in his pillow and closed his eyes, even though he knew he wouldn't sleep.

His mind buzzed. She'd tagged him as the rich boy which was the reason he avoided talking about his finances. The zeros on that paper made Emily believe he didn't need or deserve his career. He'd become the guy who'd had everything handed to him. The one who everyone assumed led a charmed life.

"Excuse me?" Emily tugged on his shoulder, forcing him onto his back. "Damn it, Aiden, I refuse to let you dismiss me."

He eyed her, unsure of what to say.

"You're not allowed to shut me out." She hovered barely inches from his face, her eyes glittering as she grasped his chin. "As your wife, I expect to be included in these big decisions. You say you want me to be your equal, so treat me that way. How long has this been going on with the firm?"

"Months." He shrugged.

"You didn't think to mention it?"

Aiden dropped a hand across his eyes, fighting the headache pounding his temples. "It started before we were back together. I first met with Tom about it that weekend you told me you were pregnant. It seemed like an inopportune moment to discuss firm business."

"Then what? It slipped your damn mind?"

Aiden sat, grasping her shoulders. "No, Emily. It didn't, but given how you're acting now, I'm glad I didn't tell you. I keep money situations to myself because it drives people insane."

"You didn't trust me?" Her eyes filled with tears.

"You're impossible. First you say you don't need to know how much I make, or what I own. Now you're all over my ass because we discussed selling the firm without consulting you. You saw the zeros on that paper and freaked out." He pushed off the bed, reaching for his jeans.

"You are not walking out on this." Emily snatched them from his hand, her green eyes blazing, her cheeks flushing a deep red. She dashed a hand across her face, blinking hard as she planted her feet, her mouth set in a grim line.

Aiden met her gaze, standing his ground. "Why is it okay to dismiss my need to have a fulfilling career?"

"What does that have to do it?"

"It has everything to do with it. You suggested I could work in some damn clinic wiping runny noses because I don't need the money. What? I'm just some pampered rich boy?"

"I've never thought of you that way. You're an amazing doctor who works hard." Emily sniffled and bowed her head, her bravado dissipating. "It hurt when you left me."

Aiden froze. They'd traveled full-circle, ending at the real reason she picked a fight. He cupped her cheeks in his palms. "I've protected you from the realities of my life. Allowing a woman in doesn't come easily, but I'm trying." He studied the face of this feisty, wonderful woman he'd fallen for. "Let's not fight. Just tell me what you want."

She stared, wide-eyed. "You're giving in?"

"Compromising with my wife isn't giving in. This isn't easy. It never has been and nothing worthwhile ever will be. Can't we live in our happy love bubble? Love our family and let the others figure out the law firm issue?"

"Happy love bubble?" The corners of her mouth twitched.

The silly expression achieved the intended results. He smiled and brushed his thumbs over her cheeks. "Never heard of it?"

She shook her head as her own smile appeared.

Aiden leaned closer. "Don't search for things to bring us down or create issues," he murmured. "True forgiveness doesn't allow take backs."

Emily rested her palms against his chest. "No turning your back. No going to bed angry, hiding, holding back, or running when things get rough. You hold things too close and keep too many secrets. Let me all the way in. I get it's difficult, but I'm trying so hard to earn the right."

"I promise. Do you?"

"I promise." Emily peered up at him.

"Riled up Emily is damn hot and sexy."

"Is she?" She brushed her hand over his hair. "Even with this big belly?"

"Your beautiful belly." Aiden rested his hands on either side, stroking it gently. "Always, Em."

She grinned. "So here we are, living in our happy love bubble. I'd love to learn the story behind that phrase. It's not something I ever imagined coming out of your mouth."

"It's borrowed. One day, I'll tell you."

"Deal. Happy love bubble it is."

The next morning Aiden wasn't as happy. The continuous dread of having to deal with James hung over him.

He didn't want to be boarding a train headed to New York, but here he was, his stomach in knots and a vague unease settling over him.

After tucking his bag into the overhead compartment, he relaxed into his seat and opened his laptop. The trip was only a few hours, but he'd work on his study. That would keep his mind off the planned confrontation.

Even a full hour of concentration was tough, and he stared out the window as the thoughts overtook him. Tom cautioned him about riling up James, but he couldn't let it rest, especially after his conversation with Jazlyn. He'd outright asked her why she'd been in the Vineyard. Her guilty silence made his anger rise.

"Seriously, Jaz? How much did he pay you?"

"It was stupid, but it wasn't a hardship. We had a good thing going for months, and I missed it. I missed you."

Even now it burned, though he shouldn't be surprised. Jazlyn had been introduced through their social circles and he'd taken a chance. She wasn't the type of girl he tended to date. He'd let his weakness for a beautiful and engaging woman overrule his common sense.

Their love affair had lasted several months before she flitted off on one of her fashion shoots and ended up in bed with the photographer. Commitment and fidelity weren't in her vocabulary. In his world, bad endings were inevitable.

Aiden squared his shoulders, keeping his charade of cool confidence as he followed the receptionist through the warren of offices, adjusting the cuff of his Armani power suit.

The receptionist raised a brow when he'd given his name, but she'd called James right away.

"Aiden?" James rose from behind his desk as Aiden was ushered inside. "I wasn't expecting you."

"You're sure about that?" Aiden ignored the proffered hand, pushing the door shut behind him. "The watchdogs inform you of my current whereabouts?"

James narrowed his eyes. The man's guilty tell was subtle but reminiscent of Thomas Hamilton. Aiden had seen it often enough in the later years of dealing with his grandfather to know he'd hit the mark.

"No more of this." Aiden tossed the envelope onto the expansive hardwood desk, keeping several feet separating them. "It didn't work."

The shutters came down over James's eyes as he picked up the envelope. "What's this?"

"Cut the crap." Aiden planted his feet and crossed his arms.

James tipped the envelope, giving it a firm shake. "What the hell?" He hopped backward as the ashes fluttered across his desk and clung to his spotless suit.

"Oh, I should have mentioned it's what's left of that magazine and the photos you sent to Emily. My bad."

"You sound so sorry." James flicked at his jacket, curling his lip as the soot smeared across the expensive fibers.

"Why should I be? You continue to try to ruin my life and my relationships. Jazlyn confessed, so don't even pretend you didn't put her up to it. One of these days your dirty little tricks will catch up with you."

"Is that a threat?"

"Never. The thing is, you've pissed off some powerful people over the years. I suspect you'll cross the line one day, and it'll be over."

"Weak. That's what you are. I saw a flash of brilliance not so long ago, but you're soft and spineless. A complete embarrassment." James leaned on his desk, ignoring the sooty mess. "Why are you here?"

"I won't tolerate any further interference in my life. Stay away from my family or you'll get to test how weak and spineless I am. You've fallen to a new low when you accost and threaten pregnant women. And the veiled threats against my daughter need to stop."

"I've heard you and Tom Grayson are selling my father's Chicago firm. I have a deal for you. You sign over your shares of the firm and I'll go away. You've always maintained you're not about the money. Prove it."

Aiden laughed out loud. "You'd like that, wouldn't you? It confirms what you consider important in your life. How pathetic. Grandfather left you a substantial trust fund, paid for your swanky New York apartment, and you've earned a decent income over the years. An apartment of that size overlooking Central Park in that location must be worth tens of millions by now. Yet you're never satisfied and you want everything I have too."

"That law firm should be mine."

"Except it isn't. Thomas Hamilton left the balance of his estate to Gramma Grace, and the firm to me. I don't know how you figure you're entitled to a damn thing."

"He was my father."

"And my grandfather. Think of it this way. Your grandchildren will never want for anything." Aiden met his steely gaze. "It's interesting you'd accuse Emily of wanting my money and play the guilt card hoping to cause a rift. You wanted her to offer legal agreements I never asked for. Very hypocritical, considering all you want from your own son is the shares of Hamilton Grayson."

"You'll regret crossing me."

"I doubt it. I know things. Things that will get out if anything happens to anyone in my family. The information is held in several locations, and if even one person I know is harmed, then it'll be out. Your friends might not slither away unscathed either. Wouldn't spending your golden years in the Federal Pen be fun? A few of your pals are itching to give you a warm welcome."

"Watch your back."

"Stay away, stop stalking us, or you will rot in hell." Aiden glowered at James, gratified to see a touch of fear in the man's eyes.

There had been a time when Aiden wanted nothing more than this man's acceptance and approval. Now he felt nothing but disgust and James shrank before his eyes. All he could hope was the man would refrain from making further trouble and let Aiden move on and be happy with his family.

He stalked from the office and headed straight for the train station. The further away he was from James Hamilton, the better.

Chapter 31

Emily

EMILY TUCKED THE LAST OF the freshly laundered linen onto the shelf in the closet and sank into the chair, gazing at the well-appointed room. Aiden teased her every time she showed up with another bag, but she couldn't help herself. After their doctor's appointment, she'd bought the softest blanket and draped it over the side of the crib, awaiting the day they'd bring their son home.

Aiden peeked into the room. "I expected you'd be in here. It's set up with every imaginable item. Now you need to take it easy and save your energy."

"It's getting there, but I can't sit still. How was work?"

"The usual assortment, but no one died, so it was a great day." He leaned in the doorway, one hand tucked behind his back.

"Well, get in here and give me a kiss." She grinned as she spotted the brightly colored bag. "Ha. And you ridicule me for buying stuff."

"I couldn't resist. It's so damn cute and now the secret is out, I can buy clothing." He kneeled in front of her and set the bag on her lap, dropping a kiss on her belly as he rubbed with warm hands.

Emily leaned down to kiss him before slipping her fingers inside, coming up with a plush stuffed bear. "Awww, it's adorable. And look, another outfit. Our child will win a best-dressed award, and we haven't even had the shower yet."

Aiden lifted one shoulder and grinned. "We should eat. I smell something wonderful."

"I had a craving for Paella. Mine's not as good as my mom's, but it was the best I could do."

"I don't know about that, mi cielo. I love your cooking, especially when you make Spanish cuisine." He pulled her from the chair.

"Let's go." She held out her hand, entwining their fingers, leading him down the hall.

Emily sighed and rolled over, her arm landing in the empty spot beside her. She'd become used to Aiden being there every morning on their honeymoon, and now it was hard to sleep after he left for work. Even after being home for three weeks, she still missed waking up in his arms.

She stared at the ceiling, taking deep breaths. Her last trimester. A mixture of excitement and anxiety flooded her every time she thought about the birth of their child.

She'd delivered babies, but she wasn't sure if her intimate knowledge of the process made it better or worse. At least Aiden wouldn't freak or pass out in the delivery room. He'd seen it all and done his share, welcoming more than a few new babies into the world during his time practicing medicine.

It wasn't yet five, and she groaned. She wiggled off the bed as a little body part pushed against her bladder. Part of the joy of pregnancy, she was making extra bathroom trips, and she was often ravenous. On her way to the kitchen she made a half-hearted attempt to smooth her wild cloud of hair, but gave up in seconds.

Aiden sipped his morning coffee as she padded in. "Hey, you're up." He smiled and set aside his cup, holding out his arms.

"Your son's kicking kept me up last night, and then this morning he performed the bladder dance. Now I'm thirsty, which means I'll be up again in an hour." She snuggled against his chest, inhaling the light tang of aftershave. It was getting more difficult to get close, and she angled her body to accommodate the bump. She closed her eyes and relaxed against him, loving the tenderness in his touch. A sweet warm greeting from this man every day for the rest of her life was something she could handle.

"That's how we're playing it? My son?" He laughed and dropped a kiss on her wild mop of hair. "You should go back to bed." He swayed on his feet, rocking her gently.

"Troublemakers belong to Daddy. Angels belong to Mommy. I'll try for more sleep. I have a half-shift today."

"We can walk home together." He brushed the hair back from her face and planted a soft kiss on her lips. "Why don't we get you tucked in? You should sleep at least three more hours. You've been buzzing around non-stop, worrying about the baby room and baby proofing, even though the baby won't be mobile for at least nine months."

"I'm aware, but that's nesting. Never thought it would happen, but apparently nobody is immune."

"Or you're too particular. I love what you've done with the room, but you need to find another outlet." Aiden led her to the bedroom and drew back the covers. "In, Mommy."

Emily smiled as he arranged the pillows, tucking them around her back, belly, and under her knees. "I forgot my water." She batted her eyes.

"Oh, allow your personal man-servant to fetch that for you." He rolled his eyes, but his lips twitched as a snicker escaped.

"Thank you, mi vida." She snuggled down in her pillow cocoon, closing her eyes. She knew he didn't mind taking care of her. It was in his nature, which was probably why he was an excellent doctor. He already involved himself, never missing an appointment and making no secret of his happiness at the idea of being a father again.

Aiden kissed her forehead, placing the water on the nightstand within her reach. He placed his hands on either side of her belly, leaning in and murmuring, "You be good and let Mommy get some rest."

"And if our little monkey doesn't behave?" Emily caressed his hair.

"No more ice cream for baby."

"Hey. That's unfair to me."

"No one said life was fair. See you in a few hours. I have to go or I'll be late." He gave her a last kiss. "Love you both. Take it easy this morning. Keep your feet up, you never know how it will be at work. Vanna's home, so call her if you need anything." After a little wave, he disappeared out the door.

⚜

Her own scream woke her. Emily crunched into a ball, tears streaming down her face at the excruciating pain shooting through her. Her palms sweated and her heart pounded as she curled up tighter, crying.

"Emily?" Savannah knocked on the door. "Are you okay?"

"Vanna." Emily forced out the girl's name, crying harder, in complete agony. "It hurts."

Warm hands landed on her shoulders. "What's happening?" The girl sniffled. "What's wrong?"

"It h-hurts. Call Aiden." She crammed her pillow against her face, one hand wrapped around her belly.

"I'm calling an ambulance. You're—" Vanna grabbed the phone from the bedside table, dialing as she rubbed Emily's arm. "I'm getting help."

"A-A-Aiden." Everything grew blurry and hazy, and Emily couldn't focus on the words, but Savannah's voice washed over her.

"They're sending an ambulance. Aiden's at work. I'll find him for you." Savannah slid an arm around her, still clutching the phone to her ear. "Hurry, please," she whispered.

The ache receded, but the burn remained, running down the side of her abdomen. She tried to move and spotted a red stain on her pajamas. "Oh, blood. Oh, no." Grief washed over her. It might be too late. She already sought answers, running through all the possible complications. "It's too early."

"There's not much blood. Relax and breathe. They'll be here soon." The girl took her hand. "I'll try Dad's cell, but I have to get my phone. I'll be right back. Keep breathing, it'll be okay." Savannah dashed from the room.

Emily struggled to breathe, only wanting Aiden to be there.

"I'm back." The girl perched beside her on the bed, now with her cell phone in one hand, the other phone still pressed to her ear. "He's not picking up."

"Keep trying. Please." Emily brushed at the tears, her cheeks damp and hot.

"I sent him a text. Hold on, the ambulance is here."

A familiar face hovered over her. "We'll move you now, Emily. How far along are you?"

"Twenty-nine weeks," Vanna said.

"Relax. We'll get you to the hospital." The paramedic assessed her, asking questions and then they were on their way out the door.

"Can I ride with you?" Vanna trailed behind, clutching her cell phone in her hand. "Please? I don't want to leave Emily."

"Come on, Savannah." The paramedic beckoned her to follow them into the ambulance.

Emily tried to relax as they made the short drive to the hospital. Savannah sat strapped into a seat, her face pale and drawn as Emily's own. All her thoughts were now focused on how she'd been overdoing it and how angry Aiden would be with her for not listening. How excited he'd been and how devastated he'd be if they lost their baby.

She sniffled, a fresh round of tears breaking free.

CHAPTER 32

Aiden

As he grabbed for the stethoscope slung around his neck, Aiden met the paramedics and listened to the rundown of the patient's vitals.

The bleeding, bullet-ridden boy lay limp and unconscious on the gurney. The fifth gunshot victim of the day and it wasn't even noon.

"Thanks, guys. We've got him." He glanced at the intern. "Can you intubate?"

The intern nodded, establishing an airway while Aiden checked the multiple wounds.

"He's what? Sixteen?" He shook his head. "Let's roll him." Aiden checked for exit wounds. "Call upstairs and tell them we're sending this kid straight up." He glanced at the nurse as she hung up the phone. "Maria?"

"Gillespie will take him. They're preparing an OR."

He snapped up the rail. "Stay with him every second until surgery takes him up," he said to the resident. "Call me if anything changes."

"Phone, Dr. Hamilton." The desk clerk waved as he hurried by.

"Take a message? They're stacking up out there."

"It's Savannah. She insisted it's urgent and I was to track you down." The clerk held out the receiver. "Line three."

Aiden frowned as he picked up the line. "Savannah. What's going on?"

"Emily." Savannah's tearful voice made his heart skip a beat. "We're on the way in. She woke up in pain, so I called an ambulance and they're bringing her into the emergency."

"What happened?"

"I don't know? I heard her scream and she was in so much pain."

"She's conscious? Any bleeding?"

"She's awake and there was a little bleeding. I was scared and didn't want to wait for you to get home. I thought she should go to the hospital right away. I'm sorry."

"It's okay, Vanna. Where are you?"

"We're pulling in now."

"I'll meet you in the ambulance bay." Aiden strode across the floor as the glass doors slid open, and he spotted the familiar blonde hair.

"Aiden." Emily peered up at him through tearful eyes framed in a pasty, pale face.

"It's okay, honey." He exhibited a calmness he didn't feel. Inside, his stomach twisted and his heart pounded at the sight of her strapped to the gurney.

"Dad?" Savannah turned a worried face his way, reaching out for him. "Will Emily be okay?"

"Vanna." He squeezed her hand. "We'll take good care of her. Wait in the doctor's lounge and I'll find you."

She nodded, staring after them as they wheeled Emily into Trauma 1.

"Get O.B. down here, stat." Aiden reached for the ultrasound machine.

Will arrived and took the wand away. "Hold her hand." The other doctor gave him a meaningful look as he shooed the student Aiden had been supervising out of the exam room.

Aiden nodded and moved to the head of the bed, giving her hand a reassuring squeeze. Will was right, he'd be useless. Emergencies required tough decisions and quick, solid medical assessments. Emotional involvement with the patient never boded well in these situations, so allowing another doctor to treat her was in her best interest.

With a mask of calm in place, he gazed into Emily's eyes. He dodged as needed, letting the team perform their duties without interference. Everyone in this room had handled an untold number of traumas, and they knew their jobs. Voices called stats, and he focused on what was happening amid the flurry of activity.

Emily's red-rimmed eyes were puffy and clouded with worry. Her rapid blinking made him realize she was close to bursting into tears. Her gaze implored him for reassurance as her forehead creased in pain.

Don't let her down. Get it together. The words rolled through his brain as he sought inner strength. Even if his stomach rolled and turned until he wanted to throw up, and it felt like everything was coming apart at the seams, Emily needed him.

"Aiden." Emily's trembling, weepy voice cut through the fog enveloping him.

It had only been seconds, but for Emily, it must seem like hours. A glance at Will and a quick interpretation of the look on his friend's face meant one thing.

He placed a hand on her cheek and stroked with his thumb. "You're in good hands. Relax." His eyes locked on hers and he squeezed her hand. The haze lifted, and the room came back into focus and a few words filtered in.

"Elevated heart rate—"

"I'm sorry, Aiden," Emily whispered.

"It's not your fault. Your heart's racing, so breathe. With me, deep inhale," he said, "and out. And again."

The frantic beeping of the monitors settled as Emily regained control, the numbers stabilizing.

"That's it." He pressed a kiss to her forehead.

"It hurts." A sob tore from her throat.

"We'll take care of that, Emily," Will said before relaying his orders to the nurse at his side.

"Breathe, honey." Aiden didn't know if he was reassuring Emily or himself. Perhaps both. His own heart raced, but he kept his expression in check, noting the pain, confusion, and distress reflecting back at him.

Emily gagged, rising from her pillow.

Aiden grabbed an emesis basin, turning her and getting it into position just in time. He supported her as she heaved, holding back her hair. Once she finished, he handed off the basin and wiped her pale, sweaty face.

"O.B. is on the way," a nurse said as she hung up the phone.

"How many weeks, Aiden?" Will glanced at him.

"Twenty-nine." He touched Emily's pale cheek. "Let me know if you feel sick again."

"It hurts so much."

"Let's look at the baby." Will adjusted her top and squeezed on the gel. The reassuring, musical whoosh of the baby's heartbeat filled the room. He positioned the wand and stared at the numbers on the monitor. "Heartbeat is elevated, but it's coming down." He guided the unit across her belly. "The baby seems fine."

Aiden blew out a long stream of air. "Hear that? The baby's okay." He stroked her hair and kissed her forehead again. "Hang in there, mi cielo."

"I hear it." Emily graced him with a watery smile.

Will allowed the wand to linger for a moment before continuing his inspection. "No abruption, fluids are good, no sign of labor." He turned the screen, allowing Aiden and Emily to see. "We'll get a second opinion from the obstetrician. That amount of pain and the bleeding, though not excessive, requires further investigation. A cyst?" He raised his brows.

"No one mentioned one during the last ultrasound, but that was two months ago. At our last appointment, the heartbeat and measurements were perfect, so the doctor didn't require one."

The obstetrician arrived. "Let's look." She ran the ultrasound wand across Emily's belly, her gaze narrowing as she inspected the placenta and viewed the baby. "You had a sharp pain? Some bleeding?"

"Excruciating pain that woke me up. It went on for a few minutes, then stopped, then there was bleeding and more pain," Emily whispered.

"How far along are you?"

"Twenty-nine weeks. She's also nauseous and vomiting." Aiden clutched Emily's hand.

"No signs of amniotic fluid?"

Will shook his head. "There was minimal blood, no fluid, and no sign of contractions, the placenta looks great and no noticeable dilation or effacement. Slightly elevated blood pressure for the mom, strong heartbeat for the baby, but she's still in pain."

"I suspect a ruptured cyst. Did they say anything about it when you were in for your last scan?"

"No. Last one was at twenty weeks."

"No pain other than the sudden onset today?"

Emily shook her head.

"That's normal with a cyst. Often there's no pain until it ruptures and then it's severe, and there can be bleeding. Labs?"

"I sent them as a rush. We ordered the standard tests to rule out infections." Will handed over the chart.

The obstetrician continued her inspection. "There we go." She wiped the wand and placed it back on the machine. "Looks like a torsion, which is why you're still experiencing this level of pain, and you have a second cyst. We need to untwist the ovary and examine it to make sure it's healthy. I'll look at the second cyst and remove it if needed." She patted Emily's arm. "We'll do a Doppler to confirm, but we need an immediate laparoscopy. We'll transfer you upstairs."

"We're not delivering the baby?" Aiden asked.

"Everything looks normal with the pregnancy. We'll monitor both mom and baby during the procedure and if there are any problems, we'll perform a c-section. In most cases, the baby goes full-term. Every week the baby can stay in utero will count. But not to worry, twenty-nine weeks is early, but viable with proper care."

"Don't leave me," Emily said.

"I won't." He kissed her hand.

She nodded and kept tight hold until they reached the double doors to the surgical area.

The obstetrician patted Aiden's arm. "I can't allow you into the OR, but as staff, you're welcome to sit in the gallery to observe. See the duty nurse at the desk for the paperwork, and we'll find you as soon as surgery is finished."

"Tell Vanna it's okay," Emily said with a wan smile.

"I'll find her after I sign everything. I'll see you soon. I love you." Aiden leaned down and kissed her.

"Love you," she murmured before they wheeled her through the doors.

Aiden leaned against the wall, tipping his head back and closing his eyes as he took several deep breaths.

"Dr. Hamilton?"

Aiden opened his eyes.

"Can you sign?" The nurse held out a clipboard.

"Sorry, yes." He cleared his throat and scanned the paperwork before signing the bottom.

"Your wife is in good hands." The nurse disappeared down the hallway toward the operating rooms.

At least he'd had a moment to regroup. The thought of losing Emily or the baby was frightening, and they weren't in the clear yet.

He returned to the ER to find Savannah.

Savannah rushed toward him. "How's Emily? And the baby?"

"They're okay. It was a ruptured cyst and Emily has to have a laparoscopy, which is surgery, but everything's all right." He wrapped her into a hug. "You did good."

"That was scary. You're sure Emily will be okay?"

"It's a low-risk procedure. Emily should be home in a few days. I'm so glad you there."

"Last time ..." Savannah dissolved into tears, sobbing against his chest. "Last time, Daddy died. Emily kept asking for you, but I didn't want to wait for you to come home."

"Shh, Vanna." Aiden swayed on his feet and rubbed her back. It couldn't be easy for the girl. The last time she called 911 was for Ross, and the end results had been devastating.

"The surgery won't hurt the baby?"

"It's a minimally invasive procedure. They'll insert a little tube through a small incision, fix the problem, and then get back out. Which means it won't take long for Emily to feel better and it won't bother the baby. The baby has a strong heartbeat, and they'll monitor them closely. Do you want to watch with me in the gallery?"

"Watch surgery?" Savannah's eyes widened. "We can make sure she's okay."

"If you think you're okay with it. If not, we can leave, but I'd like to look in at least." He patted his ID tag. "Free pass."

"Okay. I'll try."

They made their way upstairs and let the OR desk nurse know where they would be.

"Dr. Hamilton." The nurse held out a small bag. "Emily wanted you to hold on to these. We had to take off her jewelry for the procedure."

"Thanks." Aiden peeked into the bag containing her rings and earrings. He tucked them into his pocket. "Hey, Savannah, how about something to drink?" He stopped at the vending machine and bought two bottles of juice.

"Thanks. I felt a little sick and worried about Emily. I'll be okay."

"I know you will. If you don't want to watch, we don't have to." Aiden stared down into the O.R. from the gallery.

"It's fine, Dad. I'll sit with you." She grasped his hand. "They'll be okay."

⌒≼

Aiden leaned back in the chair with his eyes at half-mast. It had been a rough day, but the surgery had gone well and it seemed they were in the clear. He'd sent Savannah home, telling her to get her homework done.

Emily's eyes fluttered open. "Are you watching me sleep?"

"Sorry." He sat, stretching his arms above his head. "How are you feeling?"

"Sore." She turned her head, motioning to the monitors. "I can barely move with all these electronics attached."

"I bet, but they want to keep an eye on things." He noted the steady heart rate and regular beep of the machines. "Our little fighter is taking a nap." Aiden sat on the side of her bed.

"Thankfully. The acrobatics keep me awake." She sighed. "I'm sorry, Aiden."

"Why? Everything's fine."

"I should have listened. I've been pushing too hard."

"Don't blame yourself. It would've happened no matter what. I'd like you to slow down, but that's because I want you to conserve energy. After our baby arrives, you'll be exhausted." Aiden caressed her hand. "The Chief approved my parental leave, which means we can spend the entire summer in the Vineyard."

Her eyes lit up. "She did?"

"I'll only work on my study. Just think, over two months of lounging in the sun and laying on the beach."

A blissful smile touched her lips. "Sounds heavenly."

"It will be. We'll have uninterrupted bonding time with our new son." He ran his fingers over her belly, careful to avoid the monitors and surgical dressing. "It'll be amazing."

"Will the rest of the gang be there?"

"They booked most of the summer off before they dig in at the new firm. They all send their best for a speedy recovery. I told them you'll be home soon and then they can visit if they like."

"The offer is going through?"

"They agreed to all of Tom's conditions and added an extra incentive on top of the offer price. It's surprising how little it bothers Gramma Grace to see the firm sold, but she looked at the offer and told me I'd be an idiot not to accept."

"It's a lot of money. We don't need it, but Tom and Jenna want this."

"They do. Starting up in Boston is a huge undertaking, but with Joel on board, Tom can cut back his administrative workload and spend more time with his new family. Win-win-win for all three families."

Emily patted the bed. "Cuddle with me before you go home." She wiggled over, making space beside her.

Aiden slid off his shoes, curling up beside her. "You're wanting me as your personal body pillow."

"No ... well, yes ... but ... this is nice. I was scared."

"Me too, but the baby is healthy, you're okay, the surgery went well, and there are no concerns going forward. We have so much to look forward to over the next few months. Next thing you know, this little person will be a major part of our lives, and I can't wait."

Chapter 33

Emily

RESTLESSNESS HAD TAKEN OVER. EMILY wandered into the family room, resting a hand on her belly and staring through the wall of glass. So much had happened over the past few weeks, but now they'd settled into a holding pattern. Waiting for the birth of the baby. Waiting for Jenna's baby. Waiting for Tom and Jenna to make the big move. Waiting for the moment they could escape the city and go to their house in the Vineyard for the summer. The constant waiting exhausted her, the anticipation overwhelming.

At least she felt good, even after her stressful visit to the hospital and the subsequent surgery. Aiden had been amazing and supportive, pampering her maybe a little too much. Not that she'd complain. Not a chance.

Savannah had shown yet another side of herself—a fantastic side in Emily's opinion. The girl's level of maturity surprised her.

"I put all the groceries away, the dishes are done, and dinner is almost ready." Savannah came up beside her. "So pretty, isn't it? I'm so glad Aiden didn't pick Baltimore. It's not half as nice as Boston."

Emily glanced at Savannah. "Baltimore?"

The girl's eyes widened and a look of panic fleeted across her face. "He didn't tell you about Hopkins?" Savannah bit her lip and looked away.

"Nope, he didn't."

"I shouldn't have said anything. I'm sorry," she mumbled. "Hopkins was the better offer, but he chose Boston for me."

Emily sighed. "Boston meant a job for me. Hopkins didn't have positions. It's not your fault, it's mine." She let out a long breath. "You can say it, Vanna. I was stupid. So damn obvious, and I was too scared to grab hold and take the chance. I almost destroyed it all. I won't make that mistake again."

Savannah slid an arm around Emily's back, resting her head against her stepmother's shoulder. "Maybe it was meant to show you how much you love Aiden. I bet this baby will be extra special. I can't wait."

"Me either." Emily slung her arm around Savannah's waist. "You're smart, you know that? And thanks for doing all of that work."

"I don't mind." Savannah sighed. "Can I ask you something? There are things I have to tell Aiden, and I'm not sure how."

"Sounds serious." Emily's heart sank.

"It is, but ... hey, don't look so worried. I'm not pregnant or anything."

"Oh, thanks for clearing that up. I'm glad to hear it. I'm sure Aiden will be, too." A surge of relief ran through her. Children were wonderful, but Savannah was nowhere near ready for them. Some days she wondered if she was even ready.

"I've heard the cautions enough times. I don't think I could handle Dad looking at me all disappointed."

"He's a worrier, no question. It's because he cares, Savannah, but he'd support you, no matter what. Appreciate that he's been there. I don't have to tell you, it's a huge deal. We're married with good jobs and a great home. I'm still scared. I don't know how he handled it the way he did."

"Don't worry, Chase is paranoid and frightened of Aiden."

"Ah, right. I heard the comment on the plane."

"Like Aiden would hurt him. Something about the way Dad looks at him freaks Chase right out. He says he sometimes wonders if Dad has ESP and knows what he's thinking." Savannah giggled. "Maybe he does know. He was a teenage boy, and he admits he was trouble and got that *be good with my daughter* look from the dads."

Emily had to smile. "My dad gave him the look and I'm all grown up. I guess he missed out on giving it to all my boyfriends when I was a teenager so he had to get in at least one shot before I got married. Aiden took it pretty well."

"Something to look forward to, that miraculous day my dad accepts my boyfriend and doesn't make him feel like he might toss him out a window. Good to know." Savannah smirked.

"So this big thing you want to discuss with your dad isn't about Chase?"

"You know Tom helped me choose my courses while you two were away?"

"Did you take all the easy courses or something?"

"I took all the academic ones, but I don't know how Aiden will react."

"I'm sure he'll be fine." Emily lifted a brow. "What's this about?"

"I've always thought about journalism, but while you two were away, I spent a lot of time talking with Tom and Ryan." Savannah peered at her. "I want to go to Law School."

"And?"

"Well, I'd be a lawyer. I know how Aiden feels about it. He won't want me to be a lawyer."

"You're afraid to tell Aiden you'd prefer to study law?"

"He'll freak out."

"He didn't want to be a lawyer, but that doesn't mean he wouldn't want you to be one. Have you noticed two of his best friends are lawyers? Aiden's even part of the new firm."

"Tom said it would be okay, but I'm still nervous. Dad's done so much for me. What if I disappoint him?"

"Oh, honey. Do what you love. Pick a career you're passionate about, like Aiden and I did. We both love medicine. If for you it's law, then do it. You'll be an incredible lawyer."

"That's what Tom said." Savannah twirled a lock of hair around her finger. "In the fall, he'll hire me part-time to work in the office as an intern."

"Sounds like a great opportunity. Tom's amazing at what he does, and not everyone gets the chance to try out a career beforehand. I bet your dad will like the idea. And think of all the homework help you'll have."

"Thanks, Emily. You'll be a fantastic mom."

"I hope so." Emily hugged the girl. "I never asked how it was having Ryan stay with you."

The girl grinned. "We had fun."

"Ah, so he let you slack off. I bet you had pizza and ice cream every night for dinner and have piles of unfinished homework hidden in your drawer."

"Ha." Savannah snorted. "He's even tougher than Dad about homework and he's a health nut too, so no junk food dinners."

"How much did he pay you to say that when asked?"

"I didn't charge much." Vanna giggled, but then a thoughtful look crossed her face. "The routine with Uncle Ryan is homework the moment I get home followed by a crazy healthy meal and then we always went out somewhere."

"He did your homework?"

"He helped if I was stuck," Vanna said, "but he does his own homework. Uncle Ryan's almost completed a second degree." She shrugged. "It's always fun to stay with Uncle Ryan."

Emily smiled and nodded. "Wait." Her smile faded. "Always?"

"I've spent loads of time with him." Vanna shrugged. "He's easy to talk to, and we text all the time."

Aiden's words came back to her. His friends—including Ryan—should do anything for Savannah. Give their last breath. Maybe he wasn't so far off on that assessment. Ryan wasn't the man she thought him to be.

Alex smiled as she stepped out of the elevator. "Look at you. Ready to go for a walk?"

"Almost." Emily wiggled, struggling with her shoe. "If I could just get these on my sausage feet. Everything ballooned overnight. I can't wait to get this baby out. Am I a horrible person? Did you ever feel that way?"

"I was desperate to get this little man out. Being pregnant is amazing, but there were moments when I wondered what in the hell I'd gotten myself into. Those thoughts about being a terrible mother lurked in my mind."

"Thank goodness I'm not alone. There are days when he won't stop moving and I long to evict him from his comfy home." Emily forced on her second shoe. "I love this little guy already, but I'm terrified. It'll change everything."

Alex's eyes lit up. "It's a boy?"

"Damn." Emily dropped her chin to her chest. "Pregnancy brain," she muttered before she lifted her head. "Aiden will kill me."

"I'm so excited." Alex hugged her. "I won't tell."

She angled herself, fighting with her laces and sucking for air.

Alex's eyebrows rose. "Can I tie those? You seem to be losing the battle."

"Absolutely. I need to invest in slip-ons. Aiden ties my shoes like I'm a small child."

Alex giggled. "Pregnancy is a series of stages where the last few weeks are unbearable. Then you go into labor and you wonder if it wouldn't be better to hold the baby in a touch longer." A dreamy look appeared in her friend's eyes. "The minute Daniel appeared, my entire world changed. Every moment was worth it when I held my precious boy in my arms."

"I can't wait." Emily peered at the sleeping Daniel. "Look at him now. It's hard to believe he's already a year old."

Alexis nodded. "Joel is all *hey baby, why don't we have another one.*"

"Thanks." Emily pushed out of the chair after Alex finished tying her second shoe.

Soon they stepped onto the sunny street, strolling down the mercifully quiet street.

"So you and Joel are planning another one?" Emily tipped her face up, enjoying the warmth of the sun kissing her skin.

"Oh, no. Nooooo." Alex's eyes widened. "I nixed the idea. I refuse to manage two babies while Joel is busy with the new firm." A frown fleeted across her face. "How's Aiden been?"

"Well." Emily smirked. "He barely lets me do anything around the apartment. I'm off work now, but at the hospital he was insufferable. Always telling me to slow down and take it easy. The last couple weeks I only did light medical, and I bet he instigated it. Everyone ran interference, keeping me away from any lifting. Upside? Didn't get puked on once in my last few shifts."

"Can't say I'd fuss too hard about avoiding that." Alexis giggled. "He's always been like that. Jenna has the same complaints about Tom. Though why you girls are complaining, I don't understand. Sometimes I'm ready to trade Joel in for an upgraded model, like the ones you ladies lucked into." She waved a hand. "Aiden appears to be a damn good husband."

"He's not good, he's great." Emily grinned as Alex rolled her eyes. "It sounds like I'm complaining, but in reality, I love it. He rubs my back, massages my feet, ties my damn shoes, and fixes the nail polish on my toes. It's like there's nothing he wouldn't do, and most of it he does without being asked. Which is kind of strange, right?"

"Miraculous, you mean. There are a few hidden gems, but most guys don't get it. Some of my friends complain about cramps, or how hard it is to be pregnant or whatever, and their man is like *oh, women, so weak, must be all in their head.* Say what? I'd slap Joel silly if he made that kind of dumbass statement. Don't even get me started on the whole *that's not my job* crap men pull."

"Aiden never says things like that, but he's medically trained and knows the struggle is real. I'd kill him if he ever said it wasn't. Men are clueless, and I hear the comments some of them make to their wives when they come through the emergency. Maybe I'm still in our happy love bubble, but I wouldn't trade Aiden for anything."

Alexis laughed. "Happy love bubble?"

"Cheesy, right?" Emily flushed, her face growing even warmer than it already was.

"No ... um ... never mind. It's cute you feel that way about Aiden and your marriage. It's wonderful to see him happy, despite everything. He's opening up, and it's about damn time." She dug in her purse. "My phone's vibrating."

Emily patted her bag. "Mine too."

Alexis already had hers out. "Oh. Jenna's in labor."

CHAPTER 34

Aiden

AIDEN LAID THE CUE ACROSS the table and patted his pocket, searching for his phone. "Hey, Tom." He glanced at Joel as the man wove his way toward to the bar.

After the fifth beer, Aiden had lost count of how many his friend drank, but given Joel couldn't walk in a straight line, the man needed to slow down.

"Show time for Jenna. We're on our way into the hospital." Tom's voice crackled over the speaker. "I can't talk long."

Aiden raised a brow at Joel as he waved a bottle in the air. "Don't tell Em. She's gonna be jealous."

Jenna moaned in the background. "I doubt it, it hurts. Besides, I already texted Alex and Emily."

"How far apart?"

"Less than four minutes. She thought they were Braxton Hicks until her water broke, but her back's been aching all morning."

"She's probably been in labor for hours. Call me if you need anything, and I can fly down."

"No way. If you come here and Emily goes into labor, she'll kill you, and then me. I'll call later."

"Hope it all goes well. Joel's with me, so I'll fill him in. Tom? Relieve the back pain by applying gentle pressure with your palm against her lower back."

"Oh, you're an angel." Jenna sighed. "I wish we'd called sooner."

"I'll try that when we get to the hospital," Tom said. "Talk soon."

The line went dead.

"Jenna's in labor." Aiden chalked his cue.

"I'm sure they're thrilled. You're up next."

"Now I'm half-expecting a call from Em. Jenna's early and first babies are often late." He broke, straightening as the ball dropped into the pocket.

"You're so calm. I was a total wreck this close to Alex's due date and freaking out about making it to the hospital in time."

"The hospital's ten minutes from our house if we walk. Depending on how it goes, we might."

"Ha ha. Emily would be thrilled to walk to the hospital in labor."

"She suggested it." Aiden shrugged. "Walking speeds the process, so ..." He took another shot but missed and motioned to the table. "Your turn."

"Emily's adventurous." Joel wavered as he lined up the cue. "I suggested we work on baby number two and received a less than excited reception. Darn, missed."

"You can hardly blame Lex." Aiden smirked. "You need to learn to change a damn diaper. Besides, you're about to become a full partner in Hamilton, Grayson & Nichols. It's a huge commitment. Why do you think I've gone silent?"

"Ryan says you be whipped, my man."

Aiden sank another ball. "Ha. Whipped my ass. Some woman will cure him of his chronic bachelorhood. That'll be entertaining." He laughed, thinking about feeding Ryan his words. "I listen to my wife. We're equal partners. It's called being happily married."

Joel sipped his beer. "I change diapers."

"When Alex asks. Sure, she's off work, but you still need to help. Make her dinner or clean up the kitchen. Yes, you take Daniel to the park. You're a good dad and you love your son, but she might be more receptive to making another baby if she thought you'd be more involved and helpful with everything else."

"Chick-speak." Joel snorted. "You're channeling Alex."

"If I'm sounding like her, then perhaps ..." He sighed at the dark look from his friend. "Whatever. Listen or don't. Equal partnership, Joel. There are no his or her tasks, there are simply things that need doing. Our marriage works on the *just do it* principle."

"Then reality hits, with a baby screaming all night and the alarm set for five. You've never gone through that part, so you're rosy and optimistic. It's not fun." He surveyed the table. "Damn, you win. Again." Joel hung his cue and slid into their booth, waving down the server for another round.

"I get that, Joel, but I'm looking forward to it." Aiden sat and sipped his beer. "I don't want to miss it with this baby like I did with Vanna."

"Huh. You're a glutton for punishment, wishing for toxic diapers and sleepless nights." Joel sank back and closed his eyes. "Anyway, making babies requires sex, so it's a pointless discussion."

Aiden raised his brow. "You aren't having sex?"

"It's been months." Joel looked down. "She's always tired or busy with Daniel. And we're fighting all the time."

"About what?" Concern flooded him. This was a problem, and from the look on Joel's face, a serious one. "Thanks." He nodded to the server as she placed two more brews on the table.

Joel chugged down half of his ice-cold ale. "Everything. I don't know what to do. She's furious about not being included in the discussion about the move. She's always pissed about something."

"Em wasn't happy either, but we talked it out, though the new firm doesn't mean us moving. We've resolved our disagreements over Boston." Aiden tipped back his drink. "What can I do to help? Talk to me, Joel."

Joel shrugged, picking at the label on his bottle. "What can anyone do? Our marriage is falling apart and another baby might bring us together. She seems so excited about Jenna and Emily being pregnant."

"Well, sure. She's happy for her friends, but it doesn't mean she wants one." Aiden furrowed his brow. "Another baby won't fix things, but only make it harder. Don't be selfish."

"Why don't you tell me how you really feel?"

"Don't be an ass. You love her, right?"

"She's my forever girl." He glanced up. "I tried living without her once, and now I don't want to."

"Then try marriage counseling. Having a baby is a huge stressor, and it's not unusual for a couple to have a tough time, especially in the first year. Lack of communication and patience can make or break a marriage."

"Geez, you sound like some relationship guru or something." His friend snorted before downing the rest of his beer.

"Thanks for the sarcasm, buddy. Slow down." He pointed at the empty bottle. "I see it more than I care to admit through my work. By that time, it's escalated into violence, and one of the parties is brought in by ambulance." He held up his hand. "And no, you're not the kind of guy who'd abuse his wife but you two need to deal with your issues before it brings your marriage down."

"Says mister marinate-myself-in-alcohol. Slow the fuck down? When you about drowned yourself in a bottle after Emily left? Fucking hypocrite."

"Getting blitzed didn't help, now did it? It does nothing but make you into a hung over, stupid ass. That idiocy had repercussions for me, for Savannah, and my friends. It almost ruined our wedding." Aiden motioned to the server for menus, determined to get food into Joel before he became a sloppy, drunken mess. "I almost lost the woman I love because we couldn't communicate. It wasn't one-sided, and our relationship is far from perfect, but we're making it work."

Joel waved his bottle at the server. "Emily's got you wrapped. I'm surprised you took her back. I wouldn't have."

"Thanks for the support." *Asshole.* Aiden leaned back and folded his arms across his chest. "It's fantastic."

"I don't mean ..." Joel faltered under Aiden's cold stare. "You love her, I get that, but you've gone from a carefree single guy to having a wife, raising a teenage daughter, with another baby on the way. Less than a year and your life is unrecognizable. If you think your sex life sucks with your wife due any second? Wait until you add the screaming baby. Definite mood-killer."

"It's a lot, no argument," he said, "but there's nothing wrong with our sex life. I intend to keep it that way."

"You two are still ...?" Joel frowned.

Aiden almost laughed at the expression on his friend's face. "Pregnant women and hormones, man. She's so damn sexy. If you don't feel that way about your wife, you're missing out."

Joel tilted his head. "Stop with the bullshit."

Aiden shrugged. "Believe me or don't, but I refuse to let the physical side of our relationship fade into oblivion. My wife is a passionate woman."

"Shit. You're not kidding?" Joel shook his head. "Now you're just rubbing it in, you bastard. Beware. The newly wedded bliss will fade and the baby will kill her libido. Doesn't having another kid worry you?"

"Responsibility for a child is scary." Aiden contemplated his friend. "But it's wonderful too."

"Huh. Right." Joel accepted a menu as the server arrived. "I could eat."

Aiden perused the choices, shooting glances over the top of his menu. "Quit steering us off track. This is about you and Alex. Don't let her walk, or you'll regret it." He folded his menu. "Why don't I babysit Daniel so you can take Alex away this weekend?"

"What do you suggest I say?"

"Well, I don't know. How about I'm sorry?"

"For what? I didn't do anything." His face turned red and he narrowed his eyes. "She's the one being a total bitch. I begged her to move to Boston. Bet you didn't know that she agreed only to be closer to the gang. How about that? If you weren't here, she'd have refused."

"I'm sorry, man, but naturally, she wants to be closer to her friends. Isn't not moving more about her dad?"

Joel shrugged. "I'm still reduced to begging for every scrap of affection. Maybe Ryan's right. I'm whipped."

"That's ridiculous." Aiden shook his head. "Ryan only wishes he had a woman as great as Alex to boss him around. You know what else? I guarantee in the past several months you've done at least one thing you should apologize for. She's playing her part, but own it, man. You're defensive and have guilt written all over your smug ass face."

Joel sneered, spinning the bottle on the table. He fumbled but caught it in time to prevent the liquid from spilling onto the scarred wooden surface. "She's the one who wanted the baby."

"Uh-huh." Aiden crossed his arms. "I call bullshit. So. Invite your wife to sit down for a discussion, tell her you love her, and reassure her that you want to fix your marriage. Then shut your trap and listen."

"She'll think I've gone insane. I never talk like that."

"Maybe you should start. It sure the hell couldn't hurt." Aiden waved at the waitress. "What are you ordering?"

Joel shrugged as the server approached.

"Fine." Aiden looked at the woman. "Two burgers, with fries, two coffees, and two large ice waters."

His friend opened his mouth to speak, his gaze cutting toward the empty bottle. Joel snapped his mouth closed at Aiden's glower, fixing his stare on the table as the server cleared their empties.

"No more drinking. You aren't doing yourself any favors, and it'll make things worse if you vomit on your wife's shoes. Then she'll have two little boys to take care of, instead of only one."

"Asshole."

"Doctor Asshole to you." Aiden added a touch of cream and sugar to his coffee.

Joel sipped his black coffee, remaining silent for the longest time. "I need to apologize?" His voice was low and defeated.

"Think hard about the fights with Alex, and you'll know why she's unhappy. Even I can see you need to be more involved, and this is the first time we've lived in the same state for close to a year. She's been trying to tell you, but you haven't heard her."

"Hmm, hard not to hear all the screeching."

"Ah, shit, man. There's a difference between hearing and listening. Take it down a notch. Don't close off or get all defensive. These are her feelings, and even if you don't agree, it's how she views the situation. Take it seriously and compromise." He sighed. "Maybe you two need a referee. I'll text you the names of family counselors."

"I love spending two hundred an hour for a pile of bullshit flower-speak."

"That *bullshit flower-speak* helped Savannah. She'd tied herself in emotional knots followed by debilitating panic attacks. Now she's learned coping mechanisms, without medication. That makes it worth every single damn penny." Aiden squinted. "Do you want to save your marriage or not?"

"It's not that bad."

"You know the worst mistake people make in their marriage?"

Joel shook his head.

"Waiting too long to admit they have a problem. They let it build and eat away at everything until it's too late, then use counseling in a feeble effort to save something beyond repair. Don't wait until then."

Joel stared at him for several moments then nodded. "You'll take Daniel so we can have it out?"

"I offered, didn't I? Sort it out, Joel. If you don't at least attempt to save your marriage, you'll regret it. Forever."

Aiden stepped into Joel's dark, silent apartment, the man stumbling after him. It was barely eight-thirty, and the guy was in rough shape. Aiden saw an intense conversation with the porcelain coming in the next few hours.

Aiden flicked on the light and pointed down the hallway. "Go to bed."

"Gotta get Alex n' my baby boy."

"Don't worry, they can stay in our guest room. You need a clear head before you talk to her."

A belligerent expression settled on Joel's face. "Need to get my wife." He lurched toward the door.

Aiden stepped in his path, planting his feet and crossing his arms. "Don't fuck with me, or I'll take you down. After you sober up, you can talk to Alexis, and not a damn minute sooner."

Joel threw his hands in the air before wobbling down the hallway.

Aiden followed. He stopped in Daniel's room, packing several days worth of clothing for the boy, along with his favorite blanket and a stuffed bear. Then he proceeded to the master bedroom.

Joel sprawled across the bed, still fully dressed.

"Man, you're a mess." He pulled off Joel's shoes and draped a blanket over him. Then he located an overnight case in the walk-in closet, packing Alex several changes of clothing, and adding her personal items from the bathroom.

"Watcha doin'?" The sleepy slur came from the direction of the king-size bed. "Get outta m' wife's underwear."

"Whatever." Aiden snorted. "I'm not digging in here for fun, asshole."

"Whaaaa?"

"Never mind. Go to sleep."

"Mmmm." Joel slapped one hand over his eyes.

Aiden finished packing Alex's bag. After placing a large glass of water on the table beside a snoring Joel, he slung the two small bags over his shoulder and headed home.

⁓

"You're back." Emily said as he arrived in the living room.

He leaned in and kissed his wife. "Alex, how are you?"

"Great." Her smile didn't quite reach her eyes, which had dark circles underneath them. A squawk from down the hall made her sigh. "He's up."

"I'll get him." Aiden waved her down and headed to the guest bedroom. "How are you, buddy?" He lifted the crying boy from the playpen. After checking Daniel's diaper, he cuddled the child, who rested his head against Aiden's shoulder as he returned to the living room.

"He wants milk." Alexis rose from the sofa.

"I can pour the kid a drink." Aiden motioned her to sit.

Moments later, Alex appeared behind him in the kitchen. "Where's Joel? I thought he'd be with you."

He turned, balancing the boy on his hip. "I left him at home."

"Why are you looking at me like that? Why didn't Joel come with you? He's supposed to walk us home."

Aiden sighed and shook his head. "He needed sleep," he said. "You can talk to me, Lex."

She squinted. "So he got drunk and spilled his guts?" Tears flooded her eyes, and she sniffled. As she stroked Daniel's hair, she gave Aiden a watery smile. "He looks so comfy in your arms."

"I'm glad you're closer. I get my Daniel fix." He met her gaze. "Joel and I had a talk. I'm not judging, and I want to help. I've been so wrapped up in my own life that I missed it, and I'm sorry."

"It's not your fault that Joel and I haven't been good at communicating. So now what?"

"You talk to each other? Go for some counseling?" He stepped toward her, pulling her in for a one-armed hug. "I'll take Daniel for a few days while you two work it out. He loves you. He wants to fix it."

"What will you tell Emily?" She buried her head against his shoulder.

He rubbed her back. "It's not my place to tell her. I wish you'd talk to her yourself. You can trust her, and you need to get this out. Let us help."

"I can't face going home. Not if he's drunk and pissed off." She dipped her chin further down.

"You can crash in our guest room. Tomorrow's soon enough. He's in no shape to deal with anything at the moment."

"So he's shit-faced. Wonderful."

"I'll get your little man back to bed. Why don't you and Emily have tea, and then you can sleep? Or we can talk. Or we can sit and keep you company. No pressure, but we're here for you."

The tears flowed as sobs shook her entire body.

Emily walked in, freezing in her tracks as a frown settled on her face. Her eyebrows went up.

Aiden gave his head the slightest shake, still holding Daniel in one arm, the other wrapped around Alex as she cried.

Emily pointed at Daniel, and at Aiden's nod, she eased the boy from his hold. She backed out of the kitchen, her lips tugging downward.

Relieved of the weight of the small boy, he wrapped both arms around Alex. "It'll be okay."

"No, it won't." She snuffled, and a fresh wave of tears hit. "It's b-been s-s-so h-hard. For m-months."

"I know, honey." He rocked her, letting her cry. They stood there for the longest time, Aiden rubbing her back as she sobbed, her tears soaking his shirt.

She wound down, pulling back as she wiped at her face. "Sorry for weeping all over you."

"What can I get you?"

"That tea would be nice. Did you bring pajamas?"

"I did. Your bag is in the guest room. Freshen up and come out when you're ready. Have a bath if you like. We'll watch Daniel."

"Thanks, honey." She kissed his cheek before disappearing down the hallway.

Aiden made the tea and carried the three cups into the living room.

Emily cradled Daniel against her. "What was that about?" she whispered.

"You'll find out. Are you okay with Daniel for two minutes? I need to change and move the playpen."

"We're good. He's almost ready for bed."

"They'll stay here tonight."

Her brows rose. "That doesn't sound good."

He shook his head and went to change, moving the playpen into the master before going back to the living room. The little boy was nearly asleep and Aiden carried him to their room, settling him with his blanket and bear.

When he returned, the two women were sipping tea. Aiden dropped onto the sofa beside Emily, picking up his own cup. "Where's Vanna?"

"Out with Chase. She promised she wouldn't be late."

"Any news from Tom?"

"Nothing yet."

Alex stayed quiet, staring into her cup and taking the occasional sip. "I'm off to bed," she said.

"We've got Daniel tonight. Sleep as long as you like."

She rose, giving Emily a sideways look before giving Aiden a hug. "Thanks, Aiden. I appreciate this."

"No problem, Lex. Have a good rest."

"Good night, Emily. Can we talk tomorrow?"

Emily nodded, her gaze following the woman as she left the room, and then she looked at Aiden, confusion written across her face.

"Give her some space, and she'll share." Aiden rubbed her belly.

"Enough said. We'll be up early with Daniel." She stood and held out her hand. "Let's go to bed."

⌒≼

Aiden joined Emily in the kitchen the next morning, bouncing Daniel on his hip. A smile lit his face. "Tom called."

Emily looked up. "She had the baby? How are they?"

"He's the proud papa of a seven-pound three-ounce baby girl. Jenna and their new daughter are great. He sent us pictures." Aiden held up his phone.

"They must be thrilled. Daddy's little girl. She'll have him wrapped around her finger in no time."

"By the looks of this picture, she already does. I'm an uncle again, how great is that?" Aiden wrapped an arm around her.

Emily leaned into him. "Should I call Jenna?"

"Tom asked if we could give them until early afternoon. The grandparents are descending at any moment and Jenna's exhausted. Long day and night for them."

"I can imagine."

Savannah wandered into the kitchen. "What's going on?"

He extended his mobile. "Meet Adrianna Rose Grayson."

She took his phone and scrolled through the pictures. "Awww. Sweet. When do we get to see her?"

"Soon. Emily can't fly, but we'll work it out."

Savannah grinned. "She's adorable. I have another cousin."

"You'll have one busy babysitting service, but we get first dibs." Aiden retrieved his phone.

"Of course. I can't wait to be a big sister."

"Soon, Vanna. Very, very soon."

CHAPTER 35

Emily

EMILY RUBBED HER EYES, ENJOYING Aiden's soft breath fanning against her neck. His arm was slung over her, but the warm weather made it impossible to cuddle. Even with the air conditioning, they'd flung back the covers to combat the heat radiating from her body, and Aiden was always a furnace when he slept.

She wiggled to the edge of the bed and out from under his arm, padding through the dim morning light toward the bathroom with one hand pressed against her back. A dull ache ran around to her abdomen, and she massaged the tightened muscles. Emily sighed. This baby was taking his sweet time in making his appearance.

After splashing cold water on her face, she wandered into the bedroom, a soft smile touching her lips at the sight of her husband. The poor guy was patient about the massive body pillow sharing their bed, along with a bevy of smaller ones. He joked about the pillow Olympics as she wrestled with them, struggling to get comfortable. By now, he must be as anxious as she was for this baby to arrive, if only to regain his portion of the bed.

The man hadn't so much as twitched during her foray to the bathroom. Not that her multiple trips each night woke him anymore, plus Aiden had worked last night, not arriving home until after one in the morning. It was only coming up on five. Emily closed her eyes and relaxed, taking long slow breaths as another pain gripped her and passed.

By seven, the contractions were stronger and closer together, but Aiden was still immersed in sleep.

Emily luxuriated in a long, warm shower, and brushed her hair before wrapping in a light robe. She paced through the apartment, unable to sit still. "Come on, little one." She rubbed her more than ample belly as she ambled across the living room, back and forth, then turning for another trip. "Eviction day."

By seven forty-five, her constant movement rewarded her, and the contractions became stronger and more frequent. "Aiden." She crawled across the bed, brushing his cheek and ruffling his hair with her fingertips. "Wake up."

"Mmm, tired." He buried his head deeper into his pillow.

"It's time." She tickled the sensitive spot just below his ribs.

"For what?" Aiden asked in a muffled, sleepy voice as he caught her hand and curled up, protecting his belly.

"You need to shower," she whispered and lay facing him.

He cracked one eye open and squinted at the clock. "Too early."

"Up." She poked his shoulder. "Get dressed."

His eyes opened, and he blinked. "Why are you harassing me?"

"We have to go to the hospital later, and I thought you'd want a shower." She smiled and gave him a peck on the lips. "It's time."

Aiden blinked again and his eyes widened. "Time for the baby? You're in labor?" He sat, scrubbing at the stubble on his jaw as a grin appeared. "How far apart are the contractions?"

"About ten to twelve minutes and they're regular now. I need you." Emily took another deep breath as the contraction hit. She gritted her teeth.

Aiden rubbed her arm and fumbled for his watch. He studied it as her contraction ran its course. "That was close to twenty-five seconds. We're having a baby today."

"We are." Emily sighed and relaxed. "Get ready." She closed her eyes.

He pressed his lips to her forehead before his weight left the mattress. "About time, baby boy." With a pat to her belly, he said, "I won't be long."

The patter of water lulled her, and she let herself drift. Once the shower turned off, she wiggled onto her side and picked up her phone, scrolling down to the group chat with Jenna and Alex.

My turn. Baby day.

Moments later her phone buzzed with a reply from Jenna.

About time. Two weeks I've been waiting to hear this news.

Going as fast as I can.

Ha ha. Aiden's there?

They messaged back and forth for a few minutes before Alex's message arrived. Emily was glad to hear from her friend. Aiden hadn't been forthcoming about her troubles, only saying he needed to respect their privacy, and Alex would talk when she was ready.

She pushed it out of her mind. Today she needed to focus on the baby. A sense of peace and a surprising calmness descended upon her. It felt so right to welcome her first child with Aiden. Without a doubt, he'd be as great a dad to their son as he was to his daughter.

She tracked Aiden's progress from under half-closed lids as he entered the room with a towel slung low around his hips.

"Any more?" he asked.

"One." She scanned him. *What a lovely sight he was half-naked.* It made for a pleasant distraction. "That was fast."

"Can't keep you and our son waiting." Aiden reappeared wearing shorts and a t-shirt. "Your bag is ready." He dropped onto the bed beside her and caressed her cheek. "Want me to find you some clothes? Help you get dressed? Make you a snack? What do you need?"

"I'd love shorts or a sundress." Emily closed her eyes as another contraction hit.

"Breathe." Aiden rubbed her back until it subsided. "Let's get you dressed and moving around. Unless you'd prefer to rest?"

"I won't sleep, but I'd love something to eat." She sat on the side of the bed while he disappeared into the closet.

He reappeared with a cool, flowing blouse and a pair of maternity shorts in his hands. "Meet with your approval?"

"Perfect. Tuck an extra change into the bag if you could?" It didn't take long for her to dress and join Aiden in the kitchen. She settled on a stool while he sliced fruit and served her yogurt with granola and sweet berries. "Perfect. Nice and light." She tracked his movements as he sipped his coffee. "Vanna gone to school?"

"You look like you want this." Aiden grinned and handed her his cup. "Vanna has an exam today, and they were having an early study session. I don't want to distract her before the big test so I'll text her later."

"Good idea." She cradled the cup. "I'll get ready. It's beautiful outside."

"Do you want to go up to the rooftop garden? Or we can walk to the Commons," he said as he loaded the dishes into the dishwasher and wiped the counter.

"Let's go to the Commons. I'll have enough of being cooped up inside at the hospital." Emily leaned in for a kiss before she headed to the bedroom.

Aiden joined her a few minutes later to brush his teeth and double-check the bag. "I texted Alex and updated her. She's on standby." He held out his hand. "I have my wallet and keys, and the bag. Are we missing anything?"

"I have all I need." She stroked his cheek.

"Mmm, good. Me too." He grinned. "After the next one?"

Emily nodded and waited it out, loving how Aiden held her, talking to her in a gentle voice while rubbing her back.

"You set the pace and tell me what you need or want me to do."

As they started down the street, she stretched and inhaled the balmy summer air, thankful to be outside.

"Vanna will want to be there right afterward," Aiden said. "She wanted to be here, but the final exam is more important."

"It's better she's busy with things rather than hanging around the hospital."

"True. She confessed her plans for law school. Little sneak came by when I was at work. She figured she could spill the news and make a break for it."

Emily laughed as a picture formed in her mind. "How did you take it?"

"It's fine. She can take several undergraduate programs before she applies. Tom will involve her at the firm which will give her exposure to law as a career. If she's happy with her choice, fantastic. She got all worked up for no reason."

"I figured." Emily stopped, leaning into Aiden. "Mmm, it hurts, but the back pressure helps."

"Noted."

She took several deep breaths before straightening and linking their fingers. "You called Tom?"

"Jenna got to him first. I called Gramma Grace and Nina. They will make the other calls for us."

"So they'll descend upon us soon?"

"Yup, but Nina and Gramma have dibs on the guest rooms. Everyone else received the list of nearby hotels. I can't imagine Caroline hanging around. She'd drive me insane."

"How's Alex? She's not opening up. Is everything okay?"

He shook his head. "They've hidden their problems for too long."

"I feel awful that I missed it. We were having our own issues, and I've been so preoccupied and clueless. And she didn't say a word."

"I didn't think it was this serious. When we were at the Vineyard, there were subtle signs, but I figured it was the usual baby blues."

"It's odd because Joel's great with kids."

"He's a great dad when he's around. That's the problem. Work stress then coming home to an unhappy wife led to extra stress at home. He buried himself at work to avoid being home. The resentment grew, making Joel want to be home even less."

"And that led to Alex being even more upset and angry and resentful." Emily nodded. "Soon, you aren't talking, not spending time together, and the intimacy disappears."

"He confessed things weren't good when we were out that night. Once I got Alex talking, she told me everything. Joel resisted the counseling idea, but Tom and I talked him into it. He says he wants to save his marriage so he'd better act like it."

She entwined their fingers. "Alex talks to you. How did you get her to do that? You're Joel's friend."

"That beach house belonged to her family, not his." Aiden turned toward her. "Alex and I spent several summers hanging out before either of us knew Joel even existed."

"Now it makes sense," Emily said. "When she broke down that night in the kitchen, she seemed comfortable with you."

They continued toward the park, fingers entwined, Emily observing him with the occasional glance.

Until this baby was born, it all seemed hypothetical—*when the baby comes we'll do this, when the baby comes we'll do that*—but now? The birth of their child was imminent and their son would bind them together in a way far more permanent, and far beyond any connection she'd experienced with a man in her life.

What if they drifted apart as their child, work, and the day-to-day minutiae of life consumed them? On the surface, their friends seemed the perfect married team while underneath a storm brewed. A swirling vortex of anger and resentment surrounded the couple as they'd walled themselves off and retreated into their own corners. The two had pretended themselves right into a corner.

She pulled him onto a bench, her stomach rolling. "Can you promise me something?"

He took both of her hands, angling toward her. "What would that be?"

"Maybe it's something we need to promise one another. Our lives are changing, and after today, they'll never be the same. We're having a baby."

"I'm aware." A saucy grin appeared as he caressed her belly. "It's hard to miss."

"Aiden." Emily frowned. "I'm serious."

"Sorry." The grin faded, and he regained his gentle grip on her hands. "What should we promise?"

"That we won't ever let our love die. I never want to resent you or lose what we have. Right from our first night together, there has been such fire and energy and passion and—" She stroked his cheek with her fingertips. "On some level, I knew, and it frightened me. The uncontrollable free fall. It's a feeling I never want to lose."

He opened his mouth, but she pressed a finger to his lips.

"Swear we won't lose the desire to be with each other. The next few months will be so, so hard and we've been through so much already. What if we lose each other? What if we become another Alex and Joel?"

"No one promised it would be easy. Nothing worthwhile ever is." Aiden rubbed her hands. "I vow I won't stop talking or take you for granted, nor will I ever stop loving you. We're in this together. A team." He smiled. "Trust in us and our love. We'll make it."

"You swear?"

"I swear I'll never leave you," he whispered. "Do you?"

"With all my heart." She exhaled, letting go of the tension. The anxiety faded away. It felt wonderful and freeing to have said it out loud and to have him make those promises. She wrapped her arms around his neck and captured his lips, putting every ounce of her love into the kiss.

He tipped his head, resting his forehead against hers. "I'm with you, every single step of the way."

"We'll be more than fine." A strong contraction forced her to the present. But it wasn't so bad. The knowledge she'd get through this, that he'd be with her for every moment of this life-altering event, lightened her heart. "You see that little place right there? It sells great iced tea." Emily blinked at him.

Aiden laughed. "You want one?"

She batted her eyes. "It's hot and I'm thirsty. I'll wait here."

"Your wish is my command." He winked and glanced at his watch.

"You're not going."

"Give it a minute, and then I'll fetch your drink." Aiden pointed at the ticking second hand. Then he patted her belly. "Mommy needs to learn patience, right son?"

Emily rolled her eyes, but a strong contraction interrupted her reply. She clung to him, grateful he was there to help her through the worst of it.

"Now I'll get your iced tea." He rubbed her hand and disappeared into the coffee shop.

Emily relaxed and studied the people strolling by while she enjoyed her short reprieve. This was the easy part. It would get harder, but she figured if Aiden was this attentive during labor and delivery, it wouldn't be so bad.

Natalia had sworn how awful the experience had been, and her advice had been *take the drugs, Emily, the epidural was fabulous.* But Nat didn't have Aiden holding her hand. Natalia's useless husband had been watching ESPN while his wife gave birth to their child.

"Here." Aiden sat on the bench beside her, holding out a tall, frosty cup and a small bag. He sipped his own drink. "Excellent idea."

Emily took a long pull on the straw, sighing in satisfaction. "Good, right?" She peeked into the bag. "Yum. How did you know?"

"The smells in there made my mouth water, and I couldn't help myself. I thought I'd share with my favorite lady."

"Mi vida." She stroked his cheek and graced him with a smile.

"Why don't we find a place to sit in the shade and hang out? I'll update Alex and let her know we're fine. No rush, right? You're feeling good?"

"Sounds wonderful."

And it was. They strolled, making stops as she needed, sitting and sharing their snacks from the small bakery. They talked about everything, Aiden keeping her distracted. They even watched the world go by as she reclined against him on a bench. After a while they found a grassy spot to spread out the blanket and they relaxed in comfortable silence.

She moved closer, pillowing her head on his arm and closing her eyes, and swore she may even have drifted off for a short nap.

"Time to walk. I need to move." Emily took his hand as they ambled along, stopping whenever she needed.

"Maybe we should finish our walk?" Aiden checked his watch as her contraction finished.

"That would be a good idea." She felt amazing, but the constant walking and movement helped her progress. "Or I'll be popping this kid out in the middle of the pathway."

He laughed. "Oh, let's not do that." His expression became serious. "I'm glad I was here, and we've kept it as relaxing as possible. It's about to become intense."

As if on cue, another wave rolled over her. She propped herself against him as he ran a hand around to rub her back. "They're super close together."

"You're doing great. We're almost there." He dropped a kiss on her hair. "We'll get you into a room. The contractions are only a few minutes apart."

Emily nodded, grimacing as another strong contraction hit. Now it was getting real.

Aiden stayed calm, encouraging her to breathe. "Our baby will be here before you know it."

They signed in and the nurse escorted them to an assessment room. Emily changed into a gown and clutched Aiden's hand as everything intensified.

"Perfect timing." The nurse nodded. "Almost fully dilated and effaced. Straight to the delivery suites for you."

A nurse whisked them into the labor and delivery unit soon afterward.

Emily changed positions and swayed her hips, continuously moving. "Are you ready?" She squeezed her husband's hand after the latest and strongest contraction.

"Absolutely. Are you?" He brushed back her hair, dabbing at her face with a damp cloth.

"Yes." Constant waves rolled over her now. It was time.

"You're crowning," the nurse said after she performed a quick exam. "I'll call for the midwife. This baby is coming right now."

"Almost there, Em." Aiden guided her hand to touch the top of the baby's head.

Tears sprang to her eyes. The moment she'd been waiting for had arrived. She peeked at Aiden, trying to smile. "I need to push."

"Hold on. We have someone coming." The nurse hung up the phone.

"No, now." She inhaled, panting in short gasps to avoid pushing, staring at Aiden.

He glanced down and then at her, his eyes widening. As he tugged a pair of gloves out of the dispenser, he smiled. "Let's do it. Em, push. You can do this."

The nurse stepped in to support Emily and helped her move upright as she gave in to the urge and bore down.

"Good, breathe, breathe, hold … and when you're ready, push." Aiden's reassuring and encouraging words enveloped her. "That's it. Head's out, so take a few breaths, and … I'm ready when you are."

It passed in a blur, unreal like a dream. Not like real life at all. The nurse lowered her to rest against the pillows as Aiden laid the baby across her chest, a grin lighting up his face.

Emily touched the tiny, red, mewling infant. "He's perfect. So beautiful." A tear trickled down her cheek as she placed her hands on her sweet new son.

"He's gorgeous, Em." Aiden joined her. "Incredible." He kissed her lips while resting a hand on their baby boy.

She blinked back her tears. "Oh, Aiden." With a shake of her head, she sunk into his embrace.

"Time to get him cleaned up and then he's all yours." His lips brushed her temple before he clamped and cut the cord, giving her one more kiss before lifting the baby.

The pediatrician bustled into the room, along with the rest of the delivery team, and took charge of the infant's first exam while the midwife took over with Emily.

Aiden joined the group crowded around their baby boy.

"All good?" She strained to make sense of the murmurs.

"He's perfect and healthy." Aiden turned and grinned.

She couldn't take her eyes off Aiden as they handed him the tiny bundle. She realized at that moment how much being here meant to him.

The magical words floated to her ears. "Say hi, Mommy." Tears shone in Aiden's eyes as he tucked their beautiful baby boy into her arms. "You were amazing. I love you." He slid an arm around her shoulders and perched on the side of the bed. "Look at him, he's so perfect and adorable."

The tears trickled down her face as she rested against his shoulder. She couldn't speak, robbed of her voice by the emotions sweeping over her. His breath fanned her hair as his arm tightened, and she knew he understood. After several deep breaths, the lump in her throat loosened. "He's gorgeous." She stared down at the tiny face and the dark, unblinking eyes. The sniffle escaped as she raised her gaze to her husband's face.

He brushed away her tears with his thumb, leaning down to give her a sweet, warm kiss. "Our son. How crazy is that? We have a son, and I delivered him." He kept his arm looped around her as he ran a hand over the baby's downy head. "Welcome to the world, Kellan Alejandro Hamilton."

⌒⤳

Emily padded out of the bathroom, overcome with elation at the sight before her.

Aiden sat by her bed, cuddling the tiny bundle in the crook of his arm. His besotted grin made her weak in the knees.

There was something incredibly sexy about a strong vibrant man holding a tiny, helpless baby, unafraid to let his love shine through. Their little boy had his daddy spellbound and had stolen his heart.

"I need to feed him." Emily brushed a hand over her husband's hair before settling herself on the bed.

"Hungry, little man?" He rose to nestle the baby in her arms and plumped her pillows. "Vanna's thrilled to hear she has a little brother. Alex went to pick her up."

"Perfect. I should be done nursing before they arrive."

"Nina and Gramma are on the jet from Chicago, along with the Grayson family." He winked. "And so it begins."

Emily gazed at her son. "It'll be great. Time to meet the rest of the family. Isn't that right, my precious boy?" Her heart swelled with love as she held him close. She hadn't comprehended the hold such a tiny being could have over her. Today, they had formed the most precious memories, molding them, creating a stronger family unit.

To never experience these moments, or create these everlasting pictures etched in your mind was unfathomable to Emily. She understood Aiden's struggle. His family had stolen this incredible and special time from him when Savannah was born.

"You were wonderful. It's been an unforgettable day. Thank you for being here," Emily said.

He sank onto the bed, tucking his arm around her. "I wouldn't have missed it for anything."

Chapter 36

Aiden

The day had been amazing, incredible, and beautiful in ways Aiden hadn't expected. So often people rushed into the ER in a panicked mess, usually because something was wrong, or in cases of precipitous labor. He'd never been there for from the start of labor all the way through to the actual birth. Welcoming your child into the world seemed magical.

They'd grown closer. Another wall between them crumbled as she admitted her unspoken fears. That their marriage might bend and break. The strain a new baby brought into a relationship was a valid reason for concern.

We won't let that happen. We won't let go or stop talking. We recognize the dangers. We're witnesses to how complacency and inaction can lead to the destruction of intimacy, and how love isn't always enough to save you from reality. Something he knew all too well.

He shook off the thoughts. It wasn't over until it was truly over. Damned if he'd let Joel give up and make the biggest mistake of his life. Letting Alexis walk away would be the height of stupidity.

"Sleeping isn't allowed." Emily's sweet and gentle voice cut in on his thoughts. "If I'm awake, so are you." Her soft tone assured him she was anything but annoyed.

"Wouldn't dream of it." He opened his eyes and smiled at her. "All done feeding our boy?"

"He seems content for the moment." She brushed a fingertip over the baby's cheek, love shining in her eyes. "So sweet. Look at these teeny tiny little fingers. He's perfect."

He sat beside her on the bed, admiring his son's sleeping face. "You did a great job, Mommy."

"Now that sounds strange. Mommy. Vanna calls you Dad, so I guess you're used to it. Daddy."

"It still sounds wonderful." He'd missed so much with Savannah. To receive a second chance with his son was amazing.

"Dad." Vanna peeked in the door, a delighted smile on her face.

"Come on in." Elation ran through Aiden at having both of his children together. He'd never even imagined it until now.

"He's so tiny. Can I hold him?" Vanna focused on the baby, ignoring the photographer who had been in and out to snap pictures.

"Of course. Support his head like that ... right." Emily slid Kellan into his big sister's arms. "Meet your baby brother, Kellan Alejandro Hamilton."

"Hi, Kellan, I'm your big sister. You are too adorable. Oh my goodness, what a sweet little face." Savannah placed a gentle kiss on his downy head. She looked up with tears in her eyes. "I never thought I'd have a baby brother."

Alex peeked through the open door. "How's everyone doing?"

"Wonderful." Emily beckoned their friend. "Come and meet the new addition to our family, though I'm not sure big sister will give him up."

"No, I suppose not." Alex approached Savannah, who was rocking the baby in her arms. "Oh, he's beautiful. It went well?"

Emily grinned. "It couldn't have gone better. Did Aiden tell you?"

"Tell me what?" Alex's eyes trained on Emily for a moment, before returning to the baby's face.

"Daddy delivered him. It all happened so fast they didn't even have time to get the team in here. We have it in living color. Serena was here, and she caught the moment on camera. I can't wait to see the actual proofs from today." Emily smiled at the photographer. "No rush, I know you have lots of photos to take yet, but I'm happy you were here."

"I don't catch moments like that often," Serena said. "Cutting the cord, yes. Dad taking over and catching the baby like a pro? Never happens."

"Well, I am a doctor." Aiden shrugged, but he sported a huge grin. It thrilled him to have the moment on film. "I was only supposed to support Em today, but hey, you do what you gotta do."

Alexis wrapped her arms around him. "Congratulations, he's beautiful, and such a special day for all of you."

"Thanks, Alex. It feels damn good." Aiden planted a kiss on her cheek. "The superstar was Emily. She was amazing and so calm through the whole thing."

"Easy when you have such a wonderful and attentive husband." She held hand toward him. "I couldn't have gotten through this without you."

He felt like the luckiest man on the planet. The look on her face was even more joyous and loving than the day she walked down the aisle. How he deserved this woman loving him that much he didn't understand, but he'd make sure she knew he felt the same about her. He'd happily spend the rest of his life proving it.

Her eyes met his, and he felt the rush to the bottom of his soul.

The voices sounding in the hallway broke the connection and Gramma Grace, Nina and Jenna appeared.

"You're here," Aiden said.

"My husband insisted we leave right away. He's parking the car and will be right up." Jenna gave him a hug and a kiss on the cheek. "Congratulations."

They exchanged hugs all around, and Aiden seated Grace, placing her great-grandson in her arms.

"Look at this lovely little boy." Her eyes shone as she cradled her great-grandson. "I'm thrilled I could see him. Thank you for arranging it with Tom."

He leaned down to kiss Grace's cheek. "We needed you here to share this amazing day."

Tom appeared moments later. "Congratulations." He hugged Aiden, then Emily. "Adrianna is with a sitter. I didn't think they'd allow us to bring her into the delivery ward. You'll get to meet her tomorrow."

"Thanks for bringing Gramma and Nina."

"No problem. We were glad to give them a lift." Tom looked around. "Where's Joel?" he whispered.

"No clue." Aiden shrugged. "I messaged, but I haven't heard, and I don't want to ask Alex."

"I'll check on him. You stay with your family." Tom patted his shoulder. "Looks like I'll be fighting the ladies off to hold my nephew."

Aiden nodded, taking in the scene. The elated smile of Nina as she hugged her daughter and took her turn holding her grandson. The woman's warm and loving embrace for Savannah, who been accepted as her granddaughter. Everyone in this room was his family, one way or another, and it was so much more than he ever dreamed or expected.

The perfect ending to the perfect day.

⁓≼

Aiden crawled into bed, sinking into the soft mattress. He'd stayed after everyone had left, helping Emily with changing and tucking his son into the small clear bassinet placed beside her bed. Those peaceful moments with their son had given them time to bond as a family. With reluctance, he'd kissed them goodnight and wandered home, savoring the memories of the day.

A soft tap sounded at his bedroom door.

Savannah peeked in. "You're still awake." She padded across the room and crawled onto the bed, tossing the extra pillows off to make room. She flopped back. "How are Emily and Kellan?"

"They're great. Em ordered me to come home and sleep."

"He's precious. I can't believe you delivered him."

"It was incredible and I'll never forget it. They'll be home tomorrow." Aiden glanced at his daughter. It was funny how well he'd gotten to know her in a short time. Something was bothering her. "It'll be okay. It's a big change for everyone."

Savannah raised a brow. "You mean Kellan coming home? Sure, but it'll be great. I'm looking forward to it. I texted Leanne and Justin and sent them pictures. They both said congratulations and think he's adorable."

"Thank them for me."

"You and Emily are both so happy. I can see it in her eyes. I bet she'll be one of those cool moms everyone wishes they had." Savannah smiled. "I'm glad you married her. She's the complete opposite of the wicked stepmother's some other kids at school have. Several girls told me they're jealous." She giggled. "Some of them still think you're my big brother."

"Ah, whatever. Honest mistake. I get comments at work too. Like, *are you even old enough to be a doctor?* and it makes me laugh. That day you asked how old I was, I wondered if you thought they'd pawned you off on a medical student."

She shook her head. "I heard Emily call you Aiden, and I was putting it together and wondering if you were old enough to have a fourteen-year-old daughter."

"Barely." Aiden laughed. "So you're okay with everything?" He rolled, watching her as she looked away, avoiding his eyes. "Spill it, Vanna. You can tell me anything."

"I don't want to ruin today. It's special, and you need to sleep after being with Emily all day."

"You know what else is special? Having you here. I always have time for you. If something's bothering you, we should talk about it right away." Aiden took her hand in his. "Tell me."

"Chase and I broke up." Tears glistened in her eyes. "He wants to see other people and be free to date other people because I'll be gone all summer. Then we can get back together in the fall."

He squeezed her hand, trying to stay calm and control the anger that rose. The kid was a little shit, treating his daughter like that, and he wished he could do something about it. However, getting upset would only make it worse. "I'm sorry he said those things to you, it's not right for him to even suggest it. It's never easy to break up." They lapsed into silence and he waited to see if she would add anything.

"It blows. He's been flirting with another girl. A friend of mine said he was hanging out with her at this party last weekend. It's like he wants to break up so he can ... you know." She brushed at her eyes.

His heart plummeted. Seeing his little girl devastated by some asshole teenage boy wasn't easy. "Oh, honey." He reached across the small distance and pulled her close, letting her cry.

She sobbed. "The worst part is, I think he's already... ch-ch-cheated on me. She goes to our school."

Aiden sighed. Teenage heartbreak was something he understood only too well. Now he wanted to pummel the kid into the ground. Cheating was never okay in his books, and the boy deserved a good kick in the ass. "Teenage boys can be immature and stupid, and unthinking. You probably don't want to hear this but you're better off without him. If you don't trust him, it's over. If he'd say things like that and cheat on you? Time to kick him to the curb."

She nodded. "I told him to get lost. If he thinks for one second he can mess around all summer and I'll come running back to him in the fall, he's dead wrong. I don't want to be with someone like that." Vanna accepted the offered tissue. "Leanne said the same thing. I'm better off without him... well, she told me to dump his ass and never go back."

"I'm proud of you for not accepting his bad behavior. Someday you'll meet the right guy. Enjoy being young and free."

"And if I never find him?"

"You will. Some guy will treasure you, trust me. In the meantime, don't let it get you down. You have the whole summer away so you won't see him... or her until fall. The Vineyard is fun and there are lots of kids your age. We'll make sure you get out and meet them." He gave her a squeeze. "Better to know now, so you won't waste another second of precious time. And it leaves you free all summer, and by the time we come home, I bet you'll have forgotten all about Chase Westlake."

"It's not so easy. I liked him."

He sympathized as he'd been there too many times himself.

She glanced at him, picking at a nail. "Can I ask you something? It's kind of personal, and you might not want to talk about it."

"I can't promise I'll answer, but I won't lie either."

"How long did you and Tiffany date? You were younger than me."

"Almost two years the first time."

"The first time?" Savannah furrowed her brow.

"We were together on and off over a span of seven years. Then we separated for good. It's been ten years since we last broke up."

"You dated a long time."

"Well, yes and no. We were steady for the first year and a half. After that, it more off than on. It wasn't great, then we concluded it wasn't working, and it never would. There's too much baggage."

"You never see her now?"

Aiden shook his head. "I haven't seen or talked to her since before Christmas. We don't agree on much, aside from it being best to keep our distance. Living in Boston makes it easier."

"You say I'm too young to commit to one person, yet you were with Tiffany for so long."

"Ahh, the irony." It must be hard for her some days, considering his unruly years as a teenager, even if she didn't even know half of what he'd gotten up to. "Even as an adult, things aren't always obvious."

"I know." Savannah curled up on Emily's side of the bed. "Is Alex okay? She seemed down, and Joel didn't come. And you watched Daniel."

"I'm sure we'll see Joel tomorrow." Aiden tried to keep his voice light even though disappointment that Joel hadn't shown up at the hospital. "Get some rest, and we'll talk more tomorrow."

"Can I sleep here?"

"No hogging the bed." Aiden flicked off the light.

"Deal." Savannah rolled over, burying her head in the pillow.

The maternity ward was a hub of activity, even this early in the morning. As expected, Emily was awake and nursing Kellan.

"Good morning." He bent to kiss her, running a hand through her dark silky hair. "How'd you sleep?"

"Not that well. The nurses were in to check on me or Kellan, and the hallway is never quiet. Must have been baby rush hour." She smothered a yawn. "I was up to feed this little monkey. Please tell me you're here to take me home? I want our bed in our blissful and quiet apartment."

"Don't be so sure about peace. Gramma and Nina will fight over who makes breakfast."

"True." Emily snickered. "Hey, where's the car seat? They said they'd discharge me today."

"I'll run down and get it from the car. My hands were full." He held up the travel mugs and a small bag of muffins.

"Oh, my savior. They served breakfast, but I bet what you brought is delicious. I'm starving."

"Fresh blueberry muffins. Vanna's been baking again." He set the bag on the small table tray attached to the bed. "She broke up with Chase."

"Oh, no. Is she okay?" Emily frowned even as she reached into the bag and broke off a chunk of the fresh muffin.

"We had a long talk after I got home last night. She's sad, but I doubt she expected it to last forever."

"I'm sure not. Well, in a few days we'll be off to the Vineyard, and we'll keep her plenty busy."

"Maybe getting out sailing and down to the public beaches where the teenagers hang out will help. Perhaps we should host a barbecue or something, invite a few of the regular summer families over as lots of them would have kids Vanna's age. Leanne will be out for a visit which should cheer her up."

"You're energetic. Host a barbecue with a brand new baby in the house?"

"We could team up with Tom, Jenna, Joel, and Alex? Hire locals to help with the serving and cleanup? If you're not up for it, we don't have to, Em. We can see how it goes and decide."

"Good. It's too early for me to know how I'll feel. We need plenty of family time. Remember our promise?"

"I remember. I took the summer off so we could spend time together and create some new memories in the Vineyard."

Emily nodded. "Let's enjoy an incredible summer together."

Chapter 37

Emily

KELLAN'S MEWLING WHIMPER FORCED EMILY to open her eyes. Her eyelids were heavy weights she could barely lift. He'd been up every few hours, and the change from Boston to the house in the Vineyard hadn't helped matters.

"I'll get him." Aiden kissed her cheek and his weight left the mattress.

She sighed. A two-week-old baby meant sleep had become a thing of the past. Her eyelids drooped, subconsciously aware of the soft sounds as Aiden changed the baby and talked to him in a soothing voice.

"Em."

A smile teased her lips as Aiden cradled the tiny boy against his well-toned chest, making the tiny boy appear even smaller. She couldn't get enough of seeing her husband with their son. The way he held their baby with complete tenderness and love was adorable.

Aiden laid the baby beside her on the bed, and she positioned herself to feed him. "You awake enough?"

"I've got it." Emily stroked the baby's downy head, inhaling the sweet smell. "Thanks for changing him."

"I'll get the water." Aiden was back in moments, carrying two glasses of ice-cold water from the small fridge he'd installed in their room. He held the cup so she could sip through the straw before reaching across to place it on the bedside table.

"I'll tuck him in." Emily motioned to the bassinet beside their king-sized bed. "Go to sleep, you look like you need it." He deserved rest, considering how often he changed diapers in the middle of the night.

He nodded and plumped his pillow, burying his head. Moments later he was fast asleep, his breathing soft and even.

Not long afterward, she put the baby back into his own bed, and curled up, falling into a deep sleep.

⁓≼

Emily lounged under the large umbrella on their secluded beach, watching Vanna chase Daniel through the small waves washing up on the sand. Despite the heat, the girl had boundless energy, while Emily could scarcely keep her eyes open. The sound of the surf and calls of the gulls lulled and tempted her to close her eyes for a late afternoon siesta.

Alex stared over the water in gloomy silence, the corners of her mouth down-turned. The woman became more withdrawn with each passing day. With good reason, Emily supposed. If her husband were neglecting her and Kellan, Emily would be raving.

Emily hadn't missed the stony looks passing between the couple on the few occasions she'd seen them together. It had to be difficult for Alex to have their marital troubles playing out in public.

Emily grinned at the volley of giggles issuing from the small boy, imagining the time when Kellan would be the one playing in the surf. "Vanna's great with Daniel."

"Uh-huh."

"Alex?" She shifted on the lounger, turning to contemplate her friend. "I won't bother asking if you're okay. Clearly, you're not. You need to talk about it."

"Not sure what there is to say." Alex expelled a long drawn-out sigh. "Joel refuses to go for counseling. He's angry and intolerable, and I barely see him. My marriage is over."

"Oh, Alex." Emily reached across to squeeze her friend's hand. "Are you sure? Maybe Aiden could talk to him again."

"Joel's already pissed and he won't appreciate any more advice. He's given up on us. You're so lucky." She brushed at her eyes. "Aiden's involved in everything. And my man is where? Who the hell knows?" The words choked from her mouth. "He doesn't even have time for Daniel."

"I'm sorry." When her friend offered nothing further, she said, "Things haven't always been great between me and Aiden. I let fear rule me for a long time."

Alex glanced at Emily. "Now I get why you were reluctant to move. Nothing like a cheating bastard to turn you off men."

Emily straightened. "You think Joel's cheating?"

She shrugged. "He's never home and he can barely look at me, let alone touch me. I'm waiting for the day I find the closet cleaned out or him in bed with some woman he picked up at the bar."

Emily closed her eyes, remembering Aiden's comment. How the feeling she hadn't settled in Boston had hung over him. How he'd worried she'd bolt. She imagined Alex was entertaining similar fears. "Have you told him how you feel? I know it's hard, but once Aiden and I opened up, things turned around."

"The most I get from him these days is a few grunts. He's turned into a first-class slob. I do everything. Manage the house, pay the bills, make sure the meals are made, and care for our son."

"It seems he's avoiding everyone."

"Uh-huh. Your husband gave him a solid ass-kicking or two, and Joel resents it. Aiden's invited him sailing and Joel doesn't even bother answering. When he won't even respond to his closest friends, it's time to accept reality."

"Men." Emily huffed. "How can they be so damn clueless? If he gives you up, he's crazy."

"Or I'm crazy. I don't even know how we got here. How did you deal with the emotions, knowing about the infidelity? I understand that your father cheating differs from finding out your husband is screwing around, but how did he make it up to you?"

"The bastard never even tried. He attended our wedding and all, but since then it's back to the occasional phone call. Even when I was a teenager, he didn't make a lot of effort. My mom raised us."

"I'd move back to Chicago, but I like being close to all of you. Aiden's been great, too. I feel bad, stealing him away from you as much as I do."

"No, no. Stay in Boston, so you can be nearby. Aiden considers you family, Alex, and if you ever need help, we'll be there. That's what family does. We stick together, and we're there for each other."

Alex burst into tears.

"Don't cry." She blinked hard against her own tears.

Alex waved a hand as Emily pushed tissues on her, and then slid across to the other woman's lounger, pulling Alex into a hug.

"I h-hate him ... but I l-love him. I don't want it to be over. So m-messed up." The words barely fit between the choking sobs emitting from Alex. "He's such an a-asshole."

"Hey." She patted Alex on the back, looking up into Aiden's concerned face.

He kneeled in the sand beside the lounger, rubbing Alex's back. "What happened?"

"We were talking." Emily's tearful eyes met his, and he gave a small nod.

"You okay?" He wrapped his arms around them both.

"I'll be fine." Alex swiped at her face before regaining control and pulling away. "I thought you were up at the house, making dinner."

"Tom's finishing. I volunteered to help you ladies clean up the beach. Why don't you take the kids? It'll give Em and Jenna a chance to feed the babies before we eat."

He lifted Kellan from under the sunshade, handing him to Emily while Alexis grabbed her bag, waving at Savannah, who scooped up Daniel, bringing him over.

Emily stopped to pat Aiden's cheek and brush his lips with hers. "Don't ever change."

Emily peeked into the bassinet, resisting the urge to run a finger over her son's downy head. The baby was sleeping, so she crawled into bed beside Aiden, who was typing on his laptop.

"How's it coming?" She wiggled over, snuggling against his chest.

"Good. Just let me save." He tapped a few keys and closed his laptop, setting it on the bedside table. After turning off the light, he wrapped an arm around her.

Emily lifted her chin, accepting a long slow kiss, before resting her head on his chest. "I love it here. It's amazing we're staying all summer."

"Vanna seems to be managing, but I promised we'd get out sailing soon. If it's sunny tomorrow, maybe I'll take her out if you don't mind managing for a few hours?" He rubbed her arm.

"I'll be fine. Jenna and I planned to implement a daily walk on the beach. We'll try to coerce Alex out of her house. She needs to keep busy as things aren't going well with Joel."

"So I gather. She was a mess at the beach, and she barely ate anything. She hardly said two words when I walked them home." Aiden sighed. "I tried, but she was tired and wanted to sleep."

"Was Joel home when you got there?"

"No. I'm worried. He's never been like this ... ever. He ignores his friends and he's neglecting Alex and Daniel. If I ever get like that, give me a hard slap upside the head."

"Nah. Tom will do it for me." Her saucy grin faded as she thought about Alex and her allegations. "What if he's cheating?"

"It's the ultimate betrayal in a marriage and nearly impossible to forgive. Not sure they'd get past it." Aiden slid down further, pulling her closer. "Watching their relationship implode is painful. If he opened his damn eyes he'd see she still loves him. Short of a major intervention, I don't know how to help anymore. Talking to him failed."

"Don't let it happen to us. Please," she whispered.

"We won't let it happen. Ever." He leaned in, capturing her lips again.

Emily relaxed against him, enjoying the closeness and intimacy of their kissing and cuddling. She sighed as she curled up, listening to the steady beat of his heart.

He stroked her hair and twirled a strand around his fingertip. "Sleep, Em," he whispered before dropping a kiss on her hair. "Our little man will be up in two or three hours."

"Mmmhmm." She closed her eyes, letting herself drift off.

She awoke to Aiden running a hand over her hair, his lips pressed against her forehead. Despite being up twice during the night, he seemed wide-awake. And dressed.

"Vanna and I are heading out for a sail. It's beautiful, but later this afternoon they're calling for thundershowers. Kellan's asleep, so rest."

"Okay," she murmured, accepting another kiss. "Have fun and be safe."

"I'm always careful on the water."

She curled up, waking again as the baby fussed. As she nursed him in the rocking chair near their window, she stared over the water. It was so peaceful and amazing. These quiet little moments holding her baby boy were ones she'd never forget.

Once he was satisfied and drifting back to sleep, she sent a quick text to Jenna to arrange their daily walk, then showered and dressed.

A soft tap on the door alerted her when Jenna arrived, and she settled Kellan into the baby wrap.

"Ready?" Jenna swayed, Adrianna snuggled in her own sling.

Emily peered at the gathering clouds as they started down the beach. "I hope they're okay."

"Don't worry. Tom and Aiden are experienced sailors."

"And Alex? What's going on with her?"

Jenna shrugged. "She didn't want to come. Tom suggested we take Daniel for a few days to give Alex a break. Maybe the guys could watch the kids while we take her out. She needs to kick back and have fun."

"It's a plan. Aiden intends to track down Joel to take one final run." Emily glanced over at her friend. "He refuses to give up."

"At least someone still believes in their marriage even if neither of them does. I love his optimism."

Emily laughed. "None of you would give up on us, and look where we are now. He's returning the favor."

"They aren't you and Aiden. We're spectators, watching as they hurtle onto the reef and plummet to the bottom. There's no rescue if they refuse to grab a life preserver."

It was a sobering thought. Alex had insisted Emily fight for Aiden, yet the woman was bailing on her own relationship. Emily hoped this last effort saved them. Their marriage drowning in complacency was the last thing she wanted to witness.

CHAPTER 38

Aiden

AFTER ANOTHER GLANCE DOWN THE beach, Aiden sighed. Joel was ditching them.

He'd barely seen his friend in weeks. Even Kellan's birth hadn't gapped the growing distance between Joel and his friends. The man made only a brief appearance, relayed a surly congratulations and disappeared without even holding the baby boy.

Perhaps it wasn't his place, but he felt bound to reach out as his friends had for him. After much planning, Aiden orchestrated a meeting in a pub in Edgartown and finally, Joel agreed to sailing, but only if Vanna joined them.

Joel clearly viewed the girl as a buffer. Coaxing Joel out of his shell to find out what was happening in the guy's mind was the whole point, but Aiden agreed to the terms. There was still hope if his friend dropped his guard in the comfortable and familiar setting. Still, he prepared himself for an epic fail.

He glanced at his watch and went below to stow the last of the gear.

Vanna looked up from her spot at the table. "He's still not here?"

Aiden shook his head. "We might need to send a search party." He held up a hand at the clunk on deck.

"Hey." Joel appeared on the steps, bag in hand.

"We were about to give up on you."

"Had to get my nagging, bitchy wife off my back. Seems it's okay if I go out supervised, but otherwise I'm lectured. It's ridiculous. I'm a grown-ass man who can find his way home, for fuck's sake."

"Your enthusiasm is overwhelming." Aiden crossed his arms.

"You're stuck with me. So deal." Joel stowed his bag. "Let's go."

Aiden scrubbed his jaw. Maybe this was a bad idea. Spending hours in the close quarters of a sailboat might be more than he could bear. Only for Alex would he tolerate Joel's foul mood.

"Let's do this." Aiden cast off lines while Joel pulled in the bumpers. At least he could trust the guy if things got rough, given the number of times they'd sailed together.

Vanna helped with setting the sails, and soon they were skimming across the waves, the sun glinting off the water.

"Good weather report?" Joel sat back, gazing at the expanse of blue.

"No major weather events expected and it should be a gorgeous day. The wind will be up later, but nothing heavy, and we'll be back mid-afternoon."

Vanna stood at the wheel, her delight at being in control of the sailboat making Aiden smile.

"Your sailor girl. That must thrill you." Joel looped an arm over the back of the bench as Savannah checked the gauges, her ponytail whipping in the breeze. "She's a beauty, just like her mother."

"Mmmhmm." There were days when the resemblance took Aiden's breath away. An ache filled his soul, and an incredible sadness washed over him. Tiffany seemed blind to what she was missing and how she'd devastated this amazing and precious girl.

"Tiffany, the stunning ice-queen," Joel said. "I saw her in Edgartown the other day. She rented a house for the summer." He smirked. "She didn't seem to care you were here."

"I hadn't heard." Aiden's heart sank. Why couldn't she pick another island? "Where'd she rent?"

"Not far from our place. You'll have to tell Jenna and Alex their former bestie is in town. Her presence will be popular with the gold-digging whore." He snickered.

Aiden narrowed his eyes. "Tell her yourself. You live in the same damn house." A glance toward Savannah told him she hadn't heard Joel's remark. "I heard about the breakfast drama, so stop."

"Alex and I aren't speaking much these days, but you talk to her daily. You're spending time with my son." Joel crossed his arms. "When you relay the full report on the day, you can share the news."

Aided rolled his eyes. This was a definite bust. The guy wouldn't talk if he had it in his head that an official account would be filed with his wife. "I'm not a carrier pigeon, asshole. What the hell is up with you?"

Joel glowered, his lips setting in a thin line.

"Stop pretending this mess is Alex's fault. She's upset and someone needs to be there for her and Daniel if you won't."

"I'm sure you're *there* for her."

Shock ran through Aiden. "Have you lost your fucking mind?"

"Oh, come on. You and Alex have always been close. The question is … how close?"

"Whoa." Aiden held up his hands. "When did you get so damn paranoid?"

Joel stood, crossing his arms. "In all the years you've known Alex, you two have never?" He waggled his brows.

"We haven't. Ever. I wouldn't do that to you or my wife."

His friend's shoulders slumped and he shifted, staring at the water. "Fine," he said in a flat voice.

"You're crazy if you think Alex is cheating." Aiden sat beside him. Time to take it down a couple notches based on the concerned looks coming from Vanna. "Talk to me, man. What's going on?"

"Nothing much." His knuckles whitened as he grasped the silver side rail. "Alex ignores me. I moved into the spare room, and I hate being at home. It's so chilly all the time. She doesn't ask where I've been, or when I'm coming home, or make me meals or …" Joel threw his hands in the air. "I can't do it anymore."

"She's giving up." Aiden rubbed a hand over his face. "Now you're both so hurt and upset and angry, you've stopped trying. You need to talk to someone. Bridge the gap. Make the first move to fix it and spend time with your kid."

"Except there's nothing left to say." Joel pushed off the bench. "Let's sail." He shuffled toward the bow.

Aiden let him go. There would be more time to talk later. He joined Vanna, and they spent the next hour talking and sailing. She was an eager student, always questioning and learning. Like cooking, this was a love they shared.

At noon, they pulled into a small cove, and Aiden brought lunch from below.

"Ahh, your famous crab rolls." Joel grinned, his mood swing from earlier making Aiden frown. "Best meal I've had in a while. Vanna, your dad is an awesome cook."

Vanna giggled. "Yes, he is."

"I didn't make lunch. Vanna made everything, right down to those amazing rolls."

"What? My compliments to the chef. I guess it runs in the family. Letting your ole dad lounge around while you cook up a storm."

"Except he never lounges around. He helps Emily with Kellan, and he's writing a study for work, and helps keep the house clean."

Joel frowned. "Teaching her young, are you? She's all protective."

"We all do our part," Aiden said. "It's expected in our household."

"Subtle." Joel popped the cap off a beer and tipped it back, angling himself so his feet hung over the edge.

Aiden shrugged at Vanna before tucking the leftovers into the cooler. "How about a swim."

"It's hot out here." She peeled off her shorts and tee, revealing a pink bikini, and dove into the water.

"Joel?"

Nothing but stony silence.

"Suit yourself." It aggravated and alarmed Aiden that Joel continued with his hot and cold mood swings. This signaled a bigger problem.

Joel loved Daniel, yet was ignoring him. According to Alex, when he was around, he slept long hours, before disappearing out the door without so much as a word. The guy's clothes hung on his frame, and dark circles ringed his eyes, despite the hours holed up in the bedroom. Most concerning was how he avoided the friends he used to cherish.

"Join us if you change your mind." Aiden dove into the waves, setting out for the beach with a long smooth stroke. He'd consider his approach and revisit the discussion once he'd mulled it over.

An hour later, Aiden pulled himself out of the water onto the boat, eyeing the dark clouds hovering on the horizon. "Let's head back. That looks ominous." Pain shot through his foot and he doubled over. "Fuck."

"Are you okay?" Vanna examined his foot, grimacing at the metal wedged into the bottom of his foot. "I'll get the first-aid kit."

"Thanks. I need to bandage this." He wrapped his t-shirt around it, not looking forward to prying the bottle cap from his flesh. "It'll need stitches. Way to go asshole."

"Next time watch where you're walking. There's a plan."

"Or you could clean up after yourself. There's no room for slobs on my ship." Aiden accepted the kit from Savannah, peeling open a gauze pack before picking the metal out of his foot.

"Ewww." Savannah gagged. "Look at all the blood."

Aiden sprayed his foot with disinfectant and applied pressure with a clean piece of gauze. "It's not as bad as it looks." He sent a murderous look toward Joel. "Put on some shoes, sweetie, and watch where you step."

Savannah did as he asked, then picked up more bottle caps, frowning at the empties. "He's tanked," she whispered.

"We'll sail while he sits and touches nothing."

Joel waved a hand at him. "I can hear you."

"Good. My boat. My rules." Aiden pointed at the bench. "Sit your ass down."

The run toward home wasn't easy. The rising wind howled over the bow as the sky darkened. He hobbled around the deck, keeping an eye on Joel. Tethering the guy to the boat tempted him, but it wouldn't go over well. The man's foul mood and petulant child act prevented him from following through.

They were only halfway back and rough waves slapped the hull as they dipped and lurched across the water. Aiden's concern grew.

"Let me help." Joel wobbled upright.

"Sit the hell down. Touch nothing." Aiden forced Joel to sit. "Keep her steady, Vanna." He pointed at Joel again. "Don't move."

Vanna planted her feet, gripping the wheel. "I'm good."

The flapping sound had Aiden in motion toward the bow and he bent to tie tighten the loosened line. He'd barely straightened when the boat shuddered. Excruciating pain snaked through his back. A scream echoed in his ears as the water rushed up at him.

The moment he hit, waves sucked him under, and he kicked toward the surface, propelling himself with the one arm that still worked. It took an eternity before he hauled in a gasping breath, then spit out a mouthful of salty brine.

Another wave crashed into him, and the surf rushed over his head. As he struggled to the surface again, he caught another breath just before the pressure dragged him under.

It became a constant struggle. Each time he surfaced, he searched for the boat, but found nothing but churning ocean.

What had happened? Had the boat gone over and Vanna was in the water? Panic raced through him. His daughter might be overboard. The entire boat might have sunk, leaving them nothing.

He struggled to keep his head up and looked around, hoping for something, anything, he could cling to, for any way to escape the icy depths.

He gritted his teeth as another wall buried him, pain shuddering though him. He sputtered, sucking in as much air as his lungs would take before the inevitable next wave. The pattern repeated in an incessant loop. Break the surface, drag in a breath, hold it as the wall of water crashed onto him. Force his burning muscles into action, kicking to the surface. Again and again, then yet again, he fought the same battle, each round blending into the next.

All the while, he focused on Emily, Vanna, and his baby boy. *Keep swimming.* His arms and legs felt leaden, dragging him downward. *Don't give up.* He'd been in the water forever in a never-ending struggle for survival.

He submerged just before another wave crashed onto his head, the force tumbling him through the murk. For an endless span of time he couldn't navigate the way was up. *Was this how it would end?* When he had everything he'd ever dreamed of, he'd lose it all?

Another burst of panic flooded through him and he searched for the surface. His lungs burned, ready to explode. He peddled his legs, frantic for a breath of air, relief flooding him as cold wind swept across his face. He barely managed another breath before the next rush pounded into him.

Can't. Do. This. His sluggish mind struggled against incoherent thought. The constant assault was too much. He went limp. Too tired. Can't do this. Time to accept fate. The momentary calm as he hung below the surface was a relief to his numb body and mind.

They might never find him. Who knew how far off their course he'd drifted? Give up the fight. Images flashed. *Promise you won't leave?* Savannah's tearful face. Emily. *I promise to never leave.* His own voice echoed in his mind as glimpses of their life paraded by. Kellan. *I promise to be there, always.* A tiny fist clutched his finger as those dark eyes stared at him with complete trust.

I promise … promise … promise. Aiden rebelled, forcing himself into motion, kicking frantically. How could he be so selfish?

A long shriek carried across the water.

Not even sure if it was real, he forced his good arm into the air, kicking savagely as he dug deep for the last dregs of energy. A blob of orange bobbed in the waves and he struck toward it, throwing his good arm over and clinging tight. He clenched his eyes, nausea rolling over him.

An image of hands formed before his blurred vision. A scream tore from his throat as someone wrenched his shoulder. "Off." He sprawled on a frigid surface, dragging in rough breaths and shoving with one hand. "Don't touch." He curled up, clutching his shoulder as he gasped for air, coughing and spitting water.

"Dad." A voice rang through his head. "What's wrong?" The words echoed from miles away, through a dark tunnel. "Are you okay?"

Vanna. Safe. "Shoulder. Dislocated." He gritted his teeth. "You okay?"

"You're bleeding." She sobbed. "It took forever to find you."

"Hey." Joel's pale face hovered. "Shit, man. The boom swung and knocked you overboard."

"What? Why?" Confusion flooded his brain and spots danced in front of his eyes. If only the hurting would cease. Yet he longed to feel something. Icy wind whipped over him and excruciating pain combined with odd numbness. His mind disconnected, screaming commands his limbs refused to obey.

"You're freezing." Savannah rubbed his arm.

"Up. You need a doctor." Joel tugged at him.

"I am a doctor." Aiden grimaced, sucking for breath as Joel forced him to his feet and dragged him toward the stern. Unable to manage another step, he sank down onto the benches. "Get us back. I need Emily." He curled into a ball, squeezing his eyes closed, swallowing hard. *Make it stop.*

"Here." Savannah tucked wool blankets around him.

"Vanna." He clutched her hand, attempting to piece it together. Something nagged at him. "Joel?"

She shook her head. "No," she whispered. "But I can do this."

"Radio for help," he mumbled through frozen lips before merciful blackness descended.

⤞

A blurry white ceiling hovered over Aiden as he tried to focus. A constant beep dug into his brain.

"You're awake ..." Savannah leaned over him, brushing at tear-stained cheeks. "... hospital."

Aiden blinked, struggling to connect her words. He frowned, powerless to speak, unable to form a coherent thought.

"Emily ... Tom and Jenna are driving ..."

"Oh." Aiden closed his eyes, craving sleep.

"I'm sorry, I should've listened," Joel whispered.

This forced him to open his eyes. Joel's head hung low, but nothing the guy said was making any sense. Aiden's leaden lids drooped shut.

"Mi vida." Soft fingers across his hair. Gentle lips caressing his forehead. Lavender. Shimmering green eyes.

"Em ..." He tried to lift his hand, longing to touch this hovering angel but wincing at the sharp pull on his skin.

"Shh. Stay still." She placed her palms against his cheeks, kissing his lips. "You scared me."

"Jus' wanna go home," he mumbled. "So tired."

"Mmmm. The beauty of painkillers. Rest."

"Home ..."

"Not until the doctor clears you."

"What?"

"Everyone's okay. Sleep, and we'll talk later" Emily's warm hand nestled in his as he drifted off.

⤞

Aiden wandered into the kitchen. His eyes felt gritty and dry and his head pounded, but at least he was home. The three days since the incident had been the longest of his life.

Savannah rounded the counter, hugging him.

Aiden wrapped an arm around her, kissing her cheek before pressing his face into her soft hair. "Morning, sweetie." He held on, blinking hard.

Savannah finally pulled away, turning away as she brushed her cheeks. "I'll make you breakfast." She poured hot coffee into his favorite mug. "Emily will be back soon. She left these for you." After placing a small cup containing an assortment of pills onto the counter, she handed him a glass of ice water.

"Thank you." He tossed the tablets in his mouth and washed them down with a long drink. He observed his daughter as she worked in the kitchen. "How are you?"

She shrugged. "Fine. I didn't get hurt."

"It still wasn't an easy afternoon." Aiden sipped his coffee as she placed a plate with scrambled eggs and toast in front of him. "Thanks, sweetie." He noted her red and puffy eyes and pale face. "What happened? Everything was good, then I was in the water."

Savannah twisted her hands. "I'm sorry," she whispered. "It was my fault."

"Vanna, look at me."

She raised glistening eyes. "You almost …"

"Things happen on the water, so don't feel bad, okay?"

"You told Joel to sit, and I didn't stop him."

His heart sank. "What did he do?"

Her gaze traveled to his face, then downward. "He insisted on taking over, and I couldn't stop him. He corrected our course when you said keep her steady."

"Joel turned the boat without warning? That's not your fault."

"It is. He was drunk and wasn't supposed to sail."

"True, but he's an experienced sailor. I trusted him to sit still for the lousy two minutes it took me to tie a line." He beckoned her to sit beside him and took her hand. "Don't blame yourself. Sailing isn't risk-free. Sooner or later, something happens. We're all okay."

"You ended up in the hospital. So we aren't all okay." Her voice rose. "I was scared. It took forever to find you."

"But you did find me. I'll be fine in a few days." Aiden wondered if Joel had the presence of mind to call the Coast Guard, or if he'd hoped for the best. He didn't want to make Savannah feel worse, but he had to know. "Tell me what happened after I went overboard."

"Joel flipped out. I tried to turn us, but it was hard because we were moving so fast. Then he snapped out of it and helped. We sailed toward where you fell in. The waves were huge, but we spotted you."

"So no calls on the radio?"

"Joel called Tom when we reached the harbor."

"Uh-huh." Aiden nodded. He wouldn't say it out loud, but he was lucky to be alive. The frigid water had almost done him in. He remembered that with frightening clarity.

He clenched his fist, wishing he had something, or maybe someone, to pummel. Joel had broken his trust along with their rule to never sail drunk. His disregard for Aiden's orders had endangered them all. If something had happened to Savannah, Aiden would never have forgiven him.

Aiden closed his eyes. Sailing with Joel had been a terrible idea and now Savannah had another burden to bear.

"You're angry."

Aiden opened his eyes and faced his daughter, tipping her chin and brushing away the salty drops trickling down her face with his thumb. "Never at you," he said, keeping his voice soft and even. "Nothing that happened was your fault. Your quick thinking saved me, Savannah. You're not allowed to blame yourself. Ever."

CHAPTER 39

EMILY CHECKED HER WATCH AGAIN, twirling a strand of hair as the server left with their order.

"Relax," Jenna said, patting Emily's hand. "Vanna will watch her dad."

"Oh, right. She can really help him shower or dress." Emily lifted a brow. "The man's stubborn. He'll do it himself."

"Vanna will call if there's an issue. Besides, a shower isn't critical. He's likely sleeping."

"He almost died." Emily leaned on her hands, blinking back the tears. "That water is deep, freezing cold, and the wind was up, so the waves had to be huge. I'd bet he was in there for a minimum of half an hour and probably much longer. How did he survive?"

"They found him, and he'll recover, but not sure I'd want to be in Joel's shoes when Tom gets through with him. My husband rarely gets angry, but after he got the full story out of Vanna …" Jenna shook her head. "Tom checked over every inch of the boat."

"It wasn't mechanical failure?"

"Tom tested the response of the controls before he left the harbor to bring the boat home. He had no problem, and Vanna's story corroborates the facts. The poor thing thought it was her fault because she let Joel take the wheel."

"Did she have a choice? Joel was drunk and belligerent." Emily considered the disjointed words Aiden had mumbled to her on the ride home.

Every single syllable he'd uttered made Emily want to weep. She'd held him close, listening as she'd stroked his hair, the emerging picture making her nauseous. Aiden had banned the inebriated Joel from sailing, yet the man interfered and it had almost cost her beloved husband his life.

"Aiden's tough." Jenna rested a hand on her arm. "Pull yourself together, because he needs you to be strong, not only for him but for Savannah. Aiden won't rest if he's worrying about his family."

Emily frowned, contemplating Jenna's statement.

"Savannah blames herself, and that's dangerous for her mental health. It's your job to hold everything together and reassure her."

"The poor girl believes she almost killed him." Emily shuddered. If the boom had knocked Aiden unconscious, she'd be in her own personal hell. What would have happened out there if they hadn't found Aiden?

They'd come close to losing everything when their lives together had barely begun. Emily said a silent thanks, grateful for the miracle that had saved not only Aiden, but Savannah too.

Emily carried in the car seat, followed by Jenna and Adrianna.

"Where's Aiden?" Emily asked as she set the carrier down.

"Upstairs." Savannah looked up from her seat at the counter, flipping her notebook closed. "He took the pills, and he ate a little, but not enough." A frown marred her features.

"It's normal for him to have no appetite. Give him time to heal." Emily held her arms out to the girl and pulled her in for a hug. "How are you holding up, honey? Did you eat?"

Savannah nodded, brushing at her eyes. "I'll help Jenna so you can check on Dad." The girl waited until Jenna headed toward the car. "Alex is upstairs."

"Thanks, Vanna." Emily released Kellan from his seat and carried him upstairs. "Hi."

Alex perched on the side of the bed holding Aiden's hand. "Hey," she said in a low voice as she brushed at her red and puffy eyes. "Thanks, honey, I should go."

"You don't have to leave." Emily frowned.

Alex planted a kiss on Aiden's cheek. "I should get home to Daniel. Take care of yourself." She gave Emily a brief hug and hurried out the door.

"Something I said?" Emily laid the sleeping baby in his bassinet before reclining on the bed beside Aiden.

"She's having a rough day. It's not her fault, but she still apologized." He closed his eyes, and grimaced.

"How are you?"

"Fucking wonderful," he muttered.

"That good, huh?" She wiggled closer. "You ice that shoulder?"

"Yeah, but it still aches. I couldn't even put on a damn shirt. A shower would be great, but I can't get my foot wet, and dressing is exhausting." He motioned to his shorts. "Every inch of my body aches like someone beat me with a baseball bat. We have a brand new baby and haven't slept in forever. The last thing you need is to be my caretaker."

"It'll be fine." She rubbed his arm. "I'll catch a nap after Kellan's next feeding."

"Lucky you. Now you have two boys to bathe and dress."

"Aiden." She stroked his hair before nuzzling against his neck. "When I was pregnant you tied my shoes, made me snacks, and fixed my toenail polish. It's my turn. You're my husband, and I love you, and we take care of each other."

"It's too much to handle."

"No, it's not. This is marriage. The whole deal. If I were sick or injured, you'd do whatever I needed. I'll do the same for you." She leaned in, kissing him and caressing his face with her fingertips. "I can't live without you, mi vida."

"How do I deserve you?"

Emily rested her head on his uninjured shoulder, running her fingers up and down his chest, enjoying their closeness. "I feel the same about you. We'll get through this. Soon you'll be feeling better."

"After losing every scrap of dignity."

"Ha, tell me about the loss of dignity. Try having a baby and have everyone down there inspecting the goods every five minutes. Oh, right. You were one of the onlookers." She patted his belly. "It's me, Aiden." Emily grinned and whispered, "Tell me you won't enjoy your sponge bath."

He smiled. "Well, there is that to look forward to. Gotta love a good sponge bath."

They cuddled in silence for a few moments.

"Did you talk to Vanna about what happened?" she asked.

"I told her it's not her fault, and I'll keep reminding her until she believes me."

"Do you remember much?"

"It's foggy. I have no idea how long I was in the drink, but it seemed like for-fucking-ever. Everything hurt, and when they pulled me out, it was all fuzzy and I couldn't function. I passed out and woke up highly medicated." He sighed. "This sucks. I'm sidelined for the rest of the summer. No morning swims, no sailing, nothing. I can't help with our son and I can't work on my study, because I can't type. And I can't sleep."

"About that." She dug into her bag, coming up with two bottles. "There's enough so you can have a proper sleep and I procured stronger pain medication."

He peered at the labels. "Bless you. I'd kill for a good rest."

"These should help." It had been excruciating to see how much pain he'd been in during the restless nights. She'd done her best to make him comfortable, but there wasn't much she could do, aside from the ice and medication. "Jenna's here. Come down if you like, but if you want to nap, then take two of these."

"I vote for the drugs."

Emily tipped the tablets into his hand and held the cup while he sipped the water. "Close your eyes." She waited until he drifted off before heading downstairs.

Jenna was ensconced in a comfortable chair feeding Adrianna when Emily reached the living room. "How's he doing?"

"Sore and out of sorts. He took the sedatives, so he'll be out for hours. Last night was rough. I should have made him stay in the hospital. They would have given him something stronger."

"I'm not sure why they didn't keep him, but you seemed to have no problem getting prescriptions."

"Will Kavanaugh phoned it in to the pharmacy. Aiden can't even get comfortable in bed, the drive would have put him over the edge."

Savannah sniffled, her eyes growing shiny.

"Hey." Emily pulled her in for a hug. "In a couple of weeks, he'll be as good as new."

"You weren't there. He has so many bruises, and he almost died. It's my fault, even if he says it wasn't. I know it was."

"Focus on the fact he's upstairs, and he'll recover because of you." Emily held her by her shoulders. "No one blames you. I'm thankful for your determination to save him."

"Okay," Vanna whispered as Emily hugged her tight.

⌒≼

Hours later when Emily crawled into bed, Aiden was still unconscious. Jenna had gone home to catch up with Tom, and Vanna made dinner. It had been a quiet meal after which Emily sent the girl to bed. She suspected the teenager hadn't been sleeping either. After vowing to keep an eye on the girl, she closed her eyes and drifted off.

It seemed like only moments later her eyes snapped open.

Aiden muttered in his sleep, twitching and thrashing with his good arm. His words were unintelligible, and he gasped for breath.

"Aiden, mi vida." As she pinned his flailing arm, she stroked his face. "It's a dream. Open your eyes."

At long last, his eyes opened. Aiden stared at her for a dazed and silent moment, his breath harsh and rasping.

"Take long deep breaths. You're home, in bed." Emily wrapped her arms around him and cradled his head against her shoulder. She stroked his face with her fingertips. "You were dreaming."

His good arm slipped over her as he closed his eyes, his whole body trembling as he took a shaky breath.

"Are you okay?" Concern flooded her as she rubbed his back, hearing the slight hiss of breath as she ran her hand across the broad expanse. "Say something. Please?"

"Don't leave me," he whispered. "Stay right here."

She held him until his breathing normalized. "Want to talk about it?"

"Everything closed in." After another shaky breath, he said, "Still in the water. Suffocating. Too real."

Emily nodded. "It's not surprising you're having nightmares after your ordeal. Those sleeping pills can cause vivid dreams."

"My mouth is dry like cotton and I'm all sweaty." He slid to the edge of the bed and sat on the side for a moment before struggling to his feet.

Tears sprang to her eyes. The massive purple and black bruise across his back confirmed the force of the boom. It hurt to even look at it. She followed to ensure he reached the bathroom. "Do you need more ice for your shoulder? Something to drink?"

"Thanks, I could use both." He splashed water on his pale face before throwing the briefest glance in her direction. "You don't need to stand watch."

"Sorry, but I need to make sure you aren't—" Words failed her. She did need to stand watch, even if only for her own benefit. Aiden seemed unsteady on his feet, and not the vibrant, invincible man she knew.

"Can you give me a minute?" He hung his head, closing his eyes. "I could use the ice and water. And my pain medication."

"Right." She nodded. "I'll get the ice pack." This was one of those moments when he needed her to back off and rein in her fears, but her stubborn mind clung to the fact she'd almost lost him. Given how he looked at the moment, she wouldn't forget anytime soon.

Emily forced herself not to rush upstairs to check on him. She leaned on the counter, taking long deep breaths. Once her knees stopped shaking, she poured his water, found him an ice pack, and his pills.

By the time she returned, he'd seated himself on their bed, and was struggling to change into sleep pants. Emily hesitated for only a second before she kneeled in front of him. "Let me help." For a moment she thought he'd refuse her offer, but the fight drained out of him and he nodded.

Aiden let her dress him, plump up the pillows, and place the ice pack on his shoulder. He grimaced as he settled on the bed.

She sat on the edge, waiting as he took the pills and sipped the ice water.

He took her hand. "I'm sorry for snapping."

"Don't worry about it. You're frustrated, sore, and tired." She shrugged. "We'll get through it, I promise."

A pained look ran across his face.

"What's the matter?"

"It's nothing."

She settled on the bed and studied him. It wasn't nothing. However, Kellan's squawk followed by his shrill cry prevented her from pursuing it. "It's okay, hijo mio." She cradled her baby boy in her arms. "Someone needs a fresh diaper." As soon as she finished changing Kellan, she carried him to the bed.

She hadn't missed the longing in her husband's eyes. "Visit Daddy while I wash my hands." She laid the baby on Aiden's chest, snuggling Kellan close to his good arm. "Is he okay?"

"We're great." Aiden rewarded her with a smile.

"I'll be right back."

He dropped a kiss on the baby's head and rubbed his back. "I've missed you, hijo mio."

Emily took her time returning to the bed. She filed away the beautiful image of her son and his daddy. She'd never forget these precious moments. The past several days had been tough, but she'd get through it. They both would come out the other side even stronger.

Chapter 40

Aiden

*I*T HAD BEEN OVER A week since the sailing incident, and Aiden couldn't wait to escape the confines of the house. He let himself out, closing the door quietly behind him.

After taking several deep breaths, he slipped off his shoes, savoring the sun-warmed sand under his feet as he tipped up his head to enjoy the rays touching his face. Days like this made him grateful to be alive. His recent ordeal had been a reminder of how life could change without warning.

As he worked in an ER, he understood it deep down, but he'd learned to separate himself from the emotional reality. Focus and detachment was the only way he managed the job without being overwhelmed by the pain and suffering. Or maybe it was a self-preservation skill he'd learned at a young age to overcome his own sense of abandonment.

He stared over the water, wondering if he'd ever summon enough courage to get on his boat again. Though the chain of events remained fuzzy, he still had vivid nightmares. The suffocating weight of water rushing over him and the never-ending struggle to stay alive haunted him.

Emily held him close night after night as he gasped for breath, the cold sweat creeping over him. He'd almost lost everything, and he couldn't explain the hopelessness he'd felt in that freezing water. Not to anyone.

Aiden looked up, startled to find he'd arrived at Alex and Joel's house. Joel. The man hadn't even visited since the day on the boat, and that saddened and disappointed Aiden. It formed a dark spot in his life. Alex considered herself guilty and looked more desolate every day.

As Aiden approached the house, raised, angry voices cut through the air. Joel and Alex outright raged at each other. His concern overrode their need for privacy.

He spotted them on the patio the moment he rounded the corner.

Tears poured down Alex's face. "How could you."

"Nothing happened. I needed to talk to someone." Joel threw his hands up. "It's only a few texts."

"You've been texting for months/ Is that where you've been? Rushing off to see her while I care for our son, and our home, and you pretend to care? We need you, but you're never here."

"We're friends. Nothing more. Everyone else is on your side. Even my so-called best friends."

Aiden froze in place. Those words stung. He backed away, torn between not wanting to interfere and making sure they were okay.

Joel hurled the beer bottle in his hand, shattered glass skittering across the flagstone.

"Joel. Calm down." Alex held up her hands, palms facing Joel, inching backward toward the house.

"I get it. You don't trust me. Why don't you get the hell out? Get the fuck out of my house."

"My parents gave us this house, so if anyone should get the fuck out, it's you. Asshole."

"I've been paying the bills." Joel spun, his gaze landing on Aiden. "Fuck. Eavesdropping?"

"I heard the yelling from the beach. Calm down, Joel." He held up his one good hand, stepping forward.

Alex's eyes widened as Joel stalked the few paces across the patio toward Aiden.

"This is between me and her. I know you feel the need to rescue damsels in distress, but ... Back"—he jabbed his index finger toward Aiden's chest—"the fuck. Off."

Aiden stood his ground, riveted on Joel. "Take it easy. I'm not here to interfere, but I won't leave until you get your shit together." He hated to even think Joel might do something stupid and hurt Alex or his son. Sadly, his trust in his friend had waned.

Joel's eyes narrowed, and his hand came up, curling into a fist.

Aiden didn't move an inch. "Go ahead and take a shot. I can't fight back." He gave a one-shouldered shrug. With his arm immobilized, there was nothing he could do, but he couldn't leave Alex. If something happened to her, Aiden would never forgive himself.

Joel halted his progress, his gaze traveled over Aiden's face, then down to the arm strapped against his body. "Shit." He ran both hands through his hair. "That'd win me big points. Tom would beat the crap out of me if Emily didn't get in there first."

"Are we good?" Aiden glanced at Alex, who had tears dribbling down her reddened cheeks.

Joel shrugged and stuffed his hands in his pockets, dropping his gaze to the stone patio.

Alex brushed her face and sniffled. "I don't want to be here right now. So we're clear, this is my house, and you can't have it, but I'll stay with Aiden and Emily tonight. I'm taking Daniel. You're drunk, and I refuse to leave him here with you." Her eyes pleaded with Aiden not to leave her alone with her husband in such a foul mood.

"You're always welcome. You two can talk when Joel's thinking more clearly." He nodded, ignoring the glare leveled at him by Joel.

"Can you help me inside?" Alex motioned to the French doors leading into the house.

"Sure." Aiden skirted his way around the shattered glass.

"Thank you," she whispered as they arrived upstairs. "He's not himself. He almost took that swing at you even though you're in no condition to fight back. I love him, but I'm worried. He's never like this."

"I know. I've talked to Tom about him, too." He took her arm. "Is his drinking way out of control?"

She nodded.

"He needs help, but he's not ready to accept it."

Alex wiped at her eyes. "He's cheating on me."

"Are you sure?" His heart sank. He never thought he'd see the day, but people changed. Tiffany had proven that.

"I found a bunch of texts on his phone." Her voice shook as she pulled out an overnight bag. "Do you remember Crystal?"

"Crystal Bishop?" Aiden and Tiffany had double-dated with Joel and Crystal years ago. He'd never liked the woman much, but he'd gone along with it for Joel and Tiffany.

"Crystal McKenzie now, but that's her. He says nothing happened, and he's been confiding in her because things are going so badly with us. What if it's been more?"

Aiden held a finger to his lips and shook his head, throwing a glance toward the door. If Joel overheard it would make things worse. Better to get home and talk to her in private. "Why don't I put together several days worth of clothing for Daniel, and you pack some for yourself?"

"I appreciate this. You keep letting me stay, and you haven't given up on Joel. Even after everything."

"He's my friend and has been for a long time. It's a tough spot. I want both of you to be okay. You and Daniel need to be with us." He pointed at her bag. "Pack."

He peeked out the window on his way down the hallway. Joel sat on a lounger on the patio below. As he watched the man, he pulled out his phone and texted Emily to let her know he was bringing Alex home with him. Then he dialed Tom.

"Aiden, how are you?"

"I got out of the house today."

"Good, glad to hear it. So what's up?"

"I need a huge favor. Joel and Alex are fighting again, and Alex and Daniel will stay at our place. Any chance you can come and see what you can do with Joel? I would, but if he gets out of hand, I'm screwed. He's tanked, and came damn close to taking a swing at me."

"No kidding. Where are you?"

"At their house. I'm packing stuff for Daniel. Alex is organizing her bag and we'll go."

"Don't leave until I get there. Ten minutes or less."

"Thanks, Tom. Don't let him do anything stupid." He lowered his voice. "He's been texting Crystal."

Tom sighed. "He's cheating on Alex?"

"She seems to think so. Who knows how far it's gone? His drinking is out of control and he seems depressed. He's never gotten drunk while out sailing before that day."

"He's damn lucky because his stupidity had serious consequences."

"He and Alex were screaming at each other when I arrived. My interference wasn't appreciated, but I couldn't leave Alex. He's unpredictable. His lack of control scared me."

"I'm on my way. Pack them up, and I'll try to sober him up after you've left."

Aiden hung up, moving about Daniel's room, trying not to wake the sleeping boy. He located a bag and organized several days of clothing.

"Ready?" Alex peeked into the room. "How will we manage this? You can't carry Daniel."

"I can barely pick up Kellan." He squeezed her hand. "Tom's on his way. He'll help."

"You called Tom?"

"Yup. I'm an invalid right now. If Joel gets in your face, I can't do anything. He could take me out without even trying."

It wasn't long before Tom arrived and let himself in the front door. After giving Alex a hug, he helped them transport the sleeping boy and the bags to the car. "I'll call you later."

Aiden nodded. "You'll be okay?"

"Sure. Take Alex home, I can manage Joel. You look done in."

It was the truth. Aiden's shoulder and back ached. He needed to lie down and take more pain medication. And he'd put enough mileage on his foot, even though the cut had healed well. "Thanks, Tom." Aiden gave him a hug with his good arm before climbing into the passenger seat.

Alex drove the short distance in silence. Savannah and Emily came out as they pulled into the driveway to help with Daniel and the bags.

Aiden collapsed onto their bed, closing his eyes while Emily settled Alex and Daniel into the extra rooms.

"Dad?" Vanna came into the bedroom. "Emily said you need to take these and put heat on your shoulder." She held out a glass of water and a bottle of pills. "It's hurting, right?"

"I'm done in, and I hardly did anything."

She popped the lids off, shaking the tablets into his hand, before retrieving the heating pad and helping him place it on his shoulder.

"Thanks, sweetie."

"No problem. We'll wake you for dinner."

He closed his eyes, sliding into a peaceful sleep.

⌒≼

Hours later he awoke, feeling somewhat better. He eased off the bed and went downstairs to find Emily and Alex out on the flagstone patio with the kids.

"We were about to wake you for dinner." Emily stood to kiss him on the cheek. "I'll check on Vanna if you want to take the baby." She waited as Aiden settled into a chair and transferred the tiny boy into his arms.

"Things seem good between the two of you, despite the new baby," Alex said.

"It is. We're working at it hard. It's not been easy for her to carry a double load. There's so much I can't do." He glanced at his son, who had his eyes closed. "The medical training helps, I'm sure. She knows what to do without me explaining it, and she's not shy either, so ..."

"I won't argue there." She sipped from a glass of wine. "The two of you are lucky, but don't ignore the dangers. Joel and I grew apart, and it happened so fast."

"How long has this texting thing been going on?"

Alex shrugged. "A few months from what I can tell. She lives in Chicago, but she's here for the summer, and hanging out with Gwen Randall." She gave him a faint smile. "Wonderful, huh? He's not only spending time with his ex-girlfriend but yours too." She gulped her wine.

"Does one date make her an ex-girlfriend?" He threw a look her way. "We didn't keep in touch."

"Good. Don't be like Joel."

"Do you think he slept with Crystal?"

"Does it matter? My husband is spending time with another woman. How does he have time for lunch and endless texts but no time for me or for his son? It's wrong, and I can't tolerate it anymore." She sniffled and brushed at her eyes.

"I agree." He kept his voice soft and low. "No matter what, he should pay more attention to his family."

"He never said anything?"

"Not to me." Aiden sighed. "This is tough. The texting is wrong. It's cheating."

"Sorry for putting you in the middle. Look where it got you." She twirled her glass. "I'm ashamed of him. He hasn't come to see you, has he?"

Aiden shook his head. "I haven't seen him until today. I'm sure he's worried about his reception here, but I have to admit I'm disappointed. He's been avoiding me and now I'm his so-called friend."

"Except he always valued your friendship. I don't understand why he's pushed you and Tom away, and worse, his stupidity ..." She lifted her tear-filled eyes. "I can't even think about it. It makes me sick. You almost ..." She bowed her head, dabbing at her eyes.

"I'm okay. That's what's important. What bothers me is how he's treating you and Daniel. He needs help, and we'll try to get it for him. Get your Joel back. You can stay here as long as you like."

"Thanks, Aiden. I'm not in any hurry to go back to the house." Her shoulders shook as she cried harder. "He's not the man I married. I can't live in the same house with him. We need time apart."

⌒⤚

Aiden stepped out of the clinic, rubbing his shoulder as he wandered down the street. The doctor scanned and examined his arm, clearing him for limited and light use of his arm. It was a relief, even though he still had a lot of healing time, rehabilitation, and physio to bring it back to where it was before the accident.

"Aiden."

The familiar voice caused him to turn. "Tiffany." He tried to hide his dismay.

"How are you?" She smiled.

"Fine. You?"

"Good." She glanced up and down the street. "No Emily?"

"I'm on my way to meet her. Where's Harrison?" He looked around for the other man.

"He's not here." She brushed her long hair back from her face. "We broke off the engagement. Things haven't been good for a while as you know."

"I'm ... sorry?"

"No you're not." She laughed. "You detest Harrison. Anyway, I needed to enjoy the summer, so I stayed here. I've been catching up with people I haven't seen in years. I saw Gwen ... and Crystal, along with a few others. You remember Gwen." She raised a brow. When he frowned, she said, "I stopped by the house to see Alex, but she wasn't home."

"You should call her." Aiden narrowed his eyes, wondering how much she knew about the Joel situation if she'd been talking to Crystal and Gwen.

"Right." She studied the sidewalk, avoiding his gaze. "Aiden?"

"Tiffany?" He matched her inquisitive tone.

"I ... Damn, this is hard. Can we talk? I've been gathering the nerve to call you."

"Why? Is there anything to say?" He threw out the line she'd used on him so many times over the past years.

"Please?" She gazed at him with shimmering blue eyes. "It's a lot to ask after everything, but ... please, Aiden?"

"Five minutes. Let me tell Em." He tapped in a quick text, letting his wife know he'd meet her soon. "I was about to get a cold drink. Did you want one?"

They walked along the bustling main street sipping their icy drinks.

"This brings back memories," Tiffany said.

"Taking a stroll down memory lane, are we?" He smirked. "What did you want to talk about?"

"I've spent some time soul searching." She played with her cup, keeping her chin tipped downward. "I've made choices, most of them bad ones." After a long sip of her drink, she gazed at him. "You were right. I regret turning Savannah away."

An ache built, a sense of foreboding growing as they walked.

"I wanted her, but we closed the door and moved on. When you appeared, I couldn't handle it. It was too difficult to think about." Tiffany bit her lip and wiped her eyes with the back of her hand. "I want to see her," she mumbled.

Aiden's breath caught in his chest.

"Nothing to say?" Her teary blue eyes sought his.

"What do you want me to say? Holy shit, you're getting your head out of your ass? The problem is, it's far too late. I ... No, forget it. Go back to your life, and leave us alone. Your worst nightmare, the daughter you didn't want, and the trampy, gold-digging wife."

"You'll never let me forget." She shook her head. "I'm sorry for saying that to Emily, but admit it, you two weren't together. She was acting like a ..." She bit her lip, avoiding his glare.

"What we were or weren't is none of your fucking business. I don't appreciate hearing rude comments about my wife. At Jenna's wedding, no less. One minute you're telling me to fuck off and get out of your life, and to take my daughter with me. The next you're flirting and inviting me to your hotel room. Then you're insulting Emily or phoning to yell at me because your daddy's upset. So excuse me if I don't feel particularly friendly."

Tiffany stopped and peered up at him. "I'm sorry, okay? I don't know what else to say, except she's my daughter. I have the right to see her."

"Actually, you don't." He narrowed his eyes, waiting to let it sink in. "You have zero rights. It's just like you to forget the adoption papers you signed. You waived your rights. You don't get to make demands. You had your chance and said no. Now I'm saying no."

"You signed them too. So who made you boss?"

"Ross Phillips," he said. "He gave me legal guardianship when he passed, so I have every right to tell you to go to hell. If you think I'd put Savannah through more of your crap, you're crazy. Why? So you can flake out and disappear on her? What would you seeing her accomplish?"

"I won't," she whispered. "She can decide how much she wants to see me, or not see me, but I need to try. Please give me that chance." She opened her wallet and pulled out the photos he'd given her before Christmas. "I look at these every single day and wish I'd done everything differently. If I could take back every lousy, cruel, awful thing I've ever said or done, I would." She sucked in a breath. "I'd change it all."

Aiden stared, at a loss for words. He never thought this day would come, she seemed so set on her life, spent so much time railing against him. For her to do a one-eighty now shocked him. "Don't you understand? She's spent all this time getting over it, and we're in a good place. How can I open it up again? I'm sorry. We're done." He turned and walked away.

"Aiden." She dashed after him. "Please." Her hand clutched his arm. "Ask her. She's old enough. If she says no, I'll leave you alone. She wanted to know me, and I want to know her. Please, don't cut me out forever."

"Let go." He brushed her hand away. "What do you hope to accomplish? What's changed? Nothing." He took one last look at her. "Go back to your life, Tiffany, and stay out of ours."

CHAPTER 41

Emily

As she rocked Kellan, Emily waited for Savannah and Leanne to buy ice cream. Aiden had texted to let her know he was almost done and ready to go home.

"This is delicious." Leanne sighed. "You're so lucky, you get to spend the whole summer."

Vanna shrugged. "You'll go home soon, and then I'm on my own."

"You're making friends. Do you think Aiden will let us go to that party?"

Emily noted the looks the girls were sending her way, and she held up a hand. "Talk to your dad, Vanna. You'd need the car, right? You know he can't drive anywhere right now."

"I know." Vanna nibbled at her ice cream, but froze and stared down the street.

"Your ice cream's melting all over your hand." Leanne gave her a playful shove.

Savannah only tilted her head as she took another bite and wiped the dribble with a napkin. The girl turned away, glancing over her shoulder.

Emily turned to see what had her so interested. "Oh boy," she muttered under her breath. Tiffany and Aiden. Even from a distance, Emily could tell the woman was annoying Aiden.

"Why are you so grouchy?" Leanne's lower lip jutted out.

"I don't want to talk about it." After another long look down the street, she stalked in the opposite direction, pausing only to toss her ice cream into the trash.

Emily's phone buzzed. A text from Aiden.

Where are you?

By the ice cream parlor.

It wasn't long before he approached. Savannah and Leanne had found a bench to sit on and were whispering.

"Hi." He leaned in for a kiss, before dropping another onto Kellan's downy head. "Where'd the girls get to?"

She pointed, but restrained him with a light touch on his arm. "She saw you with Tiffany."

"Damn. The woman keeps popping up like a weed. I'll talk to Vanna when we get home."

"You sure you should wait?" Emily rubbed his back. "She's upset and you don't look happy, either."

He pressed his lips to her hair. "She wants to see Savannah," he whispered. "I need to consider the options."

"What?" Emily's eyes widened. "Oh, not good."

"No." He shook his head, keeping his voice low. "We've spent endless hours in counseling, and she's in a good place. Now Tiffany wants to stir it all up. I can't allow it."

"You have to say something to Vanna."

"Not right this minute. I'm furious and might say something the wrong way, and I'll regret it. I'd also prefer to talk to Vanna alone. I don't know how much Savannah discusses with her friends."

"I understand." She patted his arm. Knowing how much he'd gone through with Tiffany over the past few years, she understood the need to cool off. To think before he spoke. To avoid causing further upheaval and damage for his daughter.

⚓

Emily tucked Kellan into the bassinet before wandering onto the deck of the master bedroom.

Aiden sat on the sofa, staring over the water, looking troubled. He ran a hand through his hair as he shifted positions.

"Hey." She caught his fingers, brushing her own hand over his hair before leaning in to give him a long kiss.

"Hey, yourself." He tugged her into his lap, turning her so she rested against his good shoulder. An arm snaked around her, pulling her close as he tipped his head against hers.

Curling up in his lap was enjoyable. She craved the intimacy. So much had happened this summer, and she'd come dangerously close to not having him at all. There were no guarantees and holding on to what she had was everything.

"Want to talk about it?" she murmured, placing a hand on his face, stroking the light stubble that had grown over the course of the past few days. Everything seemed to take him twice the effort these days and he'd become lax about shaving. The scruffy look suited him, she decided. It looked sexy.

"I don't know what to do. Vanna was happy, but she's been moody since we got back from town."

"Is that why you let her and Leanne take the car? I was surprised you let her go, knowing about that party."

"Protecting her versus smothering her is a fine line. Ross and Jayde were wonderful people, so don't think I'm complaining or don't recognize what a great job they did raising her. They kept her close ... but maybe too close. They didn't allow her much freedom. Ross never knew half of what she got up to after she turned fifteen."

"And you do?" Emily's eyes widened.

"We do, Emily. Savannah told you many things she never told me. I never told Ross a lot of it because Vanna was interacting and asking advice. I couldn't break the trust we'd established, she'd never have forgiven me." He rubbed her arm. "Remember our talk when you first met her? We both knew she needed a woman she could confide in, and she latched onto you. I had to let her build on the security you provided."

"Ahh, of course." Emily acknowledged he was right. Savannah was a smart girl, but naïve due to Ross's overprotective nature, which had intensified after Jayde had passed. Aiden had done his best to provide the outlet the girl had needed.

"She's a good kid, but I don't delude myself. They might have sneaked out the bedroom window." He lifted a shoulder. "That's what I used to do. Grandparents said no, I went down the tree. If I even thought they might say no, I didn't bother asking."

She snickered. On her first visit to the Vineyard, Savannah had chosen the room Aiden used to have as a teenager. The tree boughs hung close to the window and were even closer now the tree was fully grown. "I can only imagine."

"You laugh, but we got into trouble and did dumbass things but we were too scared to call for help. I'd rather she used the front door and tell me where she's going, and phone or text if she'll be late or needs someone."

"I agree." Communication was a huge deal, and Aiden always wanted Savannah to be honest with him. "Better to know where she is and with who."

"Besides, she's starting her last year of high school this fall, and she has experienced little of life. So I let her go, but we also had a talk about responsibility as she has the car. That's why I brought the SUV, with a teenager we need the second vehicle."

"I remember." She snuggled closer. "What are you planning to do about Tiffany?"

"Damned if I know. The woman runs hot and cold. One moment I see the girl I knew, the next she's a bitchy ice queen. The problem is I don't trust her or her motives. Why now? And she has this ... edge to her."

"What do you mean? An edge?" A frown settled on her face.

"A sharp side. Don't know if it makes sense, but she begged to see Vanna, but then she made remarks that pissed me off. For example, I called her on the comment she made at the wedding, and she said something like *well, you two weren't together then*. It's none of her damn business, and I outright told her so. She wants to see Vanna, but she insults my wife in the next breath."

"Seriously?"

"No apology, only a demand to see Vanna, like she has the right. And she doesn't, she gave up all her rights when she signed those papers."

Emily soaked in the information, staying silent and allowing Aiden to vent his frustration.

"Tiffany gave birth to her, and wanted her at that moment in time. I know we both gave her up, signed the papers, but it wasn't our choice. So where does the moral obligation end? Legally, you can give up your rights, but morally, I don't know."

He dragged in a rough breath. "Tiffany will always be Savannah's mother and our daughter wouldn't be here if we didn't make the choices we did. We made a conscious decision to go through with it and to keep her, and Tiffany did her best. I have no idea what the right thing is. It's so damn complex."

"I know this isn't my decision, or my business, but ..." She bit her lip.

"Except for the fact you're my wife, a daily part of Vanna's life, and she looks up to you? Nope, not your business at all." He let out a small laugh. "I want to hear your opinion. Whatever I choose, you'll be dealing with the fallout. You have a right to tell me what you think."

"Is this your call?" It always felt like treading a fine line. No one seemed to mind she acted like Savannah was her own daughter, but times like now, she was conscious that she wasn't the girl's mother. "You say Vanna is growing up and you want her to take responsibility for herself. Should you be the one deciding whether she sees Tiffany?"

"It's not all about me. In fact, it's not about me at all, is it?" he said. "It's about Savannah and what she wants."

"It is her mother we're talking about. Someone she wanted in her life so badly and now it's being offered."

"I can't be impartial. At some point, I have to trust my daughter to know what she wants."

"I don't have any love for Tiffany, but for Vanna I'd make the best of it. I won't tolerate disrespect, but as you said, where does the moral side of this lead. It's not about me or how I feel about Tiffany, or you and how you feel about her. It's about your daughter. She is the only one who matters in this personal decision about her life." She met his gaze.

"You're amazing." He bent down, capturing her lips for a sweet kiss. "I love you, so much. Life wouldn't be the same without you."

Cupping his cheek in one palm, she stared into his eyes. "Every day I feel so lucky to have you. There are days when I kick myself for wasting so much time, for letting my fears get in the way. I wonder how you have the strength to deal with me and my insecurities."

"You know how I look at it?" He held her close. "We learned how much we love each other. What we have now? I don't know if it would be as strong without the lessons along the way. And we have our son, and who knows if we would have him either. Let it all go. Forgive yourself, and move forward."

"Now who's amazing." She nuzzled against his neck. "You're a wonderful husband and a great dad. I wish every day for us to keep this forever."

"No guarantees, Em. But ... we will do everything in our power." He inhaled. "Time for bed?"

"Our little boy will be up in a couple of hours." She slid off his lap, holding out her hand as he rose from his chair.

He followed her in through the French doors, leaving one propped open to let the fresh sea breeze waft through the room. They both worked through their bedtime routine, meeting up in the king-sized bed.

Emily crawled in beside him, wiggling over to be close. "Hmm, nice." Trickling her fingers down his bare chest, she tipped her head up for a kiss, before curling up against him and drifting off to sleep.

CHAPTER 42

Aiden

Hours later, Aiden awoke to thumps and muffled giggles that signaled the girls' return home.

He slid from bed, pulling on a pair of shorts and closing the bedroom door softly behind him, following the trail of soft giggles. Both girls had collapsed on the stairs.

Leanne tugged at Savannah's arm. "Hurry up before—"

"Everything okay?"

A look of alarm flashed across Leanne's face. "Aiden." The guilty glance toward her friend, who seemed powerless to walk by herself, gave him the answer.

"Help me get her to the bedroom. I can't carry her." He lifted and wrapped an arm around her while Leanne supported her from the opposite side.

Alex appeared. Her eyes widened at the sight of Savannah. "Let me help." She propped the girl up, pushing Aiden away. "Don't strain your shoulder."

It didn't take long to get Savannah to her room and drape her across the bed. Aiden checked her eyes and pulse before he shrugged. "She'll hate life in the morning, but she'll be okay after she sleeps it off. You drove home?" He glanced at Leanne, who seemed to be fine.

"Sorry, I shouldn't have driven your car, but I have my license. Vanna was too ..." She motioned to her friend.

Aiden waved a hand. "I'd much prefer you drove than allow her behind the wheel. You made the right call."

"You're not mad?" The girl looked relieved.

"No." He pulled off Savannah's shoes. This wasn't the first or the last time his daughter had gone to a party where alcohol was involved. He'd never lecture as he'd sound like a hypocrite. During his teenage years, he'd done the same things, except at an even younger age than Vanna. "The important thing is she didn't drive, and you brought her home safely. If you called, we'd have picked you up."

"My parents would yell and scream and have a fit." A frown creased her brow. "Vanna's lucky you understand her."

"Well, not always, but I try. Savannah's growing up, and testing limits." He eased her sweatshirt off, leaving her in her shorts and t-shirt. "This'll do. Let's cover her up. Leanne? Please get her a glass of water for later."

"Okay." Leanne headed out of the room.

Alex lifted a brow. "Wow, so understanding."

"You remember what we were up to every summer, so ..." He offered her a small smile. "I'd have crawled in through the window or passed out at Tom's."

She giggled. "So true. She'll be in a world of hurt tomorrow."

"Enough punishment on its own, I'd say. She's blowing off steam. I'll talk to her tomorrow." He covered Vanna with a light blanket. "Go back to bed, Alex. Thanks for your help."

Vanna appeared in the mid-afternoon and slumped onto a lounger beside Aiden, clutching a glass of ice water. "How mad are you?" she whispered.

"I'm not mad, Vanna. Did you take something for your headache? Have something to eat to settle your stomach?" He closed the lid of his laptop.

"I tried some toast." She grimaced and sipped at her water, gazing out at the ocean.

"I'm glad Leanne got you home," he said. "I'm sure this is about yesterday, right?"

"You were talking to Tiffany."

"Yes, but I didn't want to discuss it until I figured out the next move."

"Which is?"

"You up for a walk on the beach?"

She stood, stretching before combing her fingers through her blonde locks.

Aiden caught her hand, giving it a reassuring squeeze as they started across the sparkling sand. "We need to talk about Tiffany."

"Why now?"

"Everything's changed. Absolutely everything. You know who she is, and you're sixteen, not fourteen, which is a huge difference in maturity level."

"There's much more to the story, right?" She sighed. "Is it hard to talk about her?"

"Yes, but she's your mother." Now he'd put his own emotions aside and give her answers. "She wasn't always the person she is now."

"You've said that before, but you seem to hate her."

"There were times when her actions caused pain, but... I hate what she's done, not her. I'll get over my issues because being bitter and resentful is unhealthy for everyone."

"The counselor says that, too," Savannah said. "What did Tiffany want?"

He pulled her to a halt. "To see you."

"What?" Savannah's eyes widened, then she gave an audible sniffle. "Now? After all this time?"

He nodded.

"Tell her no." Savannah shook her head. "I don't want to see her."

Aiden wanted to let it rest, but he couldn't. Gently grasping her by the shoulders, he said, "Let it settle for a couple days and we'll talk again. Make sure it's what you want before you cut her off."

"You want me to meet her?" Her voice reflected the confusion written across her face. "I don't understand." Tears welled in her eyes.

Aiden pulled her into a hug. "Hey, don't cry. I'm only saying you should consider it. I can't tell you what to do. It's your feelings that count, not mine but I don't want you to make a snap decision." He released her, running a hand through his hair. "You're grown-up, and as much as I want to protect you and never watch you make a mistake, or be hurt, I have to step back."

"What's changed that she wants to visit me?" Her brow furrowed.

"Regrets about turning you away." He reflected for a moment. "She's been soul searching and wants to make amends."

"You don't sound convinced."

Aiden gave her a sideways glance. "I have my own issues with your mother."

"Do you believe she's sorry?"

"She's convinced she wants it, but be prepared it might be one or two meetings and may not lead to anything further. There are no guarantees you can build a lasting relationship with her. Just consider it without too high of expectations. Remember, it took us a while to build trust, and I was willing to be part of your life right away."

Vanna swept a strand of hair back from her face and shuffled her feet in the sand. At long last, she straightened, standing tall with her shoulders back and head up. "I'll let you know what I want to do."

A sense of pride flowed through him, and oddly, his daughter reminded him more of her mother at that moment than ever before. The determination and fire in her eyes reminded him of why he'd once loved Tiffany with a fierce and burning passion.

"Take your time." The moment had come to relay the final piece of information. "There's something else." He lifted his chin, determined to get through this, no matter what.

"It sounds bad."

He motioned to a log, a place where he'd had many deep and personal conversations over the years. "Let's sit."

She complied, tilting her head to the side. "Now I'm dying to find out." Her soft hand encompassed his. "Whatever it is, it can't be that horrible."

"Tiffany and I eloped when we were eighteen." He peeked out of the corner of his eye, not knowing how she'd react.

"You married her?" Her eyebrows shot up. "At eighteen?"

"Crazy, right? We stuck it out for two years, and then we divorced. It's been hard keeping it from you, but the entire situation's been difficult."

"Any more big secrets I should know?" Savannah leaned her head on his shoulder. "It's okay, Dad, I'm not upset. It's weird, but I understand. Thank you for being honest with me about how you feel and sharing about Tiffany."

He squeezed her hand, not letting go, relieved his revelation didn't even equate to a ripple in their troubled waters. "Let me know if you have questions. And don't feel pressured. I'll tell her to be patient." They turned toward the house. He could see she was deep in thought, and he was glad she'd agreed to weighing her options. There may be no going back.

⌒≼

Later in the evening, after a lively dinner including Tom and Jenna, everyone settled around the fire pit on the beach. Aiden glanced around, thinking how lucky he was to be surrounded by wonderful friends and family.

After a while, Leanne and Savannah left to hang out with a group of teenagers they'd befriended, with promises to behave themselves.

Not long after they'd disappeared, Aiden's phone rang. He glanced at the number, his heart sinking, but he couldn't avoid the conversation forever. "Hi," he said as he wandered away from the circle around the fire, heading down the beach. "Why are you calling?"

"Sorry, but ... Have you thought about what I asked? I'm hoping you'll reconsider," Tiffany said.

"Do you deserve the chance?"

"Clearly, you don't think so, but this isn't about me and you. It's about our daughter. All I'm asking for is a chance to make things right. For Savannah to forgive my poor choices."

Aiden's heart went out to her. Tonight, she seemed so much like the girl he'd loved and he couldn't torture her as much as he wanted to. This request wasn't about him, or the pain she'd caused, or how she'd broken his heart. That was all past, and he'd become almost whole again, with Emily, his baby boy, and Savannah.

"Please don't make me beg."

"It's in Savannah's hands. She'll be the one to say yes or no. Please keep your distance until then, and when she makes her decision, honor it."

There were a few moments of dead silence.

"You told her?" Tiffany's voice trembled.

"Can you give her some time? You can't expect her to forgive or come running because it's convenient for you. Understand?"

"I do." The long inhale carried down the line. "Thank you for giving her the choice, not forcing one on her."

"That would make me a touch hypocritical, wouldn't it? Forcing her to do something against her will? I don't want that relationship with my daughter. Once she decides, we both respect it. Agreed?"

"I'll live with it."

"If she wants to see you I won't interfere, as long as you are behaving."

"What, you going to monitor this like big brother?"

"No, I'll look out for her best interests, like her father. If you hurt her, I'll never forgive you. You've done enough damage, and if you aren't certain you can make good on your promises, you need to turn and walk away. Now. Before you do further harm."

"I won't make the same mistakes. Will you let me know?"

"I'll contact you either way, but don't hold your breath, and be patient. I need to go."

"I'll wait for your call."

Aiden cut the connection, the weight lifting from his shoulders. It was out of his hands as it should be. Now his role was to be there for his daughter and hope for the best.

CHAPTER 43

Emily

THE FINAL DAYS OF SUMMER flew by, and it saddened Emily that they'd soon pack for the return trip to Boston. She'd enjoyed her time off, watching their son grow and become more alert and personable with each passing day. And she'd done her own growing, forming a stronger and closer bond with her husband and his daughter.

She snuggled Kellan into his wrap for their daily walk on the beach. "Want to walk with me, Vanna?" Emily smiled at the girl.

Savannah seemed at odds today as Leanne had gone home. The girl had been a bundle of nervous energy, busying herself in the kitchen. Now she was storing the last batch of cookies and cleaning the kitchen after a baking spree.

"Sure. Time to get out of here." She stowed the last of the dirty dishes in the dishwasher.

Soon they were wandering down the beach, enjoying the light breeze blowing off the ocean.

"I'll miss this. Next week we'll be home." Emily inhaled the salty air, soaking up the morning sunshine. "Time to get ready for another Boston winter."

Savannah laughed. "Portland was so mild in the winter in comparison. I miss it sometimes, but Boston has great things about it, too."

"It's not so different from Chicago, except for being smaller. I like that about Boston, and I love Back Bay."

"Can I carry Kellan for a while? I've spent little time with him as Leanne's been around."

"Sure." Emily helped the girl get him adjusted in the sling.

"He's so sweet." Vanna placed a kiss on his head, supporting him carefully. "Isn't it hard, being up all the time with him?"

"If I don't get enough sleep at night, I've been able to nap. Aiden's great too, getting up and helping with him in the middle of the night, and taking him so I can have 'me' time."

"He's good with babies. Well, with all kids. Daniel adores him."

"He's like the Pied Piper with kids. I feel lucky."

"I often wonder what it would have been like to grow up with Dad and Tiffany. Maybe I'd be a whole different person. Maybe they'd be different."

"Impossible to say. It's the nature versus nurture argument, though who and how Aiden is now was affected by his experiences." Emily contemplated her own words as they ambled down the beach. She had to admit, her younger years had shaped her viewpoint. "Life has a way of changing you, forming you in unimaginable ways. Though deep down, I believe Aiden has always been this amazing, warm, and caring person."

An ever-changing array of emotions played across the teenager's face. Savannah sighed and rubbed her little brother's back. "I have a tough decision to make. Dad refuses to tell me what to do, and it's so confusing."

"I can imagine." She'd give careful consideration to her next words. If she misspoke, the issue may become clouded, or worse, she'd project her dislike for Tiffany onto Vanna.

"You're an amazing mom." Vanna peeked at Kellan. "You've been there for me, all the time. You never turned away, even when you and Dad weren't together. I appreciate that more than you'll ever know."

"With you, Vanna, it was an easy choice to stay in touch. I loved you right from the start. You're technically my stepdaughter, but I never much liked that term. If it's okay with you, I'd prefer to just call you my daughter."

Savannah nodded and reached for Emily's hand as they walked. "Can I ask you something personal?"

"Okay." Butterflies fluttered in her stomach.

"Did you always love my dad? You broke up with him, but never really left."

"That's quite the question." She shuffled her feet through the sand. "There's been something between us for a long time. Years in fact, but neither of us acted on it for many reasons. When we did?" She threw a sideways look at the girl. "Fireworks."

The girl's eyes widened. "But you kept breaking up."

"When I told you I was scared, I wasn't kidding. I'd never felt that way about anyone in my entire life and staying handed him complete power over my heart. Until I met your dad, I'd never had great experiences with guys. They cheated, lied, left, or all of the above. My earliest memories of my own father were of him leaving my mother after breaking her heart." She shrugged. "It seems illogical now, but committing to your dad terrified me. Yet, I couldn't resist him."

"You truly love him. I can see it, but I don't know how to explain what I mean."

"I understand." And she did. It was confusing even to her how she'd denied the depth of her love for so long and let fear rule her. "One day, if you meet a man who treats you as well as Aiden does me? Loves you like he loves me? Never let him go. This kind of love only comes around once in a lifetime. You can love someone, but to find the person who completes you is rare. I can picture us being together forever." She grinned. "That all sounds so cheesy and cliché, but …"

She imagined being with him, watching their children graduate school, being there for weddings and grandchildren, and loving each other into old age. It had been a bumpy ride to arrive here, but now she was holding on with both hands and all her might. There would be rough spots in their future, but that only made her more determined.

"I hope I find that kind of love someday. He never felt that way about Tiffany, did he?"

"Oh, I don't know. He cared, no question, but he was a kid. They were both young, and it was the first experience in love and all of that. I had a high school boyfriend I cared about, but we outgrew each other. I think Aiden and Tiffany were like that. They loved each other, but they were never meant to last."

"Like Justin. I care about him and he's a great friend, but it's over with us. Then Chase changed and stopped caring about me. It hurt at first, but I don't miss him now. I can go back to school and move on, and it will be okay."

"Chase was never the one for you, Savannah. You deserve someone far better, and you're only sixteen, which is far too young to tie yourself to one guy. Date, experience life, have fun, get through school, and start a career. Along the way, you'll find good and positive people. Keep them close. Cut out the toxic ones as they will make you unhappy in the long run and drag you down."

"You sound like you have experience with it."

Emily wondered how much she should share, but Savannah was growing up and seemed mature enough to handle the truth. "Sadly, yes." She looked over the water. "Two years before I dated your dad, I had this boyfriend, Jason. On the surface, he seemed fantastic. Successful, good looking, and I thought it was love. But the cracks showed, and he cheated on me." With a slight shrug, she turned to Savannah. "When Aiden and I got together, I lacked the ability to trust a man. It took a long time to get over it."

"But you did. And now you're happy."

"I'm beyond happy. You will meet good people and bad. Keep your eyes open and don't excuse bad behavior, or let it ride. Learn how to communicate and know when to walk away."

"Thanks, Emily." Savannah nodded. "Talking to you helps. I've been debating about what's the right thing to do about Tiffany. Between you and what Aiden said, I feel like my decision is right."

"Glad I could help." She hoped she hadn't said too much, but everything she'd said was true. And she'd said nothing specific about Tiffany or aired her feelings about the woman. The last thing she ever wanted to do was impede Savannah's happiness.

Emily slathered on cream as Aiden finished his call. His words were muffled, and she tried not to eavesdrop through the open patio doors.

When silence descended, Emily joined him on the patio, wrapping her arms around him from behind. She rested her forehead against his back.

After a moment, he turned and drew her in. "It's done."

"What did she say?"

"She's upset, but she promised to respect Savannah's decision."

"You're a good man for giving Savannah the power to make her own choices."

"A wise woman told me it was the right thing to do, and I had to agree. I wished Tiffany well. I hope she finds inner peace and happiness. It was harder than I expected, though, and even worse listening to her cry." He sighed, laying his cheek against her hair. "But it's for the best. She's got her art gallery to keep her busy while she gets her life together. She has a lot of issues to work through, but maybe she can find herself again."

"We'll hope she finds happiness. As much as we've been at odds, I feel for her."

Aiden brought her to sit on the wicker couch, cuddling her into his lap. "You continually amaze me. I'll never be able to express how wonderful you've been, or how much I love you." He nuzzled against her neck. "I'm sad the summer is over, but we'll have many more of them as a family."

"I love you." Emily leaned into his chest, thankful that fate had led her to this wonderful man. She was meant to be in Aiden's arms—forever and always.

Continue The Hamiltons with Book 3 - Never Let You Fall.

CHAPTER 1

Alexis

THE FAINT LIGHT OF DAWN crept through the curtains as the baby's cries echoed down the hallway. Silence fell, but my eyes were wide open. Kellan never cried for long and he wasn't my concern, being blessed with a doting Mommy and Daddy, but my maternal instinct kicked in the moment he uttered an unhappy sound.

Soft footsteps sounded on the wood floor outside my room followed by the familiar creak of the third step from the top as Aiden headed to the kitchen. Soon the deep rich fragrance of dark-roast coffee would waft through the air, combining with the fresh sea breeze fluttering my curtains.

I crawled from between the cozy sheets and tiptoed into the room next door. Daniel's deep and even breathing was broken only by the occasional slurp as he sucked the thumb he'd crammed into his mouth.

Tears sprang to my eyes as I brushed my fingers over his soft brown hair. He reminded me of his daddy with his hazel eyes and long thick lashes. I sighed and pressed a hand to my aching chest, gazing at Daniel's sweet face, so peaceful in his slumber.

"Alex," Aiden whispered from behind me. "Everything okay?"

I brushed at my eyes before facing him. "It's fine."

Aiden frowned. "Give me a minute to deliver this," he held up a glass of water, "and we can go for a walk. We'll be back long before Daniel's up."

I nodded. "I'll dress."

As he disappeared into the master bedroom, I retraced my steps to the guest room and hauled on my linen shorts and a fresh t-shirt. After a quick run of the brush through my tangled hair, I scooped it into a ponytail and examined the dark circles under my puffy red-rimmed eyes. I sighed. Not much to do about those.

I paused at the top of the stairs, closing my eyes and inhaling the expected tones of fresh-brewed coffee before trudging downstairs. "I could drink a gallon of that," I said as leaned against the kitchen counter, fixated by the wisps of steam rising from the two travel mugs.

"Then you're in luck." Aiden added a touch of cream and sugar to each and handed one to me.

I gulped a mouthful, my eagerness for caffeine rewarded with a stinging tongue. "Ouch." I pressed my fingers to my lips.

"Careful." He rubbed my arm. "It's hot."

"Yeah, you'd think I'd have figured that out." I trailed out the door after him and we ambled down the beach in the opposite direction from our house. My house? I wasn't sure anymore. Not about anything. "Emily doesn't mind me stealing you away?"

"She's feeding Kellan, and there's nothing I can do to help. I'd planned to lounge on the deck with my morning coffee, but this is better. It'll give us a chance to talk without interruptions." He gave me a knowing look. "Talk to me, Lex."

I sucked in a breath and concentrated on the cool sand squishing between my bare toes. One foot in front of the other. Keep moving forward was all I could do.

"Having trouble sleeping? Is Kellan keeping you up?"

"I can't shut it off. How can I stop thinking about Joel, and how our marriage is crumbling?" I shuffled a few paces closer to the water, allowing the cold waves to lick at my toes. I loved this beach, but this morning even the soothing rush and dawn calls of the gulls did nothing to relieve the all-consuming ache in my heart.

"I understand." He heaved a sigh. "This should've been one of those amazing summers. Our group is together again, and I'd hoped we'd start new traditions and put the past behind us. But here we are, me sidelined and you in limbo."

"Limbo." I considered his comment. "Yeah, that feels about right. Whenever I want to talk to Joel, he clams up or disappears out the door. I can't stand to even look at him. And what he did to you. How will you ever forgive him?" I sniffled. "He almost took you from us, and I'm not sure I can forgive him for that, either."

"I wish I had answers." Aiden swept a hand through his hair before reaching for mine. "He put the three of us in danger that day. The past few weeks he's been a ghost and barely acknowledges my existence. There's only one thing I'm sure of—he needs help. The catch is he has to want it and right now, he doesn't."

"Is there any way to force him?"

"Only if he becomes a danger to himself or other people."

"He was dangerous to you. His stupidity nearly cost you your life. No one wants to acknowledge it out loud, but we all know it. Emily watches you like you might fade away. Isn't what he did to you enough?"

"It's not. He's not purposely inflicting damage on other people, or himself." Silence fell for several steps. "At least, I hope he didn't do it on purpose. It was a careless, stupid, drunken move."

There it was, the thing I'd feared asking. Aiden doubted Joel's motives. "Joel's carelessness and idiotic behavior nearly killed you. Vanna said you warned him to sit still and touch nothing because you knew he was tanked."

"Yeah, I knew." Aiden stopped to pick up a rock, sending it skipping across the waves. "He rambled on about things earlier. I should never have turned my back. That's my mistake."

I clamped my teeth onto my lip, fighting the cascade of tears trickling down my cheeks. "I couldn't bear losing you. You're my brother, the one who I can always talk to, the one who's always been there. Every breakup, every crappy date, and even when my mom died, you were there. Until I married Joel, and we drifted. I have you back but almost lost you. Forever."

"But you didn't." Aiden rested a hand on my arm before he pulled me into a hug. "I'm here, Lex. Don't worry, you'll get through this." He wiped away my tears and placed a gentle kiss on my forehead.

The words stuck in my throat as a shiver ran down my spine. Every time I pictured Aiden struggling for survival in that freezing water, at the agony and hopelessness he must have felt, at how he'd almost been lost to us…

"Cold?"

"A little."

Aiden peeled off his sweatshirt and tugged the soft fabric over my head, reaching back to free my ponytail as I tucked my arms into the long sleeves.

The lingering body heat and earthy beach house scent comforted me. "Thanks."

We wandered along, finally arriving at our favorite spot. This twisted branch of Quansoo Oak had beached itself during a summer storm years ago, and many times we'd sat here and shared both our joys and our troubles.

"How can I help?" He slid an arm around me, and I leaned against his firm chest. "I hate to see you two at odds."

"You've let me cry on your shoulder, and you've been amazing with Daniel at a time he's missing his daddy. You and Tom have both stepped up, and I appreciate it more than words can express." I half-shrugged. "I should have bet on a different horse."

"Well, everyone knows men are animals." He squeezed my shoulder. "And Joel has been an enormous horse's ass."

"Ha ha." I forced a smile. "You've got that right."

The sun appeared on the horizon, creating a bright path across the ocean. The water glinted and sparkled as the first golden rays warmed my face. I lifted my chin and closed my eyes, inhaling the fresh salty air. A multitude of vivid memories surfaced in my mind. We'd spent many summers here both as teenagers and as adults, and most of them had been amazing. This year nothing felt right.

I gathered my courage. "What's up with you and Tiffany?"

"Ahh, I wondered when you'd ask." He rubbed the back of his neck. "She asked to see Vanna."

"After all this time?" I tilted my head. "How does that make you feel?"

"Not great, but I talked to Vanna and placed the decision in her hands. Tiffany's her mother, and at one time Savannah wanted nothing more than to know her. Tiffany called the other night."

"Hmm, I figured. You get that look when it's her, like you'd rather be anywhere else." I rubbed his arm. "She's put you in a tough spot. There are days when I wish we could transport back in time and fix it. Rewind that spring and summer we turned fifteen."

Aiden stared at the water with a thoughtful look on his face. "This may sound strange, but I'm not sure I'd make different choices. If someone appeared right now and gave me the option?" He shook his head. "I'd never wish Savannah out of existence. Despite everything we've gone through, I've learned and experienced so much, and I have my daughter, here and now."

His heartfelt words made me reconsider my wish. What would I do if given the opportunity to rewrite my past? I couldn't imagine my life without Daniel. Even though Tiffany had broken Aiden's heart, his precious daughter had become his saving grace. "Change even the smallest thing and the effects ripple out."

Aiden nodded. "I've accepted that the pain and turmoil in my life led me to this moment. It's meant to be this way."

"What did Savannah choose?"

"She said no." Aiden bowed his head and shuffled his feet in the sand. "Telling Tiffany was awful. She melted down."

"As in she—"

"Sobbed and ranted and screamed at me. But you know what's strange? Even after everything Tiffany's said and done, I felt sorry for her. She may never know our daughter." He dragged in a long breath and turned his head away. "She blames me for Vanna's refusal to see her. What if she's right?"

"She's not. You gave her the chance, and she refused it," I said. "But I am sorry. This summer will go down as one of the worst in history."

My heart ached for him. Aiden's life had never been easy, and now he struggled with even more heartbreak. His continuous support amazed me. He'd ensured my survival during my latest tragedy, even as he battled his own demons and cared for his newborn son. I took his hand between mine and wished I could ease the incessant pain—for both of us.

"It'll work out." The words sounded hollow, and I wasn't sure if I meant them for Aiden, or myself.

"You're right, it will." He scrubbed his hands over his face. "We should head home. Emily might need help with the baby."

We remained silent for the walk back. Aiden seemed lost in his own thoughts, and I let him be.

"There you are." Emily smiled as we entered the kitchen, swaying on her feet, Kellan cradled in his baby wrap. She tipped her chin to accept Aiden's kiss. "We planned to go into town today, Alex. Care to join us?"

The perfect couple. They looked so damn happy whenever they were together. Had Joel and I ever looked this content after Daniel had been born? I blinked hard against the burn behind my eyes. "Thanks, but I'll stay here."

"How about we take Daniel with us, and you get some sleep?" Emily raised her brows.

"No ..."

She kept her gaze trained on me, one eyebrow rising higher as she studied me. "It wouldn't be a problem."

I glanced at Aiden, who gave the briefest of nods. "Okay, thank you. I'll get him ready."

"I've got him." Vanna appeared in the doorway with a fully dressed Daniel on her hip. "I'll feed him breakfast."

A lump formed in my throat, and after giving my son a good morning kiss, I returned to my room. I hated to admit it, but I craved the break. I loved my boy, but my Daniel had become an untiring live-wire from the moment he'd learned to keep his balance. Over the summer he'd graduated from halting wobbly steps to an all-out run. Without Joel's help, every day was a marathon.

The Hamilton Series

Purchase links for these book may be found at: KateSmithAuthor.ca

Everything we Lost

Everything for Love

Never let you Fall

Everything left Unsaid

Everything we Dream

Everything we Promised

Thank you for reading!

I always love to hear from readers. I can be contacted at http://katesmithauthor.ca

Follow me on social media:

https://www.instagram.com/katesmithauthor/

https://twitter.com/KateSmithAuthor/

https://www.facebook.com/katesmithauthor/